THE architect

A NASHVILLE NEIGHBORHOOD BOOK

NIKKI SLOANE

Dormer Edition

ISBN 978-1-949409-11-6

For Nick

who made this book possible

ONE

A loud, insistent banging came from my front door, caused by an angry fist, and I froze.

First of all, it was dark and pouring rain outside. There wasn't an overhang or porch to cover whoever was knocking on my door. And second . . . what the actual fuck? I lived in the guest quarters behind my parents' house, and their property was surrounded by a fence.

So, I didn't get visitors. Anyone coming here would go to the main house first.

It meant the owner of the fist pounding on my door in the dead of night—and during a storm—had come onto my family's property without permission.

Every hair on my body stood at attention with alarm.

"Lilith?" a male voice asked, sounding urgent. "Are you home? It's Clay Crandall from next door. I need your help."

Like the snap of a pair of fingers, the tension in my body shifted and I couldn't get my door open fast enough.

He stood on the concrete path with his head tipped down to keep the worst of the rain from falling into his eyes. He was drenched, and the water molded his clothes to his body, showing off every perfect inch of him. Clay was in his late thirties, meaning he was at least ten years older than I was . . . and *exactly* the type of guy I preferred.

Jesus, he was so fucking hot. Even with anxiety stricken across his face.

I stood stock-still with one hand on the doorknob, ignoring the rain splattering my legs, and gawked at him. Behind his dark-rimmed glasses, his eyes were the same shade of brown his hair was when wet, as it currently was. He was fit and toned, and had a body made for sex. The kind I was sure could turn a smart girl like me stupid.

Which it had, because I hadn't invited him in to get out of the rain. I stepped back and gestured inside. "Come on in. What's going on?"

He shook his head. "No, I—" He struggled to find the words. "You're a veterinarian, right?"

"No, I'm a technician." It wasn't the first time someone had made that assumption. I was more like a nurse, who assisted the doctors at the animal hospital where I worked.

But this answer must have been close enough because he nodded and backed up, urging me to follow him out into the storm. "I need your help . . . at my house."

There was something odd about the way he'd said it. His voice was full of discomfort, like he was reluctant. Or perhaps he was shy.

I'd only had one conversation with my next-door neighbor since he'd moved in more than a year ago. Once he put up his curtains, I never saw him again. The guy was rarely home, and when he was, he stayed hidden. The rest of our neighbors were friendly and chatty, or nosy, or all of the above. Everyone knew each other's business. But Clay?

He was a ghost.

No one came by to see him. There weren't visiting cars parked in his driveway or the street beside his house, not even on holidays. A lawn service took care of his yard.

My mother joked he was probably a serial killer.

No way. He was too good looking for me to believe that, even when I knew serial killers could be attractive.

I put my hand up to shield the rain from my face. It was a feeble attempt to save my eye makeup as I tried to dart out into the storm, but his hand came up to stop me.

"Wait," he said.

"What is it?"

His gaze dropped to my feet. My open-toe pumps had a summery floral print and four-inch heels. I'd bought them off-season last year for a total steal.

His face took a dubious cast. "Don't you want to change shoes?"

"No, I'm good." Because I *loved* my shoes. Stilettos, or sandals, or any kind of sexy heels . . . My closet was full of them, and I took every opportunity I could to wear them.

We didn't talk as we hurried across the path that led to the gate in the fence, and my shoes were slick on the stones. The rain was cold as it pelted me, soaking my ivory shirt and squishing between my toes, but I ignored it and did my best to keep up with Clay's fast clip.

The exterior lights surrounding his large house were on, making raindrops glint, and his garage door was open. We went through it, passing by his Ford pickup truck and up the two steps to the door that led into his home.

I stood in the side entryway, dripping on the tile floor,

waiting for him to explain, but he didn't. Instead, Clay's gaze bounced around frantically as if he wasn't sure where the emergency was.

"There's a cat in here somewhere," he said.

I blinked. "Um, okay . . .?"

He rubbed the back of his neck, and his expression was full of embarrassment. At least, I assumed it was, based off his tone. I was totally distracted by the flex of his bicep peeking out from under his shirt sleeve.

He said it quietly. "I think I hurt it."

Everything in me went still, and my voice flash-froze into ice. "What?"

"It was an accident." His eyes filled with remorse. "A few weeks ago, this cat randomly showed up at my place. Maybe you've seen it? A black and white one?"

I hadn't. He peered at me, waiting for a response, but my stone-cold demeanor didn't change, and it forced him to continue.

"It keeps trying to get into my house. Every time I open a door, the cat's there, like he's been lying in wait. It rushes for the door." He hesitated. "When I got home, I didn't realize he'd followed me into the garage."

"Oh, no." I tensed. "You hit him with your car?"

Thankfully, he shook his head. "I'd just come in when I saw the cat charging for the steps, so I tried to shut the door before he made it in." Clay swallowed a breath. "I . . . wasn't fast enough. His tail got caught in it, and—shit—the howl he made was awful."

Dread and urgency descended on me. "Where is he now?"

Clay cast a hand toward the entryway and the house beyond. "I've been looking everywhere for at least twenty minutes."

My gaze left his and scoured the space, searching. "Hurt animals like to hide." I took two steps toward the living room before pausing. I should probably ask if he were cool with it before I began wandering around his house. "Is it okay if I—"

He nodded quickly. "Please." He took his glasses off and used the hem of his shirt to clean the raindrops from his lenses. "I'll take the upstairs. You search this floor?"

"Yeah," I answered. With the game plan sorted out, his feet carried him swiftly across the hardwood and toward the staircase, leaving me to begin my self-guided tour of his place.

His living room was nice, with a plush rug in the center and a matching couch and loveseat, but I didn't find a wounded cat hiding beneath them. If I'd had more time, I might have lingered by the built-in bookcases and examined the pictures displayed there, but my focus was elsewhere right now.

My goal was temporarily derailed when I turned the corner and stepped into the kitchen. Or what was supposed to be the kitchen, because the space was torn apart. An island of cabinets was perched in the center of the room, but there was no countertop. What looked like backsplash samples were taped to the wall under the space where a range hood was probably going to be installed. He was renovating the kitchen, but how come I'd never noticed a construction crew parked out front?

There were at least a dozen open boxes scattered

around the room.

I searched each one, but no luck.

"Here, kitty, kitty . . ." I called softly, but no cat appeared. It was a longshot, but I had to try, didn't I?

Once I flipped the light switch in his dining room, the chandelier warmed the darkness. This room was formal, elegant, and traditional. I got down on my hands and knees and peered beneath the side cabinet, hoping to catch two reflective eyes staring back at me, but it was empty. I'd probably wasted time looking since the cabinet was really low to the ground, but cats were also liquid and could fit into tight spaces.

I sat back on my heels and stared at the cabinet for a moment. It struck me as odd. For a guy who lived alone and never seemed to entertain, why did he need it? It was expensive and high-quality. The same for the large dining room table and its chairs.

Overhead, a floorboard creaked, announcing Clay hadn't found the cat yet either and I needed to get back to work.

Across the hall from the dining room was his study, and I checked every spot I possibly could, fighting against my curiosity to snoop. I was nosy-natured, and he was an enigma, so it was tempting, but somehow I managed to resist. Only the things out in the open were allowed to grab my attention—like the drafting table next to the bay window. There were blueprints clipped to it, except they didn't seem to be for his kitchen remodel. Whatever this building was, it was huge.

My focus had to move on.

There was a bedroom on the main floor, and once I

realized it was the master suite, it was torturous to stay on-task. This was *his* room, full of dark-colored wood and secrets only someone close to him would know. Like how he slept on the left side of his big bed.

And he wore boxer-briefs.

I knew because the chair in the corner had become a catch-all of clothes, including a black pair of underwear. I began to picture what he'd look like in them, and then immediately forced it from my mind.

Come on, Lilith. Stop thinking about banging your next-door neighbor for two seconds.

There was nothing hidden under his bed except a pair of discarded socks. Where the heck had this cat run off to? I strode through Clay's bathroom and into his large closet, but a thorough scan confirmed I was the only creature in here. Surrounded by his suits and dress shirts, it felt . . . intimate. I put a hand out, brushing my palm over the soft fabric of his suit sleeves—

"What are you doing?" His tone was brusque.

I nearly yelped in surprise, dropping my hand, and spun to face him. "Sorry." Embarrassed warmth crawled along my cheeks. He stared at me through his sexy glasses, his chest rising and falling with his hurried breath.

Only I had the strange feeling he wasn't irritated at me. The longer I gazed at him, the more I began to wonder if this was something *else*. His expression was impossible to read. Was he anxious?

Or intrigued?

I lifted my chin and pretended he hadn't just caught me

petting his clothes like a lunatic. "I take it you haven't found the cat yet?"

He set a hand on his hip and let out a sigh. "No."

Silence seeped into the space, bringing tension along with it. It seemed like he realized it at the same moment I did, just how alone we were in this small space with him blocking my exit. My brain warned me it was possible the cat didn't exist. This man was my neighbor, but he was still a stranger, and I'd walked willingly into his house. Right into what could have been his trap.

But if that were true, why did he look like he was the one who'd been cornered? His hands hung awkwardly at his sides and were curled into loose fists. Not with anger, but . . . maybe discomfort? As if my presence in this space was causing him distress.

A voice inside me whispered the cat might not be the only wounded animal inside his house.

"I don't know where he could be." He sounded defeated. "I've looked everywhere."

"It's okay," I said quietly. "We'll find him."

Clay was skeptical as he used a knuckle to push up the dark-framed glasses on the bridge of his nose, but he nodded.

"I can look upstairs—" A thought struck me. "Wait. Don't you have a basement?" Most houses in our subdivision didn't, which was why I remembered. "My mom and I walked through an open house before you bought this place last year."

If he was uncomfortable I had invaded his closet, now he looked downright terrified at the idea of me going deeper inside his home. Something like panic flitted through his eyes, and his words came out in a rush. "He's not down there. I always keep the door shut."

Well. His quick response made me quirk an eyebrow. Maybe he was a serial killer.

He straightened and attempted to act natural. "He's probably somewhere on the main floor. The kitchen, or the laundry room, or maybe the study."

"Laundry room?" Oh, I was an idiot. "It's off the kitchen, right? I totally missed it." I'd gotten distracted by all the boxes and the renovations.

He led the way, both of us moving quickly out of his bedroom, down the hall, and through the kitchen.

The laundry room wasn't much bigger than his closet. There was only space for his washer and dryer, but I put my hands on top of one of them and leaned over to look behind. Beneath the accordion dryer vent, I spotted a patch of white fur.

"There you are," I said softly.

"How the hell? He's *behind* the dryer?"

"Yup."

I straightened just as Clay went to lean over to see better, and our shoulders brushed against each other. It made my breath catch, and I wanted to laugh in surprise. I was comfortable with both my space and others'. Some might even label me as the overly friendly, touchy-feely type. I was a confident woman, the kind of girl who ate weakness for breakfast and had no problem making the first move.

So, why the fuck did something as innocent as my

shoulder brushing against his make my heart flutter?

Was it how he seemed equally affected by it? He hesitated like a scientist who'd just received an unexpected test result. His gaze shifted to the appliance in front of us.

"I can move the dryer, but not enough to get back there to get him out."

I shook my head. "Let's try to coax him out first. Do you have food we could use, like cheese or a can of tuna?"

He considered it before nodding. "Yeah, I think so."

I stayed in the laundry room as he disappeared, and a moment later there were sounds like he was rummaging around in his pantry. A whir of a mechanical can opener rang out.

"Should I put some on a plate?"

"No, just bring me the can," I answered, climbing up on top of the washing machine.

He turned the corner to find me sitting there with my legs crossed and my hands braced behind me. His steps slowed as he approached, trying to keep his thoughts from showing on his face—yet he failed spectacularly.

My provocative pose wasn't intentional, but if his mind happened to go to the idea of him fucking me on top of his washer during an aggressive spin cycle . . . Well, I wasn't the least bit mad about it.

Maybe later we could make that idea a reality.

I reached forward, took the small can from him, then turned to lower it behind the dryer. It didn't take much to entice the cat. The scent of the fish grabbed the animal's attention immediately, and two orange eyes stared up at me with interest.

"You hungry?" I asked.

I knew I had the cat hooked when I lifted the can and he followed, bounding up on top of the dryer beside me with a soft thump.

"That's a good sign," I said quietly so I didn't startle the cat. "He's interested in eating, so he's probably not in much pain."

I set the can down, and as soon as the cat took its first bite, I did a visual evaluation. The tuxedo cat had his weight evenly distributed between his paws, and when I nudged the can across the top of the washer, he hurried after it. His gait was normal.

Except—

"She's not favoring one leg over the other," I said, "so that's good."

"She?"

"Yup. This cat's a female."

I held out my hand to let her smell me, but she was far more interested in her meal than anything else. I ran a hand along her spine, checking for any signs of trauma, and when she arched into my touch, the tip of her tail wagged happily.

I grinned at Clay as I stroked the cat a second time. "I don't think she'd be moving her tail if it were broken."

As if to help reinforce my claim, the animal began to purr, and the rumbling sound grew louder as she opened her mouth to take another bite of fish.

I inspected her fur, which seemed clean and free of fleas. She was skinny, though, and there was a scratch healing on the top of her head as if she'd been in a fight with another animal recently.

"You can bring her by my clinic tomorrow and we can check her for a microchip, but I don't think she'll have one. I'm betting she was a stray until she found you."

"Tomorrow?" Clay's tone was dubious. "Wait a minute, what—"

I ignored him and gave her some scritches behind her ears. "You're too pretty and sweet to be homeless, aren't you?"

He said my name the same way I expected he'd tell me to get serious. "Lilith."

I gave him a plain look. "This cat risked life and limb to adopt you as her owner."

Anxiety and confusion tightened his shoulders. "No. I don't want to own a cat."

"Why not?" It just fell out of my mouth, loaded with double-meaning. "You don't like pussy?"

TWO

Surprise at my innuendo made Clay jolt, but the way he recovered in a blink of an eye turned it right back around to me. His gaze slid from mine, down to the thin, wet top I wore and how it molded to my breasts. My pebbled nipples jutted out, and when he zeroed in on them, desire flared in his eyes.

Then he took a deep breath and licked his lips, making heat warm my cheeks and a dull ache throb between my legs.

Oh, yes.

It was silent in the room, but the way he brazenly lusted at me was deafening. It rumbled through my body just as the thunder outside reverberated through his big house.

But his wicked look slowly faded into a serious one. "I like . . . *cats* just fine. What I meant is, I can't own a cat."

"Why? Are you allergic?"

He pressed his lips together for a half-second. "No, but I have to travel for my job."

"Really?" Confusion tugged my eyebrows together. "Seems like you're home all the time to me."

His expression shuttered. He didn't like the idea I was keeping tabs on him, and his tone turned accusatory. "Oh, am I?"

I shrugged without shame. "You're hot and mysterious, and I'm curious."

A statement like that would fluster some guys, but not Clay. He simply blinked behind his glasses. "I'm not mysterious. I'm . . ." He searched for the right word. "Private."

"Okay." I stroked the cat. "Private guys can care for cats, you know."

"So can nosy neighbors," he fired back. "You work for a veterinarian. Don't you think that makes you a better fit?"

"This cat didn't pick me, dude, she picked you. And I think you owe it to her after slamming her tail in the door." I slid down off the washing machine and was thrilled when he held his ground. It meant we were standing close enough to each other I could pick up the faint hint of his cologne. "Besides, as much as I'd like to, my landlords have a strict no-pets policy."

He looked dubious. "Don't you live with your parents?"

"No. I *rent* from them."

Yes, I was twenty-six and resided on my parents' property, but as far as I was concerned, I lived on my own. My parents' guest house was a complete space, including a full kitchen, two bedrooms, and one-and-a-half baths. I paid my rent and utilities and came and went as I pleased.

But Clay continued to look at me like I was making it all up.

"If I didn't live there," I said, "they'd rent my place out to someone else, and they'd be the ones keeping up with the main house." I pushed a swath of my dark brown hair back over my shoulder. "You know my folks are never home anymore, right? Last year my dad retired, and now they're doing all the traveling they've been wanting to since they had kids."

"Oh," he said. "No, I didn't know. Where are they now?"

"Vietnam." Wait, was that right? "Or maybe Myanmar? I don't remember their exact itinerary." Just that they wouldn't be home for another month, and they weren't planning to stay home long. South America was booked for September and October. "Anyway, my dad's allergic, and my mom's always been super anti-pet, so me having a cat is a dealbreaker for them." My mother's aversion to pets had played a big role in why I worked with animals. "Honestly, I couldn't afford a place half as nice on my salary, so I'm not about to risk it, even if this cat is adorable."

I massaged the scruff of her neck, and she purred like a motor.

Clay sighed. "It's not like I'm heartless. She is . . . kind of cute," he admitted softly. "Look, I'd take her in if I could, but I'm heading to Florida tomorrow morning, and I'll be gone the rest of the week. Maybe longer."

"What is it you do?" I asked. "All my mom told me is you're in tech."

He cocked his head in confusion, then a half-smile tilted his lips. "I'm not in tech. Architect," he corrected. "She must have misheard me."

"Oh." Well, the drafting table and blueprints in the study made a bit more sense now. "You're building something in Florida?"

"We're in phase two of a new hospital tower in Jacksonville, which, as you can imagine, is a big project. I'll be back and forth all the time for the next six months."

My gaze dropped to his tile floor while I contemplated

what to say next. The one solution I came up with was crazy, and he probably wouldn't go for it, but what was the harm in asking? I lifted my chest and flashed the biggest, most persuasive smile I owned.

"So . . . I have an idea," I said. "You have pet-friendly space, but no time. I have the time, but no pet-friendly space. Let's make a deal. I'll take care of her while you're gone. I mean, I'm right next door. It'd be easy for me to pop over and check in on her."

Clay looked at me like I'd just offered to rotate his tires. "I'm sorry, what?"

"We'll share the cat. I'll even let you name her."

His tone was dubious. "You want to . . . own a cat. With me."

"Sure, why not?"

"Because I'm a stranger?"

I waved a hand, brushing off his silly statement. "No, you're not." I smiled widely. "I know where you live, Clay. Just think of it as joint custody. We both get something out of this arrangement. I get to own a cat, and you don't even have to take care of it."

He couldn't have looked more conflicted if he'd tried. "We can't do that. That idea is . . . crazy." And yet, it was clear he hadn't ruled it out. Was he actually considering it?

"Cats are easy," I added.

His gaze shifted away from me as he thought long and hard about it. "I don't have any stuff, like cat food, or—"

Hurried excitement crept into my voice. "I can go to the store right now. I'll pay for everything."

"It's not a money thing." He lifted a hand like he could

pluck the answer out of thin air. "How would it even work?"

I tentatively placed a hand on his arm and fought the urge to squeeze the muscle that lurked beneath the damp cotton of his shirt. "I just need a key or your garage door code. I can check on other stuff for you while you're gone too," I said, "like I do for my parents. Water your plants, let you know how the remodel is going."

His attention went to my fingers resting on him, and I couldn't tell if he liked my touch or not. Part of him seemed excited by it, but a much larger part seemed guarded and uneasy. I retreated, not wanting to turn him off.

"I don't need an update on the remodel," he said. "I'm the one redoing the kitchen."

Really? I stared beyond him to the box of tiles just outside the door. "By yourself?"

He straightened. "Yes. I enjoy the work, and—as I mentioned—I'm a private person. I . . ." His voice went uneven and low. He wasn't sure he should reveal it. "This is my space. I don't like strangers in my house."

My heart quickened.

Had it been hard for him to ask for my help and let me in? He'd been uncomfortable when he'd caught me in his closet.

"I'm not a stranger," I said softly and strived for a light, playful tone. "You know where I live."

"I do," he said.

I licked my lips and peered up at him. "We could get to know each other better."

When his gaze drifted back to me, my breath caught.

The desire was back in his eyes, but there was something

else too. A strange kind of power. I'd thought I was luring him in, but it made me wonder if he was doing the same to me.

"Maybe we could name her Noir," he said.

I blinked back my surprise. "Because she's black and white?" It was a far more original name than 'Oreo,' which was what all the tuxedo cats that came into the clinic always seemed to be. I smiled. "Noir. I like that."

The first few days, my focus was solely on our new cat. As I suspected, she wasn't microchipped, and there hadn't been any recent calls to the animal shelter in town inquiring about a missing black-and-white domestic shorthair. After Dr. Johnston gave her a clean bill of health and her vaccinations, I coaxed Noir back into her carrier and took her home.

Well . . . *her* home, at Clay's place.

After we'd struck the deal of jointly owning a cat together, we'd gotten into his truck, driven to the nearby Target, and purchased enough supplies to last Noir a week. I fought him on who got to pay, but he insisted, and in the end, I gave in and let him do it.

"Can I ask a question?" I said once we were back in his truck, heading home. "Is there a specific reason you don't like strangers in your house?"

For a moment, the only sound in the car interior was the soft ticking of his turn signal. Then his quiet voice filled the space. "No, it's just a general thing."

I wasn't sure if he was going to elaborate, but he drew in a deep breath, like he was preparing for a challenge.

"Being around unfamiliar people," he continued, "makes me uncomfortable. Honestly, sometimes it's exhausting. I can deal with it when I'm at work or out at a job site, but then I need space afterward." His hand tightened on the steering wheel. "Not to sound like a jerk, but most of the time I'd rather be alone."

It was the same for me, but instead of telling him, I bit down on my bottom lip. "I'm sorry. I didn't mean to make you uncomfortable."

He took his eyes off the road for a fraction of a second so he could glance at me. "No. Don't worry, you didn't." The corner of his mouth lifted in a smile. "I mean, you should. You're one of the most beautiful women I've ever seen, and the most unexpected things come out of your mouth, but for some reason you don't make me uncomfortable."

Pleasure washed through me at his compliment, and I shifted in my seat, subtly leaning closer to him. "Why do you think that is?"

He considered his answer for a long moment, and then didn't give it to me. "Do you like people?"

"Like, am I outgoing?" I shrugged. "Yeah, sure."

"I mean, do you like being around people?"

I stared out the rain-splattered windshield and into the darkness of the night. "I like animals better, if I'm being honest. They're less, I don't know, complicated."

"Yes." He nodded.

Seduction slid into my voice. “But I like being around *certain* people.”

A short laugh punched from his lips. “If you’re in any way implying me, well—I’m about as complicated a person as you can get.”

“Oh, yeah?”

He nodded but didn’t explain.

The short drive ended as he swung the truck into his driveway, and as soon as we got back inside his house, we were focused on getting Noir squared away. After that, he walked me through the process of disarming his home security system, which was so advanced, I had to take notes on my phone.

And once we were done and Noir began exploring her new home, Clay rummaged around in a drawer in his study and extracted a key. He held it in his hand, and his gaze traced over the silver notches on one side. I understood his hesitation. This was a big step for him, and I wanted to do everything I could to make him feel comfortable with me—not just in his home, but as a person.

“You can ask me anything, you know.” My tone was playful. “I’ve heard communication is super important when you’re co-parenting.”

A smile twitched on his lips, and Clay’s fingers unfurled, holding the key out to me in the palm of his hand. “Okay. Can I ask how old you are?”

Instinctively, I straightened, trying to make myself look more mature. “Twenty-six. You?”

If my age surprised him, he didn’t show it. He simply

nodded. "I'm thirty-five."

It was a question I probably should have asked sooner. "Have you owned a pet before?

"Yeah. My mom had a cat when I was young. She was pretty—all-white—but she only liked my mom and merely tolerated the rest of us."

"What was her name? Wait, let me guess. Snowball?"

"No, it was way more original than that. It was Kitty."

"How creative." I laughed lightly. "So, Noir will be your first pet since then?" When he nodded, I grinned. "Well, I'm glad I get to share her with you."

Clay looked pleasantly surprised. "Me too."

We lapsed into silence, but it wasn't uncomfortable. If anything, it was warm and inviting.

When our shared moment was over, his gaze turned to the window, and he moved to pull an umbrella out of his entryway closet. "Can I walk you home?"

It wasn't raining nearly as hard as when he'd dashed over to my place to ask for help, and as we walked together, fat raindrops pitter-pattered against the large black umbrella. I loved being under it because it gave me an excuse to linger close to him.

But when we reached my door, he announced he needed to pack for his work trip, thanked me for my help, and said good night before I could invite him in or make a move.

I was able to quickly temper my disappointment, though—he'd given me both his number and a key to his place, and I'd have ample opportunities over the next few weeks to learn what made him such a complicated man.

I went over every day the first week and got in the habit of texting him pictures of Noir. Sometimes I had to be quiet and sneak into the house to catch her curled up on a couch cushion in the sun. If I made too much noise, she'd run and hide at first. Like Clay, she was shy in the beginning, but warmed up quickly when she realized it was me.

I did my absolute best not to snoop through his house.

He'd said he was a private person, and I was determined to respect that. But— damn—I felt like one of the wives in the Bluebeard folktale every time I walked past the door to his basement. Was there a bloody chamber behind it, full of all his dead wives?

Why had he been so nervous when I'd mentioned going down there? My curiosity grew each day. At least he'd be back tomorrow, and when I stopped by to say hello to both him and our cat, I'd find a way to casually bring it up in conversation.

Except I didn't get a chance. I was sitting on the rug in his living room, scratching Noir's chin exactly the way she liked it when a loud bang came from below, startling both of us.

"What the fuck was that?" I demanded.

Noir looked at me with the same question in her eyes as she leapt to her feet, her body on high alert.

The bang had been loud enough it sounded like something

heavy had crashed to the floor. I ran different ideas in my head, from a light fixture breaking to the water heater malfunctioning, and all of them warranted investigation.

Or at the very least, a peek down the stairs.

My heartbeat kicked up a notch as I wrapped my hand around the doorknob. The anticipation had been building all week, and excitement zipped through me like nervous electricity. I turned the knob and pushed the door open, only to stare down the dark and disappointingly normal staircase.

I wasn't the only one curious, though.

A half-second later, Noir bolted down the stairs and turned the corner at the bottom, disappearing out of view.

"Well, shit."

I flipped on the light and descended the stairs after her.

Last time I'd been in this basement, more than a year ago, the space had been set up as one large bonus room, a couch on one side and a play area for kids on the other. When Clay had moved in, he'd changed it dramatically. The carpet was gone, replaced with laminate floors, and more lights brightened the room.

He'd converted it into a workshop, sectioning it off into stations. One corner was an impressive work bench and table saw. Another held materials stored in tidy, labeled compartments, and beside it—the items too big to go into drawers or bins, like lumber and reams of black and red fabrics, which were either vinyl or leather.

I forgot all about my cat as I walked through the space, marveling at the sophisticated organization and flow of the work room.

Clay built custom furniture, and by the looks of it, it wasn't just a hobby—it was a side business. An order form was pinned to a board, the specs highlighted, and handwritten notes were inked in the margin. Materials for the 'pillory stocks' build had been ordered and were supposed to arrive next week.

My gaze slid away from the piece of paper, moving toward the finished piece that stood in the corner behind the stairs. I was immediately struck by its sleek lines, but it also took me a moment to make sense of what I was looking at.

When I did, my mouth dropped open, and heat rushed through me.

"Holy shit," I whispered.

THREE

Clay had told me he was a complicated man, and as I stared at the sexy piece of furniture he'd crafted, I peeled back one of his layers.

This St. Andrew's cross was slightly different than the ones I'd seen online, but there was no mistaking its purpose. The beams still crossed in a giant X, but this one also had crossbars at the top and bottom, so it was more like two triangles kissing.

The hourglass silhouette of it was outlined with metal, and rings were placed at every intersection. There'd be multiple places to hook on to. Spots to attach handcuffs, rope, or chains. The cross itself was covered in black and accented with red, and I couldn't help myself. I reached out to touch the leather and found it buttery-soft.

It was so fucking sexy and stunning, it stole my breath.

My quiet, studious looking neighbor built custom, high-end BDSM furniture.

I marveled at the craftmanship as I walked around the St. Andrew's cross. It was angled back just a bit, and a support beam jutted out the back, probably to give it extra stability. It was impossible to look at it and not imagine what it'd feel like to be bound spreadeagle to it. I wouldn't care which way he'd have me—either facing him or away, my body exposed for whatever he wanted to do to it.

Would he spank me?

Flog or whip me?

Fuck me?

I burst into flames at the idea. I'd never explored any kind of kink before, but I was a 'try everything once' kind of girl, and this had always fascinated me. A quick look at my internet browser history would reveal my sexual appetite was healthy and I had wide tastes.

And to do it with Clay? I imagined him delivering a sexy spanking, and then using that same hand to push his glasses back up on the bridge of his nose. He'd evaluate me with an exacting look and then adjust my positioning or correct the arch of my back with a firm hand or a dark tone.

An ache of need radiated through my body.

There was a W-shaped logo carved into the back of the cross, matching the letterhead of the order pinned to the board. I trailed my fingertips over the carving.

"Wicked Architecture," I read aloud.

I dug my phone out of my back pocket, typed it into Google, and found the company website in the search results. Like the piece of furniture in front of me, his website was slick and sexy. When I clicked on the portfolio page, I stared at the pictures of the various pieces he'd created.

Some of them were easy to understand how they were used. There was a barrel shaped horse and a spanking bench that sort of reminded me of a small, padded picnic table. He'd already done a more traditional cross, and then something labeled a milking table, which was long and padded, had a hole cut out of the center of it, and sat on top of a cage.

I got how the kneeler and the item described as Catherine's wheel worked, but what was a queening chair? The licking bench looked complicated, and I couldn't figure out who went where or what was even being licked. His portfolio was full of gorgeous pictures of furniture, showing off his high-quality work, but having a model in some of the images would have been helpful.

My curiosity carried me back toward the order form. The price tag for the stocks he was building was seven hundred dollars. The figure didn't surprise me.

Clay may have used math to build it, but his architecture was more like art to me.

Noir had finished exploring the rest of the room, and she cautiously prowled toward the cross, eyeing it with skepticism. She sniffed it once, slinked around one of the beams, and then stretched up, latching her claws into the leather.

"Noir, no!" I cried, scooping her up into my arms, and extracted her claws as delicately as I could. Thankfully, it didn't seem like she'd damaged the leather; I'd gotten her just in time. From now on, I'd make sure to keep her out of here and the door to the basement closed.

She squirmed in my hold, since she was a cat and preferred her independence, and reluctantly I made my way to the stairs.

It was then that I noticed there were thick planks of wood standing upright, resting against the wall, like they'd been stained and then left there to dry. Only one of them was on the floor at a strange angle. The board must have slipped.

"*That's* what fell," I told the cat.

She didn't care. Noir was far more interested in being released. I hurried up the stairs, closed the door, and set her down. She skittered away, temporarily annoyed with me for confining her.

My gaze drifted back to the door, and my mind wandered down to what Clay was building in his workshop. He'd made pieces of restraint and confinement, and—fuck—it was so sexy. I wouldn't be annoyed with him if he wanted to confine me . . .

In fact, I was sure I'd be thrilled.

Saturday morning, I had a shift at the clinic, as did my best friend Cassidy Sheppard. We'd meet two years ago when she began interning, and although she was a lot younger than I was, age was simply a number when it came to her. She'd turn twenty-one in a few months, but I'd swear she was in her thirties, maturity-wise.

Cassidy was an old soul, and I wasn't the only one who thought so. Her boyfriend was in his early forties.

I spent the afternoon desperately fighting back the desire to tell her what I'd found in Clay's basement. It wasn't that I worried she'd judge him. I mean, she got up to all kinds of shenanigans with Dr. Lowe—or *Daddy,* as I sometimes called him. I'd sort-of-jokingly-but-also-seriously nicknamed him that behind his back, which she hated, but then again, she *was* sleeping with a guy who happened to be her ex's father.

I didn't confess my discovery to my friend because every time I thought about it, a voice in my head would pipe up.

Clay's a private person, it scolded.

So, I kept it a secret, no matter how much I was dying to talk about it with her. Plus, I didn't tell her how I'd spent last night studying every piece of BDSM furniture in his portfolio. Or how this morning I'd devised a plan to broach the subject with him next time I saw him.

"What are you doing tonight?" Cassidy asked me as she finished wiping down the table in exam room two. Had she sensed the excitement I was trying to hide, or was she simply making conversation? *Daddy* wasn't on-call this weekend, and that was such a rare thing, I knew she'd be occupied.

"Not sure." I played it cool. "I might go over to Clay's."

She stopped what she was doing so she could stare at me like I'd just said I hated wearing heels. "You're going to spend your Saturday night alone with your cat?"

A sly smile curled on my lips. "Hopefully not alone. Clay got back last night."

"Oh, I see." She grinned. "I'd say good luck, but I doubt you'll need it."

"Meaning?"

Cassidy tossed the paper towel in the trash can, and then made a production out of looking me over. "You asked a stranger if he wanted to own a cat with you, and he said yes. Trust me, he's interested."

"That's the thing, though. I can't tell if he is."

She turned skeptical. "You're super hot."

"Thanks." I laughed lightly. "Except I've been super hot for the past year, and he never noticed me before," I mused.

She was well aware of the way I'd lusted over Clay when he first moved in, and she shrugged. "I am kind of surprised the cat made a move on him before you did."

Cassidy had a point. Usually, if I saw something I wanted, I went for it. "Maybe I've been playing the long game with him."

She feigned seriousness. "Uh-huh, sure."

It reinforced my plan for this evening, and once my shift was over and I was seated in my car, I thumbed out a text message to Clay.

Me: Hey! Is it cool if I stop by for a visit?

Clay: Yeah. I won't be home until later.

I frowned. That wasn't part of the plan.

Me: Hot date?

As soon as I sent it, my frown deepened, because now I was terrified I'd just made it weird, or worse—he'd tell me the answer was yes.

Clay: Ha ha. I'm in Smyrna, picking up cabinets.

I brightened with relief. Smyrna was only thirty minutes away. I could make that work.

Me: Okay. I might still be there when you get home.

He sent me a thumbs-up emoji, and I grinned wickedly to myself.

It was June, and already one of the hottest summers on record for Nashville, and yet I shivered.

I was sitting on the leather wingback chair in Clay's study, the one that had wooden armrests, and it was directly under an air conditioning vent, so the frigid air was blasting me. Also not helping my situation . . . I was naked except for my favorite pair of high-heeled sandals. The sexy black straps crisscrossed over my feet and all the way up to my ankles.

I'd been seated like this for a while, sitting in the chair with my legs crossed and my dark brown hair loose around my shoulders as I waited for Clay to return home. Noir had come to say hello to me, but once the air kicked on, she slinked away in search of a less drafty place.

This was risky plan, and I'd been shivering long enough in my spot to begin to second-guess myself. It could backfire and embarrass me, but at the same time, I thought it was unlikely. Clay was attracted to me. He'd said I was one of the most beautiful women he'd ever seen, and his desire had been unmistakable the night I'd talked him into adopting Noir.

He wanted me. He just needed a little push.

And I'd make it as easy and clear as possible I wanted him, too.

I had confidence, but it threatened to run away from me the moment I heard the mechanical hum of the garage door. The sound came from all the way across the house, which meant I had time. I could grab my stack of clothes and dart into the hall bathroom, then emerge once I was dressed. Clay would never know I'd been naked in his study, my bare skin pressed to his leather chair.

A door opened, and the alarm system chirped.

Footsteps crossed the tile floor of his kitchen, followed by a clatter as keys were dropped on a counter. Then, silence . . . as if he had paused.

"Lilith?"

No turning back now. I straightened my posture, lifted my chin, and spoke like my heart wasn't threatening to beat out of my chest. "I'm in here."

Clay followed my voice, his feet carrying him down the hall toward the study. I sucked in a preparing breath, leaned an elbow casually on an armrest, and curled my lips into a provocative smile.

When he stepped into view, every muscle in my body tightened. He wore a simple gray t-shirt, jeans, and his sexy black-rimmed glasses. Shit, he looked good. But he pulled up short at the sight of me.

His eyes went wide, and his mouth dropped open, but he didn't produce a single sound. It was like everything in him had shut down and quit working, including his brain.

"Hey, neighbor." My tone was sultry. "Welcome home."

He didn't blink, and his chest wasn't moving. Had he forgotten how to breathe? Everything inside me buzzed, thrilled at how I'd stunned him speechless.

I'd hoped to surprise him, and I certainly had, but . . .

It had been cold under the vent, and the longer he stood there and stared at me without moving or saying a word, the worse the chill on my skin became. Time dragged, and dragged, and I swallowed thickly.

"Clay," I whispered, "are you okay?"

Behind his glasses, his eyes clouded over before his gaze dropped to the floor. "What happened to your clothes?"

I wasn't prepared for his harsh tone, and it cut through me like a knife. Of all the different emotions I'd anticipated, anger hadn't been one of them.

"I . . ." My confidence tumbled off a cliff, and I shot to my feet, blood rushing hotly to my face. "I thought you'd like this, but I must have misread the situation. I'm sorry."

I reached for my clothes on the desk, but his sharp command froze me into place. "Stop."

The stillness of the room was oppressive, and I was sure if he didn't say anything else, I'd be frozen like this forever with breath halted in my lungs.

"You thought," his voice was as precise as the blueprints spread out on his drafting table, "that I'd like this? Seeing you naked?"

Oh, God. My mouth went bone dry, preventing me from speaking.

When he lifted his gaze to mine, it rose slowly up the length of my body, evaluating each curve and every inch of bare flesh.

"You're right," he said finally. "I like it a lot." His

expression heated as he took a step closer, but he arched a disapproving eyebrow. "But I don't do well with surprises. I don't like the unexpected."

I had no idea what to say. "Oh. I'm sorry."

He acted like he hadn't heard me, because his expression remained stern. "I don't like my plans being disrupted."

It bubbled up out of habit. "I'm sorry."

"And I had plans for you. This," his gaze swept over my nude form, "is way ahead of my schedule."

If he had sounded playful or teasing, I would have laughed with nervous excitement—but he hadn't. If anything, his tone hinted at his annoyance, and it had a strange effect. I was eager to please him, to alleviate his irritation with me, even when I had no fucking idea how. I was already naked and throwing myself at him. It spun me for a loop that he was upset about it. Especially when he'd said he had plans for me and getting naked was on his schedule.

I crossed an arm over my stomach and gripped my elbow, wanting to reach for him but unsure of how he'd feel about it. I regrouped, shifted on my heels, and let go of my elbow so I could put my hand on my hip.

"Oh, yeah?" I tried to achieve the same sultry tone I'd used earlier. "And did your plans include us going downstairs to your workshop?"

My question caught him so off-guard he reared back a step and tension flooded through his frame. "Excuse me?"

Oh, shit. I'd misread his reaction. He wasn't surprised by my question—he was *offended*.

His eyes narrowed, and I shrank perfectly in time with

them. My brain fumbled and searched for a way to fix it. "It's beautiful, you know," I said quickly. "The cross you've built, and all of the—"

"I don't remember giving you permission to go into my basement." He was hard and cold, even as his eyes burned with outrage. "That's my private space, and you had no right to be there."

"That's not entirely true." I didn't like his accusation. "You kept the door closed, and I respected that all week, until I couldn't avoid it. Yesterday, when I was over here, there was a huge crash, and I needed to make sure something terrible hadn't happened."

He paused. "What?"

"Those boards you'd left leaning up against the wall? One of them fell over. I had no idea what that sound was, so you can't blame me for checking it out. What if it had been part of the ceiling falling or a beam collapsing or something?"

Clay's gaze slid away from me as he considered this new information. We had to look ridiculous, me standing there buck naked in his study while he was fully clothed.

"I wasn't snooping, I promise," I added. "I was trying to be helpful. Trying to be good."

He repeated the word like it was unfamiliar. "Good."

"Yeah. I didn't plan to go down there and find your workshop, but"—I shrugged—"you can't blame me for looking. I was interested. Don't worry, I didn't touch anything, even though I wanted to."

He looked at me cautiously, unsure if I was telling him the truth.

"And I'll say it again." I wanted him to hear the honesty in my words. "The stuff you've built? It's gorgeous. Like, the fucking sexiest art I've ever seen."

His shoulders lifted as he drew in a deep breath, and when he pushed his glasses back on his nose, Clay seemed to collect himself. My compliment had a powerful effect on him, which he tried not to show. He straightened. "It's not art."

"Why not? Because it serves a function?" I smiled wickedly. "Okay. Let's go downstairs and you can show me."

He scrubbed a hand over his mouth, mostly to muffle the "*fuck*" he muttered under his breath, but the action gave him back some of the control he'd lost. Curiosity lurked in his expression. "You'd be up for that?"

When I nodded, he walked the few steps toward me until there was no space left between us, and he peered down with a discerning look. The shift in him strengthened until power radiated from him. It was formed like a question, but it rang in my ears as a demand. "Can I touch you?"

I nodded.

Rather than put his arms around me, he slid one of his hands into the hair at the nape of my neck, cradling the back of my head and angling it up. His voice was as smooth as warm honey. "You want me to strap you to the cross and do what, exactly?"

His gaze traced over the curves of my face before landing on my lips. My pulse raced, and he was so close, I could barely breathe.

"You can do whatever you want to," I uttered.

"Hmm." It was the perfect answer because sinful

darkness danced in his eyes. "Maybe I want to punish you for screwing up my plan."

Did he mean his plan of getting me naked?

The air in his study was thick with lust, and Clay's strong hand cupping the back of my head made it hard to think straight. I pictured myself in cuffs, bound to his beautiful St. Andrew's cross downstairs while he teased and tortured.

He tilted his head a single degree, adjusting to a better angle to plant his lips over mine. "Would you like that?"

My body was clamoring for it. "Yes."

A smile curved his mouth. He already knew my answer. "Is that what you need? A little bit of discipline?"

Awareness lurked in the back of my mind. He was older and obviously more experienced, but my eagerness made me ignore the warning. I was hungry for his kiss, looking forward to whatever punishment he wanted to dole out. "Yes," I whispered.

He slid his hand away and stepped back so abruptly, I swayed at the sudden absence of him.

"All right." His tone was cool and indifferent. "Then, you'll get dressed right now and go home."

FOUR

My heart thudded to a stop. One second ago, Clay's lips had been a scant inch from mine, and now he was gone.

"What?"

He said it plainly. "You wanted to be punished. I'm punishing you," he casually tossed a hand toward me, gesturing to my nakedness, "and I don't want to encourage this behavior."

My body refused to move, so I stood there dumbfounded and with my mouth hanging open. "Are you kidding me?"

"Do I look like I'm kidding?"

No, he certainly didn't.

His expression was fixed, and all the heat between us dissipated in an instant. My brain couldn't process what had just happened. How had he turned himself off so quickly? Disappointment descended on me like an avalanche, and hot irritation quickly followed.

I closed my mouth with an audible snap, and as I reached for my clothes in a huff, the last thing I expected to hear from him was a deep, satisfied chuckle. But that was what he did, and the sinful sound reverberated through me.

"Look at you," he said darkly. "All upset you didn't get your way."

My hands slowed. What the fuck? He was being an

asshole, and I glared at him, ready to unleash my tongue—

"God, you're even hotter when you pout." Seduction threaded his voice. "You're so fucking hot, Lilith, I can't even stand it."

What?

He gave me emotional whiplash, and I blinked rapidly, trying to understand him. But it was impossible because he stared at me now like a starving man, his expression dripping with desire, and all thoughts emptied out of my mind.

"I've changed my mind," he declared. "Turn around. Put your knees on the seat of the chair."

I was still processing his command when he grasped my elbow and guided me to the leather wingback chair I'd been sitting on when he came home. He set his fingertips on my back and eased me forward, until I had my knees buried in the cushion and my forearms draped over the top of the chair.

It caused an arch in my back, and my bare bottom jutted out toward Clay, and he skated a finger along my spine, tracing a line from my shoulders to my hips. And then his featherlight touch was gone.

"You want to be punished." It was a statement, but it was clear he was waiting for confirmation from me, so my head bobbed in a nod. "Good," he said. "I hope you're not fragile."

His hand came down quickly, and although the smack of his palm against my ass sounded loud, his blow fell painlessly across my skin. A stunned smile buzzed my lips. I'd never really been spanked before, and this was what I'd hoped for. Part of me was disappointed I wasn't bound to the beautiful cross he'd built, but the rest of me was pleased. I'd yearned to sexually explore, and it didn't matter that much where or how it happened.

I was grateful he was willing to partner with me.

Clay spanked my ass again, and this one had more of a kick to it, but I bit the inside of my cheek to keep from giggling. Was that supposed to hurt? Because it didn't, not by a longshot. I understood, though, how he was testing me. Better to start soft and build up to it, rather than do too much, have to back down, and potentially scare me off.

His palm cracked against me once more, and this one was serious enough to make my body jolt—but it was simply from the force of it and not in pain. My breath came and went in quick bursts, but otherwise I didn't make a sound. Could he tell my short breath was caused by anticipation and not discomfort?

He sounded begrudgingly impressed. "You're awfully quiet."

"Guess I'm not fragile." For added effect, I wiggled my hips.

He let out a short laugh, and it sounded very much like, *"We'll see about that."*

The wood floor beneath his feet creaked as he adjusted his stance. Then the sharp smack of skin meeting skin punched through the quiet of the room, quickly followed by another slap.

And another.

He alternated between sides, spreading the blows around, varying tempo and placement.

I gasped at the rhythm he created, the warmth that bloomed over my skin, and a muscle deep in my belly clenched in pleasure. When a moan slipped from my lips, he hesitated, making it possible for me to hear he'd become as out of breath as I was.

"It feels good," I said quietly.

He sounded surprised. "It doesn't hurt?"

I turned over my shoulder to glance at him and subtly shook my head. Fucking hell, he looked so incredibly sexy as he stood behind me, desire hazing his eyes.

A moment stretched heavy between us before he asked it. "Do you want it to?"

His posture was rigid, announcing everything hinged on my answer, and a dark voice inside me spoke up, encouraging me to try something *new*.

I'd always had a high threshold for pain—at least that's what I'd been told. I didn't mind a blister or a shoe strap cutting across the top of my foot. I dealt with the discomfort because I loved my heels and enjoyed both the ache and the release of slipping off my shoes at the end of the night.

Would it be the same now? Would the pain he gave me, followed by the absence of it, be pleasurable? I was eager to find out. He'd asked me if I wanted him to make it hurt, and it was startling how confidently my answer came.

"*Yes.*"

He exhaled loudly, and with deep satisfaction, and the sound gave me a delicious shiver. I licked my dry lips as his focus swung to his desk, and then on to the drafting table. Whatever he'd been searching for, he found it there.

He strolled to the table, picked up a long, silver ruler, and seemed to evaluate its weight in his hand. It wasn't a flat, normal ruler—it was one of those triangular drafting things with three sides, each ending in a point.

If I had any doubt about what he planned to do with it, it vanished as he smacked one end of the ruler against the palm of his other hand. He hadn't done it as a threat. In fact, he wasn't even looking at me. He studied the ruler and his open palm, evaluating it. Satisfied, he turned toward me.

Oh, my God.

Blood rushed loudly in my ears, dulling the sound of Clay's footsteps as he came close. My gaze was fixated on what was clenched in his hand, and goosebumps burst across my arms and legs.

While I was focused on the ruler, his gaze burned into me. "You understand what I intend to do with this scale?"

Was that what the ruler was called? "Yes," I said, squeezing it out between my short breaths. "I do."

"You'll show me you're okay with trying this," he said, "when you cross your wrists behind your back."

The feeling coursing through me was the same one as stepping onto a rollercoaster and pulling the bar down to lock me in place. I knew what was about to happen. It would probably feel scary but exhilarating, and I went to it willingly. Eagerly, even.

I leaned forward, resting the flat of my chest on the top of the chair back, and put my hands behind me, stacking one wrist on top of the other. My long brown hair draped down over my face and toward the floor, and I shut my eyes, mentally preparing myself for what would come next. Not that I had any idea what that triangular-shaped ruler was going to feel like when it—

The cold metal kissed my skin, and I flinched reflexively. Both of my hands resting on the hollow of my back curled into fists.

He hadn't actually spanked me.

All he'd done was set the scale against my ass, creating two chilly lines on my bare skin, and my overreaction to it caused a chuckle to roll out of Clay's throat. But then his voice turned serious. "Have you ever done something like this before?"

My eyes popped open and my hair shimmered as I shook my head.

The cotton of his t-shirt and the heat of his body was abruptly warm on my back as he leaned over, bringing his mouth right beside the shell of my ear. "I'm glad I get to be the first."

I swallowed a breath as he straightened, and a split second later, the ruler slapped against me in a sharp, quick strike.

It *stung*. The sensation of it forced me to suck in a breath through tight teeth.

But apparently this wasn't the reaction he'd been hoping for, because Clay repeated the action, and this time the crack of the ruler brought fire. Pain throbbed and lingered in the aftermath of the metal biting into my skin.

"*Fuck*," I swore.

His tone was sinister. "*Now* we're getting somewhere."

My head spun at this version of him. Up until yesterday, he'd been my shy and quiet next-door neighbor. I'd never expected him to be assertive. Or so . . . dominating.

And, shit, I hadn't expected to like it so much.

I wished I had known sooner, because I would have come over asking to borrow a cup of sugar. Except I would have been hoping for something other than sweetness.

He struck my ass again, hard and unapologetic and right across my cheeks, and the pain from the contact seared through me. As it radiated down my limbs, I whined and squirmed, trying to make the feeling dissipate faster.

"Does it hurt?"

"Yes," I groaned.

It was like his dark voice was inside my head. "Do you want me to stop?"

"No," I said softly. My emotions were fractured, all over the place. But I felt strangely more aware and present in the moment than I ever had before. I didn't want him to stop, but my voice was barely a whisper. "Is that weird?"

His answer was resounding and excited. "No."

I turned as best I could to see him and marveled at the way his lips were parted so he could drag heavy air in and out of his lungs. The ruler was clenched in a white-knuckled fist at his side, and an impressive bulge pushed at the zipper of his jeans, tenting the front of them.

"You like the pain?" he asked, studying me. "Does it turn you on?"

Yes? Well, more like *maybe*. I didn't know the answer with certainty, so I stuck with the truth. "I like the way you look right now."

That was what was turning me on. How he was in complete control of what we were doing. The way he gripped the ruler at the ready and stared at me with excited urgency, willing to do what had to be done to his naughty neighbor. He was prepared to get me back in line.

I shouldn't like what he was doing. He was hitting me hard enough to leave marks, and I was aware I was in way over my head with him. And yet, why wasn't I nervous? Why did I feel . . . safe?

Perhaps it was because he hadn't done anything I hadn't agreed to or asked for. The unforgiving ruler was exactly what I'd been craving.

I had to strain over my shoulder to see him as he grabbed a handful of my skin where the raised red lines crisscrossed each other, and he squeezed until I clenched my teeth. His grip intensified the lingering ache in my sensitive, welted skin, but it was oddly pleasurable. The connection of his touch only turned me on more.

He grunted a sound of approval as he grasped my tender flesh. "I like the way you look right now, too."

When he released his hold, I sighed in contentment, only for him to bring the ruler crashing down with a brutal slap. I cried out, canting my hips to run from the pain, and dug my nails into my palms.

But just like the way he stared at me, the hurt and the longing for him to do it again was inescapable. I was adrift and fell further under his spell as he used his free hand to undo the button of his jeans and drop his zipper.

It was clear that, just as I did—he *ached.*

A look of desire twisted on his face as he dug his hand inside his undone pants. I gasped at how hot it was, both the visual and the idea that he was getting off on what we were doing.

A yelp ripped from my mouth as I took another hit, and I lifted a foot, all the way until the back of my stiletto heel touched my burning skin. It offered me some protection and a reprieve, and Clay stroked himself. He twisted his grip and pumped his fist, and the edges of his jeans and underwear worked down over his hips until his dick was exposed.

While he wasn't exactly naked, he was where it counted, and it was satisfying he was nearly as vulnerable as I was. He fucked his fist with vicious need, like a man who had no other choice. I watched the head of his thick cock turn white as he thrust through his tight fingers, stoking the fire raging inside me. The throb pulsating in my flesh shifted, sliding down to the center of my legs.

And with it, the atmosphere in the room changed, like the sun outside had suddenly been blotted out by the clouds. Everything closed in around us. I sensed the reckless hunger building inside Clay, and I quivered in anticipation, my heart thundering along at breakneck speed.

The *whoosh* of the ruler cutting through the air announced how fast it was traveling, and I heard the smack of it before the pain registered. Agony stormed through my body, white-hot and cruel, and there was no time to consider how to react. I groaned and recoiled from his merciless ruler, using one hand to brace myself and grip the chair's armrest, and my other hand to shield me from another blow.

There was no need to tell him to stop or utter the word *no*. When I'd uncrossed my wrists, it had announced that for me. Clay's tool of punishment clattered to the floor, and as I struggled to heave air into my body, he dropped to his knees behind me.

"Oh, *fuck*," I gasped.

Because he flattened his palms to my hot, irritated skin, peeled me apart, and pressed his mouth right between my legs, where I was soaking wet.

And desperate with desire.

The tip of his tongue coursed through my pussy, found my clit, and focused in, fluttered over it. I jolted from the shocking, acute pleasure. I loved it when a guy went down on me, but this? It was insanity, and it'd *never* felt like this before. Each lush stroke of his tongue caused static in my body. It was so good, it short-circuited my brain, and my body didn't know how to handle the overload.

I clenched my hand on the armrest, my fingers straining. It felt like I needed to hold on to something while I endured this new type of lashing, where instead of a cold, metal ruler, the instrument of torment he used was the velvety-soft flat of his tongue.

My legs quivered, and when he increased the pressure of his strokes, moans seeped from my mouth. His lips closed around my clit and sucked gently, feeding my building pleasure until the only thought pounding in my mind was my approaching orgasm.

I was primed to explode, and I detonated when Clay's fingers curled inward. He raked the sharp edge of his fingernails over the swollen lines his ruler had caused on my skin, and the pain mixed with my pleasure, setting me off.

My orgasm was an electric shock as it traveled up my spine and burst out through my limbs. It was icy cold and scorching hot, and my cry of ecstasy filled the room. I reached my hand back to him—either to touch him or push him away from my overly-sensitive body—I wasn't sure. The climax swept through me violently, draining and weakening and taking until it felt like I had nothing left.

But I wasn't allowed to touch him, or perhaps he wanted me to stay exactly as I was, because his hand closed around my wrist and pinned it to my back in the same spot it'd been when he'd used the ruler. And he climbed quickly to his feet, moving with efficiency.

His one hand on me wasn't much of a restraint, especially since my other was free. The thing keeping me in place was the powerful sensation he'd given me, which was still making me shudder with bliss. As it began to diminish and my breathing slowed, his ramped up. He had his fingers wrapped around my wrist, but his other hand worked himself over at a frantic tempo.

Holy fuck, it was hot.

Intense concentration etched his handsome face as he stared down at his furious hand, watching himself jerk off right over my bare ass—the one he'd marked with both his ruler and his fingernails. His chest rose and fell dramatically as he pumped his fist, the tip of his cock brushing against my knuckles of the hand he held down.

When he came, Clay exhaled an enormous breath, groaned loudly, and his fist slowed to a measured tempo. Hot, thick liquid splattered onto my back in spurts, and dripped onto my fingers. His grip on me had tightened nearly to the point of pain, but tension went out of him as he recovered from his orgasm, and I wondered if his hold on me was more about connection than anything else now.

The cadence of his breathing gradually returned to its unhurried pace, and as that happened, awareness rolled through me. I'd come to his house and gotten naked in hopes of seducing him. And yeah, he'd gone down on me, but . . . we hadn't had sex. I hadn't touched him. In fact, he'd barely touched me in a way I was used to.

And we hadn't kissed.

Instead of his mouth pressed to mine, he'd given me red, angry welts on my ass and his cum splashed on my skin. I wasn't upset about what we'd done. Just disappointed we hadn't done . . . *more*.

"Stay still," he said softly when I attempted to move.

My muscles were taxed from being in the same position for so long, not to mention the amount of tension I'd had while maintaining my posture, but I did as he asked. His fingers slid away from my wrist, and I left my hand where it was, resting awkwardly on my back.

There was a box of tissues on his desk, and Clay went to it, pulling several out, and then returned to me, gently cleaning up the mess on my back and fingers.

His voice wavered, less confident than before. "How are you feeling?"

I wasn't sure how he meant.

Physically? Emotionally?

The truth was I didn't know. The welts on my body were

still smarting, but I kind of liked it. It was an aching reminder of what he'd done, and mentally, my head was foggy. Not exactly dreamy, but sort of . . . floaty.

It was nice and made me bold.

"I'm feeling," I said, "like I wish we had kissed before we . . ."

He let out a tight breath. "I can fix that."

Then his hands were on my shoulders, easing me back off the chair. For the first time in ages, I tottered on my heels like they were brand new. Like I wasn't comfortable standing or walking in them, even though I wore high heels every chance I could since I'd turned twenty.

Shit, this floaty state was distracting.

I shuffled in place, turning beneath his guiding hands to face him. Clay studied my lips with the same focused look he'd given me earlier, and it didn't allow my racing pulse a moment to slow down. This time when he touched me, he used both hands. He slid them into my hair so he could cup my face and hold me still, then lowered his mouth to mine.

Like everything else had been, his kiss was not what I expected. It wasn't controlled or restrained, but it wasn't deep or passionate either. It felt . . . calculated. It gave me a strange thought that he'd drafted how he'd approach kissing me, even down to the specific angle he'd use. Had he designed it to the exact degree? If I went poking around in his papers, would I find it sketched out somewhere?

His kiss felt *planned*.

It wasn't a bad thing, though—just different. It still had heat and intimacy, enough to make me feel lightheaded.

There was just a hint of tongue, and as soon as I tried to reciprocate, it was gone.

The kiss was over.

He drew back, keeping my face cradled in his hands, and an emotion I couldn't place drifted through his eyes. Regret? I hoped not.

"I had planned," he said, "to have a conversation with you before we went any further, but—"

"I disrupted your plans."

He nodded, his expression serious. "We still need to have it, but before we do, you didn't actually answer me. Are you hurting? Do you want ice or a pain reliever?"

I wasn't hurting, mostly just uncomfortable, and I was too curious about what he wanted to talk about to care much about the dull heat banding across my skin. "I'm all right."

His discerning look said he didn't believe me. His hands slid away, did up his jeans, and collected my stack of clothes off the desk. "Come with me."

I wasn't given a choice, but I didn't need one. I was just like the cat slinking around his house—too curious for my own good.

He led me into his bedroom, not bothering to turn on the lights. The evening sun was setting on the far side of the house, making the room dark and moody and sexy. He deposited my clothes on the top of his dresser and motioned to the unmade bed. "Lie down on your stomach."

He wanted me to get into his bed? I didn't need to be told twice. I put a knee on the mattress, crawled along the sheets in a way I hoped he found seductive, and lay down with my head on what I suspected was his pillow. The sheets smelled faintly sunny and woodsy, like the scent of his detergent battled for control over his cologne and body wash.

I'd expected him to join me in the bed, but instead he disappeared into his bathroom, flipping on the light and moving deeper inside, out of my view. There was the sound of a door opening, perhaps the linen closet, and then the faucet ran for a moment. I propped myself up on my elbows and peered through the doorway to watch him wring out a towel.

It was only a few moments later when he brought it into the bedroom and draped the cold, damp towel over the marks on my skin. I flinched, but the coolness of it soothed me instantly.

"Thank you," I said.

Clay sat on the side of the bed, turned toward me with one leg tucked on the mattress and a contemplative look streaked his face.

"What did you want to talk about?"

He drew in a heavy breath. "Remember how I said I'm complicated?"

I nodded. I'd thought he meant the BDSM furniture, but the way he was now made me unsure. He looked more nervous than he was the first time he'd used the ruler on me.

"I can do relationships," he said. "I completely understand the need for commitment and trust. And even monogamy if that's what my partner wants." He frowned, like the next part was difficult for him to say. "But I don't do romance, Lilith." His gaze trapped mine. "Which means I don't date."

FIVE

I blinked, trying to digest what Clay had just said. "Why?"

"I'm no good at it, and more importantly, I'm not interested. I've never been."

The look he'd given me before—the one I couldn't place—made sense now. It had been guilt.

"I'm sorry," he said quietly. "If that's what you're looking for from me, I can't give it to you." He pushed up his glasses and straightened his shoulders. "As a rule, I don't scene with someone unless they know already. I'm sorry about how I handled that."

I swallowed a breath. "So, what you're saying is . . . you don't want to be my boyfriend?"

He went utterly still, but when I laughed and he realized I was joking, he returned to life.

"Don't sweat it, Clay." I grinned. "I'm not looking for any of that right now." My last several relationships hadn't gone so well. Maybe I was like him. "I'm not any good at dating either."

My response was so unexpected to him and, God, the way he looked at me. As if I were a structure he wasn't able to figure out, a puzzle he couldn't solve.

I mashed his pillow beneath my chest. "Do you do this a lot?" What was the word he'd used? "Scene?"

He hesitated, but it didn't seem to be reluctance. More like he was trying to word his answer carefully. "I haven't in a while." He reached out, tracing his fingertips over the curve of my shoulder. "You liked what we did?"

"Yes."

His tender touch was disarming. "I'm meeting a client tonight at Club Eros." He pushed a lock of my hair back and his tone was cautious. "Are you interested in coming with me?"

"Club Eros," I repeated. I'd never been to a BDSM club, and suddenly now I was dying to. What would it be like? I said it teasingly, even though I was serious. "Are you going to show me your world?"

His gaze snapped to mine, and his intensity made me shiver with excitement. "Yes."

I wore a black corset top, paired with a teal skirt, and the same black heels from earlier. The strapless satin corset was the sexiest thing I owned, and I'd never been brave enough to wear it before tonight.

I sat beside Clay in the back seat of our Uber as it drove us toward the club. He'd given our driver the address, and I wondered most of the drive there if the guy knew what kind of club he was going to deliver us to. Clay was dressed in a black suit without a tie, and the collar of his white shirt was unbuttoned. He looked nice and professional, and not at all like he'd be the type of guy to spank me with a metal ruler hard enough that sitting was still uncomfortable hours later.

But I liked the sensation. I spent every quiet moment thinking about who had caused my discomfort, and heat flushed through me.

When I climbed out of the car and stared up at the club, I was surprised at how unassuming it looked. The rest of the block was warehouses, but this building was a house. Two-stories tall and brick, it was set back a little from the road, and had no signage other than a backlit chrome E glowing beside the door. I wouldn't have even known it was a club if it wasn't for the black-suited man standing on the porch out front. He was clearly security. Otherwise, the place was dark and quiet.

I strolled alongside Clay, moving across the sidewalk and up the porch steps to the entrance.

The security man seemed to recognize Clay, because the guy smiled and opened the door for us. He gave me a casual once-over. Not leering at all, more simply curious. Clay said he didn't date, but he'd probably brought other women here before me. Maybe the bouncer was interested in who this new girl was at this regular customer's side.

The guard gestured politely for me to go first, and I stepped across the threshold into the club.

The walls and ceiling of this small entry room were painted black, and subdued lighting lit the woman sitting behind the counter. She was older, but had a bright, youthful smile.

"Welcome back," she said warmly to Clay before her gaze turned to me. "Can I see your IDs?"

"She's new," he explained as we both pulled out our drivers' licenses. "Not a member yet."

I set my ID on the counter, and the woman's smile widened. "That's great. I'll get you all squared away, honey."

She scanned our IDs and typed into her computer, nodding along to the soft thump of music that could be heard coming from deeper inside the place. I was handed a clipboard with a release to sign and date, which I did.

After the paperwork was completed, she looked pleased. "Your membership's been approved," she said, handing back my license. "The new member fee is twenty."

Clay must have been expecting this because he dropped a credit card on the counter, right next to his ID. She picked up his license and got to work scanning it in.

"The cover for her will be ten," she continued, "and for you—"

The scan of his license popped up on her screen, and the title 'Preferred Member' flashed along the top.

"Oh." She straightened in pleasant surprise. "So, the total will be just sixty."

I blinked. *Just* sixty? I lowered my voice to a whisper so only he'd hear. "How much is it regularly?"

His expression was fixed. "For the guys who are regular members, it's a hundred a night."

"Jesus." That was a lot for one night, not to mention sexist, but also . . . it didn't surprise me. The strip club I went to years ago with my guy friends had no cover charge for women. Maybe this place wanted to entice as many women as possible like other clubs did.

The woman turned her attention to him. "Do you want to give her the tour, or would you like me to call someone from staff?"

"I can give it to her."

She nodded and focused on me. "All right, the rules are easy for women. Really, the only one is no phones are allowed. If you get caught using one, you'll be asked to leave. You're allowed to go anywhere inside the club, except staff areas, behind the bar, or the restroom that's opposite the gender you identify as. Also, if anyone makes you feel uncomfortable or unsafe, just let someone on staff know immediately and we'll take care of it. Staff is all around the club. They're the ones wearing gold nametags."

Done with her spiel, the woman swiped Clay's credit card, tore off the slip, and passed it to him to sign.

"If you're interested in watching," she added, "Mistress Theia's show begins at eleven thirty. Any questions I can answer for you?"

It was clear she was asking me, but my brain was buzzing over what she'd just said. *Show? Mistress?* I was anxious to go inside. "No, I don't think so."

"Okay. You two have fun." She slipped her hand under the counter and must have pressed a button, because the door to the club buzzed softly.

Ever since I'd been told about this place, I'd tried to picture what it'd be like. In the movies, sex clubs always seemed either scary industrial, full of metal and leather, or elegant and opulent, with red velvet drapes and flickering candles.

Eros wasn't like either of those.

At first glance, it was like any regular nightclub. There was a bar along the back wall and a dancefloor in the center, complete with strobing lights and music that was heavy on the bass. There were elevated platforms at the edge of the dance space. One was a cage and the other a pole, but currently both platforms were empty.

It was relatively dark in the large room, and subdued lighting was cast down on the individual tables scattered on the carpeted area.

There weren't many people out on the dancefloor, but I couldn't tell if it was because it was too early in the evening, or the cause was the song that was currently playing. It was sexy, but it was also slower. Too slow to make me want to dance.

Several couples and groups of friends sat at the low tables, talking and drinking while watching the handful of people moving to the music on the dancefloor.

My gaze followed theirs, and I did a double-take.

One of the women out dancing lifted her dress clear up to her waist, flashing the crowd with her perfectly bare lower body. When I turned to Clay to see his reaction, he wasn't surprised. Only a faint smile hinted on his lips.

He had to lean close so I could hear him over the music. "Guys have to be dressed in the common areas on this floor, but not women. Once you're through the front door, you can take everything off if you want to, Lilith."

It was suddenly difficult to catch my breath. Obviously, I wasn't shy, but I'd never been a true exhibitionist before, mainly because I worried getting naked in public would get me in trouble. My gaze went back to the dancefloor and the woman who swayed her hips, teasing the couple closest to her as she showed off her pussy. Was I interested in that?

I didn't have time to consider it right this second, because there was still a lot to take in.

I found the clientele interesting and unexpected. There was a huge range in ages—people of all shapes and sizes and levels of attractiveness—and the vast majority of them were dressed up like Clay and I were. Fancier skirts, dresses, and suits seemed to be the standard, rather than leather or latex.

"Let's get a drink, and I'll give you the tour," he said.

When I nodded, Clay gestured toward the bar. One side of it was occupied by a few guys who sat on stools, and their gazes were fixated on the dancefloor—until I walked by.

Awareness trickled down my spine. I looked good tonight in my corset, short skirt, and stilettos, and these men had noticed. The atmosphere surrounding me thickened.

It was the same experience as a group of guys zeroing on me at a bar when I'd been separated from my friends.

It felt like I was being watched by predators. As if these men were a pack of wolves and I was fresh meat plunked down in front of them. Had Clay sensed it too? He set his hand on the small of my back, and my heart tripped over itself. Maybe it was just a helpful gesture to guide me, but I doubted it. He'd done it to lay claim.

And I didn't mind that one bit.

While we waited for the bartender to mix our drinks, I ticked my head toward the men on the other end of the bar. "What's the story with those guys?"

"Single men are only allowed at the bar."

"They can't go anywhere else?" Confusion made me press my lips together. "They pay a hundred bucks to, what? Just sit at the bar all night?"

He found my question amusing as he tipped the bartender, grabbed our drinks, and handed mine to me. "No. They can leave the bar if someone invites them to join them."

"Oh, I gotcha. If a woman picks them up, then they can—"

"Yeah, except it's almost always couples."

"Really?" I grinned scandalously. "Threesomes?"

He was so matter-of-fact about it. "Sometimes, or the husband just wants to watch."

Oh, my God. My gaze flicked to the men perched on their barstools who looked like they were waiting for someone to punch their dance card. "If I hadn't come with you tonight, would you be sitting with them?"

Not that he'd have to wait long. He had the whole Clark Kent thing going on, which was incredibly sexy. At least, it was to me. I'd always thought Superman was the hottest when he was hiding behind his plain clothes and glasses.

"I've been a member for more than five years," he said, "and I've been vetted, so I have the same freedoms as you."

"Yeah?" I lifted an eyebrow and pretended to be skeptical. "Why don't you get naked and prove it?"

It was so much fun to catch him off guard. His eyes would widen behind his black frames, and I could see how disoriented he became when things didn't go exactly as he planned. He recovered quickly, though.

"I stand corrected. I have *almost* the same freedoms as you."

He took a sip of his drink, then motioned beyond the dancefloor. There was a doorway on the far side of the room that led to the rest of the club, and I was eager for the tour, but before I could take a step, my heart lurched.

There was a man seated alone at one of the tables with his hand wrapped around a tumbler of amber liquid, although the drink looked untouched. He wore a beautiful gray suit and blue tie, and when he lifted his hand to wave, a brilliant smile broke on his face.

I didn't know him, but blood rushed through me, heating my body regardless.

Clay was handsome and sexy, exuding intelligence and competence. He was like a Hollywood version of a hot nerd.

This stranger waving at me was the Hollywood version of a hunk, and even though I usually liked Clay's brand of guy best, it was impossible to ignore how good this man looked.

He was younger than Clay, but older than I was—maybe the guy was thirty. He had sandy-colored hair that was perfectly unruly, the ends curling as they fell to brush his ears. And—sweet Jesus—his friendly smile. It lit up the room.

I waved back, keeping my gaze locked on him, even as I whispered to Clay. "Why is that guy waving to me?"

He chuckled. "He's not."

When Clay waved back at the man, embarrassment slammed into me. How freaking cocky had my question been? To just assume the guy was interested in me, and not Clay? He'd told me twenty seconds ago he'd been a member at this club for more than five years. Surely, he'd met other regulars and become friends.

Another idea dawned in me. "Is he the client you're meeting?"

"No." I'd expected him to say more, and the long silence prompted him to reluctantly continue. "He's a . . . friend."

"Oh?" Interesting. "Let's say hi before we start the tour."

But he didn't move. Instead, his gaze sharpened on me. "Why?"

What did he mean, why? "Because it's polite?"

"Hmm, is that it?" His slight smile was teasing. "I'm sure the fact that he's attractive has nothing to do with it."

I played dumb as my gaze drifted back to the man. "Is he? I hadn't noticed."

"Right." He laughed at my outright lie. "Maybe we can say hello after the show if he's still here. I want to make sure I have enough time to show you around before my meeting."

"Okay," I said. It was clear he had a plan, and it didn't include introductions with the hottie in the gray suit. The guy's gaze followed us as we strolled past the tables and dancefloor, but he never made a move to rise from his seat or motion us over to him.

The next room was a swanky lounge. On one side, a couch and several cushy chairs were gathered around a glass table. On the other, there were two open doors, leading into rooms that were dark.

"If a door's closed," he said, "it means the room's in use."

He stuck his hand in and flipped on a switch, lighting up the room that contained two couches that were so small, they were more like loveseats, and a side table that was only big enough to set drinks on. It was tight in the room, but the couches were deep and inviting, and it wasn't hard to picture what probably went on in here.

Clay turned off the light and led me down the short hall. To our left was a gorgeous L-shaped wooden staircase, but he went right, taking me into a room with a glossy black floor and dark red walls. There was a small platform, like a stage, at the end of the room, and a strip of exposed brick served as the backdrop, framing the St. Andrew's cross mounted to it.

I swallowed a breath. I didn't need to see the logo carved in the side because I recognized the style instantly.

"Yours," I said.

There was a hint of pride from him. "Yes."

This cross wasn't like the modern one he had at home. It was the traditional X, made of wood and decorated with iron bands and rings. The warm oak looked great against the brick, and it fit the space perfectly.

"It's beautiful," I said.

"Thank you."

The cross had drawn my attention since it was the focal point, but my gaze shifted to take in the rest of the room. I got the feeling that the black folding chairs were typically set up in rows facing the cross, but tonight they were placed in a circle, leaving the center of the room empty.

Whatever the show was, it'd be happening there, rather than on the stage.

Disappointment skittered through me. "They're not using your cross for the show?"

The corner of his sexy mouth quirked up. "No, it doesn't look like it tonight." He jerked his head toward the doorway.

"Come on. Let me show you upstairs."

The wooden staircase was ornate and had to be original to the old, converted house. The stair treads creaked and groaned loudly as we ascended. I didn't know if it was a stupid question, but I was too curious not to ask and lowered my voice to a hush. "Is everyone gonna be naked up there? Will people be fucking?"

Amusement dashed through his eyes. "I doubt it. I mean, it's still pretty early. Things usually start happening around midnight."

He was right.

No one was having sex or even naked. It was because there wasn't a soul on this floor, other than a staff member sitting on a stool at the top of the stairs. The second story of the house was smaller than the main floor, and the few rooms were basically more lounge areas. The only doors on this floor were for the bathrooms.

The biggest room had an impressive stone fireplace and a huge black leather sectional in front of it. An oversized matching ottoman rested in the center of the U shape the couch formed. Like the rest of the club, the space was tasteful. It was sexy with mood lighting and sultry music wafted from speakers mounted in the corners.

The biggest difference between this lounge and the one downstairs was what rested on the side tables. Tissues. Antibacterial wipes. And . . .

"Is that lube?" I asked.

"I think so, yeah." He gave me an evaluating look, maybe as curious about my reaction as I was about him. "So, thus ends the tour." He took a sip of his Manhattan. "Thoughts so far?"

"It's," I had no idea how to put it in words, "interesting."

He understood. "Not what you were expecting?"

I nodded. "Not in a bad way. Just . . . different."

He shifted on his feet, bringing him close and cutting down on the space between us. His voice dipped low, making it sound impossibly sexy. "Don't be disappointed. The night is young."

"I'm not disappointed."

His gaze roamed over my face before settling on my eyes, and I'd swear he could see right past the lie I'd just told. "Sure you are. You thought there'd be whips and chains. Maybe a dungeon, or an orgy." A gentle smile tilted his lips. "There's nothing wrong with wanting that stuff, but it's better this way. There's a lot I'd like to show you, and it's easier to learn how to swim in the shallow end."

How did he do that? His words filled me with this dark, impatient craving.

Clay's hand slid onto my back, then down over the curve of my ass, squeezing me just hard enough to remind me of the marks he'd put there.

"I really like your enthusiasm, though," he whispered.

Fuck, I nearly melted.

But instead of doing anything else with me, he glanced at his watch and announced it was time for his meeting. I followed him back down the noisy staircase and into the main floor lounge, then sat down in the chair he directed me to, while he sat on the couch.

While we waited, I surveyed my surroundings in greater

detail. The music was loud as it streamed through the open doorway to the nightclub room next door, but I could also hear activity in the red room down the hall. Perhaps they were finishing setup for the show.

One of the doors to the private rooms across the way was closed now. *In use,* he'd said. There was a tall, narrow window framed between the two doors, but it was dark. Was it a functional window where the shade was drawn, or had it been painted black? I couldn't see any bodies moving beyond it, and suddenly that was all I wanted.

I'd been at this sex club for thirty minutes, and other than the woman who'd flashed her pussy on the dancefloor, I hadn't seen any sex. It was so much tamer than what I'd done with Clay this afternoon, not to mention . . . this all felt normal. It only ramped up my sex drive.

And I felt like I was fucking starving.

Clay's client was a skinny man in his fifties, who had a ponytail and wore black leather pants over his lanky legs. The guy's southern accent was thick—much deeper than a Nashville one, and I wondered what he sounded like when he ordered his submissive around.

As he evaluated the different swatches of fabric Clay had given him, the man talked about wanting extra padding on the kneeler. His sub was older, he said, and he wanted to be careful of her knees.

That little detail caused unexpected warmth to slide through me.

Up until now, I only knew the commercialized stuff when it came to BDSM. Porn and countless movies had conditioned me to think only young, beautiful people were allowed to play, to enjoy. But this guy and his older sub were *real* people—not the manufactured stories I'd seen. I was surprised by how much better I liked reality.

So, I wouldn't call Ponytail Guy good looking, but . . . was it strange I found him sort of attractive in his own way? His confidence and ease were undeniable. Or maybe it was the level of care he had for his partner. As the men continued their conversation, the guy revealed his wife was currently at the table in the other room with their friends. He'd snuck away for this meeting, because he was having Clay build the custom piece as a surprise for her.

While details were hammered out, the window across the room abruptly lit up, and my gaze flew to it like it was magnetized.

Holy shit.

SIX

The woman was curvy and, although she was larger than I was, she had beautiful proportions. She wasn't entirely naked because her skirt was bunched around her waist, and a black collar wrapped around her throat, but everywhere else she was bare. Her large, sexy tits swayed each time the man behind her slammed his hips against her ass. Since she was bent over, she braced herself on the window with her hands, her fingers splayed out on the glass.

Had she sensed me? The woman peered out through the glass, her gaze searching, and when she found I was watching, she locked in on me. A sultry smile bowed on her lips, wordlessly announcing how she wanted me to watch.

Jesus, I was on fire, but I didn't dare look away.

The way the man fucked her was rough. The slap of his body rippled and reverberated across her skin, and his face twisted with pleasure. The woman definitely liked it, but it seemed like she was enjoying me even more. To put a finer point on it, she leaned forward and flattened her breasts to the glass. Her tits became two perfect circles of pale skin surrounding her dusky nipples.

Clay's voice was sharp enough to break through. "Lilith."

My attention snapped to him, only to discover both men on the couch were looking at me expectantly. Clay had been sketching something on a notepad he must have been carrying in his suit pocket, but his pen was frozen mid-stroke.

The client laughed. "Your sub didn't hear a word I said."

I jolted. He thought I was Clay's submissive?

Was I?

I didn't correct the guy. Instead, I pinched my knees together and squeezed against the ache the thought of belonging to Clay caused. "I'm sorry," I said. "I, uh, got distracted."

Clay helped me out. "He was complimenting your shoes."

"Oh, thank you." I smiled, hoping to appear grateful and not embarrassed.

I smoothed my hands down my skirt, suddenly not sure what to do with them. Even though my gaze was fixed on the men, I could feel the man and woman next door fucking against the window. It was like they were pressed against me, trying to get inside my brain.

Clay's pen resumed moving, and it gave me something else to focus on. He drew in bold, confident strokes as he explained where he'd place the attachment rings.

"Good." The client nodded. "She still hasn't mastered how to stay still."

The understanding look Clay exchanged with the man made goosebumps lift on my legs. God, did I want to know what he'd do to me if I couldn't stay still. Would he give me a disapproving look over the top of his glasses? Maybe use the ruler again? Or would it be something with an even sharper bite?

I clamped my teeth to hold in my moan.

When the discussion finished, Clay promised to email

over a rendered proof by the end of next week, and once he had approval, he'd be able to come up with a delivery date. The men shook hands, I nodded my polite goodbye, and then the man was off to return to his unsuspecting wife.

My gaze darted to the window. The couple was still there, still fucking, and her gaze was still pinned on me.

"I'm surprised," I tried not to sound breathless, "that you like coming here."

Clay pocketed the notepad and pen and settled back in his seat, his drink in hand. "Why's that?"

"You said you're a private person." I motioned to the window. "Doing something like that's not exactly private."

"No, it's not." He smirked. "But I don't do that."

"What?" I asked. "Lift the shade when you—"

"I don't fuck while other people watch." His tone was serious. "I'd rather do the watching." He blinked slowly, his eyes heavy with desire, and swirled the drink in his glass. "What about you? Is that your kink?"

"Watching?"

He paused, and—shit—his intense look trapped me in place. "Being watched?"

This question was too hard to answer while looking at him, and my gaze fell to the glass tabletop. Even there, I saw his muted reflection watching me. He was so good looking, it wasn't fair.

"Maybe," I said. "I'm not shy."

Had he been holding his breath? His chest rose and fell like he'd let out a deep breath. "No, you're not."

I lifted both my gaze and my shoulder. "I'll try

anything once."

"Is that so?" Electricity crackled between us, and it intensified as his attention swung to the window. "Prove it."

Oh, Jesus. My mouth went dry and my voice faltered, even as I wanted it to sound strong. "How?"

"She seems to like you. Why don't you go to the window and give her a kiss?"

I nearly laughed with delight. It wasn't just easy and safe—it was sexy too. "Okay."

The woman watched me with interest as I stood and sauntered toward the window, and a smile grew on her lips as I closed in. When I put my hands on the glass, she followed suit, placing her hands on the other side right where mine were. Like we were touching.

I leaned forward and planted my lips against the glass, leaving behind the faintest stain of lipstick. As soon as I drew back, she eagerly leaned forward, parted her lips, and dragged the flat of her tongue over the spot. It was as if she wanted to lick up my kiss, and it was erotic. I turned to see what Clay thought about it, only to find him standing beside me.

His fingertips glided across my bare shoulder as he moved to cup the back of my neck with a hand. He didn't speak, but I swallowed thickly. This simple action of his hand on me felt possessive and controlling, and God, did I like it.

His voice was quiet but powerful. "That was my fault. I wasn't specific about where I wanted you to kiss her."

"What?"

The dominating hand on me began to press down. "On your knees."

Fuck. Was it possible to shiver from heat? Because that was exactly what I did.

Clay urged me down to kneel in front of the window. The couple on the other side hadn't slowed down. If anything, my participation had turned them on even more. The man's thrusts were relentless, making her tits jiggle and bounce violently.

My knees abraded on the stubby carpet as I stared up at Clay, awaiting his instruction, and watched his lips part to take in a breath. Having me on my knees and under his command was so satisfying to him, for a moment he looked overwhelmed. But he blinked away his haziness and leaned over me, bringing his mouth right against the shell of my ear.

As he spoke, his hot breath brushed against the sensitized skin of my neck. "I want to watch you lick her pussy."

There was a power that took hold of me when he issued his command. It was a need I didn't know existed until he put it into words, and now it was real and living. There was no indecision or questioning if I wanted this. He wanted it, so now I did too.

I pressed my palms to the glass, tipped my forehead to the cool pane, and waited. It announced to the couple what I needed, and as soon as they realized, the man shoved her forward. Her hips and the delta of her thick thighs pushed to the window.

I'd kissed a girl once when I was in college at a house party. The upside-down margaritas had been flowing freely, and someone had dared us to do it. Maybe she'd been the one who'd dared me . . . the night was fuzzy. I remembered the kiss as being nice but not earth-shattering. Kissing girls wasn't any different than kissing boys, I'd discovered.

And for as curious as I was in life, it was surprising I wasn't more than mildly curious when it came to women. I'd always been far more attracted to men. And I was certainly interested in this self-proclaimed complicated man whose demand made me shudder in excitement.

Following his order would be easy, and I wondered if it was possible the simulated sex would be even hotter than the real thing. I tilted my head, opened my mouth, and slicked my tongue across the glass, right over her neatly trimmed landing strip.

"Fuck," Clay groaned appreciatively. "Again."

Satisfaction washed down me in waves. I did as asked, dragging my tongue along the smooth glass that was damp and smudged from my first pass.

"Look at you," he said, "being such a good girl now. I think you should stand up and show her what happened when you weren't."

He extended a hand to help me up, and I took it. "You want me to—"

"Show her the marks your bad behavior earned you earlier today."

It was intoxicating being with him, and exhilaration simmered in my blood, like I was high. As soon as I was on my feet, I turned around, bent slightly at the waist, and lifted the back of my skirt.

Cool air drift over my exposed cheeks. I'd worn a thong tonight, not just to prevent panty lines, but to avoid putting anything over my irritated skin. As soon as his handiwork came into view, Clay let out a deep sigh of satisfaction. Like I'd done earlier, I wiggled my hips, showing off my ass, and that earned me a spanking.

It wasn't mean or harsh—it was playful, and I nearly giggled.

There was a dull bang that came from the window, and although the woman had probably raised her voice, it sounded muted. "Join us!"

But Clay shook his head, pointed to the nearly empty glass in his hand, and then gestured toward the main room, telling them we were going to get fresh drinks.

"The show's going to start soon," he said as we made our way back to the bar. "We should get in there if you want a seat."

A quick glance revealed Clay's friend was gone, which was disappointing on several levels, but I tried not to show it. I brushed a lock of hair over my shoulder. "What's it going to be like?"

"The show?" His smile was cryptic. "It'll be interesting. I think you'll like it."

There were only a few seats left by the time we stepped into the red room, and Clay urged me down into the first available chair while I was distracted by what was on the center of the floor.

Or more appropriately, who.

The girl looked like she was in her early twenties. She had her dirty blonde hair twisted back into a bun, and that along with her slender frame made me think of her as a ballerina. She was pretty in both her face and her body, and colorful artwork was scrawled all over her skin. I could tell because she was completely nude.

The girl had a lot of ink, plus a piercing in each nipple. She was lying on the floor, and as she took in a breath, the studs glinted faintly beneath the latex blanket covering her that was so thin it was nearly transparent. It was strange. The blanket was draped over a rectangular frame that surrounded her and the latex cinched around her neck in a thick black collar.

I'd just gotten settled in my seat when a woman dressed in black stepped forward, and every conversation in the room ceased. She was probably already naturally tall, but the huge platform on her stiletto boots exaggerated her towering height. Her shiny 'wet look' bodysuit hugged her gorgeous figure, accentuating her in the right places. The woman was statuesque and incredibly beautiful.

The braids of her dark hair were pulled up into a high ponytail, then they cascaded down her back like a beautiful tassel. Her latex bodysuit covered everything up to her chin, and even her hands were wrapped in the black PVC fabric. It left only her face visible, showing off her strong cheekbones and flawless brown skin.

Mistress Theia looked otherworldly. Like a goddess from a planet where sex was a religion.

A simple silk blindfold dangled from her fingertips as she strutted to the girl lying prone on the floor. There was power and confidence in every step she took, and she was catlike as she crouched by the girl's head. The blindfold was slipped on and adjusted until both women seemed satisfied with the placement.

While that was happening, more couples came into the room, hushed and respectful, like the show had already begun. Maybe it had. I was surprised, yet pleased, when Clay offered his seat to a woman and moved to stand behind my chair.

The dominating woman's voice was deep and seductive, drawing my attention back to her. "Ready, pet?"

The girl shifted inside the latex, spreading out her arms and legs so they were a comfortable distance from her body. "Yes, Mistress."

A loud mechanical whirr rang out, sounding sort of like a vacuum cleaner.

Oh . . .

Wow.

That was *exactly* what it was, because the girl wasn't covered by a blanket—she was encapsulated in a bag, and once the machine sucked out the air, she was locked in place. As the latex molded tight to her body, it became even more see-through and gave her skin a smooth, plastic sheen. And as soon as the air was gone, the machine powered down and the room went utterly silent.

A smile twitched on Mistress Theia's lips as she gazed down at her pet like trapped prey. The dominant savored the scene before her. Then, she strolled to the girl's side and knelt.

I sipped in air as her black hands smoothed over the girl's latex-bound skin, touching her with reverence. She coursed her palms over the girl's hips, up over her taut stomach, passing across the pretty patterns of ink. The girl's breathing instantly went ragged, and although she was immobilized by the sealed latex around her, her chest heaved.

Jesus, it was fucking sexy.

Mistress Theia shifted over her, putting one knee down between her sub's parted legs, so she could touch more places. Her hands caressed, gliding in slow, luxurious strokes, working up and down the girl's body. It looked like she varied the pressure she put down too. As she passed over the girl's breasts the first time, it was featherlight, but her stroke downward had more drag.

I didn't know if it was solely meant to prime the girl, or the audience too, because anticipation coiled low in my belly as the black hands inched down over the blonde's waist. My gaze tracked them all the way until her fingers slid between the girl's thighs and began to massage.

The moan she issued flickered through my body like a lick of heat.

And it was at this moment, I glanced up and discovered a pair of eyes watching me from across the circle. Breath halted in my lungs. The gorgeous man in the gray suit—Clay's friend—hadn't left after all. He was here for the show, but while everyone else was watching Mistress Theia play, this guy was watching me.

SEVEN

The man in the gray suit stared at me, his deep-set eyes brimming with curiosity. Was he wondering who I was? How I knew Clay? Or maybe it was simpler, and he was questioning why I was gawking at him.

I averted my gaze back to the scene playing out on the floor.

Mistress Theia had one hand resting on top of the girl's pelvis, and her thumb dipped down, rubbing circles against the girl's clit, while her other hand wandered from breast to breast. A longer, louder moan drifted from the girl and swept through the room, making the woman in the seat next to me ball a hand into a fist.

I understood. Watching the scene was turning me on, too. It wasn't just the sexual stuff, either. It was the power. Mistress Theia chuckled wickedly when the girl tried to writhe inside her prison and the latex wouldn't allow it.

Faster and faster that sinful thumb moved, and even though the girl couldn't escape, Mistress Theia leaned over and set her forearm across the girl's shoulders to pin her in place.

She cooed softly to her sub. "Such a good pet. Are you going to come with all these people watching?"

The girl's moan was desperate with need, but before

she could answer, Mistress Theia clamped her hand over the girl's mouth. The words came out muffled beneath her black plastic glove.

Mistress Theia's smile was evil. "I can't hear you," she whispered.

Lust snaked through me, tightening every muscle in my body. It was ridiculous, but I felt like I had to sit absolutely still, otherwise everyone would know how uncomfortably turned on I was. Making it worse on myself, I risked a glance across the way to the stranger in the gray suit.

Fuck, he was still looking at me, and this time he had one eyebrow arched and the corner of his mouth lifted in a sexy smile, which told me it didn't matter if I moved or not. This guy somehow saw all my desire, right into the heart of me, and maybe even down to the marks Clay had put on my ass.

As if to remind me of his presence, cool fingertips grazed across my skin, making me flinch. Then Clay's hand was there, cupping my shoulder as he stood behind me. Maybe he was just resting it there casually. But like the other times he'd done it at this club, his touch felt possessive. Had he noticed the way his friend was looking at me, and wanted to assert ownership?

Everything fed into me, building like a pressure valve. The way the stranger's unabashed lust for me dripped off his face. Clay's subtle domination as his fingers encased my shoulder, keeping me in place. It made me shudder with satisfaction.

On the floor, whimpers of pleasure escaped through Mistress Theia's fingers, forcing my attention back to her.

As she slowly dragged her hand away from the girl's panting mouth, she also withdrew her hand from between the girl's legs. That earned her a cry of desperation, but Mistress Theia rose onto her knees and gave her sub a look of disapproval. It didn't matter that the blindfolded girl couldn't see it.

"Shh," she ordered.

The girl squirmed as much as she could while sandwiched between the sheets of plastic.

Mistress Theia lifted her attention to one of the men seated nearby and held out an expectant hand. Had they discussed it before the show began? The guy reached into a bag near his feet, pulled out a cordless wand vibrator, and passed it to the waiting mistress.

Her thumb pressed the button on the handle, and just the dull hum caused the blonde to whine with need. She knew what was coming and was eager for the pleasure the vibrator would give her.

The head of the vibrator was ghosted over the girl's nipple, and although she couldn't see her domme's smile, surely she could hear it in her voice. "Hmm. Do you want this?"

"Yes, Mistress."

"Where? On your aching, little clit?"

The girl swallowed so hard it was audible. "Yes, please."

"All right." She moved the wand down, slipping it between the girl's spread legs, and stroked the head once over her clit before lifting the vibrator away. "How was that?"

The girl's gasp began in pleasure and ended in frustration. She'd only been given a teasing hint and wanted much more. Once again, she tried to squirm, but the only thing it did was make the flexible frame of the bed around her bend slightly.

"Mistress, *please.*"

Mistress Theia giggled in delight, and the sexy sound shot right through me. It was stunning how much I liked hearing her satisfied, like secondhand pleasure.

This time when the vibrator was pressed between the girl's thighs, Mistress Theia left it there. She dragged a fist over her ponytail, smoothing the braids together, and pulled her hair over her shoulder so it would be out of her way. Then she leaned forward and set her hand flat on the girl's chest, directly between her breasts. It was so she could brace herself as she knelt over her submissive and hold the vibrator tight to the girl's clit.

Short, gulping breaths were punctuated with her moans, and it was obvious how the pleasure was building inside her. The girl tried to move her knees, so the frame warped ever so slightly, and one corner lifted off the ground before quietly knocking back down to the floor. Only her chest could move as she gasped for air.

The stillness and smooth latex coating made her look like a plastic doll. And it was sort of the same for the woman perched over her in the glossy bodysuit. She was like the other side of a coin. Covered in opaque black while the girl beneath her was covered in sheer white. Free to move and control, versus restrained and completely at someone else's mercy.

Top versus bottom.

I never would have thought I'd be into something like this, but good lord, it was fucking hot.

Mistress Theia ground the buzzing head of the vibrator against the girl, moving it in a tight circle, and liquid heat poured through me. Was it wrong to want to trade places with this girl? Because I did. I craved to feel the roll of the wand against my clit, to get relief from all the tension building inside me. I was sort of worried I might come right here in this chair, in a room full of people and the only touch was Clay's hand resting on my shoulder, his fingers brushing over my collarbone.

Would he like it if I did?

Would the man across the room from me like it?

Mistress Theia leaned further forward on her knees, which made her feet come off the floor, and the spikes of her boots lifted into the air. She didn't notice. She was intently focused on what she was doing and determined to bring her submissive to orgasm.

It seemed as inescapable as the vacuum-sealed bed. As the girl trembled, the sheet of latex stretched across the frame began to vibrate. Needy cries tore from her lips, sounding sort of like panic, but it was clear it was pleasure.

"I'm coming, Mistress," she gasped. Her chin lifted as her head tipped backward, and then the orgasm consumed her.

I clenched my teeth to keep from making a sound, leashing the moan I wanted to set loose. But a few others in the room didn't stay quiet. There were noises of approval and whispered words of encouragement to both the domme and the submissive.

And as the climax rolled through and began to recede, Mistress Theia didn't let up. The shuddering sighs from her submissive changed in pitch and urgency, swinging from satisfaction to dread. Because she was overly sensitive, and now the vibrations no longer felt good. The head of the wand wasn't bringing pleasure—it was discomfort.

This time when she squirmed, it was with real effort to escape.

A pleased, dark look splashed across Mistress Theia's face as she turned off the vibrator and dropped it to the latex stretched between the girl's legs. Her expression said that just because she'd stopped with the toy, didn't mean she was done with the girl. She shifted so she was sitting on her heels, kneeling beside her submissive, and slapped her fingertips against the girl's overstimulated clit.

A sharp sound of surprise punched from the girl's lungs. I don't think it had hurt that badly, it was more that it hadn't been expected. But her mistress's second slap? That one wasn't friendly, and the girl jolted. Each subsequent spanking increased in intensity, and the harsh sound created a song with a rhythm in pain.

Mistress Theia swung her hand with purpose and skill, striking the girl exactly where she meant to, and this time when the blonde bucked against her cage, the lower half of the bed began to twist.

But the domme's laugh was as dark as the suit she wore. "That's so cute. You think you can run from me."

She reared back and drove her hand down with a vicious slap, and the girl made a keening sound. It was like it had stung too badly for her to stay quiet, even though she was supposed to.

The cold grip on my shoulder tightened, and I knew in an instant what this meant. Clay probably hadn't done it on purpose. He was fighting against the arousal swelling inside him. If the first part of the show was for me—then this part was made for Clay.

He got off on pain.

Movement caught my eye. Earlier during the show, a couple had ducked out of the back, either no longer interested . . . or too turned on to stay. I wondered which it was for the man in the gray suit as he stood, keeping his chin tucked to his chest, and politely left.

I stayed where I was, pinned under the tense grip of a man who said he liked to watch, all the way until the show was over and Mistress Theia had the girl cradled lovingly in her arms.

Clay's hand slid away, and he dropped down into now-empty seat beside me, his expression shuttered and giving nothing away. "What did you think?" His voice was forced casualness. "Did you enjoy the show?"

"Yes." I was breathless, and my heart was still racing. "I liked it a lot."

A relieved smile broke on his face, reaching all the way to his eyes trapped behind the dark frames he wore. I turned in my seat so my knees touched his, and set my hand on his thigh, not too close to make this private man uncomfortable, but high enough he couldn't misinterpret my meaning.

His gaze dipped down and evaluated the ballet pink nail polish at the ends of my fingertips.

"Why don't you take me home," I said provocatively, "so

you can fuck me?"

"I don't have to take you home to fuck you, Lilith." His gaze rose oh-so-slowly to meet mine. "We'll go upstairs."

Excitement fluttered inside me, then halted. Wait a minute. Hadn't he said he didn't fuck in front of other people? Everything was open on the second floor. "Are there private rooms up there?"

He was already up, out of his seat. "No."

There was no explanation as he moved toward the doorway. It was clear I was supposed to follow. Was it possible his mysteriousness was intentional? He knew I was a curious person, and maybe he was playing that up, using my desire for answers to guide and control me.

The stairs whined as we ascended them, but this time when we entered the main lounge, it wasn't empty. People mingled in small groups, and some sat together on one side of the sectional that dominated the room.

Clay led us to the empty side of the couch and sat down, gesturing for me to sit on the ottoman directly across from him. As I took my seat on the leather, I sensed that the room was watching us.

"I feel like I'm," I said quietly, "on display sitting here."

He angled his head, intrigued. "Does it bother you?"

"No," I admitted.

"Can you blame them for looking?" His eyes were magnetic. "You're the hottest girl in the club tonight. Maybe the hottest girl to ever come here."

I sucked in a breath, which tightened my corset around me. My breasts pushed against the boning, and the sensation was enjoyable. But I gave him a dubious look. "Hotter than Mistress Theia?"

My question pleased him. "She's hot," he agreed, "but she's a domme." His gaze skated down my body like he was appreciating fine art. "For someone like me? You're *far* more attractive."

"Because I'm submissive."

"Yes, you sure seem to be." There was an electric current running between us, and the voltage increased when he sat forward and used a finger to nudge me to uncross my legs. "Did you like it earlier when I told you what to do?"

My knees were now side-by-side, but I kept my thighs pressed tightly together beneath my skirt. "Yes."

"Are you turned on?" There was music playing in the room, along with conversations and laughter, but his voice was all I could hear. "Is your pussy wet?"

"Yes," I breathed.

He sat back, relaxing in his seat, and casually draped an arm across the back of the couch. "Show me."

Thoughts vaporized in my brain for a moment. I tore my gaze away from him, checking to see if anyone had heard his command. Would I care if they had? As I scanned the room, no one appeared all that interested in us. The two couples on the opposite side of the couch had finished their conversation, because both women were slumped down in the cushions, their legs hooked over their husbands' shoulders. Or maybe they'd swapped partners, and the guys were going down on each other's wives.

There was a sharp bite of pain on the top of my thigh,

and I yelped with surprise, my gaze flying back to Clay. A red mark bloomed on my skin.

"Did you just pinch me?"

"We'll have to work on your focus." His tone was straightforward. "I said I want to see your pussy."

I exhaled loudly. He looked so stern and serious that more heat poured into my body. I was going to liquify under his watchful stare, and I was sure I'd love every minute of it.

So, I wasn't nervous when I leaned back on one arm, spread my knees, and hooked my fingers in the crotch of my thong, pulling it to the side. He'd seen plenty of me this afternoon, but this was more thrilling. I wasn't just bare to him—anyone could see.

I let Clay get his fill of looking before I spoke. It was supposed to be teasing, but my voice came out hushed. "Happy?"

His gaze flicked to mine, and power flared in his eyes. He *was* happy. Beyond pleased with how I'd followed his directions. His hand on the back of the couch curled into a loose fist, like he wanted to touch me but then thought better of it.

I let go of my panties and closed my legs, sitting up straight. "Are you going to fuck me here in this room when we're not alone?"

His aversion to the idea lasted only a blink of an eye, but it was unmistakable. Which didn't make a lick of sense. Why'd he bring me here? His shields went up, hiding whatever thoughts were going through his head. "Do you want that?" he asked. "To be fucked while everyone watches?"

I had an immediate answer of *yes* but didn't want to blurt it out until I gave it real thought. In my peripheral vision, I could see the woman in the corner of the room, crouching in front of a man who had his pants down around his ankles and his dick in her mouth. They didn't care I was watching them, and neither did the couples behind me. The men were still on their knees, heads moving between the women's thighs, but now the women had their tops off and their lips locked together.

There was a fog of lust in this room, and it seemed everyone was susceptible to it, including me. Everyone, that was, except for him. Clay's eyes were focused and clear and promised to give me whatever I wanted.

"Yes," I whispered. "I want them to watch."

His smile was hesitant but genuine. "Okay."

Blood rushed hotly through my veins, bubbling with anticipation. I nearly burst when he stood up, expecting him to push me down onto my back on the oversized ottoman but . . . he didn't. His attention swung toward the hallway. "Will you be all right on your own for a minute? I need to use the restroom."

"Oh," I said, trying to get hold of myself. "Uh, sure."

He nodded and strode to the hallway, disappearing behind the door to the men's room. With him gone, there was nothing to do but watch the people around me, and it didn't take long to understand why Clay enjoyed coming here.

Even as a spectator, it was incredibly hot.

I turned around to face the couples across from me, where one of the men was now fucking the woman he'd been going down on. His pants were down just enough to cut across his bare ass, and his muscles flexed and hardened with each of his thrusts. And since I was turned halfway around, when the cushion I was sitting on flattened beneath me, I spun, expecting it to be Clay.

"That was fast—oh," I said.

The woman had a toothy grin and lipstick that was bright red, and for a moment it was all I could see. Her tone was sugary-sweet. "Hey, you."

"Um, hi." I pushed out a friendly, confused smile. I didn't know this woman. She was quite a bit older than I was, wearing a lowcut black dress that was so tight, it looked like her boobs were going to pop out at any moment.

"You're new," she said, running a hand through the strands of her wavy brown hair. "We haven't seen you before."

"We?"

She giggled and flicked a finger toward a man standing nearby. "Me and my boyfriend. He's cute, right?"

Uh . . .

He looked like he was the same age as my dad. The guy had his hands in his pants pockets and a lewd smile plastered on his face, like he'd sent his girlfriend over to warm me up. I squeezed out a polite smile, but my tone was cool. "Sure, he looks nice."

She was about to wave him over when Clay reappeared, and a scowl formed on his lips when he saw the woman at my side.

"No, thank you." His tone was gruff. "We're not interested."

Her mouth dropped open, her lipstick forming a perfectly red oval, but she didn't say anything. Instead, she got up in a huff and scurried away with her boyfriend in tow.

"That was kind of rude," I told him when she was gone and he'd returned to his seat across from me.

"Was it?" His expression was plain. "You think it would have been better to make polite conversation for the next half-hour and waste everyone's time? Or were you interested in either of them?"

"No," I said. "But you were really direct."

He looked at me like I was being naïve. "I've come here long enough to know that's the only thing those two understand. If you're not clear, they think they have a chance. You're so far out of their league, I'm a little offended they tried, and a lot offended with how they waited until I wasn't around to do it."

"Well, they're gone now. You've successfully run them off." I gave him a lopsided smile. "Where were we?"

"We were going to talk about how this is going to work."

My smile hung. "Talk?"

He flashed an amused look, like he found derailing me entertaining, but then he turned serious. He leaned forward and took my hand. It was the first time he'd touched me where I didn't feel any motive behind it, other than he just wanted a connection.

"I'd like a relationship with you."

"Okay," I said before realizing he wasn't finished.

"Our relationship isn't going to be like what you're used to." He studied the way he played with my fingers, as if fascinated by them. "And it might not be long before you realize it's not enough for you. I can give you a lot of things you'll like." His gaze had been focused on his fingertips tracing my hand, but it snapped to mine. "Pleasure. Pain. Even euphoria. I can show you how good you are at things you don't realize you're capable of. But I know my limits, Lilith."

His fingers urged mine apart so he could lace our hands together.

"We'll trust each other and enjoy being together. And I'll care for you, but . . . I won't fall in love. It's not something I do. So, if that's your end goal," sadness hinted at the edges of his eyes, "we might as well stop now."

I filled my lungs with air as I considered what he'd said and how to respond.

"It's not my goal," I said softly. His discerning gaze tightened like he didn't believe me, but I squeezed his hand. "Look, I've never fallen in love, and honestly? I don't plan on doing it—at least not anytime soon."

Once again, I caught him off guard, and he struggled with how to regroup.

"So," I continued, "if you want a relationship that's just sex and kink . . . I'm game."

"It's more than *just* that," he said.

I gave him a sinful smile. "I'm sure you'll show me, then."

Clay's surprised reaction told me he didn't think I'd accept his offer, and pleasure seeped into his expression. "If your goals change, or you start to develop feelings, you have to be upfront with me."

"Fair enough. Same for you."

He looked at me like I'd just told him the sky was green. Him developing feelings for me wasn't a possibility as far as he was concerned, but he humored me anyway. "Yes."

With that settled, he began to relax and return to the man he'd been earlier when he'd told me to get on my knees.

"So, now that you know my limits," he smoothed a hand down the line of buttons on his shirt, "what are yours?"

It felt oddly like negotiations, and I considered some glib answer, but in the end, I went with the honest one. "I'm not sure."

It was as if he'd hoped I'd say that, because a smile widened on his lips. "I have an idea. Something we can test and see if it's a limit for you."

"Oh? What is it?"

He let go of my hands so he could cup my cheek and draw my ear close to his mouth. Like it was important, and he didn't want me to miss a word. His voice was low and devious, sliding into me like a hot knife through butter. "Ask the next man who walks by if he wants to taste your pussy."

Whoa.

"What?" I jolted back from him, and my eyes went wide. "What if he says yes?"

There weren't words to describe how Clay stared at me. If there were, I wouldn't be able to find them, because I flash-boiled and everything inside me became steam. His eyes were lidded with desire.

He likes to watch.

His shoulders rose with his uneven breath. "Would that be a limit for you?"

The steam fogged around in my head, and I blinked my eyes rapidly, trying to get it to disperse. Was it a limit? Could I let a total stranger go down on me while Clay watched?

The depraved part of me hungered to find out. A runaway freight train had replaced my heart, barreling out of control, chugging away at a million miles an hour.

He'd asked if this was a limit, but I'd been waiting for him naked in his house this afternoon. He knew what my answer would be.

I subtly shook my head. "It's not a limit."

Excitement crackled in his eyes before his gaze turned toward the room, surveying the crop to see who'd be the lucky man.

Hyperawareness traveled up my back like faint pinpricks. My body sensed what was happening, while the rest of me struggled to catch up. Had I subconsciously willed this into existence?

No, I realized. This was too perfect to be anything other than designed.

At some point, the man in the gray suit had come into this room. Now he stalked toward us, and his intense gaze was fixed on me.

EIGHT

All the sound in the room faded out, and my heart leapt up to my throat, cutting off my airway.

The man in the gray suit moved deliberately and with focus, ignoring the groups of writhing bodies scattered around the space. There was an easy swagger to him as he walked. If Clay was a man drawn with sharp angles and precise measurements, this guy was beautifully sketched by freehand.

I dry-swallowed. As he approached, so did the moment I'd have to speak to him. I wanted to—part of the fun was the challenge of it—but that didn't mean I wasn't nervous. What if my question, like, offended him?

And what if he said no?

He reached the end of the couch, stopping a respectable distance away from us, which meant I couldn't whisper my question. I'd have to say it loud enough for him to hear me over the swelling noise of the room.

It wasn't just music and conversations in here now. There were throaty moans. Cracks of palms against asses. Steady thumps of hips beating against hips.

The man didn't notice or care. He was focused only on me.

I opened my mouth to speak, but when the words didn't come, the guy cocked his head, puzzled.

His voice was deep and hushed. "You have a

question for me?"

I knew it. Clay was an architect. He made his living by planning and designing, and that extended into the other areas of his life. I glanced at him, but his expression was fixed. I'd have to ask him later how he'd accomplished this, but I suspected it'd happened when he'd stepped away to use the restroom.

"Yes," I said, "I have a question." I was grateful it came out confident and clear.

And why shouldn't I be? I wanted this. Even if nothing came of my offer, just making it to a complete stranger was wild and exhilarating. I uncrossed my legs and pressed the front of my skirt down in the hollow I'd created between my knees, my hands curled around the hem.

He peered at me expectantly as I took in a preparing breath.

"Do you want," I said, "to taste my pussy?"

Disbelief knocked him back a half-step, and as soon as he finished processing the question, his attention snapped to Clay. Was it to check with him if this was all right? To see if my date would allow it? The two men exchanged a long look, and God, what I would have given to understand their wordless conversation.

But I didn't.

Satisfied, the man's focus swung back to me and swept downward, taking in my outfit, my legs, my heels . . . A slow, wicked grin spread across his face. It made me smolder, but then the word he uttered? It set me on fucking *fire*.

"Sure," he said.

Oh, my God.

My pulse went erratic when he stepped into the space between the couch and the ottoman I was sitting on, blocking my view of Clay. I stopped breathing altogether when he knelt on the floor between my parted legs, bringing him perfectly into my eyeline.

Time suspended as this handsome stranger stared at me. Did he see the same curiosity he had reflected in my eyes? I was fascinated by who he was to Clay and what he'd been told about tonight. There weren't answers in his eyes, though, only more questions.

His gaze drifted down and came to a stop on my hands holding my skirt in place. "Can I touch you?"

It was the same question Clay had asked me earlier, and the flashback to the ruler striking my skin was unavoidable. I shuddered with a pleasurable aftershock, but hopefully the man didn't notice.

I pressed my lips together and nodded, too anxious to speak, because I worried what might come out. This whole night had been intoxicating and obliterated what few inhibitions I had. If I wasn't careful, I might tell this stranger he could fuck me.

The man's palms were warm when he gently set them on my knees, but they didn't stay there. Up his hands went, sliding along the tops of my thighs, and showers of goosebumps burst across my legs as he pushed back my skirt.

I had to force air in and out of my body, making my corset heave. Then I put my hands down behind me on the ottoman and leaned back, making room for him. Over his shoulder, Clay was there, supervising us with a hungry look.

The man reached my hips, and he rested his hands on them, hesitating. He searched my eyes, confirming I was comfortable with him going further, so I gave him a tiny nod, then lifted my hips to make it easier for him to peel my underwear down.

When he bent to push my thong past my ankles and shoes, Clay's expression filled with power. "You'll watch me while he does it. Understand?"

Oh, God. The idea was scorching hot. I bit the inside of my cheek to stay quiet and gave another quick nod.

The man in the gray suit didn't have any objections or comments about Clay's command. Instead, he discarded my panties on the ottoman beside me, slid his palms up the insides of my thighs, and pressed me shockingly open, revealing my bareness to him, and everyone else in the room.

"Fuck," I uttered under my hurried breath. Anticipation turned me into a livewire. I was supposed to watch Clay while it happened, but my gaze bounced between the two men as the stranger dropped his shoulders and slowly lowered his mouth to me.

"Oh, *fuck*," I repeated as his lips made contact.

The faintest brush of his mouth over my clit caused my legs to tremble. His warm hands gripped the insides of my thighs, and I stared at Clay through my lust-hazed eyes. It was impossible to catch my breath.

There should have been a voice in the back of my head telling me this behavior was wrong. That I wasn't supposed to let a stranger fuck me with his tongue while my brand-new boyfriend watched.

Boyfriend?

Was that the right label to use for Clay? Partner was a better fit.

The voice that was supposed to make me feel shame was silent tonight, blotted out by the inferno burning inside me from this erotic act. Or maybe Clay had deactivated that part of me earlier when he'd wielded his ruler.

The man's tongue was velvet as it slid across my damp skin. Shit, that felt amazing. It rolled over my clit, spinning circles of bliss that clouded my vision. I was breathing so hard, I became lightheaded, and I had to press a hand to the center of my corset, leaving myself propped up by one precariously shaky arm.

I gasped with pleasure as the man's grip on me tightened and the tip of his tongue fluttered.

And while he was physically pleasing me, the expression that hung on Clay's face announced the stranger was currently satisfying us both. He enjoyed the way I trembled as his friend's lips sealed around my clit and sucked. He drank up my moans like his favorite brand of liquor, savoring each gasp and whimper.

"Does it feel good?" he murmured.

I was sure I was going to rattle apart, or my supporting arm was going to give out, or I would come without warning while Clay watched me through his sexy, serious glasses. So, it was hard to speak, and I had to concentrate to get the word out. "Yes."

His hand had been resting on his thigh, and although

the move he made was subtle, I didn't miss how it turned slightly inward and tension filled his fingers as he squeezed. He wasn't going to touch himself when all these people were around, but oh, how he wanted to.

Watching me with his friend's head between my legs turned him on, and the thick line of his cock pressed against the inseam of his pants.

I wanted to understand him better, but the stranger's mouth was distracting, pulling my thoughts in a million directions. I gave a loud moan when the man used his thumbs to peel me apart and focus on the spot that would bring me the most pleasure.

"You like this." It wasn't a question from Clay—it was a statement of fact. "You like how everyone's watching."

Were they? On some level, I sensed there were eyes on me, but I hadn't glanced around to check. My gaze never deviated from Clay's, because he'd given me instructions, and I was determined to follow them.

But nerves made my voice go uneven. "I like," I rasped, "how *you're* watching."

I had nothing to be nervous about because my confession earned me the biggest grin I'd seen yet from him. If I'd had any air left in my lungs, his gorgeous smile would have taken it all.

The man's tongue created a flurry of sensations, and it felt way, *way* too good. How long was this 'taste' supposed to last? His mouth was heaven, so I wanted him to keep going, but I worried he'd stop right as I got to the edge.

"I bet he wants to fuck you," Clay said. "He hasn't been

able to take his eyes off you all night."

The man's tongue hesitated for a fraction of a second. Was he going to deny it? Or was it the idea of fucking me had short-circuited his brain like it had mine? No protest came from the man, and when he resumed moving, the strokes of his tongue were more deliberate and needy. He pushed one of my legs up onto the ottoman, forcing me to fall back onto my elbow.

It was better and so much worse like this, because now both men were in my line of sight. I could see the man as his pink tongue slicked over me, and Clay behind him. My partner looked down on us like a lion watching his offspring feast on its first kill.

My moans competed with the sounds of pleasure in the room, and we weren't in the club anymore. The space had transformed into a pit of hedonism. It was full of naked bodies that thrashed and writhed and clawed at each other for release.

Clay's voice rose over the growl of the sex surrounding us. "You told me you wanted to fuck while other people watched. Do you want him to do it?"

The man's eyes had been closed, but they blinked open, and when his gaze connected with mine, it had to mirror my surprise. But beneath his shock, I saw through to the truth. I didn't know a thing about him . . . other than he wanted me to say yes.

It wasn't like I'd never had a one-night-stand before. I'd gone home from the bars with a poor decision more than once when I was in college, and sometimes I slept with a guy on the first date, knowing it wasn't going anywhere and I'd ghost him in the morning. I liked sex—like, a *lot*—and finding a partner wasn't hard. But finding someone I wanted to hang out with long-term? That was much more of a challenge. Once the newness of them wore off, so did my interest.

So, if I let this guy fuck me, it would be an extreme one-night-stand. We didn't know each other's names and had barely spoken. Right now, the only thing we had in common was the man watching us from the couch.

That's not true.

You want to say yes to this as badly as this stranger wants you to.

It was wild and reckless, but when had I let that stop me before? Was this really worse than getting naked and ambushing Clay in his house?

I panted for air, needing to build up energy to speak, but I didn't get the chance. Clay sat forward, rested his elbows on his knees, and delivered a look so sexual it was indecent.

"If you don't want him, then don't come." He said it like it was simple. "You'll tell him 'thank you,' and he'll know this is over and he should go back downstairs." Behind his glasses, his eyes blinked slowly. Whatever he was about to say was so appealing to him, it was difficult to get the words out. Desire choked his voice. "Or he uses his tongue to give you an orgasm, and then he gets to try for another one using his cock."

My shoulders shuddered as I exhaled a sharp breath. The concept was so powerful, I melted and collapsed flat on my back. As I lay on the leather, the stitching on the center seams rough against one of my shoulder blades, the man kneeling between my legs froze in place.

He was waiting for me to make my choice.

I'd already made it, hadn't I?

But I was so overloaded with heat, I needed a moment to collect my thoughts. When I propped myself back up on my elbows and stared at the men, I found them waiting with bated breath, both hoping I wasn't going to thank the man and dismiss him.

My hand shook with anxious excitement as I reached out and threaded my fingers through the man's wavy hair.

It took him a moment to understand I wasn't pushing him away, and his eyes widened with surprise before lidding with satisfaction. I tugged gently, urging him back to me and to use his mouth again. I wasn't going to send him away.

Beyond him, my partner's lips fell open, and he let out a pleased sigh. The sound of it was the best kind of foreplay. It turned me on even further, not that I needed any help there. The need inside me was dire.

The man's tongue whipped at me, causing waves of bliss to crash through my center. I held Clay's gaze, and his drilled right back into me, and my pulse sped until it felt like my heart was going to explode.

Jesus. The stranger was like a human Hitachi, and he'd just flipped the setting up to 'high.'

"Fuck," I groaned. My hips moved without thought, rocking against his face. My body was desperate to get off. I'd been existing in a prolonged state of arousal all night, and it had grown to a critical level during the show.

Time blurred. It mixed and swirled until it no longer had

a shape or meaning.

But the man in the gray suit was relentless. When he paused to catch his breath and give his tongue a few seconds of rest, the pad of his thumb took over, rubbing back and forth on my sensitive clit.

"I'm going to come," I whispered, although I wasn't sure which man I was speaking to. No, that wasn't true. I was letting them both know.

Clay's eyes lit up. "Do it."

This was a command I had no trouble obeying, not even when I knew some of the people in the room were watching. If anything, that just made it better.

I clenched a fistful of the man's hair to hold on, and let the orgasm take me. Pleasure poured through me like lava, igniting every nerve ending. It made my muscles contract and flinch, and a cry of ecstasy rang from deep in the back of my throat. It left no doubt what had happened.

Dear lord, everything was tingling.

But the man didn't slow down. His strong hands clamped around my hips, pinning me to the leather and preventing my escape. He was shameless as he licked and caressed, disregarding the way I bucked and bowed from the acute pleasure.

It wasn't until I whined and let go of his hair that he finally released me, and—holy shit—he grinned like the devil. I'd just come, but I nearly did it all over again. His smile, coupled with his sexy hair that I'd disheveled, was lethal.

I was still recovering when Clay spoke, his words for the man. "She'll sit in front of me. I want her between us while you fuck her."

Oh, my God. *Yes.*

Clay watching me with the stranger was hot enough, but being between these men? That would be incendiary.

In my post-orgasm fog, my limbs were sluggish and shaky, but the man seemed aware. He straightened on his knees, helped me to sit upright, and then his arms circled around me, bringing us chest-to-chest.

I stared up at him and his breathtaking mouth. We were close enough it'd take no effort for one of us to kiss the other. It was so strange. He'd gone down on me and given me an orgasm, and yet kissing him felt like too much. Too forward.

Not to mention, it seemed shockingly dangerous.

The threat of his kiss didn't last because one of his hands moved down and slid beneath my bottom, and then I was hoisted up into his arms. He turned and lowered me into the empty spot at the edge of the couch, directly between Clay's spread legs.

As soon as I was seated, Clay put his hands on my waist and eased me toward him, so my back was against his hard chest. It was stunning how quickly everything had flipped. Now he was the one doing the touching and the man was the one watching us. As Clay gathered my hair and swooped it over a shoulder so it would be out of his way, I rested my hands on his knees.

It was nice, being up against him.

He tipped his head down, pressed his mouth to the pulse point just below my ear, and as he spoke, his lips fluttered against my skin. "Tell him to take his dick out. You want to see it."

It was involuntary how my hands clenched on him, my body's response to the heat of his order. I repeated his words as a tight, urgent plea to the man. "Get your dick out. I want to see it."

The corner of his mouth hooked up like he was about to reveal a big secret, and it was sexy as hell. While he undid his belt and the fly of his gray suit pants, Clay shifted behind me. His arm snaked between our bodies as he retrieved something from his jacket pocket.

Then, a foil packet was slipped beneath my palm.

Well . . . if that wasn't approval of what he wanted to happen, I didn't know what was. My fingers curled around the condom while I watched the stranger's methodical fingers work on undressing himself.

His pants were undone, but not down. He left them open and on his hips because his hands were busy pushing the tail of his tie over his shoulder, and then those efficient hands moved to undo the bottom few buttons of his dress shirt. It parted to reveal defined abs and the black waistband of his snug underwear.

I swallowed hard as he pushed a hand inside and dug out his cock—

Oh, he *was* hiding a big secret.

Warmth spread across my cheeks as I stared at the thick, hard dick in his grasp, his fist stroking ever-so-slowly back and forth. Like me, he wasn't shy about being naked, and didn't seem to care who was watching. Maybe he got off on it too, like I had tonight.

"Look at that," Clay whispered in my ear. "You want him

to put all that inside you, don't you?"

I bit my lip to hold back my moan. Thankfully, his question was rhetorical. He was aware how much I desired the man, and his fingertips traced lines over the back of my palm, reminding me of the condom he'd pressed into my hand.

"Put this on him."

There was freedom in being under Clay's direction. I didn't have a problem taking initiative or making a move, but his guidance meant less guesswork for me. I was still in control and knew I could say no or change my mind at any point. I didn't have to do anything I wasn't comfortable with. But it also felt like while my boundaries were expanding, the consequences weren't.

I had to shift forward in my seat to reach the man in the gray suit, and his eyes were brimming with lust as I tore open the wrapper with my unsteady hands. Once I had the condom out, I stared at him in silent question. It seemed silly to ask if I could touch him, but . . .

He understood my hesitation because he nodded and moved his hand out of my way. His dick jutted out from his body, waiting for me.

I couldn't help but smile when my fingers closed around him and he jerked in response. The muscles in his jaw flexed as I tentatively pumped my fist over him. Not that he needed help getting warmed up—he was already rock hard—but I wanted to touch him before there was anything between us.

He held perfectly still as I fitted the condom over the head of his dick and rolled the ring down, but he let out a tight groan like he was enduring exquisite torture from me.

When I finished, he stroked a hand over himself, adjusting the fit so it was how he wanted it.

Cool fingers were set on my shoulder, and Clay urged me to lean back against him once more. At the same time, the man hooked one of my legs over his elbow and pulled my hips closer to him. My ass was barely on the edge of the couch, and I was lying with my head resting on Clay's chest.

It meant the men could stare down at me, and the moment was intensely powerful. They must have felt it too because both of them drew in a breath and held it. My gaze darted from Clay to the center of my legs and the man who held himself steady but hadn't advanced on me.

"He won't without your consent," Clay said. "So, tell him what we want him to do."

He'd said *we* and not *you*, and knowing Clay wanted this as much as I did made my heart skip and stumble.

I peered up at the man and held his gaze while I lifted a hand toward Clay. I curled it behind his neck to hold on to him, and the words came from me drenched with need. "I want you to fuck me."

Permission granted, the man inched forward, and the sheathed tip of him brushed against my entrance, the head of his cock sliding back and forth in luxurious, teasing strokes.

Did both men understand the trembles cascading down my legs weren't anxiety, but anticipation? Excitement flooded my system, overwhelming me and stealing my breath. So when he lined himself up and began to push inside me, my mouth rounded into a perfectly silent, *"Oh."*

He was thick and long and a lot to take, but he moved

slowly, and the sensation of fitting my body around him had my toes curling into points inside my shoes. Sheer concentration was etched in his expression as he eased deeper, like he was struggling mightily to keep control.

Inch by inch, he slid inside . . . all the way until I put a hand on his bare stomach, signaling for him to stop. That was as far as he could go. He might have been the biggest guy I'd ever had, and I was going to have to work up to being able to take more.

"Shit," I groaned when he withdrew his hips and then pressed forward again at a painstakingly slow pace. Pleasure swamped my brain, graying out the rest of the room so only these two men I was trapped between remained.

"You like it?" Clay's tone was provocative. "Tell him."

The man's tempo picked up to a steady, perfect pace. Fast and deep enough to drive into the right spot, but just slow enough so I could feel every movement—even the subtle flex of him when I gasped with satisfaction.

"Oh, my God," I said. "It feels so fucking good."

The man's jaw tightened. He liked hearing that, and maybe he wanted to reply, but it looked like he was holding it back. Perhaps he worried how that would go over with his friend, the one who was in charge of this scene and could end it at any moment.

"Yeah?" I didn't have to see Clay's corrupt smile to know it was there. I heard it in his question. "Is he stretching you out?"

"Yes," I whispered.

I sank further into the couch and back against his chest

as the man clamped a hand on my hip, leaned closer, and held me in place so he could fuck me better. It was madness being sandwiched between these two men, and there was hardly any space between us. The man was inside me, and Clay was wrapped around me, so it felt like we were all connected. One unit, rather than three separate people.

It was *indescribable* how much I liked the concept.

Since he still had his suit on, a bead of sweat formed at the man's temple and trickled down. I understood. I was sweating as well beneath the boning of my corset. Did Clay somehow know? His hands went around me and slid up the front of my top . . . stopping when they reached the top slide-clasp.

He undid the first one, then another.

It wasn't enough to expose my breasts to the man or anyone else in the room. He'd only done it to make room for himself, so he could slip a hand inside and cup one of my breasts. I moaned when his fingers found my nipple and began to pinch.

"Everyone's watching you," he said, squeezing harder. "Just like you wanted. You look so fucking sexy, they all wish they were him right now."

I tried to picture what they saw. How the man's thrusts were pushing deeper inside me, little by little. The way my legs were wrapped around his hips, one hand splayed out on his chest and my other still bent behind me to hold on to Clay. He had one hand down the top of my undone corset, and the other at my waist where my skirt was bunched.

And while my gaze was locked on to the man in front of

me, my attention was split equally with the one at my back. The man was physically inside me, but Clay was inside my mind, stoking my wicked thoughts.

The pinch on my nipple grew in intensity right along with the man's hurried tempo, and Clay's grip was no longer pleasant. It turned achy and white-hot as it went on. Even when I whimpered and my breath went ragged, he didn't back down. His unrelenting pinch rode the rise and fall of my chest, never losing tension.

It *hurt.*

And yet . . .

Like his ruler, I liked the pain. It focused me into the moment and made me experience both men physically at the same time. One was pleasure, and one was pain, and my body had no idea which one it liked more.

Clay shifted beneath me, and I could feel he was aroused. The man's thrusts were hard enough they reverberated through me, making me rock against the erection at my back. Did the man realize as he was fucking me, he wasn't just giving Clay pleasure through the visual—he was causing it as well?

"Fuck," I whined. The pain in my nipple was agony and would have scrambled my thoughts—if I'd had any left. I didn't because the man drove into me at a mind-numbing pace. All I could do was experience.

Since my mind was voided out, Clay moved in and took over the space.

"I'm the one who made this possible." His hand on my waist drifted up, and for a split second I panicked that he was going to put his other hand inside my corset. I wouldn't be able to take it if he decided to pinch me on the other side too. But his hand continued to travel upward. "Everything you feel right now is because of me. All this pain, all this pleasure. His big cock filling you up? That's *me*."

I heard Clay's words while I stared at the handsome stranger, and it only further blurred the two men together into one.

My body was desperate and aching for relief. An orgasm had been a distant dream but suddenly closed in as a *very* possible reality, and heat built in my center. My soft moans swelled into gasping, urgent cries. When I grew shamefully loud, Clay's hand went over my mouth, his fingers catching and muffling my needy groans.

I dangled right on the cusp for a second and an eternity, the moment suspending between wanting it to be over and begging for it to never end.

The man's hips beat furiously into me, and Clay dropped his head into the crook of my neck. In my heightened state, everything was more sensitive. His whiskers were sharp, scraping against my skin as his lips parted, and then he sank his teeth into my neck—right where my pulse pounded.

His bite wasn't any worse than his merciless fingers twisting my nipple, but the new source of pain crossed more wires inside me and caused exquisite chaos. The final push I needed came just after, when the man adjusted my leg draped over his arm. The change in the angle was delicious, but it was where he had put a hand down to brace himself that detonated the pleasure in my body.

He gripped Clay's thigh, and both men seemed comfortable with the placement.

"I'm coming," I cried.

"*Yes,*" the men said at the same time. Or maybe they had a singular voice now, speaking as one.

Fireworks blasted up my spine and shimmered through my limbs. My breath cut off as my lungs shut down and my heart jerked to a sudden halt. It was like every function in my body had to power down to weather the storm of my orgasm.

Which was shockingly intense. So fucking powerful, tears welled in my eyes.

Pain shifted onto its side, morphing into something else. Clay's pinch was gone, but the burning ache became pins and needles as blood rushed back to my skin. The harshness of his bite on my neck softened into a kiss.

I was left quaking when the most intense orgasm of my life began to recede, and it left me only vaguely aware the man was close to coming. It wasn't until his brow furrowed and his expression twisted with a carnal hunger that I realized what was about to happen. The muscles rippling beneath my palm tightened, and a huge gasp of breath burst from his lips.

His thrusts fell out of rhythm, turning jerky and erratic before slowing nearly to a stop. "*Fuck.*"

His face left no doubt he was orgasming, but there were also the pulses inside me to signal how much pleasure was rolling through him. Wave after wave, diminishing until there was only his uneven breath left in the aftermath.

God, he was beautiful like this. His eyes were clear but

unfocused, and he looked at me like I held all the secrets he'd been searching for his whole life. Didn't he know that wasn't possible? He knew more about Clay's world than I did.

I suspected I was staring back at him in exactly the same way.

"Thank you," a cool male voice interrupted.

It broke the spell between us, and the man blinked, turning his gaze toward the person who'd just spoken. Irritation flitted through his eyes as he peered at Clay, but it vanished a heartbeat later.

Once again, the men conducted a wordless conversation as they exchanged a look, and the result of it did not make the man happy. He withdrew from me and slid his hand away from Clay's leg, until he was no longer touching either of us.

We were silent while he pulled up his pants and clenched them closed with a fist. What had happened? The mood had turned cold as soon as Clay had thanked him—

Ecstasy and agony no longer lingered in my system, but my brain was slow to restart. What was it Clay had said earlier? How if I told the man *thank you*—it meant it was over and he was supposed to go downstairs?

Oh.

He'd just told his friend to leave.

The man climbed to his feet and cast his gaze down on me. It looked like he wanted me to say something, to ask Clay if he could stay, and I opened my mouth . . . but nothing came out. I was out of sorts and hadn't a clue how to put what I was feeling into words.

So, the man turned and walked away, but rather than

head for the stairs, he went the other way and disappeared into the restroom.

Clay extracted his hand from my top and refastened the clasps of my corset as I remained leaning against him, too stunned to move. Once my corset was closed, he pushed down the sides of my skirt so I was decent again, then shifted me in his arms so I was seated sideways. I stared at my legs draped over one of his, my heels on the couch.

He used a hand to turn my head toward his, and his mouth sealed over mine. His kiss was slow and methodical. Once again, it felt designed, and I couldn't help but think it had an agenda. He used his kiss as a tool to pry everything else out of my head, to force my focus onto him.

And only him.

It worked. I was unaware the man had reappeared and was standing in front of us with his hands on his hips and a firm look on his face. His gray suit was back in place, and I was dressed, and we looked like we had earlier. As if the experience we'd shared hadn't happened.

But it had. My underwear was still resting on the ottoman where he'd dropped it.

The man stared at Clay with demanding eyes, but the body beneath me filled with tension. Clay was displeased the man had returned.

"Thank you." This time it was more forceful and a clear dismissal to his friend, who I was starting to suspect wasn't exactly a friend.

The man's tone was an even mixture of disbelief and offense. "Clay."

"We had a nice time together," he said. "Let's not go ruining it." When that didn't get the results he wanted, Clay's expression hardened. "Okay. Do you want your privileges revoked?"

The man jerked back as if Clay's threat had physically landed on him, his face soured, and he threw a hand up in the air like an angry surrender.

Whatever, his eyes screamed.

Then he exhaled loudly, turned, and marched off like he couldn't get away fast enough.

What in the world? I swallowed a breath and my tone turned skeptical. "You said you two are friends?"

"We are." Clay's arms settled around me, and some of the tension he'd had relaxed away. "It's complicated."

Obviously. When it was clear he wasn't going to explain, I fought the urge to pry. He was private and not in a forthcoming mood right now. If I were easygoing about it, maybe he'd be more likely to open up to me later. "All right. Does your friend have a name?"

His shoulders lifted on a heavy breath. "No, he doesn't because I was the one you were with tonight. There was no one else."

Did Clay think the man would only become a separate person if I had a name assigned to him?

His mouth pressed to mine, erasing all my thoughts except for one. I was curious to a fault, and this complicated man was irresistible catnip to me. He was a mystery, and I would solve him, one way or another.

NINE

Clay flew to Jacksonville first thing Monday morning, and was gone all week.

Noir didn't seem to mind. She was settling in nicely to her home and no longer hid from me when I came over for my nightly checks. In fact, it wasn't long before she was trained to come running when she heard the chirp of the alarm system each time I opened the door.

Thursday evening, she was hopped up on catnip and purring like mad when my phone rang, and Clay's name appeared on screen. He wanted to FaceTime me? I tapped the screen and pushed out a bright smile.

"Hey, there," I said. "Are you missing this pussy?"

I was lying on my back on the floor beside our cat, so I panned the camera over to bring her in frame.

His laugh was short, and I couldn't tell if he was amused or just caught off guard by my joke. He appeared to be sitting on the bed in his hotel room, leaning against the headboard. "Hi. I see you're keeping her company."

"I check on her every day."

"I know," he said. "I see the notifications on my phone."

I paused. His security system was fancy and probably had cameras too. "Yeah?" I teased. "Are you watching me?"

His eyebrow edged up into an upside-down V. "Is that

a problem?"

God, his playful sternness got me hot. "You know it's not."

But whatever dirty thoughts I was about to have were interrupted when Noir rolled over. As she stretched, her claws came out and reminded me of what I needed to mention. "I'm worried she might be scratching on your furniture. Any objection to me buying her a scratching post?"

"Why would I object to that?"

"I didn't know if you were thinking about building something for her."

"Oh." His gaze drifted away as he considered it, then returned to the camera. "I can't."

I nodded in understanding. "You've got your kitchen renovation and that kneeler you're working on. I just figured I'd check before I went and—"

"No, it's not that." He closed his eyes and rubbed the center of his forehead. "I can't because I don't know when I'll be home next. That's why I'm calling."

I sat up with a start. "What?"

"Somehow the wrong specs went to the fabricators, which means now we have to change the configuration of the rooms. And that means the outlets have to move, plus the cabinets . . . It's a cascading change and a fucking nightmare." He opened his eyes, and disappointment made his shoulders slump. "I have to stay onsite until we have it sorted out."

I pressed my lips together and did my best to control my emotions. He was supposed to come back tomorrow, and since he was only set to be home for the weekend, we'd made plans to spend Saturday night together.

Well, he'd said he'd handle the planning, but I'd agreed to come over.

I'd been eagerly wondering what he had in store for me. I wasn't just terribly curious about him, but also wanted to know how he'd help me explore BDSM. What kind of enjoyable pain was he planning to put on the menu for our evening?

And also, we hadn't had sex yet—not when it was just us, so I was desperate for that.

"How long do you think it'll be?"

He hesitated. "At least another week or two."

I forced out a smile, trying to downplay my disappointment. "That's not that bad."

"No, but it's not," he weighted the word, "ideal." He was just as frustrated with the situation as I was, and that helped ease the sting a little. "I had plans for us, and you know I don't like it when my plans get changed."

Warmth spread through me at the memory. "You don't have to change them. This is just a delay." I lifted an eyebrow and strove for a sexy tone. "I'll still be right next door whenever you get back."

Noir rested her head on top of one of her arms as she curled up into a ball and began to fall asleep. I panned the camera down so she was in the frame.

"I bet she was looking forward to seeing you again," I said.

When I moved the phone so I was back on screen, his guard seemed down and his tone genuine. "Trust me, I was looking forward to seeing her, too."

It was perfectly clear he wasn't talking about the black and white cat we shared.

Instead of spending Saturday night with Clay as planned, I commiserated with Cassidy. Her boyfriend Greg was on-call all weekend, which meant he was stuck at the hospital and we were both without our partners. We did dinner and a movie, and then she 'crashed' at my place afterward—at least, that was the version she told her mother.

It really meant she parked her car at my house, then walked to Greg's place that was a few streets over and slept in his bed, because there was a chance he'd come home in the middle of the night, and they took every opportunity they could to be together, especially when she was home from Vanderbilt for the summer.

I suspected she wasn't fooling anyone, but Cassidy wouldn't turn twenty-one until August, and her mother liked to pretend her daughter wasn't spending the night with a man who was twenty years older.

I'd given my friend an edited version of last weekend, telling her how my naked surprise for Clay had worked, and that after we'd fooled around, he'd taken me out to a club later that night. I left out the ruler he used, what kind of club we'd gone to, and that I'd let a stranger fuck me while he watched.

Lying wasn't something I was comfortable with, but I'd sort of jumped into the deep end with Clay and didn't know how Cassidy was going to react. Telling her would be better if I did it in smaller pieces and gradually. Plus, this would give me time to gauge how my partner would feel about me sharing with her what we did.

I'd told her about Clay's offer of a non-traditional relationship.

"And you're okay with that?" she asked me as we ate. "A relationship that's just sex?"

I laughed lightly. "Oh, yeah. I'm more than okay with it." If anything, I preferred it. "I just get all the good parts. I don't have to meet his family or pretend to be interested in his stuff if I'm not."

I left off the biggest perk. If we didn't let our feelings get involved, then maybe my eventual break-up with Clay wouldn't be as messy as my previous ones had been. And I wasn't being defeatist about needing to break up with him down the road—I was being a realist.

He didn't do romance or love, but I didn't do long-term.

Cassidy gave me a dubious look but didn't say anything. I hadn't judged her when she'd hooked up with her ex-boyfriend's father, and so she wasn't going to judge me . . . but that didn't mean she thought what I was doing was all that smart.

It probably wasn't, but I was already in too deep. I was too focused on getting to know everything about him. Why was he so private? Why didn't romance interest him?

After the weekend, Clay and I fell into a surprising pattern. He'd caught on that I'd go over to his place every night after I'd eaten dinner and check in with Noir. My visits usually were about thirty minutes, but once he started calling during them, I often lost track of time. We spent more than an hour chatting most nights—although he let me dominate the conversation. I tried to steer the focus toward him, but he was masterful at sidestepping it.

His mysteriousness was like a new kind of foreplay. Or torture.

"Okay," I peered at him through the screen of my phone, "I've put this off as long as I can. We need to talk about this haircut."

I walked over to the fireplace in his living room and pointed to the framed photo resting on his mantel. It looked like it had been taken years ago, maybe even a decade prior, and seemed to be his younger sister's graduation from the University of Tennessee. She was pretty in her black cap and gown and was flanked on either side by her parents. Beside her mother stood Clay, wearing a suit, thinner frames, and an unfortunate buzzcut.

"It was hot as hell that summer." He flashed a rueful smile. "It grew back."

"Thank God for that," I teased. "When was this?"

The light in his eyes began to dim. "Eleven years ago."

"Your sister's really pretty. She favors your mom."

Even on the small screen of my phone, I could see the exact moment he shuttered himself away. His expression went flat. "Yeah."

"Hey," I said quickly. "I wasn't snooping. This picture is out in the open, and with your lack of hair in full view . . . I can't *not* look at it."

I padded on my bare feet to the entryway. I couldn't tell if he had a 'shoes by the door' policy inside his house, but his floors were beautiful hardwood, and I didn't want my heels to damage them.

"And I wasn't snooping through your mail either," I continued.

Irritation sliced down his face. "Excuse me?"

"You know I watch my parents' house for them, right? One of the things I do is bring the mail in every day and go through it for them." I gave him an embarrassed smile. "I grabbed yours today. It's habit, sorry. And your mailbox was pretty full." I showed him the stack of letters and mailers. "I didn't go through it, I swear," I explained quickly. "I only brought it in and dropped it off here, but . . . there's a letter from the HOA on top."

His displeasure drained away. "Oh."

"My parents got one too."

The homeowners' association used to be nothing more than a small annual fee to maintain the sign at the front of the subdivision, but last year Judy Maligner had taken over the board. Her lifelong goal was to be a giant pain in the ass—and she was currently living her dreams.

I couldn't stand the woman and had yet to meet anyone who could.

Clay paused as if considering something. "I guess . . . do you mind opening it?"

"Sure."

I set the phone down on the table, propped up against the wall so he could still see, and then tore open the top of the envelope. He waited patiently as I unfolded the single sheet of paper and scanned the contents.

"Fucking Judy," I mumbled under my breath.

"What is it?"

I let the letter drop onto his stack of mail. "It's the same one my parents got. The HOA has adopted a new 'night sky' policy."

He took off his glasses and ground the palm of his hand into one eye.

"You know what that means?" I asked.

"Yeah. Is this just letting me know about the policy change? Or is it a warning?"

I pressed my lips together for a moment. "It says you have thirty days to change your landscape lighting or you're going to get fined. Lights can only point down, not up anymore." I glanced at the date at the top of the letter. "Sorry. You have twenty-six days left."

He put his glasses on as he let out an enormous sigh.

The policy was bullshit. Half the houses in our subdivision had soft up-lighting and had been that way for years. She wanted everyone to redo their exterior lights to—according to the letter—prevent light trespassing into the sky and causing pollution.

"This is all Judy," I said. "The rest of the board is terrified of her. They let her do whatever she wants, including harass Dr. Lowe."

Clay looked confused. "Who?"

"Dr. Lowe? His house is a few streets over, and he unfortunately lives next door to Judy Maligner. She's pissed he's dating my friend Cassidy, so she fucking weaponized the HOA against him." I glared at the letter. "I guarantee he's got landscape lighting that points up. Everyone else that does in this subdivision, like you and my parents, are collateral damage."

He digested the info. "Why's she pissed he's dating your friend?"

"She says it's inappropriate because Cassidy's a lot younger than he is. But I really think it's because she wanted Dr. Lowe for herself." I picked the phone up and stared at him, not wanting to think about stupid Judy for another second. "How's it going at work? You think you'll be home soon?"

He put a hand on the back of his neck and leaned against the headboard of his hotel bed. It was an hour later for him in Florida, and he was wearing a simple white t-shirt, so I got a view of his toned bicep. He seemed unaware of how good he looked or the effect he had on me.

"Maybe another week. It was my department's fuck up, and the hospital system won't put up with a delay over something like this."

Another week wasn't the end of the world, I told myself. I could sulk later after we'd hung up. "What are you going to do about your lights?"

He let go of the back of his neck and lifted the hand like he had no idea. "I'll deal with it when I get back, I guess."

The idea quickly took shape in my mind, and I slathered on my best salesman smile. "Okay. I have a proposition for you."

My smile had been too thick because he looked wary. "Yeah?"

"I'm already handling this for my parents. If you want, I could have the company that's rewiring my parents' house come quote your yard too."

"I feel like there's a catch coming."

I laughed lightly. "All you have to do is tell me something about yourself. Something I don't already know."

He wasn't amused. "Like what?"

"I don't know." But I *did* know. My tone was innocuous and casual. "You could tell me how you got into the lifestyle."

Rather than look nervous or displeased, he relaxed, and his expression was . . . strange. Almost smug, like I'd aimed way too low. He shifted on his bed, getting more comfortable. "Porn."

"Um, what?" *Was he saying he did porn?*

Like he could hear my thoughts, Clay shook his head. "A few years ago, I was watching a video that had this spanking horse in it. The whole time I'm looking at the video, instead of watching the performers, I'm staring at the piece and thinking, 'I could build that better.' So, I did some research and," he lifted a shoulder, "some testing of my design."

A wide grin spread across my lips. "You got hot for furniture while watching porn?"

"Yeah." His unexpected laugh was warm. "After I built that first one and sold it, the client wanted another piece, plus they told some of their play partners about me, and I developed a reputation for my work. There's not a big market for BDSM furniture, but the stuff I build is high quality, and it's important to me that it doesn't just look good—it meets every one of the clients' needs too."

"Form *and* function," I said.

"Yes, exactly." Somehow, with five hundred miles between us, the air around us thickened. Smoke filled his voice. "It didn't take me long to realize I enjoyed the research. I liked watching people play together at Eros, and it took even less time to figure out how much I liked testing my pieces out with a submissive."

His words were a puff of air sweeping across the embers inside me, rekindling the fire that had been dormant the last week. "I'd be happy to help you with that."

"Thanks. I . . ." He frowned and glanced away. "I haven't done that in a long time."

"How come?"

His gaze snapped back to mine and sharpened, maybe evaluating whether to go any farther with this conversation. I pleaded with him with my eyes. Didn't he know the fastest way to build trust was to share with each other?

He took a deep breath. "Things didn't end well with my last partner."

All the desire in me was shelved, and a heavy feeling sank in my stomach. I was sure the answer was no, but I asked it anyway. "Do you want to talk about it?"

"No, not really." Clay couldn't have sounded more honest if he'd tried. He fidgeted, suddenly uncomfortable, and the words spilled from him. "She wanted more. Needed things I couldn't give her." I'd never seen him truly look sad until this moment, and it was heartbreaking. "I was upfront from the very beginning," he said, "but she thought she could change my mind. I cared for her a lot, but I wasn't going to fall in love, and when that didn't happen, she kind of lost it."

Ice crept down over my body, freezing me in place. "What happened?"

"I told her it was over, but she refused to accept it." His expression was grave. "She wouldn't respect my boundaries, so last year I sold my place and moved to the other side of the city where it's pretty unlikely she's going to find me."

"Holy shit," I breathed.

He didn't just like his privacy—he *needed* it.

"Believe me when I tell you, when you showed up naked in my study," he admitted, "it nearly killed me. It'd been more than a year since I'd wanted to play with anyone. One look at you and I threw every fucking plan I had out the window."

I sagged against the hallway wall. It was incredibly powerful that he was opening up to me, and that I'd been the first person he was willing to play with in such a long time, after a relationship that hadn't ended well.

My voice fell to a hush. "I'm glad. I really liked it."

"Me too." He straightened, blinking back the fog I seemed to create in his head. "I'm sorry if I'm slow to share things. I ignored my instincts last time and ended up causing her a lot of pain."

I understood how he meant it. He got off on pain, but not the emotional kind, and I suspected he'd left himself out of the equation. He'd cared about his former partner, and seeing her suffer had hurt him too, even if he didn't admit it.

"It's okay." I hoped he could see my honesty. "I meant what I said before, so you don't have anything to worry about. I'm not going to fall for you, and . . . I can prove it."

"What?"

He'd shared with me, so it only seemed fair. I brushed my hair back out of my eyes and gave him a serious look. "I've dated a lot of guys, and it always ends the same. I'm not built to go the distance." My tone dipped low, pulled down with shame. "This is going to sound awful, but the harder a guy falls for me? The faster I want out."

Clay stared at me with disbelief.

"My final year in college," I added, "I was with this guy for a year. My longest relationship by a mile, and it's possible I only stayed with him so long to see if I could. I thought maybe—I don't know—the feeling would go away."

I was a magnet. Desire pulled me in, but then the power of it flipped me over, turned everything upside-down. Suddenly, the thing I'd been attracted to repelled me with the same amount of force.

Tension held my shoulders tight as I recalled the memory. "I didn't realize while I was fighting the urge to leave, he had no idea, and was falling deeper." I hesitated. "He bought an engagement ring."

His eyes widened with alarm. "Uh-oh."

"Yeah." I swallowed a breath. "Like your partner, this guy didn't handle the breakup well." There had been tears, and angry words hurled at me, followed by apologies and more tears. He'd been as sure of his love as I was of my desire to bolt. "He tried all sorts of ridiculous things to get me to stay or win me back. I mean, he wrote letters to my parents. Fucking letters. Who does that?"

Sympathy painted his expression, but he stayed silent as

he listened.

I put my hand on my hip and lifted my chest, standing tall. "I'm not going to fall in love with you, Clay. The arrangement we have works just fine for me." I made a face. "Well, except I'm here and you're down in Florida."

"I agree, but at least it's temporary," he said. "In the meantime, I have an idea."

My interest piqued. "Oh?"

"How would you feel about trying some long-distance play?"

I didn't know what exactly that entailed. "Like, web cam sex?"

His smile was sly. "Something like that, yeah."

I grinned. He liked watching and I had no problem being watched. "I'd be into that."

"Good," he said. "Maybe we can try that next time."

I acted like it was an innocent question. "How about now?"

He laughed and shook his head. "No. I want to plan it first."

Shit, the idea of that turned me on so much.

Somehow, I survived the weekend without burning out the motor in my vibrator. Every quiet moment alone, my thoughts would drift back to my night with Clay and the stranger, and then I had no choice but to seek relief from my battery-operated friend.

I'd just finished sorting Clay's mail with him when his expression turned serious. "Do you have plans tonight?"

My pulse jumped. Had he finished planning it out? Were we going to play? "It's just a regular ol' Tuesday for me. Why?"

"It's unfair," Clay said.

"What's that?"

"That it took a year for me to discover you, and now that I have, I'm stuck five hundred miles away."

Whoa.

For a guy who wasn't interested in feelings, that had sounded awfully romantic. It sent tingles up my spine, and the sensation was alarming. He wasn't supposed to say stuff like that.

And I wasn't supposed to like it, either.

"But I thought," he continued, "we could try something to tide us over until I'm back. Are you up for that?"

I shot him a sexy smile. "What'd you have in mind?"

Tonight, he'd FaceTimed me through his laptop, so it was strange when he picked up his phone and thumbed something out on it. Message sent, he set down his phone and turned his attention back to me.

Mischief lurked in his eyes, but he hadn't answered my question. When I tilted my head expectantly, he lifted a finger, signaling me to wait, to give him a minute—

The doorbell chimed, and its loud two-toned gong startled me.

He wasn't surprised. Instead, he smiled like the Cheshire Cat and used that same finger to point to the door. "Answer it."

What on earth?

I picked up my phone, carrying it with me as I left the living room and strode into the entryway. It was after eight p.m. and the evening sunlight was fading fast, plus the side windows surrounding Clay's front door were beveled. It obscured the large figure on the porch.

I suspected—or hoped—who I'd find waiting for me, and when I pulled open the door, I wasn't disappointed.

The stranger from the club lifted his gaze to meet mine and flashed his dazzling smile.

TEN

Breath hung awkwardly in my lungs at the sight of this sexy stranger, while the rest of my body lit up. He wore dark jeans and a stone-gray button-down shirt with the sleeves rolled back to his elbows, which gave me all the forearm porn I could ask for.

"Hi," he said in his deep voice before his gaze shifted to the phone in my hand. His posture stiffened like a person interviewing for a job and wanting to make a good impression.

It came from me breathlessly. "Hi."

"I thought the three of us," Clay said on screen, "could have a conversation. Do you want to invite him in?"

It was at that moment I realized I'd been gripping the door handle so hard, my hand ached. I stepped back, making room. "Come in."

The man crossed the threshold, keeping a polite, cordial distance. While his gaze remained on me, I sensed he was completely aware of the other man, even if Clay wasn't physically in the room. I closed the door behind the man, then looked at Clay for what was going to happen next.

"This is Mr. E," he said.

Seriously? I grimaced at the fake name. "Mystery?"

"No." Clay's eyebrow shot up, and he weighted each syllable. "Mister. E. I've already told him to call you L."

Had Mr. E not understood like I had? Did he think my name was Elle? Either way, it didn't matter. I was pleased to have at least a sliver of information about him, even if it was only an initial.

Clay's tone was friendly and not bossy. "Go sit together on the couch, and I can explain what Mr. E is doing here."

Breath was held tightly in my lungs as I walked toward the living room and E trailed behind me. Had he been in Clay's house before? It didn't seem like it. When I sat down and rested the phone in my lap, he surveyed the room like everything was unfamiliar.

Except for me, which was ironic. Yeah, we'd had sex, but we barely knew a thing about each other. Not even names.

His gaze zeroed in on Noir, who bolted the moment she realized there was a stranger in the house. His reaction was odd. Was he amused? Or was he not a cat person?

"What's wrong?" I asked.

He was amused, or at least he found my question funny, because a smile tilted his lips. "I didn't expect him to own a cat."

I was going to explain she was *our* cat, but Clay cleared his throat in a way that demanded our attention, and E's smile drained away. The large man sat down beside me on the couch and kept a respectful space, as if he weren't allowed any closer.

"Since the three of us have already played together," Clay announced, "I asked Mr. E if he'd be interested in a temporary arrangement." There was a gravity to his voice, hinting this was a big deal. "He said yes."

I swallowed thickly. "What kind of arrangement?"

"Until I'm back, he'll be me."

"What?"

"I'll still control the scene, but it'll be remotely for now. He's agreed to fulfill the physical part for me."

I nearly dropped the phone. Every muscle inside corded like a tightly twisted rope as I struggled to process what he'd said. "Like . . . he'll be your stand-in?"

The sinful look in Clay's eyes was seriously hot. "Yes. You'll think of him as an extension of me. He's another way for us to play together."

I focused on the man sitting beside me and how he held himself perfectly still. His chest rose and fell with uneven breaths, but otherwise, there was no way to tell what he was thinking or if he was nervous. His expression rang of forced emptiness.

I tried to understand why Mr. E agreed to this. "You'll take directions from Clay?"

"There are rules," my partner interrupted. "I'd prefer if you only spoke to me, and not with each other."

I stilled. "Why?"

He put a finger on the bridge of his glasses and pushed them up. "Because I think it'll be easier for you to imagine it's me." He wasn't sure if he should say the next part but decided to go for it. "No personal information, which is why you have initials instead of names. This is temporary, and I'd like to minimize your connection to each other. That way, when it's over, it's not difficult for anyone."

I didn't miss the way his eyes shifted E's direction, like

he faintly worried the man he'd invited into his house might get attached to me.

"So, I can't talk to him," I said with mixed feelings, and my tone turned dubious. "Do I call him by your name?"

"No. I'll be onscreen, so if you have a question or need something, just ask it."

I mashed my lips together as I considered this completely bananas idea. I saw the appeal of it for Clay because he enjoyed watching, and I did see the appeal for E, because he'd get to carry out all of Clay's plans.

This arrangement was *all kinds* of attractive to me. We'd make lemonade out of the lemon Clay's job had handed to us.

I took a breath. "What are the other rules?"

"You can't see him if you're not seeing me."

Meaning if Clay wasn't on video, E wasn't allowed to be with me.

"I trust Mr. E," he added. "You should feel comfortable and safe with him, so don't think this rule has anything to do with that. It's only because he's my surrogate. He'll act as I would if I were physically there."

I nodded slowly. "I understand."

"Also," his expression was intensely serious, "no kissing on the mouth."

God, that sent the strangest thrill through me. Surely, this rule was just meant to support the idea of no personal connections between Mr. E and me, but there was a possessive undertone to it. Did Clay want something only for himself? That he'd be the only man allowed to press his lips to mine?

Once again, it felt like he was being unintentionally romantic.

"Do you have any questions?"

I probably did, but I couldn't think of any, except for one. It beat loudly in my brain like a racing heart, picking up momentum as it went. My voice was tight, choked with need. "When do we start?"

My question gave the men so much pleasure, I could taste it. I felt it in shimmers across my skin, prickling up my spine, and blood rushed warmly to my face.

Clay's word was an order for both of us. "Now."

And as soon as the command had been given, E snatched up the handle to his bag, was up on his feet beside the couch, and had his hand extended to me in invitation. Hopefully, he didn't see the subtle tremble of mine as I set my hand in his. His grasp was gentle but firm as he pulled me up.

I couldn't imagine what I looked like to him as I stared up wide-eyed, clutching both my phone and his hand. This couldn't be real. It was too much like a perfect fantasy to be happening.

Yet, it was.

Clay didn't tell his stand-in where to lead me, but I suspected it was because he'd done it earlier. I tried not to rush as we made our way toward the basement door. Every step we descended pumped more desire inside me, and by the time we reached the bottom of the stairs and I set my gaze on the St. Andrew's cross, I was ready to burst.

E surveyed the room, and when his focus landed on the gorgeous piece of furniture, he let go of me and stepped forward to admire it better. I lifted the phone and turned it so Clay could see then turned it back to face me.

"I'd forgotten how beautiful it is," I said softly.

Clay's Adam's apple bobbed in a thick swallow and his shoulders lifted. My compliment had caught him off-guard and he struggled not to look affected. "Thank you." His tone evened out. "Hand the phone to him. I'd like everything off, please."

Him telling me what to do was sexy, but the way he did? Fuck, it was seriously hot. His *please* was so proper and polite, making it sound like I was doing him a favor, when as far as I was concerned, it was the other way around.

When I held my phone out to E, he set his bag on the nearby workbench and took it, tapping the screen to reverse the camera. And then both men waited to watch me undress, making the air in the room go thin.

Clay had seen me nude, but the man in front of me hadn't, and although his focus was pointed down at the screen he held out in front of himself, I was acutely aware of how I had his attention.

My black tank top went first, my dark brown hair swishing as it was pulled off, revealing my black bralette. I cast my shirt aside and gave the sexiest smirk I could manage, and then my fingers went to the button of my jean cutoffs. I bent at the waist, keeping my gaze locked onto the phone while I pushed my shorts down my legs. It exposed my green panties trimmed with black lace, and thank fuck I'd decided to change into them before coming over to Clay's tonight. They were one of the sexiest pairs I owned.

I wasn't shy, and I didn't waste time teasing the men. The faster I got naked, the quicker E could strap me to the St. Andrew's cross and carry out Clay's orders. I crossed my arms, gripped the bottom of my bralette, and lifted, freeing myself from the lace until my breasts tumbled into view.

There was a joint deep breath from the men, almost as if they were the same person. Wasn't I supposed to think of them like that? The muscle along E's strong jaw flexed, and his gaze flicked to mine. He wasn't allowed to speak, but he didn't have to say anything to communicate. He liked how I looked.

When I hooked my fingers into the waistband of my underwear, Clay's voice was abrupt. "Wait," he said. "I like those. Leave them on."

"Okay." I withdrew, letting my hands hang at my sides, and turned my head toward the cross. But Clay's instructions weren't to step up to it. They weren't even for me at all.

"There's a mount for the phone on the shelf," he said to E.

The phone screen was tapped, turning the camera around again, and I stood motionless as E found the stand, clipped my phone into it, and positioned the camera so I could see Clay. The stand rested on the workbench, and now that his hands were free, E turned his attention to his bag.

The zipper was pulled in an unhurried, steady stroke, mirroring the slow reveal when I'd undressed, and a fist reached inside my chest at the same time E reached inside the bag. A coil of black rope was pulled from inside, and the invisible fist tightened.

Clay's question was echoed in E's eyes. "Yes?"

Like I'd been with the scale ruler, I should have been nervous, but I wasn't. I only had eagerness to see how he'd use it, and so I nodded slowly.

"Good. Hold your hands out in front of you."

I did, and when E began his approach, I wasn't sure where to look. Was I supposed to keep my eyes on Clay? It was impossible because he was on a tiny screen resting on the workbench, and E was right in front of me, seeming larger than life.

He dropped one end of the long rope, and the coil unfurled, landing with a quiet thud in a pile at my feet. There was a pause, only for a second, as if he were giving me a chance to change my mind . . . or maybe he was deciding to truly commit to whatever he was about to do. I stared up at him, searching his face, but his gaze fell to my wrists and the end of black rope stretched in his hands.

My arms were bent so my elbows were at my sides, and I laced my fingers together. Was this what he'd been waiting for?

He wound the rope around my wrists several times before knotting the end off, and then began feeding it between my bound wrists in a figure eight pattern. It wasn't tight, but snug and inescapable, and my pulse quickened. And once he'd repeated threading it between my wrists enough times, he guided the rope up to my shoulder.

I dry-swallowed as he slipped it behind my neck and leaned in, scooping a hand in to sweep my long hair free from the rope. The texture of it wasn't unpleasant against my bare skin, but my heart clattered to a stop when E continued to wrap the rope around my neck. Shivers cascaded down my arms as it was looped a second time around my throat, and he repeated the action, pulling my trapped hair free from beneath it.

"If it's tight at all," Clay said, "let me know."

I was disoriented by what was happening; it felt like Clay was right here and not miles away. The black rope circled my throat for a third time, and although it wasn't constricting, I felt its dominance on every inch of my body, all the way down to my toes. This time, when E adjusted my hair, he was more thorough and lingered close enough I could feel the heat of his body. His fingertips brushed over my skin as he fluffed my hair, ensuring no strands were caught.

The rope was brought back down to my wrists, and the loose end of it was no longer on the floor. It brushed against my knees before he wrapped it a final time around my bound wrists and tied it off. He'd used all the rope without running out of it or having too much to spare. There was no need to undo his work and start again, because this was a man who had practiced.

Who knew what he was doing.

His pause this time was far more pronounced, and I peered up at him, desperate with questions I knew better than to ask.

"Tell me you're ready," a voice demanded.

I was in a delirious haze, unable to tell which man had spoken, but when it registered it was Clay, my gaze shifted to him. He was framed perfectly so his handsome face filled most of the screen, and it made it so I could see every drop of lust coursing through him.

"I'm ready," I said.

E ran his fingers over the ropes strung between my wrists and my throat, like he was examining a necktie, but abruptly clenched them in a fist and jerked it forward. It was so startling, I stumbled and crashed into him. Since the rope was wound around my neck multiple times, the tension distributed evenly, barely tightening against my throat. And as soon as the pressure had come, it was gone, and my collar relaxed.

He'd had to let go to steady me in his arms.

God, this guy was *solid*. His chest was a wall, and his arms were warm stone, and I liked the way they felt around me. But I didn't get to enjoy it, because he gripped the ropes again and used them to lead me to the workbench, pulling me along like an owner using a leash.

Heat blasted up my legs, thickening in my center. The juxtaposition of his tenderness with my hair to his rough yank of my harness had me spinning in the most exhilarating way.

There weren't words from Clay to tell me what to do. E tugged the ropes and pulled my hands to the top of the workbench until my arms were stretched across it and I was bent over the table. My forearms rested on the surface that was faintly gritty with sawdust, and I peered into the camera, seeing the miniature version of myself in the corner of the screen. The black rope draped across my throat, reminding me of a collar, and it looked so fucking sexy.

E stood beside me and rummaged once more in his bag, and then a new item was presented to me. The black leather paddle was squared off at one end, rounded at the handle, and accented with beautiful red stitching. It wasn't large, but I suspected it was plenty big enough to get the job done.

"Yes?" Clay asked again.

I imagined my consent was as much for E's benefit as it was Clay's, so my answer was breathy but sure. "Yes."

He sat back in his chair and got comfortable as he waited for the show to start.

On screen, I could see E standing behind me with the paddle gripped in a hand. He studied my body, but I couldn't tell if he was figuring out placement . . . or simply admiring the view. My green panties were cheeky cut, exposing the bottoms of my ass to him.

I drew in a slow breath when E set the paddle against the back of my underwear, and he rubbed the flat side of the paddle in circles on my ass, each rotation growing wider and quicker. It felt nice, but also like he was winding me up. Priming me for what would happen next.

Since I could see onscreen, I knew when the first strike was coming, but it surprised me all the same. It didn't hurt in the slightest. For such a strong guy, I'd expected him to put more force behind it. It hadn't been a spanking. This had been a kiss.

When a smile bowed on my lips, Clay smiled too, but I got the impression he was smiling for an entirely different reason—like he knew something I didn't. He did, didn't he? He'd scripted this evening.

E slapped the paddle against me again, this time on the other side of my ass, and I swallowed back a giggle. "Is that supposed to hurt?"

E's gaze flicked to the screen, and he cocked an eyebrow in question.

Clay laughed lightly. "No," he said. "Not yet."

Was he answering me? Or speaking to E? Maybe both.

E's strikes increased both in intensity and frequency, heating me inside and out. My skin warmed from the rush of blood, and I watched the screen with fascination. It was one thing to hear and feel the sharp slaps of the leather while my hands were tied and my bare breasts were pressed to the table, but that was just the first layer. I could also watch E as he swung the black paddle through the air and see how he enjoyed the reverb of each strike as it rippled across my flesh.

And at the same time, I got to see Clay's reaction to it and the way his eyes hooded behind his glasses. He stared at us with so much hunger, it should have been frightening—but of course it wasn't to me. It only turned me on more.

The blows alternated sides, and even though my panties were still on, the whisper-thin fabric didn't give me any protection when E really began to spank me. He reared back and brought the paddle crashing down on me hard enough that the smile on my face dried up.

It didn't hurt, really.

The discomfort was like sitting on too-hot leather seats in the summer, only more focused.

The man who loomed over me had his attention locked on to what he was doing, and his jaw was set. It wasn't until a soft moan slipped out of me that it broke his focus. His gaze flew to the screen, checking in with both me and Clay, and when he determined my moan was in pleasure, he resumed his work.

He looked even more beautiful like this. All the power was supposed to be Clay's, but E was the one wielding it, and satisfaction streaked across his face as he delivered blow after punishing blow. The loud, uneven tempo of his paddle filled the room, and my skin began to burn all over from his relentless paddling.

Clay asked it even as he already knew my answer. "Do you like it?"

"Yes." I dropped my head forward, resting my forehead against the bindings around my wrists.

"No." His tone was stern. "Eyes up and on me."

I lifted my head and peered at him through the strands of hair that had fallen into my face. Behind me, the paddling had paused. It was so E could grab the back of my underwear and wedge it up between my cheeks, exposing more of me to his spankings. My skin was the prettiest shade of pink I'd ever seen.

I groaned with both pleasure and discomfort when he swung again. The blow was so hard, I lifted on my toes and my back arched, but that made E scowl. He put his hand on the small of my back and shoved, pushing me back down into position. His corrective hand stayed where it was like a warning, and I burned even hotter at his touch.

Oh, my God. Could he see how turned on this was making me? My underwear had to be soaked, and more heat flooded my face. The paddle cracked against my skin, and I pushed air out in a hiss through my tight teeth.

E's spankings were merciless, but so was the way Clay

stared at me, and weren't these spankings really his? He'd drafted and designed this scene, probably down to how many strikes I'd receive and how hard I'd get them.

"Shit," I groaned. Pain banded across my cheeks, and I tried to shift under the weight of E's hand, encouraging him to find a different spot for his next blow. And yet . . . even though it hurt, I still liked it. The prickly heat left after the leather was gone felt intoxicatingly good.

Clay's lips were parted so he could pull in a deep swallow of air, and his shoulder moved rhythmically. What was he doing? Oh, my God. The paddle was so distracting, it took me a moment to realize he was jerking off.

My fingers curled into fists at this idea.

He was turned on, and I was the cause of it.

And what about E? It was hard to tell if he was breathing hard from the scene, the exertion, or a combination of the two. He seemed far too focused on his task to think about anything else right now.

As I whined and wiggled, it had a polarizing effect on the men. Clay's hand pumped at a faster tempo, but E's face took on a dark cast. It looked like he wasn't enjoying it quite as much as he had been when we first started.

"You've got an ass of steel." Clay's expression was sinful. "I guess I need to find someplace *new*."

His tone was deceptively casual, but the way E went still announced this was an order. He contemplated what to do, then rested the paddle across the small of my back so he could unroll his shirt sleeves. It was odd that the leather was cool against my skin, when it had created fire all over my backside.

Once he had the line of buttons down the front of his shirt undone, E pulled it open and off his shoulders, revealing his tan, sculpted chest. Even better? His jeans sat low on his hips, showing off the notched V that disappeared beneath his waistband. I thought Clay had a body built for sex, but E had one built for fucking.

He tossed his shirt on top of his bag, snatched up the paddle, and swung it so quickly, I didn't have time to brace.

"Oh, fuck," I babbled. "*Fuck.*"

Because he'd aimed lower, and I discovered through searing pain that the backs of my thighs, unlike my ass, were *not* made of steel. I jerked my head back, only for the rope to go taut and yank my bound hands with it. The agony of E's strike went on and on, no matter how I tried to run from it. And there was his other hand, which pressed down on my hip and pinned me to the tabletop. I collapsed forward with a thud, surrendering to—

"Fuck," I swore again, only this time in pleasure, because E's hand moved and was now between my legs, his fingertips massaging my clit.

The distraction gave me much-needed relief from the pain, and the stroke of his fingers on my damp panties was so good, if he kept doing it, it wouldn't take long to bring me to orgasm. It was like the pain was a shortcut, a way to bypass foreplay or prepare my body in seconds.

"Look at me," Clay demanded, but there was an edge of a plea to his words.

Endorphins pumped through my system, and my head

was a chaotic mess, but hearing him centered me, and as I raised my fuzzy gaze to find him, E pulled my panties to the side and slid a finger deep inside me.

My moan was low and throaty, and onscreen I watched both men enjoy the effect they had on me. E's mouth hung open with lust, and Clay's hand moved fast enough it made his shoulders vibrate.

I tensed the muscles in my arms and back when E added a second finger and began to fuck me with them. He wasn't done either. He raised the paddle and returned to swatting my ass, where the skin had graduated from pink to a brilliant red.

"It was worth it, wasn't it?" Clay's voice was hypnotic. "Taking the pain to get the pleasure?"

"Yes," I whispered. A thousand times over, yes.

"You look so fucking good like this. Your ass painted red and tied up for me to use any way I want. You want that, too, don't you?" His hand moved faster still, and pleasure dripped from his face. "You want to be used?"

"Yes," I moaned.

He looked thrilled but feigned a scowl. "Naughty girl. You're going to make me come."

"Show me," I begged.

As Clay reached forward and tilted the camera down, I shifted my focus to E for a fraction of a second. He'd paused the paddling, perhaps to focus on what his fingers were doing, or maybe to catch his breath. He had a faint sheen of sweat on his face and chest and was breathing hard. I understood. All I had to do was lie across the table and take it, and

I was sweating, too.

Clay's lower body came into view. His pants were undone and around his ankles, and he ringed his thumb and forefinger around his cock. His light grip pumped up and down in short, shallow strokes, focusing mainly on the tip. These weren't maintenance strokes to keep himself hard—these were edging ones. Like a full fist wrapped around himself would be too much and he wasn't ready to lose control.

"See what you do to me?" he asked, although his question was rhetorical. He pushed the screen up so his face was back in the camera's view, and his attention drifted to E. "Again."

The fingers inside me retreated, and E's deep breath in was so heavy, it was audible. He had reservations, but Clay did not, and he looked irritated at how his stand-in was hesitating.

"Again?" Clay asked me. If I wanted it, that should help with E's unease, wouldn't it? And I did want it . . . because E had stopped touching me, and with the pain I'd get pleasure.

"Again," I confirmed.

ELEVEN

E's inhale had been loud, but his sigh was so quiet, I doubted the microphone picked it up. Clay didn't seem to hear it either. He was pleased when E adjusted his grip on the paddle and prepared.

Trepidation swirled in my stomach, and shivers broke down my legs. Would it be worse this time? And if so, would the 'after' be even better? Or would the strike of the paddle be less intense than the anticipation of it?

On top of it all, there was my strange fascination with the experience. A large part of me wanted to see how much I could take. It hoped for the vicious slap of leather in a place that would make tears spring into my eyes. I sank my teeth into my bottom lip and held my breath, bracing for the blow I knew was coming while my gaze was fixed on both the man who'd ordered it and the man who'd carry it out.

The paddle swung so fast, as it cut through the air it made a *whooshing* sound, and I heard the crack of it against my skin before the impact registered. The pain entered my body through the back of my thigh and stormed up my body, filled with fury. It consumed me with its white heat, the strength of it so powerful I couldn't breathe.

Agony carried me away, but this time instead of fighting it, I let it sweep through me. A sob welled in my throat, but I cut it off, so it came out as a startled cry. In my misery, I was only vaguely aware of the paddle dropping to the floor and the hands on me.

I stared at the screen through blurry eyes, seeing one man while being touched by another, and the two of them began to morph into one. He told me I was beautiful while his fingers stroked my clit, and as the pain gripping me started to relax, I began to float.

"Such a good girl," the man cooed. "You've earned this."

He pushed his fingers inside me and reached around with his other hand to rub my clit, and a long moan poured from my mouth. My ass and the backs of my legs were on fire, but everywhere else was lit up and singing.

In my floaty space, time seemed to slow to a crawl. Even my thoughts slowed, as if my brain had been powered down to conserve energy and only the critical systems were still operating. It was nice and dreamy.

But it couldn't last forever.

A sense of urgency grew and swelled, spinning my mind back up and making me aware. Oh, my God, I needed to come. The fingers plunging inside me, working together with the ones massaging my clit, created an ache that rivaled the one throbbing in my skin. I had an irrational fear that all the tension inside me was a bomb, and I had to get it out before it detonated and killed both me and the man at my side.

"Oh, my God," I gasped, shifting my hips against the table so his fingers could drive deeper and hit just where I needed them to. "Oh, God . . . *oh, God . . .*"

"Yes," he encouraged, although it came in two separate

voices, one echoing the other.

The orgasm swelled as a tidal wave of ecstasy and crashed into me, wiping all thought away. It was far more devastating and amazing than anything that could be done with just a paddle or a pair of hands between my legs.

I writhed against my restraints, making the cords wrapped around my throat constrict, but the sensation only added to my enjoyment. Just as I couldn't escape the pain, I couldn't run from the pleasure either. Not that I wanted to.

The orgasm crested and started to recede, and the man began to peel apart, splitting back into two separate bodies. Clay and Mr. E were equally responsible for my pleasure, and as they shared the credit, they also shared the same look of satisfaction.

My knees were jelly, and I lay on the top of the workbench, not caring how my breasts were flattened against the rough surface as I struggled to catch my breath. There was movement behind me as E stepped back and disappeared out of the frame. I turned my head, resting it on my outstretched arms, and watched as he pulled open the door to the storage closet.

It was big enough, it was nearly a room and had a light, and when he flipped it on, my mouth would have fallen open if it weren't already. This closet had to be where Clay stored unsold pieces or prototypes because it was packed with furniture. Some pieces were upside-down and stacked on top of others.

E must have known what he was looking for, but not exactly where it was, because he stood in the doorway with his back to me and scanned the closet for a long moment. It gave me time to admire the sculpture of his body. He was broad and toned, and the tan of his skin said he'd spent a lot of summers shirtless.

Whatever he'd been looking for was found, and he disappeared inside the closet, making noises like he was moving things around. When he emerged, he was carrying a large . . . panel? The rectangle was padded, covered in black leather or vinyl, and three sides of it were outlined in red. He carried it by a strap handle, and once he reached the center of the room, he laid it cushion side down, revealing the other side was cushioned too.

Oh.

I finally understood when E squatted, unlatched the side, and opened the piece. It uncovered the dark-stained wood legs that were inside, and I realized I was looking at the underside of a folding table. As he locked the tabletop in place and worked to unfold the legs, I pushed myself upright. With my hands tied and my body still recovering from the spectacular orgasm, I couldn't help him set it up, but he didn't need my help, anyway. Instead, I used the time to brush whatever dust I could off my chest.

Once E had everything done, he grabbed a leg, tilted the table on its side, then lifted and set it on its legs.

Of course the table was sexy and beautiful, but it couldn't compete with the man standing beside it. His gaze landed on the phone before drifting to me, and then he sauntered my direction, looking far more confident than I'd seen him before. Right before he reached me, he veered to the stand that was holding my phone and moved it to the edge of the table. He bent slightly, making sure the newly set up table was in frame, then straightened and grabbed the ropes at my wrists.

Both men were silent as he tugged me to the edge of the table, so the only sound was our shuffling footsteps. E's hands slid up the ropes, all the way to my throat, then parted to smooth over my shoulders. He leaned in, setting his mouth against my neck, just above the place where the rope was wrapped.

Any recovery I'd made was instantly wiped out by his soft kiss. My knees went soft again, and I tried not to sag into his arms while his damp, warm mouth created wonderful shivers. His hands continued to move, sliding down over my chest, and cupped my breasts. As he brushed his thumbs over my hardened nipples, my gaze was on the screen of the phone.

Clay studied me as I studied him. E's mouth followed his hands, his head dipping down so his lips could capture one of my nipples, and heat snapped through my body.

"Have you," I said between gulps of air, "ever done anything like this before?"

E hesitated, like he wanted to answer, but knew he shouldn't. We weren't allowed to speak to each other, so my question was supposed to be for Clay.

"No," Clay said. "The night at the club was a first for me." He was still stroking himself, but his movements had slowed, and his tone was uneven. Unsure. "I've never shared a partner before."

E steadied my other breast in his hand and focused

his mouth on it. The sharp edge of his teeth bit, just hard enough to feel amazing, and my heart beat in double-time. "Do you like it?"

"Yes. I do." One corner of Clay's mouth turned up in a smile. "What about you?"

"Yes," I whispered.

It was getting difficult to stand, but E had an arm around my back for support, holding me upright while he feasted on my flesh. My eyes were heavy with desire, but I fought to keep them open and my gaze on Clay. Since my question had echoed his when we'd been in his study, the first time we'd played together, I also echoed his response.

"I'm glad I get to be your first."

E's teeth latched down, even harder this time, and I squeaked with surprise. My wide-eyed stare dropped to the man whose tongue spun a circle on my nipple while he watched me. It felt like he wanted my attention, to remind me he was here too. I expected punishment from Clay, but not E, and it was both dangerous and thrilling. Clay was in charge, but that didn't mean E was submissive.

And perhaps to prove it, he picked me up in his arms, and put one knee, then the other up on the padded top, climbing onto the table. My legs went around his waist, and he lowered me onto my back on the leather, dropping me so quickly I landed with a thud and my head bounced.

He was perched over me on his hands and knees, and because I was under him, there was nowhere else to look but at his victorious smile. Oh, he liked having my full attention. My bound hands were in front of me, so he grabbed them and flung them up over my head, out of his way. I had to turn my head to the side so the rope connecting them to my throat wasn't stretched across my face.

The table wasn't all that wide, but it was long, and E had more than enough room to maneuver. He kissed and bit a line down my body, pausing over my breasts before moving on, working lower. The table beneath us didn't shake or make a sound as he shifted on his knees and backed down off it. Then he hooked a finger under the lace trim, pulled my panties to the side, and set his mouth on me.

It punched a moan of satisfaction from my center, and my back arched off the tabletop. His mouth—oh, my God—it made me quiver. It poured fire over my body, injected it into my bloodstream, heating me like an inferno.

Nearby, my phone sat on the table, its camera catching it all for Clay to enjoy. He watched how I writhed and bucked, heard how I gasped and whimpered. He saw E straighten, grasp the sides of my underwear, and jerk my panties off. I had to put my legs together and lift them straight into the air, but as soon as the fabric was free, E slapped my ankles apart and lunged down between my spread thighs.

It was feral, the way he attacked me with his tongue. Aggressive and rough, as if having to remove my underwear was an interruption he couldn't afford to have. An unfair obstacle thrown in his way.

Clay had told me he hoped I wasn't fragile, and since I had proved to them both that I wasn't, E didn't treat me that way either. He nuzzled into me, his head moving side to side as his tongue lashed and flicked and fucked.

I had to heave air in and out of my lungs.

Sweat coated my skin. I could feel it on the back of my neck, trapped beneath the rope. I could barely make us out in the small box in the corner of the screen, but I saw what I wanted to. Me naked except for the black rope. E's head between my legs—although one of them blocked his face. He had his arms under my thighs and his hands on my stomach, his fingers laced together.

It was fucking erotic.

Live-streaming porn for Clay, and he gazed at us with so much lust, it filled every pixel of the screen.

He didn't speak, though. There were no questions for me or directions for E. Clay was an observer now, not an active participant, and the thought materialized in my head. This was why E had looked so confident when he'd brought me to the table.

What he was doing right now? This wasn't scripted. It was his time.

And he was efficient with it. As he fucked me with his skilled tongue, he started to work on undressing himself. He toed off his shoes, then jerked off his socks, one after the other. When that was done, his hands went to his waist and worked to undo his jeans.

He moved with urgency. It wasn't like he was under a time limit—at least, I didn't think—his hurried hands seemed to be propelled simply with need. Did he feel like I had earlier? Was he gripped with the same irrational thought that there was a bomb ticking inside him, and if he didn't get what he wanted, he'd die?

Dark gray underwear was all that was left to be removed, but he didn't take it off. Instead, he went to his bag and retrieved something from one of the pockets before walking over to the end of the table where my hands rested.

The condom was dropped to the leather beside me, left within reach for when he'd need it. But right now, he was focused on turning me so I was on my stomach. As I rolled over, he urged me backward on the table, forcing me up onto my hands and knees. It was so there was space for him to climb up on the padded tabletop and join me.

E was on his spread knees, but upright, and there was nothing submissive about his posture. If I had any doubts about what he wanted, he cleared those up by pushing his underwear down until it stretched across his thighs, set his impressive erection free, and canted his hips toward my face.

Since my hands were tied and I needed my arms for support, the only thing I could do was open my mouth and let him push his cock inside. His strong hands gathered up my loose hair, keeping it out of my way, but also using his grip to hold me in place.

You want to be used.

It was what I'd said I wanted, and E was happy to oblige. His grip was firm on the back of my head as he sawed his cock in and out, fucking my mouth like he didn't care if I enjoyed it. I was there for his pleasure. He was so freaking big and hard, it was a lot to take. His hips pumped furiously, pushing deep enough that I choked and gagged. He eased off but didn't retreat entirely, and his shallow, slower thrusts gave me just enough time to recover before picking up the pace again.

It was messy. Saliva dripped from my lips, dangling in a thread onto the leather, but it was ignored. I wondered what Clay thought. From his angle and with my hair held back, surely he could see everything. My jaw began to ache from how rough and big E was, but . . . shit.

It was so freaking hot.

I gasped for air as he abruptly pulled back and released his grip on my hair, and my head hung down while I tried to catch my breath. The condom was snatched up as he got down off the table and shed his underwear.

"Turn around," Clay ordered. "I'm going to fuck you now."

A shift went through the room. E's time was over, and we were back under Clay's direction. It was awkward following the order since I was tied up, but I managed it, and once I was on my hands and knees facing the other way, E climbed up behind me and rolled on the condom.

A gasp burst from my lips when he buried himself inside me.

"Shit," I groaned at the abrupt intrusion. Like last time, he pushed deep enough it was right at the edge of discomfort. How the fuck did girls take a big dick in porn like it was easy?

I attempted to watch us on the screen, but the last thing I saw was E tangle a hand in the hair at the crown of my head before he jerked me back, forcing my gaze up toward the ceiling. Was this how Clay intended to fuck me? Rough and urgent?

As E tugged my head back, it made the rope between my neck and my wrists go taut. The cords wrapped tighter around my throat, and my back arched, allowing him to drive deeper inside me.

My moan was a mixture of dissatisfaction and pleasure, and my brain was in total conflict. How did something that was uncomfortable also feel good? Like, *really* good?

Careless hips slammed against my ass, creating hot, stinging slaps on my irritated skin. His hand fisting my hair was harsh, inadvertently twisting and pulling strands with each thrust he gave, and my scalp ached, but the gasps and moans he twisted and pulled from me were more deliberate. His other hand was locked on my waist, tight and merciless, steadying me so he could maintain his punishing rhythm.

As his intensity built, so did the aching need inside me. I'd already had one orgasm, but my body was greedy and begged for another. E's hand on my waist came off, only so he could pause his tempo for a split second and crack his palm against my ass. It sent heat up my spine like lightning.

And then he had both hands in my hair, pulling me back farther as he sat back on his heels. I'd been up on my straight arms with just my fingertips planted on the table for support, but I sank back into his lap, my back against his chest. In this new position, he couldn't thrust quite the same, but he let go of my hair and put his arms around me.

Now that his hands were free, he used them to touch. One cupped my breast, and the other gripped the rope stretching down the center of my body. I turned my head toward the phone, wanting to see what we looked like, but also . . . What did Clay think about this?

Did he like watching another man fuck me on the

furniture he'd built?

The answer was a resounding *yes.*

Clay's shoulders moved violently as he jerked off, his face coated with desire, and it was so sexy, the muscles inside me clamped down. It brought me oh-so-close to coming.

It was beyond strange my partner was so far away, yet it also felt like he was right here. He wasn't physically in this room, and yet he flooded every inch of it with his dominance. Even as the man at my back moved inside my body and his warm, ragged breath filled my ear, I saw Clay. All this pain and pleasure I'd been given, it came from him. He was fucking me just as much as E was.

There were short, hurried swallows of air that mixed with moans of satisfaction from both men, but E's were louder and more urgent. His muscle-bound body flexed and contracted as he pushed me to rock my hips on him, then wedged a hand between my thighs, urging them apart. It was so he could smack his fingertips against my clit.

"Oh," I moaned. His slap wasn't hard or cruel. Its intent was to bring pleasure, which it absolutely did.

Clay was breathless as he growled his order. "Harder."

E didn't hesitate. His next slap was more aggressive, and I jolted, both from the sting of it and the acute bliss as the sensation dulled away. His strikes against my swollen clit, in combination with his deep thrusts, were going to send me over the edge, and both men sensed it.

"I'm gonna fucking come," Clay warned.

A single breath later, pleasure twisted on his face and his eyes slammed shut. It looked like he was enduring exquisite torture as the orgasm took him. It was violent and beautiful, and I gasped with enjoyment. Sometimes pleasure was like a gift—better to give than receive, and some of the ecstasy coursing through him ran through me as well. He'd gotten off not just watching, but having his plans carried out on me.

The fingers buried in between my legs changed tactics. The biting slaps became erotic caresses, and within mere seconds, E's strokes set off a charge in my body.

"Oh, God," I cried. "Fuck, I'm coming."

Arms locked around me to hold me in place. There were grunts and strained moans from behind as I rode out my orgasm on him, my whole body trembling. It sounded like he was holding back, but then gave in. I was still coming when he shoved me forward, face-down onto the tabletop. I caught myself on my forearms, but my cheek pressed to the soft leather.

Since everyone else was coming, E must have decided to join in.

His hands captured my hips, and he rutted into me, ruthless and primal. As if he were a man driven to the edge of madness and he no longer cared what he was supposed to do. There was no right or wrong, no desire anymore to stay within the rules. He pumped furiously, and his thrusts wracked my body.

God, I loved it. He'd given me so much pleasure, he earned the right to take some of his own. To use me however he needed. A few more powerful thrusts, and then he pulled out. Onscreen, I saw how he moved to yank the condom off and hurl it to the ground, then lifted on his knees so he was perched over me, his fist sliding back and forth over his dick.

He came in sputtering bursts, and the hot liquid flicked onto my back and my ass. It dripped from his tip as his hand slowed, wringing the last of his orgasm from his body while his chest heaved for air.

The way he looked at me when he came? So undeniably sexy, it rivaled watching Clay.

In the aftermath of our joint climax, no one moved.

One breath at a time, I came down from my high and began to return to reality. My back was wet, my legs were sore, and it was uncomfortable with my hands pinned beneath my body, but I stayed still. I expected a command from Clay at any moment, but he just gazed at me with a dreamy stare.

It was so nice, the floaty feeling from earlier returned and a shy smile warmed my lips. What we'd done was wild, and I was in awe of him. How willing he was to share and trust. That he'd given me a fantasy and gotten off on it just like I had.

E's hands were damp, and when something cold wiped over me, I flinched. I'd been so out of it, I hadn't realized he'd climbed down, cleaned up in the bathroom nearby, and returned with a damp hand towel. It glided over my skin in soothing strokes, and he took extra care on the lower half of my body.

I'd only heard E speak a handful of times, but his voice was deeper than before. "Are you all right?"

Clay cleared his throat, the sound loud and angry. It was his reminder to E about the rules, and E shot him the briefest of irritated looks before bending over to retrieve his underwear and pull it on.

"How are you feeling?" Clay asked.

I rolled onto my side to face the camera. "I'm good, but . . ." I lifted my bound hands.

He nodded. E understood, too, how I wanted to be untied, because he moved to the side of the table, took hold of my shoulders, and helped me sit up. Luckily, as long as I didn't move and my skin stayed as it was on the leather, it didn't hurt. His broad back blocked my view of the screen, so there was nothing to look at except the bead of sweat erratically trailing down his toned chest as he began to work on the knots at my wrists.

It had been sexy and provocative when he'd tied me up, but I wasn't prepared for how sensual the process would be as he undid his work. Skilled and methodical, his fingers loosened the knots and unwound the rope, and since he was focused on that, it gave me a chance to really look at him.

His deep-set eyes were sharp and inquisitive, hinting at his intelligence. What did he do for a living? His hands were gentle now, but he'd been rough with me earlier. His smile could be brilliant, or his expression contemplative, like he could be whatever he wanted. Maybe he was an entertainer. A lot of folks in Nashville were in the music industry—the woman who lived next door to Dr. Lowe was some bigwig agent.

When E began to unwrap the rope from around my neck, his gaze met mine, and I swallowed a breath. He looked at me like I was one of the most beautiful things he'd ever seen, and it was incredibly powerful.

Like last time, he leaned in close, and it was unstoppable the way I craved the heat of him. I lifted my chin, jutted out my chest, making my nipples brush against his warm skin. It caused him to let out the softest sigh of contentment, and it made me even bolder. I didn't know what was allowed, but since I couldn't see Clay, it meant he couldn't see me, so I flattened my hands to E's chest.

He stiffened, but I got the feeling it wasn't from my touch . . . like me, he wasn't sure if this was allowed. But it was clear he wanted this. His eyes went hazy as I dragged my hands down, trailing fingertips over the ridges of his defined abdomen.

It was a stolen moment between us, because once more, Clay cleared his throat. In response, E shifted to one side and finished undoing the ropes, and now the phone screen was visible again. Clay was relieved to see me, and guilt flashed through me. He'd given me this gift. An amazing experience with someone other than himself, plus an enormous amount of trust. The least I could do was think about him and not the man at my side.

The rope fell to the floor, and my hands were free, and I marveled at the indentations left from the thick cord. It was a gorgeous pattern—like woven bracelets tattooed across my skin.

While I was looking at them, E went to the workbench, removed my phone from the stand, and brought it to me. I took it, and he sat beside me, close enough that our legs touched.

"Are you cold?" Clay asked.

My body was cooling off, and I was going to answer, but

E abruptly scooped me up into his arms.

"What—?" The rest of my question died as he dragged me into his lap. I was now sitting sideways on him, and his thick arms circled around me. My gaze bounced from the man holding me to the phone in my hand.

"How was this for you?" Clay's focus was on me and his tone curious. "Did you like being tied up?"

"Yes."

It was distracting how E's hands smoothed over my skin while I talked to Clay, but I enjoyed it. He not only kept me warm, but the connection was nice. Plus, I was tired like I'd just run for miles and had the overpowering desire to cling to him.

"And the paddle?"

"Oh, I liked that a lot."

Behind his glasses, Clay's thrilled smile reached his eyes. "At any point did it get to be too much? More than you'd want in the future?"

I shook my head, and my voice went soft. "It was just the right amount."

My words affected both men. E's hands skimmed up my back, over my shoulder, and down my arm until his fingertips skated along the rope pattern.

"Anything you didn't like?" Clay leaned closer to the camera like he wanted to be closer to me. "Anything you wished we'd done?"

My gaze went to the St. Andrew's cross like it was magnetized, tracing the lines and lingering on the rings where restraints would be clipped. "I thought we'd use the cross."

Clay gave a surprised half of a chuckle. "Maybe next time."

Next time.

E lifted my wrist and pressed his lips to the underside, kissing the indentations there. It made my heart flutter. He was supposed to be a surrogate, giving me what Clay physically couldn't, and although my partner had been attentive last time after we'd played together, this tender kiss from E seemed out of character for Clay.

It was half-teasing, half-serious from me. "You weren't like this last time."

"No," Clay sucked in a heavy breath, "but sometimes the sub isn't the only one who needs aftercare."

There was so much meaning in what he'd said and how he'd done it in a measured tone. Clay was a dominant who didn't need to snuggle or bond afterward . . . but he wasn't going to ignore the needs of the other person in the room. Even if he wanted me to pretend the scene had only been between us.

I watched E as he continued to rub and kiss the marks on my wrist like he was worshipping them. So, I wasn't sure who I was speaking to when I made my announcement. "I love the way the marks look."

"Mm, me too," Clay said. "The ones around your throat are beautiful."

It was like E hadn't been aware of them until then, and his hot mouth lifted from my wrist so he could set his lips against the side of my neck. I shuddered with pleasure as he kissed me.

While I stared at Clay onscreen, E's kisses carved a path,

following the line of the rope, and I went weaker with each one, sinking further into his arms. Clay's expression was fixed. It seemed like he was trying very hard to stay indifferent, and I was struck with the thought.

With all we'd done today, the way I'd been shared between the men, it was only E's innocent kisses that caused worry to pool in Clay's eyes. Wait a minute . . . It wasn't worry.

It was jealousy.

TWELVE

After Clay and I spent Wednesday night talking about things we wanted to explore with each other, Thursday's session was more . . . intense. E arrived not long after Clay had called, and I'd been eager to head down to the basement.

Once again, the St. Andrew's cross was ignored, and I stood beside it in my disappointment while E disappeared inside the storage closet. He emerged a moment later, carrying a piece that looked heavy and confusing—until he set it on its front foot and unfolded it.

It reminded me of a weight training bench. It had a small seat and a tall adjustable back that could be set up at different angles or lay flat. Plus, there was a metal bar at the base of the front foot with rings at either end. Like Clay's other designs, this one was sleek and elegant, covered in black vinyl with sexy red accents.

While E finished setting the chair up, I was instructed to get naked, and when I had my clothes folded in a neat stack on the workbench, E pulled leather cuffs from his bag, dropping one pair of them on the floor with a loud thud beside the chair.

My breath caught.

Whatever Clay had planned for us, I sensed it was a level up from what we'd previously done. There was a different mood than last time, and the air crackled with electricity. E's posture wasn't awkward, but it was stiff. As if he were anxious.

He stalked toward me with the other pair of black cuffs in his hands and a stern expression. It was seriously hot, and I was giddy with excitement, holding out my wrists eagerly.

The thick leather was lined with faux fur. It was fitted around me and buckled, one wrist then the other, and the metal clasps tinkled as they dangled down.

"You won't need a safe word tonight," Clay said from the screen of E's laptop, which rested on the workbench. Our conversation tonight had started on my phone, but once we'd moved downstairs, E had pulled his MacBook from his bag, linked into Clay's WiFi, and called him through Skype. It allowed us to see everything on a bigger screen—not just Clay, but what E was doing to me too.

"Okay," I said, somewhat confused. We hadn't discussed safe words yet, so it seemed unnecessary for Clay to tell me I wouldn't need one.

Last time we'd played, he'd sat at the desk in his hotel room, but tonight he had his laptop beside him on his still-made bed. He was dressed in jeans and a t-shirt and lay on top of the covers, his back against the headboard. Everything appeared casual and relaxed, but there was no doubt who was in command.

"You might say the word 'no' during the scene when you don't mean it." He said it like a professor giving a lecture. "'Stop' will *always* mean stop. But if a 'no' happens, I've told Mr. E to use his best judgement on whether or not to keep going. Is this something you're comfortable with?"

I swallowed thickly and my tone was skeptical. “And why might I be saying ‘no’ when I don’t mean it?”

Clay’s chest lifted with a deep breath. “It could be a coping mechanism to the pain.”

Holy shit.

Since he’d finished with my wrists, E had gone motionless, and my gaze drifted from the laptop so I could glance up at him. Was that apprehension lurking in his eyes? No. It wasn’t dread; it was like . . . restlessness. He waited for my answer like a person waiting to parachute out of a plane. Nervous but excited.

“Yes,” I said, my gaze fixed on E because he was the one who most needed to hear it. “I’m comfortable with it.” And then I spoke to both men equally. “I trust you.”

Because our unconventional arrangement wouldn’t work without it.

E’s shoulders softened as he let out a tight breath of relief, and the unease faded from his expression.

“Good,” Clay said. “What word do you say when you want to stop?”

My pulse raced. “Stop.”

His tone was pleased. “Have a seat.”

The seat portion of the chair was so short, only my ass fit on it, making it more of a place to rest the weight of my body, but once I was laid back against the angled chair, it was comfortable, and I didn’t worry I’d slide off.

E grasped one of the clasps on the cuffs I wore and lifted it over my head, then clipped it to the ring behind the chair back. He had to lean over me to attach the other cuff, and I took in the faint, woodsy smell of him. Fuck, he smelled good.

Once it was done and my hands were restrained, he went to the laptop, adjusted the angle so I was centered in the frame, and returned to me. He took a knee, scooped up the cuffs he'd dropped beside the chair, and began the task of securing my ankles.

I stared straight ahead at the screen, watching on one side the man who lounged on his hotel bed, and on the other side, the naked, breathless brunette bound to the chair and the man on his knees in front of her. Since my hands were overhead, my breasts were high, and my nipples hard.

Clay's stare was as inescapable as the leather cuffs holding me in place.

There was a faint metallic click as the last clasp was hooked to the bar at the base of the chair. Since I was restrained, I expected E to stand up and get started on whatever was next, but he remained kneeling in front of me, his gaze pinned on my ankles.

He grasped the bar with both hands and pulled outward, spreading the telescopic rod out and forcing my ankles with it. The action was so surprising, I gasped, and heat pooled in my center.

"If you have trouble staying still," Clay's voice was seductive and not threatening, "I can belt your waist to the chair too. But let's see how you do without it first."

E climbed to his feet, stood back, and admired the view. His gaze trailed over my curves, drinking in all my bare skin, and lingered at the nakedness between my parted thighs. I was vulnerable, completely at the mercy of both men, and

I—fuck—I *loved* the feeling. Every nerve ending in me was tingling with anticipation, sensitized with waiting.

Blood rushed in my ears, and my heart pounded as E went to his bag to retrieve something. What would we be using tonight? A flogger? A crop?

The black velvet bag he produced was much too small for those things. The bag had drawstrings and was roughly the same size as the palm of his hand. How could something so small cause me enough pain that Clay worried it'd be too much?

"Open your mouth and then bite down," Clay ordered. "You're going to hold on to this bag while I get you ready to use what's inside."

An evil smile twitched on his lips. He knew I was curious about the contents of the bag, and he was purposefully keeping it a secret. I did as told, though. I opened my mouth and waited patiently for E to hold out the top of the bag for me, and then bit down.

Whatever was inside didn't weigh much, but I clenched my teeth harder when E skimmed his fingertips over my breasts. He drew designs on my skin as he moved along, caressing my arms and my stomach. He bent at the waist to go lower, brushing his fingers on the insides of my thighs.

Goosebumps pebbled across my legs in waves, and my breathing went short. It took no time for the bag and its strings in my mouth to become damp with my saliva, even as I tried to swallow it back. E's sensual touch was the opposite of pain, and just the faintest edge of his fingernails scraping over me caused sparks of pleasure to cascade up my spine.

My back bowed as he pressed the pads of his fingertips to my clit and rolled them in one slow, grinding circle. It was wild how quickly the men made me out of my mind with need, and my moan of encouragement was muffled under the velvet bag.

Clay's voice was so sinful, it sounded like he was right beside me, whispering. "Ready to see what's inside?"

When I nodded, whatever was inside the bag clinked.

E pulled it from my mouth, opened it, and dumped the contents into his palm, showing them to me. There was a pair of black-tipped alligator clamps, complete with small screws to adjust the tension, which I understood, but . . . I blinked at the rest. There were several silver balls, each the same size as a pea, and I had no idea what they were for.

He grasped two of the little orbs between his thumb and forefinger, then closed his fist around the rest of the items so he could use both hands to separate the balls. My heart skipped as he released one and it flew back to its mate.

Magnets.

And by that demonstration, they looked to be powerful, too.

But he opened his hand, fished out the two clamps, then put the magnetic balls back in the bag before stuffing it in the back pocket of his jeans. I balled my hands into fists as he took a knee beside the chair, cupped a breast, and captured my nipple between his lips.

Or more specifically, his teeth.

I tried to stare at Clay onscreen, but E's soft bite grew hotter and more intense, stealing my focus. It became too much, and I whimpered, trying to move away. But escape wasn't possible, and there was a jangle of metal from the clips as I strained against my cuffs.

It had the desired effect, though, because E broke the latch of his mouth. His eyes were bottomless tonight, like midnight ink as they evaluated me. He tested the pinch of the clamp on one of his fingers, adjusted the screw, and then seemed satisfied with the force it'd apply.

Air came and went rapidly from my lungs as he squeezed the clamp open, fitted the jaws around my nipple, and eased off his hold. The pinch of the clamp was white-hot, but pleasurable, and I liked the way it looked. He'd attached it so it was flush with my skin, rather than jutting out from my body.

The sweet ache of it built as he repeated the whole process on my other breast. The gentle bite of his teeth swelled toward pain, and he gauged how much I could take, then tested the clamp to find its matching tension.

I exhaled loudly as he clamped the second one down. It hurt, but felt good too, and the men could tell. It was written all over my face, expressed in my sighs, and told in the way the muscles of my arms flexed.

I was rewarded with a stroke of E's hand between my legs, and my moan was deep and grateful. But like last time, I only got one circuit of his hand before it was gone, which was crueler than the persistent pinch of the clamps. My body was taut from the physical restraints but also the throbbing need the scene was causing.

Onscreen, Clay unbuttoned his jeans, dropped his zipper, and wedged a hand inside. I licked my lips, feeling parched.

I couldn't tell if E was aroused because he was still on his knees beside me and dropped his head to the first breast he'd attached a clamp to.

"*Oh*," I groaned. His tongue flicked over the nub of my skin trapped between the metal jaws, creating a sensation that nearly split me down the middle. It was pain and pleasure, and my mind fractured.

He bit the underside of my breast, but it wasn't until he brought his fingertips down across my pussy in a sharp slap that I jolted. Even though my ankles were restrained, the rest of my legs weren't, and my knees turned inward, instinctively blocking him from repeating the action.

"Open," E growled, jammed a hand between my knees, and flung them apart. Hearing him speak when he wasn't supposed to was the biggest shock of all, and my gaze darted to the screen, anxious of what Clay thought of this development.

But if he was unhappy with it, it didn't show. Perhaps he was too distracted watching the scene and stroking his fist over his cock. Or maybe it was exactly what he would have said, and this had been the most efficient way to correct me.

Or . . .

The men were melting back into one, becoming a singular dominant to master me.

The next blow struck me right on my swollen clit, and I jerked against my restraints. That one *hurt*, and I blinked rapidly as the pain radiated and dissipated. There wasn't much of a reprieve. E's fingers slapped against me repeatedly, varying in force and tempo, so I was constantly on edge.

Clay said it like he was accusing me. "You're so fucking

wet. Why's that?"

"Because..." I started, but the next strike was hard enough to steal my thoughts. I had to focus on not whimpering.

"Because," he finished for me, "you like those clamps on your tits."

I didn't need to confirm it. He knew it was the truth, because both men could see the color of heat splashed across my cheeks and the desire smoldering in my eyes.

His tone was so wicked, it bordered on sinister. "I bet you'll like it when they come off too."

It was his signal to E, who gripped the ends of the clamp and released my nipple from its hold. I flinched and cried out when pins and needles stabbed at me, the unfortunate side effect of my blood rushing back to the area where the clamp had temporarily disrupted circulation.

It hurt way more than the ache of the clamp, or the sting of E's slaps.

So, the word *no* flitted through my mind and nearly escaped when his mouth latched onto my nipple and sucked, hard enough that it carved hollows in his cheeks. I bucked on the chair, nearly coming off it.

"Hmm." Clay shot me a disapproving look. "I guess you'll need help staying still."

I choked back a groan as E replaced the clamp and the rubber-tipped metal bit into my tender nipple. It made my head spin at how it hurt—yet it turned me on. The delicious misery primed the rest of my body as easily as flipping a switch.

I was breathing heavy as E stood and moved to his bag

on the workbench, and pride flooded my center as I caught sight of the bulge pressing against the fly of his jeans. He was just as turned on as everyone else in this scene.

The black Velcro strap he retrieved was cinched around my waist, plus the back of the chair, lashing me in place. To test it, E tugged at a clamp and pulled it free. The pain stormed in, but no matter how I tried to squirm, I could barely move.

He'd looked unsure before we'd begun, but that emotion was gone. As he watched me unsuccessfully attempt to wriggle away, power flared in his eyes and his palm drifted down to his erection, squeezing himself through the denim.

Fuck, it was hot.

The pain from him removing one clamp was still fading when he loomed over me and his fingers toyed with the ends of the other. Chemicals pumped through my system, urged along by my galloping heart, and my legs trembled with apprehension. I understood what was in store for me once the clamp came off, and I dreaded it, but also wanted relief from the ache it was currently causing.

He tugged the biting metal piece off, and I slammed my eyes shut, burying my face as best I could in the side of my arm. It throbbed like I'd been hit with a hammer, and I breathed through each pulse, drinking in air in slow, measured sips.

When I finished evening myself out, I opened my eyes and found both men staring at me like statues. Was it concern for me that had made them go motionless? Because if so, there was no need. In the absence of pain, I became warm and tingly, and a dazed smile spread across my lips. It felt similar to a post-orgasm high. Like everything was dreamy and happy.

E returned slowly to life, pulled the velvet bag from his back pocket, and dumped the magnets into his palm.

My tone was teasing, but my voice sounded far away. "What are you planning to do with those?"

His expression was an enigma, but Clay's was pleased, and his fist resumed its unhurried strokes along the length of his hard cock. The way he twisted his grip from his tip down to the base and then back up again was hypnotic and distracting. I wasn't aware E had separated the magnets and held one in each hand until he leaned in.

I sobered and my eyes widened when he placed a silver ball on either side of my nipple and then let go. The pull between the magnets was strong. It was a more intense squeeze than the clamp, and I set my jaw. This ache was acute enough that I sucked in shallow breaths as he prepared to place a second pair of magnets on my other nipple.

"I don't know how long I'll be able to take it," I whispered.

It was like I'd just told Clay the sexiest thing ever. He pushed up his glasses, and his eyes glittered behind the lenses. "I know it hurts," his tone was reassuring, "but it feels good too, doesn't it? Like a good pain?"

When E finished setting the magnets, it was too overwhelming to find words. Even thoughts were difficult, but I managed a short nod. Clay was right, though. It *was* a good pain, and when E straightened, I got a glance of myself on the screen.

The small silver balls gleamed like piercings.

And I fucking loved the way they looked.

Clay's tone was deceptively nonchalant, like it was just that simple. "I'll take them off as soon as you come."

My discomfort turned my mind into a void, making plenty of room for the men to fill it. The pain and pleasure they created were all that existed, and I eagerly focused on E as he knelt in front of me. His hands roamed over my body, teasing and enjoying how I shifted mindlessly within my restraints.

It was clear I wasn't the only one who liked how my tits looked with the magnets pinching my pink skin. He squeezed one of my breasts, plumping my skin between his fingers, and the air in the room thickened.

"Do you want my mouth or my fingers?"

Clay asked the question, but I'd been focused on E, and it reinforced the feeling they were the same. Two different bodies, but one purpose. The fingers and mouth physically belonged to E, but they operated under Clay's direction.

"Both," I breathed.

Because I needed to come, and that would be the fastest way to get there.

Clay chuckled. "Greedy."

E dragged his hands down my stomach as he settled in on his knees, getting comfortable. His palms smoothed along the insides of my thighs, pushing my legs wider. He already had enough room—he'd done it to exert control. Didn't he know that was unnecessary? He had complete rule over me.

His gaze stayed locked on mine as he lowered his mouth to my pussy, and electricity jolted up my legs. I moaned in relief while his tongue fluttered, and I gasped in satisfaction when two thick fingers speared into me. He pulsed them deep and rough, and the fracture inside me widened. Everything hurt yet also felt like bliss, and the conflicting emotions threatened to burn me to ash.

There was a faint edge of concern in Clay's words. "Are you about to come?"

I was panting and had to force it out. "Oh, God, yes."

"Stop. It's too soon."

E froze, and I gawked at the camera, both confused and irritated. "But you said you'd take them off when—"

"Slow her down."

My heart flipped upside-down because Clay's order to stop wasn't for me. It was for the man on his knees, and I whined with frustration when E followed the command. Both his mouth and fingers retreated, leaving me right on the edge. And when the pleasure was gone, so was the war for focus. It was all pain now.

"Clay," I hissed.

He wasn't deterred. "I want to see if you can come through the pain."

"*What*?"

E's gaze drifted down my body as if he felt guilt. Was it because he'd gotten me close too quickly for Clay's liking? Or for what he was about to do?

One of the clamps was pulled from the black velvet bag, and my mouth went bone dry. I had an inkling of where he intended to use it, and just the thought of it made it so I couldn't catch my breath. The word *no* echoed loudly in my head, but I kept my tongue leashed. Maybe he planned to use it somewhere else or—

Oh, no. I whimpered in trepidation as E drew in a deep, preparing breath, then pinched my clit between his forefinger and thumb. His gaze flicked to mine, either checking in or perhaps waiting to hear the word *stop* tumble from my lips. But every muscle in my body was tense and strained, and I was frozen with my intense curiosity.

What would it feel like?

Would it hurt worse than the magnets? Or would it be an even better 'good pain?'

The long seconds suspended between us, and when it was clear I wasn't going to stop him, E pushed forward. The rubber tips of the clamp closed around my clit, and he eased off his grip, increasing the bite on my sensitive, swollen nub of skin. It went on, and on, and I clenched my fists so hard, I was sure there were half-moon indentations in my palms from my fingernails.

"Fuck," I groaned. My head lolled to one side, and panic bubbled in my stomach. The amount of pain was . . . staggering. Tears burned the edges of my eyes. I had to focus on drawing air in and out of my lungs, because if I thought about anything else, I'd fly apart.

It was surreal to see myself on the laptop screen. It exaggerated the feeling like I was outside my body, witnessing this the same way Clay was, rather than experiencing it in the moment. E shifted to one side between my legs so his torso no longer blocked Clay's view, and the man on screen let out an appreciative sigh.

"Look at yourself," Clay said with rich satisfaction, "squirming and whining as you try to hold it together. You're so . . . *achingly* beautiful."

Aching was right because everything throbbed and clamored for mercy. I shifted my hips as much as the belt around my waist allowed, futilely trying to get free. "Please . . ." I pleaded. Sweat dampened my temples and tremors rattled my body. "I can't . . ."

E plucked the clamp off me, and the sharp pain was like a knife slicing down my clit. I hissed through clenched teeth and my vision blurred. It drove the two men into one shapeless figure, both my tormentor and my savior. He leaned in, licking the spot that was white-hot.

"Fucking *fuck*," I gasped. "No."

But I didn't mean it, because as his tongue continued to caress and massage, the prickly sparks of his indecent kiss morphed into something else. My pain turned upside-down, tumbling into pleasure, and my *no* flipped along with it.

"*Yes*," I cried.

I blurted it again as the man slipped his fingers back inside me. The hot ache in my nipples flooded across my skin and seeped in, making my muscles liquify and my bones melt.

"Look at me," he demanded.

For a moment, I wasn't sure how the man meant. There was only one of them, after all. But I blinked through the fog of everything and refocused on the screen. His hand jerked up and down in rapid strokes, and while his eyes were lidded with pleasure, the rest of him was filled with authority.

"It sounds like you're close and need the clamp again."

The lie came from me in a rush. "No. I'm not close."

His smile was knowing. "I think you are."

There was a flash of silver in his fingertips, and while the word *no* was a loud, angry chant in my head, the word *stop* was nowhere to be found.

"You made it once before," he said, "you can do it again."

"No," I whispered, but it was too late. The intense pinch was back, swelling until it blocked out everything else. All the blood had run out of my arms and they'd gone to sleep, but it was ignored. The pull of the magnets no longer bothered me either. Because the clamp on my clit enveloped my body like a vice, squeezing until I thought I might die.

In this agony, I began to dislike the man. It was cruel how he stroked himself like he was taunting me.

Look how much pleasure your suffering gives me.

I hated him as his tongue whipped at me. He fucked me with his mouth and his fingers as the clamp bit at me with teeth of fire. He gave contented sighs of satisfaction like he was feeding off my pain. He threw his forearm over my stomach so his free hand could spread my pussy wider to his brutal tongue.

Only . . .

The pressure of the clamp began to ease.

"Yes," he encouraged. "That's a good girl. You can come even when it hurts, can't you?"

The men had twisted into one, but as the pain in my clit started to subside, they separated. Clay was onscreen and far away. He wasn't able to see how the clamp was being removed because E's head blocked his view.

The gradual release of the clamp's grip meant it didn't hurt nearly as badly as coming off in an instant, and when he finished, E tightened his fist around it, then focused on his task.

My head swam with thoughts. Did Clay know what he'd done? E had been told he could use his own judgement, but this felt . . . like a secret. I didn't feel guilty about that either. Clay kept nearly everything about E a secret from me. Wasn't it fair I kept one from him?

My chest heaved as I gasped for air. The tip of E's tongue seemed to know exactly where and how I wanted it, and his fingers slid in and out of me with the same precision. Fuck, I was going to come, and as my orgasm closed in, I worried the force of it might make me scream.

But instead, I was utterly silent as ecstasy burst inside and channeled out through my limbs. It was strange and wonderful to come like this while I was unable to move. It made the sensations linger, prolonging my enjoyment. Was this how it'd been for the girl trapped in latex under Mistress Theia's dominance?

"Are you coming?" Clay asked.

"Yes," I gasped.

He gave a choked-off sound of pleasure, and seconds later he joined me. His fist slowed, focusing only on his sensitive tip, while he erupted and cum dribbled down over his clenched fingers.

E's mouth had ceased, but his fingers were still lodged inside me. Could he feel the rhythmic pulses of my internal muscles squeezing more pleasure from him? He studied me like he wanted to know everything about me, and—God—could I relate.

I was still cooling down when he withdrew, stood, and set about removing the magnets. I could tell he was trying to do them slowly, but it wasn't as controlled as the clamp, and I sucked in air through my teeth.

Once everything had been put back into the black velvet bag and pocketed, E unclipped one of my wrists and gently guided it down. There was tension in my neck and back, and my arms were still asleep, so I was grateful for his carefulness. I'd expected him to undo the cuff, but he clipped it to a ring beneath the seat, and then repeated the process with my other hand.

I shot Clay a look, wordlessly asking him to explain.

He still had his dick in his hand, unbothered by the mess. "You were so amazing. Now I show you how much I appreciate you."

E marched over to his bag on the workbench and produced a cordless wand vibrator, announcing the scene wasn't over.

But there was a definite shift in tone. The first half had been pain.

The second one would be absolute pleasure.

THIRTEEN

I was out late on Friday with Cassidy when my phone rang, and my pulse kicked when Clay's name flashed on the screen.

"Hey, there," I said into my phone as I flashed an apologetic smile to my friend. She waved a hand, and I stood from the table, heading off to a quieter section of the bar that served just enough food to qualify as a restaurant.

"Hi," Clay said. "So, I just got home and—"

"Oh, yeah? How was your flight?"

"It was fine." There was something in his voice I couldn't identify. Curiosity? Confusion? "Any idea where the food in my fridge came from?"

I laughed softly. "Yeah. You told me you wouldn't be getting in until late, and since you're only home for forty-eight hours, I bought some stuff to get you through the weekend. I thought I'd save you the time of having to go out."

"Oh." He paused, and then pleasant surprise clung to his words. "That was . . . nice of you."

Even though he couldn't see me, I smiled and shrugged. "It was kind of self-serving. This way you have more time to decompress," I filled my words with extra meaning, "and, you know, work on your *projects*."

I could hear his smile in his voice. "I see."

This corner of the lobby was quiet, but all the sound

faded out until it was just him. He was back. When I went home this evening, he'd be right next door. No more two-dimensional Clay to play with. It'd be his hands on my body.

"Thank you, Lilith." His gratitude made warmth bloom in my chest. "You should come over tomorrow afternoon so I can work on my new favorite project."

My heart skipped.

I stood in Clay's workshop, drinking the glass of lemonade he'd poured me, and watched him work, but anticipation vibrated as nervous energy inside my body. He wasn't aware. He was busy gluing and clamping pieces together of the kneeler he was building for the client we'd met at Club Eros. While I studied him, I also had one eye on the St. Andrew's cross.

"Did you ever think about using a model for your pieces?" I asked.

He tightened the final clamp. "Sometimes I do before I scale up. I want to make sure the proportions are right."

What?

Oh. I gave a half of a laugh at the misunderstanding. "I meant like a person. I think it'd be helpful for your potential customers to see your stuff in use." I walked over to the chair we'd used during our last session. "There are a lot of options here. Different places to clip onto, and then there's the spreader bar. You can put a bunch of pictures in the gallery for this, but without someone sitting in it? It's hard to get a sense of what it's capable of."

He made a face. "I get what you're saying, but I wouldn't even know where to start with that."

Because he was private, and he wouldn't want a stranger coming to his house, and definitely not down to his workshop.

But I wasn't a stranger.

I affected a dramatic, wistful voice. "If only you knew someone who loved your work, especially when they're handcuffed to it . . . Wherever could you find a girl like that, I wonder?"

His attention was no longer on what he'd been doing, it was set on me and he asked it with total disbelief. "Are you volunteering?"

"What if I am?" I ran a fingertip seductively across the chair back.

It was interesting to see how this excited him as my partner, but also as a businessman. His gaze turned to the storage closet as he considered my offer. "I have a lot of pieces."

"And I have all afternoon," I said.

"You *want* to do this?" He put a hand on his hip and shifted his weight to one side. "I can blur your face, but you're okay with these pictures being shown to other people?"

I laughed. "Yeah. Remember when I was waiting naked for you when you got home? I don't mind who sees me. Hell, if I had more time, I'd probably make an OnlyFans account." My cousin Heather made good money there. "You don't need to blur my face. I assume you have a blindfold."

"I do."

This hadn't been on his agenda for us today, and he visibly struggled with what to do. He hated being surprised, but he didn't want to miss out on an opportunity.

"This doesn't have to derail your plans," I said. "You can still do all the things to me you want to." I nodded toward the St. Andrew's cross. "As long as your plan includes using that."

His eyes filled with dark heat. "Oh, it does."

Decision made, he took the glass of lemonade from me, plunked it down on top of the tool cabinet nearby, and gave me a discerning look.

"Before we start," he said, "I want to talk while your head's clear. Rules can become flexible when you're deep in a scene, and I don't want you agreeing to something you might end up regretting later."

I nodded. My reservations went out the window fast when something I wanted happened to dangle in front of me. "Okay. What do you want to talk about?"

"Are you on birth control?"

I blinked in surprise but recovered quickly. "I've been on the pill since I was fifteen." I took the continuous one because who had time for that period bullshit? "Why?"

He shifted his weight, and I didn't miss the way he subtly leaned toward me. "I was tested before my last relationship, and I haven't had any sexual partners since. I'm clean, so if you're safe and interested in it, I'd like to go without a condom. It's easier, and—"

"More fun?" I teased.

Oh, his smile was delicious. "Yes, it's more fun." He turned serious again. "But I understand and respect if you'd prefer to keep using them. Also, I'm asking that this is only with me. Any scenes with Mr. E—if it requires it—will use protection. I've been clear with him about that."

I understood the need for condoms, but I disliked them. The smell, the taste, the way putting them on could interrupt the flow of sex. Plus, I disliked the miniscule layer between my partner and me, separating us from each other.

"I'm okay going without them if you are," I said.

He was pleased, which meant I was pleased too.

While I undressed, he set up the lights and gray backdrop in the far corner of the room, and then carried the chair over. I left on my bra and underwear, which was a simple set of black lace I'd put on with hopes I'd be able to sell him on my modeling plan. I also wore my high heeled black sandals, where the straps flowed from the front of my ankle strap down over my toes, leaving the sides of my feet totally bare.

He had to go upstairs to retrieve the blindfold, and while he was gone, I wandered around, examining the different pieces in greater detail. His work was so beautiful. I couldn't wait to experience it during play. Whatever we didn't get to today, I was confident I'd get to it eventually with E.

My mind drifted to him. What was he doing right now? It felt wrong to think about him, but I was so damn curious. The floor overhead creaked and footsteps came down the stairs. When Clay came into view, it reminded me the best-looking piece of art in his house was the one currently walking toward me with a blindfold in hand.

I slipped it on, keeping it pushed up on my forehead so I could watch as he went to the bottom drawer of a cabinet and pulled out leather cuffs. They looked identical to the ones E had used. Were they the same brand? I didn't know anything about BDSM supplies. Maybe there was only one company, or perhaps all the styles were similar.

We started our photoshoot with Clay's chair, and I don't think either of us were prepared for how sexy this would be.

Like my session with E, I was restrained at the wrists and ankles, but now I also had the blindfold pulled down over my eyes. It prevented me from knowing what Clay was doing, and it allowed my imagination to run wild.

Goosebumps lifted on my arms and my breath went short.

I was trapped here, waiting, and completely at his mercy.

We hadn't played together, not physically, since the day he'd used his sharp ruler on me, and desire moved thickly through my veins. Oh, how I craved his hands on my body.

Instead, he took his pictures.

I heard his feet as he moved around, adjusting to different angles, and listened as his breathing seemed to hurry along. Was this turning him on as much as me? Was the anticipation killing him?

He teased me too as he adjusted my positions. He unclipped my hands at the base of the chair and latched them up by my head, then skated a finger down between my breasts. It glided down over the hollow of my belly button and lower still. I moaned and shivered as his fingers brushed over the crotch of my panties.

"So wet for me." His voice was hushed, and the heat of his mouth ghosted over my lips, but when I tried to kiss him, he retreated. "Not yet. I'll make you earn it."

We didn't do every piece he had. Some, like the padded folding table, were self-explanatory. The queening chair didn't take long to photograph. I posed on the low, U-shape seat that allowed my partner to lie in comfort beneath me while I was perched over their face.

Clay's voice was all-knowing. "What are you smiling about?"

"I'm thinking about how this could be the other way around." My ankle cuffs were currently hooked onto the sides of the chair, but . . . "It would also work if the sub was beneath and their hands were attached."

"Yes. I could put you like that and if you're not rimming me to my satisfaction, I could correct you with a riding crop against your tits."

I jolted at the visual. It sliced down through me and poured lava inside. "Holy fuck."

"What?" His tone was patronizing and sexy. "Do you like the sound of that?"

I was wound so tight I was going to explode, so I said it the same way I'd murmur a *yes*. "Maybe."

"Interesting." Even with the blindfold on, I could picture him making a mental note.

He saved the St. Andrew's cross for last, because of course he did. He knew I wanted it, so he had to drag it out.

There'd been a longing ache in my body, and once he had me splayed out on the cross—the cold, padded vinyl pressed against my belly—relief swept through and uncorded my muscles. There was just something about the position I hungered for. It whispered of darkness, of something old and basic and carnal.

"I don't know if I'm going to be able to use any of these pictures," he said.

I went on alert. "Why? What's wrong?"

"Do you have any idea how fucking hot you are? No one's going to look at anything else but you. I know I can't."

I grinned. He made me weak, and I was glad for the restraints on my wrists that were pinned up. I couldn't collapse even if I wanted to.

His words were so distracting, I wasn't ready when the feathery tails of something played over my back. I flinched. It hadn't hurt; it had just startled me. The sensation was pleasant.

Clay's mouth was abruptly right by my ear. "This is a flogger."

The heat of his body vanished as quickly as it had appeared, and his next strike was more intense. Not painful, but attention-getting.

As he had E do with the spankings, Clay warmed me up. All the wispy tails of the flogger stroked and whipped against my skin, and since I was still blindfolded, I focused in on it. He built in speed and force, moving around so he didn't hit the same place twice.

"Do you like it?" he asked.

"Yes."

"I thought you would."

Immediately, there was a loud *whoosh* as the leather cut through the air, and this time, he wasn't playing around. I sucked in a sharp breath as thirty tiny whips hit me. I didn't get time to recover because he did it again. Pain bloomed across my skin, and beneath my blindfold, my eyes fluttered shut.

It hurt in such a good way.

I whimpered with pleasure and sagged in my cuffs as he settled in, finding a pace, and creating fire that spiderwebbed across my nerve endings. It made me contract after each blow and pulled gasps of breath from my lips.

He'd talked about euphoria, and as the pain got stronger, the absence between his blows—the microsecond before the flogger struck me again—was heaven. I shuddered with bliss when he paused to unhook my bra and expose all of my back to his tool of pain and pleasure.

And in these moments of quiet, I pictured E there too, standing in the shadows as he watched the scene unfold.

There came a thud like the flogger had been dropped, followed by rustling, and then a zipper going down, tooth by tooth.

"I'm so goddamn hard, I have to fuck you."

"Yes," I cried.

His warm, bare chest flattened against my back, which was scorching from the flogger, but I didn't care. He was naked, and pushed his cock between my legs, rubbing himself against the crotch of my panties in teasing strokes. It made me tremble.

One of his hands pressed on the small of my back, urging me to arch and jut my ass out back toward him so it'd be easier to bring us together. He hooked a finger in the side of my panties, lined himself up, and pushed in.

My moan was guttural but muffled under his louder one. It felt like he'd made me wait years for this, so did he feel like he'd been waiting his whole life?

He was thick and hard, and satisfaction grew as he continued to advance.

I'd expected a rough fuck, and he didn't disappoint. His hands were mean and intrusive, and nothing was off limits. I bowed and stretched and struggled, wanting more. Lust was a drug that I couldn't get enough of when I was with him.

I pictured us in my head as his violent thrusts racked my body, but the cross didn't budge an inch. I imagined how his ass flexed and contracted as he drove into me. Sweat dampened the temples of my hair, and when he grabbed a handful at the back of my head and yanked me toward him, I groaned my approval.

"I'm going to come inside this pussy," he said between labored breaths, because fucking me this intensely was a full body workout. "But you have to come first, Lilith. Don't make me wait."

"Oh, my God." It didn't take me long after that. The tendrils of ecstasy started pulling me up, and up, and . . .

I could hear the smile in his voice. "Yeah?"

I moaned, unable to speak, while the orgasm had me in its grasp. It was powerful and exhausting, and when it began to fade, I was utterly drained. I became a ragdoll tied to his beautiful art, nothing more than a vessel for him to fill with his pleasure.

Fuck, I loved it.

When he came, he sank his teeth into my shoulder, but

his bite was painless. I was too focused on how it felt as he lost himself inside me. It was wonderful but ended too soon.

"You've earned this," he declared, just before he turned my head to him and sealed his mouth over mine.

His kiss was hot and dominating. In its wake, some far off voice in my head began to whisper. It warned me if I wanted to keep Clay, it was better not to get too close.

Don't let him in.

I worried it was already too late.

FOURTEEN

Two days after Clay returned to his jobsite, E met me at the house, followed me down the basement stairs, and proceeded to carry out the detailed plan Clay had crafted for him. I wore nothing but a pair of open-toed polka dot heels that had an ankle strap, and while E couldn't say anything, I was fairly certain he liked them.

Once I started wearing my shoes during our sessions, I began to think of them in a new way. My green crocodile pumps had been the riding crop. I'd worn my gray and red plaid heels the first time I'd felt the sweet agony of a cane. Each design became paired with a scene.

I wanted to wear a new set each time, but at this rate, I'd have to go shoe shopping by the end of the month.

What a terrible burden.

I smirked.

Clay noticed my shoes too because he loved details and didn't miss much.

Clay: Wear your red stilettos with the metal heel tonight.

He meant my ruby suede shoes with a rose gold heel. Last time I'd worn them, E had placed a line of clothes pins on the insides of my thighs. Would I be seeing more of those this evening?

The answer was yes.

And my pattern continued that whenever my pain or my pleasure reached its highest point, the two men would blur and become one. It was my favorite part of the session, the moment where I felt . . .

Complete.

It was two more weeks and six pairs of shoes later when we hit our first snafu. Up until that point, everything had run smoothly—just as Clay had scripted—until the night I'd spent twenty minutes petting Noir while waiting for his phone call.

Had something happened? He was *never* late. If we said eight o'clock, my phone always buzzed a few minutes before. I could tell he liked to talk to me prior to Mr. E's arrival.

Worry grew much larger when E didn't show up. The doorbell never rang, and his hulking figure didn't appear at the front door.

Was it possible I'd gotten my days mixed up? I began to thumb out a text when finally a FaceTime call popped up on my screen.

"Hey." I did my best to sound light and casual. "I was starting to worry about you."

"Hi. I'm sorry for keeping you waiting." Gone was Clay's normal confidence. He looked flustered. "There's been a change in plans."

He'd told me, more than once, how much he disliked that, and my stomach flipped over. "What's going on?"

"Mr. E had a work emergency."

"Oh. I hope everything's okay." It was a force of habit. "What does he do?"

His expression locked down. "I'd prefer not to say."

I pushed out a breath that may have sounded frustrated, and when Clay's expression filled with disappointment, I couldn't hold it in any longer. "You can't expect me not to be curious about him."

I mean, I'd been fucking him for weeks, although Clay would have probably argued I'd been fucking *him* for weeks.

His shoulders sagged as he rubbed the crease developing in the center of his forehead. "I know, Lilith, but this is new territory for me, too. He's with you all the time, and while this arrangement works for now, it's temporary." His eyes sharpened, etching over my face. "I just want . . . some distance between you two. In case I haven't been clear, I'd rather be the one with you." His voice fell to a hush, as if hesitant to reveal it. "Sometimes I wish I could have you all to myself."

There was a pang of longing in my heart. It was nice to hear, but was he worried about losing me? I got that he figured the less I knew about E, the better, which would decrease the risk—however unlikely—that I'd fall for the other man. Clay wasn't just protecting himself, either. He was trying to protect me from being hurt when the time came for E to exit the relationship.

Except . . .

That tiny voice whispered again it was already too late.

I loved what we had—and I didn't want it to be over.

Clay and I had made a deal. No feelings, no attachments. Was I supposed to tell him that was happening now, when my feelings weren't only for him?

For the last week, I'd tried to convince myself I wasn't

interested in E beyond sexual attraction. The pull toward this mystery man was just my insatiable desire to know more about him, but I was kidding myself.

When I thought about my future with Clay, I couldn't picture us without E there too.

Oh, I was in trouble.

In my fear, I stayed silent, and I fought to rationalize it away. Clay shared me physically with E, but not emotionally. So, I spitefully kept my emotions from him.

I slathered on a brave face and a sexy smile. "Well, you've got me all to yourself tonight, don't you?"

His mood lifted. "Yes."

As usual, he was sprawled out on his hotel bed, and when he drew in a heavy breath, the shift visibly went through him. There was the confident dominant I was familiar with.

"That's why I was late calling," he continued. "I had to revise my plan for the evening."

"Yeah?" I perked up. While I was disappointed E wouldn't be joining us, I wasn't unhappy to have some one-on-one time with my partner.

And it was a wildly different experience than anything we'd done before.

While I wasn't physically tied up during the session, there was still plenty of restraint placed on me. There were the rules Clay doled out in his exacting voice, plus the way I had to control myself. It was so much easier when there was rope or cuffs. Making myself stay still was hard. But making myself stop when I was close to orgasming?

That was a real challenge.

He decreed tonight I was to vocalize everything. He wanted me to be loud and communicative. Clay demanded I show him all my visual cues when I was right on the cusp of coming.

So I did, over and over again.

He studied me like a student eager to get a perfect test score, watching me as my fingers played with my clit, mentally cataloguing every moan and sigh I made.

It was erotic performing for him, yet surprisingly intimate too.

I'd gotten myself off at least twice, but he drew my final one out. My body pleaded for release, and when he finally allowed it, bliss rushed through me in a hot wave. I collapsed back on his couch, swallowing gulps of air, and stared up at the nothingness of his vaulted ceiling.

A terrible realization dawned inside me.

My orgasms had been satisfying . . . so why didn't I feel satisfied?

Since E and I weren't allowed to talk to each other, I liked to think that we were able to communicate other ways. Body language, or breaths too soft for Clay to hear, or an exchange of looks.

Hi, I said, when E stepped through the front doorway. *I missed you.*

I missed you too, I imagined his eyes saying back to me.

Clay was oblivious to the conversation going on between us, too eager to get started. "Let's head downstairs."

We'd done it enough times, preparing for the scene came naturally to all of us. I undressed while E set up his laptop. He connected with Clay, then took my phone from me and hung it up, setting it on the workbench beside his computer. He adjusted the angle of the camera until Clay said it was good, before both men set their sights on me and . . .

Then the scene truly began.

It'd been a long, especially hard day at the clinic this afternoon, and I was emotionally drained, but my exhaustion and everything else melted away when E approached. I gave a startled, then relieved sigh as he fisted my hair, jerked my head back, and sank his teeth into the side of my neck.

It took no time to fall under the spell of their dominance.

Not long after I was bound to Clay's prototype chair, did I understand why Clay had been studying my cues in our previous session. E teased me mercilessly with the cordless wand vibrator, taking me right to the brink, only for Clay's sharp order to ring out and bring me to a screeching halt.

While the impending orgasm slipped away, E undid his jeans and pushed his hardened cock into my mouth. I wasn't able to move my head much because tonight there was a collar locked around my throat, which was hooked into the chairback, but that didn't slow E down one bit. He firmly held the sides of my head as he fucked my mouth, and his ruthless way was exactly how I imagined Clay would do it.

I was left struggling to catch my breath, a trail of saliva

hanging from my lips as he retreated and picked up the vibrator. As soon as it made contact with my clit, its buzz sent pleasure pulsating through my center. It dragged a grateful moan from deep in my chest and got my orgasm back on track.

The basement wasn't cold, but a shiver glanced down my spine. There hadn't been any pain tonight. No stinging cracks from a paddle, or lines of fire created across my skin with the thin plastic cane Clay sometimes wanted used on me.

Dark anticipation welled in the bottom of my stomach.

He had something else planned, I just knew it. Clay didn't give pleasure freely. I liked how he made me earn it. So, as the tingles of my approaching orgasm crawled along my skin, I held my breath and waited for the other shoe to drop.

The tension inside me grew until it was tight enough to snap.

"I'm gonna come," I gasped.

"No, you're not," Clay growled. "Stop."

A frustrated whine seeped out of my mouth as the vibrator was ripped away and its buzzing went silent. God, I'd been so close. I tried to shift and twist in my bindings, searching for something to press against. My ankles were attached to the bar by my feet and my knees were held open by another spreader bar that E had pulled from his bag of fun. It meant I couldn't close my legs and squeeze against the pleasure humming in my body.

Clay's smile was wicked as he watched me squirm against my restraints, and his voice was patronizing. "Did you need something?"

"Yeah, the vibrator back where it was."

I was a half-second too late to correct myself. He wouldn't like my tone, and E's hand was quick to deliver my punishment. The pinch of his fingers on my nipple wasn't all that bad, but he used his grasp to pull hard, lifting the weight of my breast away from my body. It was a delicious shot of pain. As soon as he let go, my breast snapped back, and he slapped his fingertips across my distended nipple.

It wasn't cruel, but it wasn't nice either, and I liked the way the discomfort ricocheted through me. I enjoyed it so much, I considered giving Clay some more lip so it'd force E to do it again.

"You don't *need* the vibrator," Clay's tone was pointed, "you just want it."

"Yes," I said.

It was sexy and infuriating how he sat on the other side of the screen looking smug and powerful. "Well, that's too bad." He took off his glasses and proceeded to polish the lenses with the bottom hem of his shirt. "You had enough orgasms yesterday. I don't think you need any more tonight."

The word echoed through my head, but E said it out loud. "What?"

His eyes were wide and his posture stiff. It announced this wasn't part of Clay's plan—at least not the one E had been told, and he wasn't too happy hearing about this change.

Clay slipped his glasses back on and gave a hard look to the man who was his surrogate, and—holy crap. This flex of power was just as much for him as it was for me. A few sessions in, I'd determined that while E liked dominating me and carrying out most of Clay's orders, he much preferred giving me pleasure.

Now it'd been taken off the table.

Was this punishment for missing the session last night . . . or something else?

Clay's voice dripped with condescension. "It's called denial. Have you not heard of it?"

E's eyebrow lifted sharply. "I know what it is."

The mood in the room devolved and became fraught with tension. The men typically didn't speak much to each other during a scene, and when they did, it had always been cordial. They were teammates working toward the same goal.

For the first time, they were two predators fighting over the same kill.

Clay was determined to make clear he was the alpha. "Great," he said dryly. "That's what I want to do with her tonight."

His declaration didn't sit right with E, and he stepped in between me and the camera, blocking my view of Clay and forcing my gaze up onto him. It was clear he was considering how to proceed. Did he bow down, or make his stand?

This isn't what I want to do, I imagined him saying to me.

I didn't know what to tell him, or how to convey my thoughts without words. Of course I didn't want to be denied, but . . . playing with these two men had awakened something inside me. Plus, I trusted Clay. He'd given me so many amazing experiences, the biggest of them all being E. He'd broadened my sexual horizons. He knew what he was doing.

If there was frustration tonight, then he was making a promise of satisfaction later.

Maybe E wanted me to push back, but it wasn't possible. I was strapped down to the chair, naked and exposed and totally immobile. Couldn't he see I was already committed to the scene?

My gaze dropped to E's feet.

Decision made, he moved to my side so he was no longer in the way, and cast a begrudging gaze toward the computer. "All right." His tone was flat. "What's next?"

It was three more tormenting cycles with the vibrator. I'd climb the hill toward orgasm, and as I approached the edge, it was taken away, leaving me breathless and bereft.

And since I wasn't experiencing release, E didn't either. During one of my cooling off sessions, he tucked himself back in his underwear and pulled his pants on. Perhaps it was out of respect to me, or maybe it was the only kind of control he could exert in the scene. Yes, E submitted to Clay, but he did it with reservations.

He didn't seem to be a switch, and if Clay took the leash off, I was certain I'd find out exactly how dominating E could be.

I moaned under my breath as he set the head of the vibrator against me. It felt good, but it'd stop the moment it started feeling great, and I'd rather not have it at all when I knew there'd be no release at the end.

"Maybe if you beg me," Clay said, "I'll change my mind."

I clenched my teeth against the enjoyment humming through my body. "No. I don't beg."

He flat-out grinned, like it was the most exciting thing he'd ever heard. His smile was so huge, it seemed to fill the entire laptop screen.

"Oh, you don't?" He was arrogant and powerfully sexy. "I'll test that theory the next time we're together. I'll give you so many orgasms, I think you'll be begging me to stop."

"*Fuck*," I whispered. It was more threat than promise, and so hot, Clay didn't need to warn E that I was close. The vibrations ceased as the wand was turned off and pulled away, only seconds before I tipped over into ecstasy.

I panted as I clung to the edge, and E's mood turned stormy. He strode to his bag, shoved the vibrator inside, then returned to me and began to undo my restraints. He wasn't rough or cold with me—I wasn't the source of his frustration. Whether Clay was ready for it or not, it didn't matter. E's actions announced the scene was over.

The denial had broken E much faster than it had me.

Since it hadn't been physically intense, there wasn't much aftercare. E rubbed away the indentations his rope had left on my skin, but his gaze barely met mine. His eyes stayed silent.

It'd been the tamest scene so far, and for the first time, it felt awkward when it was over. We dressed, Clay switched his call from E's laptop to my phone, and once everything was put away, we shuffled up the stairs.

"Do I need to remind you," Clay asked, "that I said no orgasms tonight?"

I squeezed the phone tightly and bit it out. "No, sir."

While I would follow his order, he hadn't said shit about me needing to like it. The evil part of me taunted he'd never know if I ran home and finished off the job myself. But *I* would know, and that was what Clay was banking on. Just like last night, the real test would come when there weren't restraints.

A pleased look flashed through him and he nodded subtly at my promise. He adjusted his posture, straightening his shoulders. "Can you move the phone so I can speak to Mr. E?"

I did, moving to stand beside him and angling the phone so we could both view the screen.

Clay's tone was genuine. "Thanks for tonight. I'm sorry for changing the agenda on you. That won't happen again."

E didn't have a response, other than his chest lifted with a heavy breath. Whatever he wanted to say, he must have felt like he couldn't right now. His expression was cryptic, almost as if he were struggling not to get lost in thought. But his deep breath must have been enough of an acknowledgment for Clay, because the matter seemed settled.

"Goodnight," he said.

"Yeah." E's tone was guarded. "Night."

He strode to the front door, gripped the handle, and pulled it open before turning to finally, *really* look at me. My pulse went into overdrive. Shit, he was so handsome, and interesting, and I ached to know more about him. The ache was even more acute than the one I'd felt earlier when I'd been desperate to find release.

We held each other's gaze for a beat too long, because he did nothing to disguise the desire that lurked inside him, and I liked how it looked. It made me swallow hard.

Goodbye, he seemed to say.

"Goodbye," I echoed back, only mine had been out loud.

He froze.

Was he wondering if I were talking to him, or the man he could no longer see? My phone was turned so the screen was facing me. Or was he nervous because I had spoken directly to him, which was against the rules?

Static swirled around us, creating heat and electricity. It increased exponentially when he pushed the door shut, and remained inside, putting his hands squarely on his hips as he challenged me.

Oh, my God.

My heart thumped so loudly, I worried Clay would hear it and I'd give away what E had done. My gaze dropped to the screen in my hand and I tried to block everything else out. I would pretend E had walked out the door and shut it behind him, because Clay believed he had.

"Is he gone?" he asked.

Blood rushed through my head like a freight train, drowning out all other sound. I didn't stop to consider my answer. The lie simply burst from my lips. "Yes."

FIFTEEN

On some level, I was aware of my guilt over lying to Clay, but I refused to think about it. I was too curious, and honestly, it was a miracle I'd made it this long without breaking any of the rules.

I was just too weak.

"I know tonight was a little . . . off," Clay said. "In my head, it played out differently." He made a face, displeased with himself. "I'm sorry. When it comes to you, I need to learn to expect the unexpected."

I stared at my phone, trying to focus on what he was saying. He'd changed the design on himself—something he never did—and had inferred I was the cause. If I weren't so distracted by the man who lingered silently by the door, I might have realized what a big deal this was. Instead, I held breath tightly in my lungs and forced myself to act natural.

"It's okay." I added a shrug and a smile for additional effect.

"Good." Although he sounded slightly less than convinced. "Well, I should probably let you go, unless you want—"

"Yeah, I'm kind of tired." Maybe he wanted to talk about the scene, and I could be missing an opportunity for him to open up, but I felt E's gaze on me like a giant magnifying glass. "Think I'm going to say goodbye to Noir and then head out."

He nodded in understanding. "Have a good night." His lips curled into a smile. "But, you know, not too good."

My nervous laugh was overly loud, but he didn't seem to notice. "Right. Talk to you tomorrow."

"Bye."

As soon as I pushed the 'end call' button and the screen went black, chaotic energy hummed through my veins. I took my time setting my phone down on the side table, right beside the stack of mail I brought in nightly for Clay, because I wanted to pause in this moment before I crossed the point of no return.

Betrayal was something that couldn't be undone. And even as I knew that—I also knew I was going to do it regardless.

He'd set his bag down beside him and his hands had returned to rest on his hips, but his posture wasn't confrontational. It seemed anxious.

I'm nervous, his expression said.

Me too, I answered back.

I breathed the word. "Hi."

His lips parted. His hands moved to hang at his sides, and his greeting was as tentative as mine had been. "Hi."

The room felt uneven, as if there were only pockets of air to breathe here and there, and they shifted and swirled unexpectedly around us.

It'd been nearly two months since our first night together at the club, and I'd wondered about him relentlessly since, but as I peered at him now, my mind faltered. I'd wanted so badly to talk to him, and yet I wasn't able. Perhaps all the questions I wanted to ask had jammed together in the rush to get out, and shut me down completely.

Was it the same for him? It looked like the tension-filled silence threatened to consume him.

"There are so many things I want to ask you," I whispered, "I don't know where to start."

Suddenly, he was moving. He charged forward so abruptly, I took a half-step back, but it wasn't enough to outrun him. Not that I wanted to anyway. His arms caged around me, locking me in his embrace.

"There are things I want to ask you too," his voice was as strong and sure as his hold on me, "but there's something I want more."

He leaned closer so his mouth was only a breath away from mine. My heart skittered around inside my chest. I had a good idea what he meant, but I asked anyway. "What is it?"

He closed the space between us, not just with our mouths, but with our bodies. I was pressed to the length of him from our lips, to our chests, and down to our knees. His kiss smoldered and then burned through my body in the most amazing way. It was so strange it was the first time, after everything else we'd done together, we'd connected this way. Unscripted and more intimate than the marks he'd put on me or how I'd welcomed him inside my body.

His tongue dipped into my mouth and the slow, seductive slide of it injected passion into my bloodstream. And with it, came an insatiable need, so powerful that I vaporized and became a slave. I lifted onto my toes, deepening our fiery kiss, and fisted handfuls of his hair.

It broke whatever restraint he had on himself.

For a moment, I wasn't sure which one of us was leading, or if we moved as one. I stumbled in my heels as I was blindly urged to shuffle backward into the study. I felt wildly out of control when my fingers clawed at the snap of his jeans, but he had enough control for both of us. He caught my wrists and pinned them behind my back, slowing me down.

It was so he could kiss me how he wanted to, with my full, undivided attention. I sighed into his mouth, grateful with how he'd taken charge because I struggled so desperately with self-control.

He crossed my wrists and kept one hand on them but lifted the other to cup my cheek. His mouth moved against mine, and he persuaded me with both his lips and his hold to adjust the angle of our kiss.

I'd spent the evening being teased without satisfaction, but he kissed me as if he'd spent the last two months being taunted by my lips and now he was going to take what he was fucking owed.

His palm slid down along the edge of my jaw, his fingers trailing behind, and as his hand curled to rest on the center of my throat, the kiss ended. He brushed the pad of his thumb over my lips, and it was reminiscent of the way he rubbed at the indentation his ropes left on my skin. Did he think I needed soothing after something so intense?

Because he was dreaming if he thought he could wipe away the mark his kiss left on me.

His beautiful eyes were bottomless as he stared down into mine, and although there was no tension in his hand, it wrapped around my throat as a collar. Power flared through his expression like fire, and although I didn't know his name, I knew *this* man. I'd met him plenty of times downstairs.

He was one half of the man who made my body sing and cry with agonizing pleasure.

I was still drunk from his kiss when he let go of my wrists and tugged at the waist of my shorts, popping the button free and then focused on dropping my zipper. And then it was a mad dash to get each other's clothes off—or at least out of the way. We moved as if we were running down a steep hill, our hands struggling to keep up with the force of our momentum.

He got on his knees and jerked down my panties, but as they fell to my ankles, I stepped out of them and my shorts, and then joined him on my knees. His shirt was off, and his jeans were undone, but he hadn't given me a chance to get them down off his hips. I'd had to stop when he'd pulled my shirt up over my head.

His mouth claimed mine and his fingers hooked one of the straps of my black bra, tugging it until the cup peeled down and my breast was exposed. A panicked whine drifted out of me. I'd had so much foreplay already, I wasn't sure I could survive any more.

Had he sensed that? His arms went around me, lifted, and when I folded my legs around his hips, he leaned forward to set me down on my back. The smooth wood floor was cool against my feverish skin, but it wasn't enough to tamp down the inferno raging inside me.

I was naked except for my half-off bra and my burnt-orange heels, and I clawed at his undone jeans, trying to get inside. By the time I had my hands beneath the stretched waistband of his underwear and wrapped around him, he was already hard. A hiss of pleasure came through his clenched teeth.

Earlier, I'd told the men I didn't beg—but right now? I was *close*. A plea simmered just behind my lips. The need for him was fucking critical, like an unseen force was hurling us together and we had no choice.

Shit, I was half out of my mind, and he was too, so I didn't stop him when he pushed his clothes down over his hips and out of our way. In fact, I encouraged him, lifting my hips to adjust the angle so he could slide deep inside with one urgent thrust.

"Oh, God," I moaned with relief, louder than his gasp of pleasure. I threaded my fingers through the hair at the back of his head and held on when he began to move.

It felt incredible.

So different than the other times we'd done this. And that made sense because this was the opposite of our carefully designed sessions. Those scenes had been deliberate, planned to each detail, whereas what we were doing now was hurried and mindless.

No, worse.

It was *thoughtless*.

E's thrusts were just as demanding as his kisses, and my bare skin squealed against the polished wood floor as he drove into me. Even when his mouth wasn't on mine, his lips didn't stray from my skin. They roved over my cheekbone, down the curve of my neck, and wandered to my breasts. It was like he loved the taste of me and couldn't get enough of it.

His hips beat against me as his body pumped into mine, and my hands played over the muscles of his chest and arms. While his insistent mouth explored, I reveled in touching him.

Trapped under the heat of him, it took no time for my skin to become slippery with sweat. It was hard for him to get traction with his knees since his jeans cut across his thighs, so as we writhed and thrashed, we inched along the floor.

His groans of satisfaction filled my ear, and I raked my nails down his powerful back until I could clench a hand on his ass. I loved feeling the flex of him as he drove into me, and my hold, plus my legs wrapped around his, helped keep me from shifting too much.

Because the angle was just right.

Tingles began in my center, and goosebumps lifted on my arms. My heart raced along. All the warning signs of my orgasm were there, but it lingered frustratingly just out of reach. Maybe all the edging before had made my body reluctant and defensive.

I was too desperate and frantic to see any other reason for why my orgasm was being so elusive.

The sex was so aggressive, it was taxing on both of us, and I sensed his confusion on why he hadn't been able to push me over the edge. He'd done all the things right. He was thick and hard, pushing deep inside me with a punishing rhythm that should have made my toes curl and my eyes roll back into my head.

And it wasn't like it didn't feel good. It felt amazing.

But it had felt amazing since the moment he'd gotten inside me, and this sustained high point had become a plateau.

So, I drew one of my knees up, and urged him to let me hook it over his shoulder. It allowed him to slip even deeper, past the point of comfort for me, and I welcomed the sensation.

His eyes widened and then hooded with pleasure. When he slowed and ground himself against me, he gauged my reaction carefully. Or maybe he was trying to even himself out and make it last.

"Oh, fucking *yes*," I groaned.

The aching fullness of him was just enough to break up my plateau and I finally crossed the threshold. I came in a rush, shuddering all around him, and he smothered my cry of pleasure under a devouring kiss. Like he wanted to drink in my moans.

The connection of our mouths went unbroken as he came too. The muscles beneath my hands solidified into rock, making him jerk to a stop, and the rhythmic pulses inside flooded me with heat. I sighed in enjoyment at the sensation.

My orgasm had been short, and evaporated from my body nearly as quickly, and as the man over me went still, déjà vu descended on me. Like yesterday, my release had only given me temporary satisfaction. There was a large part of me that wasn't satiated.

It left me feeling incomplete. Like I'd been treating a symptom but not the underlying cause.

Instead of warming as he usually did afterward, tension gripped E and it was cold.

"Shit." His tone was pure dread. "We didn't use . . . I forgot to—"

Oh. Well, that was another reason why it'd felt so different. I'd completely lost my head about using a condom, and he had too. His gaze was on me, but his eyes were unfocused, and I squeezed his arm to bring him back and assure him.

"It's all right," I said. "I'm on the pill, and I'm safe."

It took him a moment to process and he relaxed with a sigh, melting into the crook of my neck. "Me too, I swear." He planted a kiss at the spot where my pulse pounded. "Fuck," he whispered, "I can't believe I did that."

Did he mean forgetting the condom . . . or was he talking about the sex we'd just had?

"Yeah," I said.

Icy slush seeped through my veins, making me cold all over. What the fuck had I just done? No, that was a stupid question. I knew exactly what I'd done. My betrayal would shatter all the trust I'd built up with Clay, and I'd destroyed this incredible partnership.

Hope it was worth it, a bitter voice said in my head, and the pain of it was so sharp, I had to tear my gaze away from E. I stared blindly at the bottom of the beautiful drawing table I was fairly certain Clay had built himself while E shifted, moving to lay on his side next to me.

I was aware he was looking at me. Perhaps he was assessing my mood or hoping I'd turn to him and give a shy smile. But I didn't move. I couldn't do anything because my guilt was crushing.

His fingers were warm as they gently grasped my chin, and he pulled my focus back to him. His expression was full of concern, and whatever look I had on my face made his worry deepen.

Now it was his turn to reassure. "Hey, it's okay." He slid his palm up and down my arm as if trying to warm me up. "It's going to be all right, L."

Displeasure made me press my lips together. How the fuck was this going to be okay? Even though I was in a sexual relationship with both Clay and E, we'd gone behind my partner's back. I'd effectively cheated.

E raised up onto his elbow and his expression was serious. "This wasn't your fault—it was mine. I'll explain what happened, how I took advantage of the situation."

"What?" What was he talking about?

He struggled to assemble the words. "I was so frustrated, I stopped thinking and I let my emotions take over. All I wanted was you alone, to talk to you." His voice dipped low. "I wanted to kiss you. I didn't give a damn about the consequences."

"Hey, I didn't either." His hand on my arm had slowed to a stop, so I set mine on top of his. We'd done this together, and the blame was at least as much mine as it was his. "What are we going to do?"

His answer was immediate. "We tell him."

I swallowed a breath and nodded, but my head was a mess. I loved what the three of us had. Was there any chance I hadn't fucked it up beyond repair? The way E looked at me now, I felt lost. Now that I'd slept with him outside of my arrangement with Clay, what did he think? Would he expect me to leave my partner and become his?

My voice wavered. "How do you think he'll react?"

"I don't know."

"Will he end the arrangement?" Panic made my heart flutter. "What if I never see you again?"

"That won't happen." His brow furrowed. "Clay's a good guy. Yeah, he'll be pissed, and he's got every right to be, but . . ." He sighed. "Look, I'm new to this and all, and I'm not trying to shift blame, but his rules set us up for failure."

Had they? And what did he mean?

"New to this kind of," I wasn't sure how to define it, "group thing?" I found a better word. "Dynamic?"

His gaze slipped away. Even without Clay, I think we both still felt him there, and it was obvious E was hesitant about what to reveal.

"Yeah, but also, like everything." His attention snapped back to me, as if tired of fighting it. "I've had girlfriends. I've gone to the club a few times and played before. So, I've done some scenes, but this?" He tangled his fingers with mine. The air in the room slowed, making dust motes suspend in place. Like the whole world crawled to a stop. "You're the first person I've done this with more than once. You and Clay," he said, gravity filling his voice, "you two are my first partners."

"Oh, my God. Really?" Warmth rolled through me, but his statement was hard to believe. "But you're so good at it."

His smile was temporary. "Thanks, but if that were true, I wouldn't have stayed. I would have had some fucking control." He rolled onto his back and jerked up his pants, his hands doing up his fly and there was tension all through the muscles of his chest and arms. "I thought I had more self-control, but if this was a test, I failed."

"Yeah? Well, I did too." It was sweet, but also kind of annoying how he once again wanted to take all the blame.

He shifted back onto his side, put his arm around me, and pulled me up against his chest, where it was warm and distracting. "I'll talk to him," he said. "I'll explain what happened and apologize."

"Um, I think you mean *we'll* talk to him. We made this huge mistake together, so we can apologize together."

It was a careless word to go along with all my thoughtlessness, and when he stiffened, I felt even worse. The atmosphere in the room plummeted twenty degrees. "I didn't mean—"

"Yeah, good point." He did little to cover the hurt in his voice and he ignored my attempt to correct myself because the damage was done. His arm slid away, and he sat up, his unfocused gaze not meeting mine. "If we tell him it was a one-time thing and won't happen again, maybe he can look past it, and then everything can go back to how it was."

We both knew it was a lie, but I didn't call him on it.

He reached for his shirt and jammed an arm inside. "I need to think about what I want to say first, so we should do it next time we're together."

He was slipping away, but I didn't know how to stop it. My voice was as weak as I felt. "All right."

I was all out of sorts as we both got dressed, and the awkwardness between us only grew more painful as the silence dragged on. Once again, all the questions I wanted to ask clogged my throat and nothing came out.

My heart hammered in my chest when the last of my

clothes were back in place and there was nothing left to do but face him. He stared at me expectantly, unsure what to do, but I felt the same.

"I should probably go," he said.

Say something, a voice in my head screamed at me.

He moved toward the front door and picked up the bag he'd left there.

"Wait." Finally, I found my voice. "Tell me your name."

His shoulders rose with a deep breath. "I think we broke enough rules tonight, don't you?"

Oh, God. My hands tensed into fists, and my voice broke on the word. "Please."

My plea visibly went through him, piercing through the hurt and reaching beneath. His throat bobbed with a hard swallow. "It's Travis."

And then he pulled open the door and walked out without saying another word.

SIXTEEN

The clinic had closed half an hour ago, but Dr. Johnston was still in exam room three with Morpheus and his owner. The black Labrador was going to finish his recovery at home after surgery because everything had gone smoothly, and I suspected the reason this was taking so long was because the doctor was giving Morpheus's owner some pointed advice.

This was the dog's third surgery to remove a foreign object from his stomach. Today, it'd been part of a belt, complete with metal grommets, and the doctor had to fish through several feet of intestine to find each one.

Morpheus was a sweet two-year-old, but he was high energy. If he didn't start getting daily exercise and more attention from his dad, this was going to keep happening, and next time the outcome could be different.

My eyes flicked to the clock on the wall. The team from Grassmere Zoo would be here soon, and the doctor had mentioned she wanted to greet them when they arrived. Hopefully, she was wrapping up and I wouldn't have to figure out whether to interrupt if our guests showed up early.

Cassidy stood beside me as we worked to finish cleaning up the surgical area. There was still a lot to do after we finished sterilizing tools and wiped everything down, and I was grateful she was interning again during her summer break from Vanderbilt.

"You okay?" she asked.

I slowed as I shut the door to the autoclave and pushed the button for it to start its cycle. "Yeah. Why?"

She shrugged. "I would have thought you'd be excited about tonight, but you seem kind of down."

She was talking about the care team from the zoo coming in. I was excited, but it'd been a long, grueling day, and it wasn't over either. Not to mention, what I'd done with E—*Travis*—my brain corrected, had been stealing my focus every waking minute. Guilt laced around me, making the burn from his kiss linger.

If there was an award for "Most Efficient Fuckup" I was sure I'd be declared the winner. I'd betrayed Clay's trust, and then hurt Travis by saying that being with him was a mistake.

"I'm just tired," I lied, which only made my crummy mood worse. She was my best friend, and I was supposed to be able to tell her anything. "Okay, so I'm tired because I couldn't sleep last night. I screwed up."

"What?" She stilled and concern flooded her eyes. "What happened?"

"I like Clay," I admitted.

She looked confused, as if this were common knowledge. "Um, aren't you sleeping with him?"

"Yeah, but we have that arrangement where we don't do feelings. It's just sex and it's so perfect, because it's what we both want. You know what happens to me when I have a boyfriend."

She understood how I lost interest and wasn't built to go

the distance.

"So," she said slowly, "you like your fuck buddy, and that's a problem?"

I sighed. "It is, because I *like* him."

She nodded, finally getting what I meant. "And that's breaking the rules."

Just one of the many rules I've broken.

"That's not even the really big problem. Everything was going great," my tone was glum, "and then I had to go and fuck it all up."

Cassidy smoothed her hands down the front of her maroon scrubs. "What'd you do?"

I couldn't contain it any longer. "I went behind his back and had sex with someone else."

My friend couldn't have looked more confused if she'd tried, and her tone was dubious. "If you slept with another dude, um . . . how sure are you that you like Clay?"

I frowned. "It's complicated."

His words from our first conversation came back to me in a rush. *I'm about as complicated a person as you can get.*

The door to the operating room swung open, interrupting my thoughts, and Dr. Johnston stuck her head in. She was a short woman in her fifties with thick glasses and long bangs, but they couldn't hide the excitement dancing in her eyes. "The truck's pulling up, ladies."

Cassidy and I followed her out to the side entrance of the clinic, along with the rest of the doctors and staff, and waited in the hot evening sun for our guests to arrive. A white, unmarked commercial truck lumbered through the clinic's empty parking lot and pulled to a stop with the soft hiss of its brakes.

For a moment, I forgot about everything else and remembered how much I loved my job. Even the bad days where I came home covered in fur or had stains on my scrubs from sick animals, taking samples, and lab work.

Animals always kept it interesting, and I loved the variety of patients we treated, big and small. Being one of the largest clinics in Nashville meant we had a lot of specialized machines, and that included an open-air MRI. It was image diagnostic equipment big enough for horses and cattle.

And today it'd be used to scan a Sumatran tiger.

There'd been several cars following in a line, and while they parked, the truck driver and passenger worked to get the back door up. There were two people inside, a man and a woman who were both wearing dark gray scrubs with the zoo logo over the pocket. They must have ridden along in the back to monitor the sedated tiger.

The metal rolling cage had circular holes for airflow, so I only got a glimpse of the orange inside as zoo staff brought the cage down via the truck's liftgate and then began rolling it toward the entrance.

"Dr. Eckhart?" Dr. Johnston asked the man, looking for the vet in charge.

He craned his neck and looked around. "He rode behind us. I think he's still in his car."

They couldn't stop moving because they'd lose momentum, plus there was an incline to get in the building, and the tiger inside was at least two hundred and fifty pounds. I sprang into action, putting my hands on the back of the cage and helped push—

"Lilith, wait here and show the rest of the team where to go," Dr. Johnston said.

I wanted to grumble in disappointment, but I should have expected this. I'd become the face of the clinic, and the doctors had praised me for my excellent 'people skills.' Whenever an owner was being difficult, I was the one who had to get on the phone or step into an exam room to assist.

So, I stood in the walkway and watched as everyone else got to head inside. It'd be crowded in the MRI room, and this meant I'd be one of the last ones in. Fuck, I was going to be stuck in the back.

I sighed, turned, and ran face first into a chest covered in gray, which was a wall decorated with a stethoscope.

"Whoa," the man said. As I bounced off him, his hands instinctively came up and grasped my arms, steadying me. His sharp intake of breath made my heart skip, and then stop altogether when I lifted my gaze to his.

"Oh, fuck," I gasped.

He'd been introduced to me as Mr. E. Why hadn't he corrected Clay and said it was Dr. E? It was right there on the name badge clipped to his scrubs.

Dr. T. Eckhart, DVM.

Thoughts flew threw my brain at a million miles an hour, and the dumbest one won out. I looked like shit. The makeup I'd put on this morning was long gone. Rather than heels, I wore a pair of slip-resistant rubberized shoes. My hair was up in a messy bun, with extra emphasis on messy.

And no matter how careful I was, it seemed like every day I ended up with poop, pee, vomit, or blood on me . . . and today I had the full compliment.

He was a veterinarian though, so maybe he understood. He gazed at me like he didn't see any of it, he only saw me. And while I looked like garbage, he looked impossibly good. All confident and sexy and like a man who worked in my field and loved the same things I did.

I was almost too stunned to speak, so it came out hushed. "Travis?"

It was the first time he'd heard his name in my voice, and while his eyes softened, his hold on me tightened. Had he done it to prevent himself from pulling me deeper into his embrace?

He opened his mouth to say something, but a woman in a matching uniform appeared at his side and gave us a curious look. He let go of me and straightened, and even though it was hot in the sun, it was instantly cold when his touch was gone.

The woman didn't have a stethoscope around her shoulders like he did, and her name badge only had her first name on it, so she was probably a vet tech like me. Her tone was light and friendly. "You two know each other?"

Yes.

But also, no.

"Yeah." Travis lifted a hand my direction as if he were going to introduce me, and paused, realizing he still didn't know my name. His gaze dropped to my silver nametag and he studied the print there. "Lilith and I . . . have a mutual friend."

His face contorted with displeasure at the inadequate statement.

Well, at least it was true, wasn't it? I pressed my lips together.

The woman was oblivious to the tension between us. She nodded and glanced impatiently toward the clinic, wanting to do the job they'd come here for. So, I plastered on a smile and hoped he couldn't hear how affected he'd made me. "Welcome. Let me show you where the MRI is, Doctor."

As I suspected, by the time we made it into the room, there was barely any space left. The team from the zoo was assisted by some of our staff as the pad beneath the tiger was used to lift him onto the table.

I squeezed in beside Cassidy, and as Travis spoke with Dr. Johnston, my focus was drawn to the big cat. God, he was beautiful. A brilliant orange with vivid black stripes and a distinguished ruff that looked like a beard. It was amazing to be so close.

The tiger's name was Harta, and for the last few months he'd been experiencing sporadic seizures. His episode on Tuesday wasn't any different than the others, but he shared an enclosure with his sister Eka. She'd been so concerned, staff worried the female tiger might accidentally hurt him while trying to help or protect her brother.

My gaze drifted from the sedated animal to the group of doctors discussing symptoms and what they'd look for on the scan. Travis listened thoughtfully as Dr. Johnston spoke, but I couldn't focus on what she was saying.

He'd cancelled our Tuesday session because he had a

work emergency. Had he told Clay what that emergency was? Because tiger seizures would not have been my first guess. But—oh, God—this new information was almost too much to bear. It felt like, at least on paper, Clay had unknowingly picked the perfect guy for me.

Or maybe he'd done it knowingly. It added another layer as to why he'd been reluctant to tell me anything about Travis.

During the MRI, he glanced my direction, and when he caught me looking, I quickly dropped my gaze to the floor. Two months ago, I would have simply smiled back at him. It wasn't that my confidence was gone now. Taking my gaze off him was a safety measure. If I looked at him long enough and saw how good his scrubs fit around his toned frame, it was possible I'd be pushing people out of my way in my struggle to plant my lips on his.

Thankfully, Harta's scan was clear. There were no tumors or lesions, and after consulting with the other doctors, Travis announced they'd manage the seizures with medication.

It was the best possible outcome, and I felt the same relief he did, judging by his expression. As the team prepared Harta for his return trip to the zoo, I slowly worked my way toward the man I'd broken rules with last night.

He thanked everyone at the clinic for their time and help, and when his attention settled on me, I subtly ticked my head toward the door.

"Can we talk?" I wordlessly asked.

He turned to the vet tech beside him. "Excuse me. I'll be right back."

My pulse moved much quicker than my feet as he

followed me out of the MRI room and into a nearby consultation one. Luckily, it had already been cleaned for the night. He ignored everything else in the room, including the wallpaper border of cartoon cats chasing balls of yarn, and turned to face me as I shut the door behind us, closing us in together.

"I'm sorry," I blurted. "Being with you wasn't a mistake. I still feel your kiss, and it's burning me up inside."

His eyes went wide with shock.

The dam had been broken and now that it was out, the rest poured from me. "I like Clay, but I like you too, and I love what *we* have. The problem is I don't know if I'm allowed to like you, and I know I'm not supposed to like him, so it's just really confusing." I frowned. "I'm not like this. Usually I know what I want, and I say what I mean, but with this arrangement, everything's different."

He pulled his shoulders back like the information had been overwhelming and confusion washed over his face. "Wait. You're not supposed to like him?"

I swallowed a breath. "I'm not supposed to, like romantically. We agreed no love or feelings. It's only supposed to be a sexual relationship, and he promised to teach me about, well, all the stuff we've been doing."

Something flitted through his eyes like a glimmer of hope, but it was gone too quickly for me to be sure. "But you like him romantically," he said. "And you're saying it's the same for me?"

He'd asked his question as if he suspected the answer, and I was too distracted to pick up on his subtle approach until his hand gently cuffed my wrist. His touch was disarming, and I spoke more to myself than to him. "I don't know if it's allowed."

My voice had been feather-soft, but his was solid and confident. "Then we should find out."

His statement seared deep inside, filling up the space around the kiss he'd given me last night, and as soon as it did, I had to make even more room because he tugged me toward him and lowered his lips to mine. His mouth stifled the gasp I made, which shifted into a content sigh, because this kiss?

It was blistering.

Everything else ignited and burned away in the fire of it.

"Clay's house," he said as he came up for air. "Eight-thirty. We can talk to him then."

It was more of a request than a question, but that was fine with me. I'd fallen so deeply under his spell, I didn't care that I was at work or what I looked like. All I wanted was his kiss. "Okay."

His tongue slid into my mouth, caressing mine, and pleasure rushed between my legs. For a brief moment, I was angry with how he'd been kept from me, but his hand was on my waist, and he tilted the angle of our kiss, increasing the intensity of it, and all was forgotten.

"Dr. Eckhart?" a female voice called from behind the door.

It was like a needle dragging across a record and instantly his lips were gone, severing our kiss. He stepped away, pulled open the door, and cast a glance back at me. "See you tonight, Lilith."

My face was warm and my lips still tingling as I watched him go, and I didn't move until the hallway drained of people.

But Cassidy was there, lying in wait for me, and one quick look told her something had gone down while Travis and I had been alone.

Her tone was hushed but playful. "What was that about?" Her mouth curled into a smile. "I swear, that's got to be some kind of record."

"What?" We trailed behind the rest of the team, and it was highly unlikely they could hear us over the rattling wheels of the cart.

"You always get hit on and that guy got you alone in, like, ten seconds." She shook her head in amused disbelief. "Not that I blame you. He's a hot *and* a doctor."

"And we all know how much you like those," I teased, then sobered. "I know him. His name's Travis and . . . he's the other guy I'm sleeping with."

"Oh, wow." She pulled to a stop just inside the doors, while the rest of the group continued down the walkway to the truck. "Wait. *Sleeping* with? You did it more than once?"

My gaze followed Travis as he supervised the cage being loaded and shook hands with the clinic staff. I took in a shallow breath. "Only one time," I said, "when Clay wasn't watching us."

Her head swiveled to me and her jaw dropped, but she didn't produce a sound. My admission hung awkwardly until she closed her mouth with an audible snap.

"You weren't fucking kidding," she gave me a wide-eyed look, "when you said it was complicated."

"No, I wasn't."

And I was beginning to think what I had with Clay and

Travis was exactly the right kind of complicated.

At eight-fifteen, I went down the stone pathway in front of my house and out the gate, heading toward Clay's with a new pair of red strappy sandals on and a head full of worry. Travis had said to meet him at eight thirty, but I planned to use the time before to play with Noir while I rehearsed what I was going to say.

But when I unlocked the front door and pushed it open, the alarm didn't chirp as it normally did. Oh, God. With what had happened with Travis yesterday, had I forgotten to set the security system before leaving?

No, wait—I had. I remembered doing it, plus Clay had his app on his phone. If I'd forgotten, he would have eventually noticed and armed it himself. I only made it a few steps through the entryway before seeing the light on in the kitchen.

Awareness prickled through me. Someone was in the house.

"Hello?" I called.

"I'm in here," Clay answered back.

What the hell?

He was in the kitchen, wearing jeans and a fitted polo shirt, reminding me of the preppy guys I used to gravitate toward years ago in high school. But in contrast to his look, he was stooped down with a drill in one hand and appeared to be working on a sliding drawer inside one of his cabinets. When I entered, he set down the drill on top of the newly installed counter with a thud, rose, and turned to face me.

His expression was guarded and unreadable.

It was stunning to see him when it was the middle of the week, and he hadn't mentioned yesterday he was coming back. My breath caught seeing him. Not just because he looked so good, but at the realization it meant we could talk truly face to face.

My throat was tight with anxiety. "What are you doing home?"

He gazed at me for a long moment and stood absolutely still, making awareness tingle in me once more.

Finally, he spoke. "I told my team I had an emergency and needed a couple days."

Oh. No.

He knew.

SEVENTEEN

Guilt drove my gaze to the floor, and I stared intently at the drill Clay had abandoned there.

"A drawer's not that urgent," I attempted to joke, but my voice lost power as I went. "It probably could have waited."

"Lilith."

He said it in the same tone he used when he told me to look at him. I dragged my gaze up, dreading the hurt or anger I deserved to find in him, but it wasn't there. His face remained an emotionless mask.

"I'm so sorry," I whispered. Remorse was a thick lump in my throat, making it hard to swallow. "When did Travis tell you?"

He flinched at hearing Travis's name come out of my mouth. "He didn't."

It was like it was suddenly too difficult to look at me and he turned slightly, blinking against the sensation.

"Then—" I started, confused.

"I saw you two on the cameras."

I'd completely forgotten about them, and—oh, God—now I felt *even* worse. I flattened a hand to my chest as if I could smother the guilt raging through me. Hearing about what we'd done was bad enough. Witnessing it was extra cruel.

"I stopped watching," he added quietly, "once it was clear

what was going to happen."

"I'm so sorry," I repeated.

He shook his head and his gaze returned to me. His expression finally had an emotion, but it wasn't anger or jealousy or sadness. It looked like shame.

"It wasn't your fault, Lilith," he said. "It was mine."

His admission was jarringly the same as Travis's had been, and kind of ridiculous. Why was it both men wanted to take complete responsibility for my actions? "What are you talking about?"

He took a tentative step my direction, closing some of the space between us. "I kept you siloed off from each other, and I tried to do the same with the way I felt about you, but I . . . got jealous." He took another step, moving closer still. "So, then I overcorrected, and I pushed you toward him."

My heart stumbled and beat faster. Was that true? Clay knew how curious I was, and Travis said he felt like we'd been set up to fail.

"I convinced myself I wanted it to happen," he said. "Once I saw you two together, I thought it'd—I don't know—cure me of the way I was feeling." He made a face like he thought in hindsight the idea was stupid. "Or maybe I'd see how badly I was standing in the way."

I licked my dry lips, unsure of what to say, but thankfully he wasn't finished.

"In a way, it did both." He lifted a hand, and I stood utterly still as he cupped the back of my neck and gently drew me toward him until I was only a breath away. "You like him," he said softly, "and that's okay."

I let out a tight breath. "I like you too, though. And . . . I *really* like what we have." My voice fell to a whisper. "I'm terrified of losing it and terrified these feelings won't last."

Rather than be surprised or disappointed, the corner of his mouth turned up into a pleased and sexy smile. "You're worried you're going to get bored?"

He'd said it like it wasn't possible, but I knew myself. As much as I wanted it to, this feeling wouldn't last. I'd get through the honeymoon stage of the relationship, and then feel like it'd run its course.

"It always happens," I said.

His hold on me was stable and supportive and reassuring. "If your feelings are temporary, I'd like to remind you—so is my arrangement with him."

I frowned. "Is that a threat?"

"What?" He softened. "No, no. I just meant it's possible your feelings about Travis might go away before my project's even finished. Or maybe we change our minds about our arrangement with him. It's not exactly something I can plan." His eyes deepened, filling with gravity. "I like what we have too, Lilith. Enough to fly home today and try to work this out so I don't lose you." His shoulders straightened abruptly because he hadn't meant to phrase it that way. "So we don't lose what we have," he corrected.

Oh, wow. I swallowed a breath because his admission made excitement flutter inside me.

"I'm not Travis," he continued. "There are things he can give you that I can't, so if I'm standing in the way of you two—"

"You're not," I said in a rush.

Maybe it was true that Travis could offer me things Clay couldn't, but it went both ways. Clay gave me an experience Travis didn't seem capable of, at least not without Clay's direction.

Relief scrubbed away Clay's worry. "Okay. Good."

When he leaned in and slanted his lips across mine, it momentarily voided all thoughts from my mind. His mouth was warm and his tongue lush, and even though this kiss was clearly scripted, I melted all the same.

His skilled mouth pressed to mine while his hands caressed the curves of my body, moving as if he had complete ownership over me. Didn't he? Like Noir, I felt jointly owned. And Clay's domination wasn't what I expected it to be. Sometimes it was subtle persuasion, not force. Requests instead of demands.

It was fucking irresistible.

I'd been filled with trepidation coming over here and admitting what I'd done. The last place I expected to end up was in his arms, him kissing me and acting like there was nothing to forgive.

"You're not mad at us?" I asked.

"No, I'm not upset with you."

His meaning nearly slipped past me because his touch was so distracting, but I paused. "And Travis?"

He exhaled, reluctantly straightened, and gave me a pointed look. "I'm disappointed with him."

I was compelled to defend him. "But why not me?"

"Because he's supposed to have more self-control."

I lifted an eyebrow. "Didn't you just tell me you wanted

it to happen?"

"I did, but he's a dominant and I trained him better than that. He shouldn't have given in to what he wanted so quickly."

I sucked in a surprised breath. Clay had trained Travis? The idea was . . .

Hot.

Oh, my God, it was so hot. What had that been like?

For once, Clay was oblivious to the effect he could have on me. "I'll discuss it with him when he gets here." His gaze traced over my lips as if considering kissing me again. "When I called to set a time with him tonight, he told me you ran into each other at work today."

"We did."

"Nashville's a big city, but I knew there was a chance it'd happen since you're both in the same field."

"It was pretty surprising," I said pointedly, "coming face-to-face with Dr. Eckhart."

Clay matched my tone. "And it was pretty surprising when I asked last night if he'd left, and you said yes."

I pressed my lips together. "I'm sorry about that."

He turned serious. "I shouldn't have withheld information from you, and I'm done doing that. We both need to be better about communicating."

I was about to speak when the doorbell rang out, making my heart skip. Travis was early.

"Go downstairs," Clay said calmly. "I'll get the door."

I hesitated. "We said we were going to talk to you together."

His eyes stayed fixed on me, even as he began to move

toward the doorway that led to the entryway. "It's all right. I have a plan."

Warmth spilled through my limbs. "Of course you do."

I went down the steps slowly, trying to hear what was happening at the front door, but it was quiet. Had Travis been as surprised as I was to see Clay was home? Or had Clay already told him? Everything had happened so fast when I'd discovered him in the kitchen, we hadn't gotten much of a chance to talk details.

I was still kind of hazy on where things stood with the three of us. Clay had said it was okay for me to have feelings for Travis, but he'd also told me he was jealous. Plus, he'd been worried enough about losing me he'd declared an emergency to his work and rushed home.

My feelings for both men were getting more complicated by the minute.

The prototype chair had been moved to the corner and the folding table we'd used the first time we'd played together stood in its place, waiting. I walked to it and skimmed my hand across the top, letting my fingers trail over the soft, smooth material, my fingertips following the line of a seam.

I hadn't been able to do much admiring of it last time, but like all his other work, the table was exquisite. Steam filled my body as I remembered how the scene had played out. Would his plan for tonight be similar to what we'd done last time?

The stairs creaked as two pairs of footsteps came down them, and then Clay appeared, followed by a pensive-looking Travis.

The muscles in my center tightened. It was the first time we'd been together in the same room since the night at the club, and things were so different now. Travis's gaze swept the room, found me, and zeroed in, which made my muscles squeeze harder still.

The men were both incredibly handsome, but in their own way. Travis's hulking frame and strong jawline made him more widely accepted as attractive. He was the magazine cover hunk, whereas Clay was leaner. There was more mystery surrounding him, hidden behind his glasses and his cryptic expression.

It was impossible to decide who was more appealing.

"We have some things to talk about," Clay said, casting a glance toward the other man. "I thought we could work through it with a scene."

My pulse skittered into overdrive and I was so into the idea, I could barely get my words out. "All of us, playing together?"

He drew in a deep breath. "No." He made a face and amended his statement. "Not exactly. We've each had a session one-on-one, and I've gotten to enjoy watching the two of you together. I think if we reverse the roles tonight, it could be helpful."

All the air was sucked out of the room and the thermostat cranked to a million degrees. I felt flushed as my gaze bounced between the men. "You want Travis to watch us?" He'd told me he was a private person and he'd shied away from physical stuff with me at the club, but . . . he was clearly comfortable with Travis. He'd said he'd trained him, after all.

"Like, a demonstration?"

Clay shook his head, and his posture was stiff. It announced whatever he was about to say, he was uneasy revealing it. "I think it would be good for him to see us together, to remind him that I am your partner too."

His tone was so even and measured, it was impossible to know how he meant it. Was this supposed to be punishment for Travis? Or was it Clay's attempt to prove he deserved equal status in our developing trio?

"And it'd be good," he added more directly, "for him to work on his self-control."

The newly discovered submissive part of me shivered with pleasure at his scolding tone, and Travis looked away. He wasn't happy with himself, or the way his mentor had called him out.

"What about you, Travis?" I asked. "Do you want this?"

It was the first test to see if Clay's rules were officially gone, and the atmosphere was tense until Travis's attention turned to me. He set his hands on his waist and shifted his weight to one side, striving for a casual stance.

"Yeah," he said. "If that's what it takes for him to accept my apology."

The intensity of his stare was absolute. He'd trained to become a dominant, but there was clearly some God-given talent Travis had been born with, because I had to hold in my shudder of enjoyment. He looked at me the same way Clay did.

Like I belonged under his care and nowhere else.

In the silence, it became apparent both men were waiting on me, so I lifted my chin and leveled a look at Clay. "Are the roles completely reversed? Travis is directing the scene?"

Clay did his best to hide his flinch because the idea filled him with disdain. He wouldn't take orders from someone else, but he played it off like there was a simple reason. "No. I already have the scene planned."

"Hmm." I murmured it as a thinly veiled, *how convenient*. "All right."

He looked pleased, went to the rolling stool tucked under the workbench, and pulled it out, gesturing to it. "Travis."

The taller of the two men didn't look all that comfortable as he walked past me toward Clay. He watched his mentor as if he expected the stool to be rolled out of the way at the last second as he sat, but thankfully that didn't happen.

Satisfied that Travis was settled, Clay's attention went to me, and I held breath tightly in my lungs as he approached. He moved to stand behind me, making sure not to block Travis's view as his hands closed on the back hem of my shirt and began to lift.

I raised my arms and let him pull it over my head while my gaze was fixed on Travis. His hand that had been resting on his thigh balled into a fist. I wore a simple white bra that wasn't at all sexy, and he'd seen me naked several times, but it was like I surprised him every time with how good I looked. I couldn't help but wonder if he was already struggling to keep his hands to himself.

"I'll accept your apology," Clay's hands encircled my waist, and his fingers worked the button of my pants, "when you accept mine."

Travis gave him a dubious look. "For what?"

"The rules I made you follow. I'd thought we'd only need them that first time," his voice was shaded by embarrassment, "but I enjoyed how they gave me all the power. That wasn't fair to either of you."

My pants were undone and coasted down my legs, and he held his arm out for me to use as support while I stepped out of them. Travis's gaze traced every inch of the white silk covering me.

Clay wasn't as distracted as the other man; he was intent on getting me naked. "Lilith and I talked a little before you arrived, and I told her it was okay if she has feelings for you."

Surprise made Travis's eyes widen. His lips parted to speak, but then the clasp of my bra was undone, and my breasts tumbled free. As the bra fell to the ground, Clay's warm hands closed around me and squeezed hard enough to make me melt back into him. Travis stared at us, transfixed.

"And then what did you say to me?" Clay's head was beside mine, and he tilted down to drop a kiss on the place where my neck met my body.

I shivered and my breath went shallow. Travis was a statue as he watched another man's hands on me, and his expression said he both loved and hated it.

"I said I have feelings for you too," I admitted.

One of Clay's hands moved down, his fingertips skimming over my taut stomach, then slipped inside the top of my panties. My heart beat faster and faster as he continued his descent.

"And I like what we have," I whispered. He stroked his fingers between my legs, and I moaned. "Oh, my God—I like it so much."

Clay gave a grunt of satisfaction while he rubbed where I was hot and damp, sending a shower of goosebumps down my legs. "Yeah. I like it too."

Travis watched the hand inside my panties as if he were hypnotized, and his Adam's apple bobbed with a thick swallow.

"What about you, Travis?" Clay's tone was full of seduction. "Do you like what *we* have?"

The question carried double meaning. On the surface, he was asking about the arrangement. But beneath, he could be talking about me. That the 'we' meant he and Travis were a pair and they possessed me *jointly*.

There was no hesitation, and although the word was quiet, it detonated like a bomb. "Yes."

My underwear was pushed down across my thighs so it was out of Clay's way, and perhaps as a reward to Travis, who could see now exactly how the other man was touching me. It was tame in comparison to all the things Clay had seen Travis do to me, but it was somehow just as intense. The role reversal made everything feel brand new.

"Good," Clay said. "Since it's been working for us, let's modify the arrangement."

I swallowed a breath and my eyebrows tugged together. "How?"

"I was thinking Travis and I could be equal partners. If he wants to lead a scene with you, I'm okay with that." He tacked it on to the end like he'd just thought of it, even though I highly doubted it. "As long as I get to watch. Would you like that?"

Oh, my God.

"Yes," Travis and I said together.

Lava pumped through my veins at the idea, and I worried I was going to combust as I watched desire flood Travis's expression.

"And, obviously, you can talk to each other going—"

"Can I kiss her?" Travis asked in a rush.

The hand teasing me froze. Was it the interruption that bothered him, or the question? Clay's tone was biting. "You did yesterday, didn't you?"

Travis's gaze shifted away, and he cleared his throat. "And, uh, this afternoon."

"Doesn't sound like you care if you have my permission."

The heat of Clay's body behind me slid away, leaving me cold and lonely. It felt like punishment, and I deserved it, didn't I? With what Travis and I had done, it seemed like our kissing had bothered him the most.

"I'm sorry," Travis said. "You gave me clear boundaries, but I did what I wanted anyway."

Clay went to the workbench and retrieved the coil of black rope that rested there. "Yeah. That's why we're going to work on your self-control tonight." He came back to stand in front of me, and his voice dropped low. "Hands together."

As I complied, it improved my posture, and my underwear slipped down to my ankles. It was strange to be naked while both men were dressed, but it wasn't uncomfortable. It helped with how Clay stared at me, and the way his shoulders rose and fell with his uneven breaths.

The rope was tied around my wrists, and it wasn't surprising how efficiently Clay moved as he threaded the thick cord back and forth in a figure eight, creating layers up my forearms like cuffs. When he seemed satisfied, he knotted it off, but left a long tail.

His voice was deep and commanding and meant for me. "Yesterday, I told you I'd give you so many orgasms you'd beg me to stop, but you didn't keep up your end of the deal, did you?"

I was uncomfortable with my guilt. "No, I didn't."

"There has to be consequences for that." Dark anticipation lit his eyes. It said I might not enjoy what he had planned, but he certainly would. "On the table," he ordered. "On your back."

For emphasis, he gave a tug of the ends of the rope he was holding, pulling me along like I was his captive. Was it wrong to like how it made me feel? Because I did. I left my underwear behind on the floor as I marched toward the beautiful piece he'd set up in preparation for the scene. When I reached it, I turned and sat, my skin quietly squealing against the cool leather as I shifted into position.

I hadn't finished settling down before Clay threaded the loose end of the rope through the metal handle at the table's end and pulled, stretching my arms up. The cord was taut, vibrating subtly as it was tied off.

Clay could have asked for Travis's help with securing me to the table, but he didn't. Maybe he liked doing it himself, or perhaps he wanted the other man to feel like an outsider, looking in. Clay wasn't able to do anything when he watched from Florida, so maybe he wanted Travis to experience the same thing.

Clay stepped back and his gaze swept over my body, which was naked except for my heels, and it stoked the fire that had been flickering inside me.

I waited to be punished.

Was eager for it, even, because I suspected it'd release all the negative feelings I'd been struggling with. The guilt, the shame . . . the tension of wanting both men and worrying how that'd make the other feel if they found out.

As I stared up at the ceiling, I wondered what form my consequences would take. A cane? Nipple clamps? Clay turned and strode across the room, and I lifted my head to watch him go. Travis studied him too as the man approached. Although we could talk to each other now during a scene, it felt disrespectful to do it, and he looked at Clay with anxiety.

Like he worried he was going to be asked to deliver my punishment.

But Travis wasn't Clay's destination. A mini fridge sat to the side of the workbench, which he opened and pulled out a Ziplock bag from the freezer compartment. I only got a glimpse of what was inside before he shut the fridge, set the bag down on the workbench, and picked up a leather work glove.

The inside of the bag seemed to be ice, only it wasn't shaped in a cube.

An icicle?

My stomach bottomed out and my mouth went dry as he opened the bag and pulled the thing out. It was long and shaped like a popsicle, rounded at one end, and there was no doubt in my mind what he intended to do with it.

It scared me how much the idea turned me on.

EIGHTEEN

Did this idea turn Travis on too? He eyed the shaft of ice in Clay's hand and shifted, making the stool squeak beneath his weight.

Clay slipped on the glove, probably to prevent his fingers from getting too cold, but also to help him keep his grip. The ice was already glossy, as if it had begun to melt in the freezer. He carried it around the table to the far side, so that once he began, he wouldn't block Travis's view.

He'd said they were going to work on his control, and I got the feeling it was about to be tested.

Clay cast a glance down at me on the table, my bound wrists above my head. "I assume you haven't done temperature play before."

My voice was hushed. "No."

He turned the icicle over so it was tip-down, and dangling over my chest. "I asked you to do something for me, and you said you would, but you didn't. So now we have an issue of trust."

A droplet of water formed on the bottom of the icicle and broke free, landing just to the side of one of my nipples. I flinched at the cold and the damp track it left as it dripped down my side.

"I'm sorry," I said.

He asked it in a hypnotic voice. "Do you trust me?"

I peered up into his eyes, and for the first time, I wished he weren't wearing glasses. Even though I could easily see through the lenses, I didn't like anything between us. His intense stare was so deep, it went on forever.

"Yes," I breathed. "I trust you."

I'd been so focused on him, I'd forgotten about the ice hovering above until a new drip splashed onto my skin, this time hitting its target and making me startle. A faint smile twisted on his lips just before he bent at the waist and licked the drop from my hardened nipple.

I sighed with contentment. The cold water followed by his warm tongue felt so nice—

"Fuck," I gasped, jolting hard enough the table beneath me gave a groan.

While he'd distracted me with his mouth, he'd also run the frigid tip of the icicle down between my legs, making the ice skate over my hot, sensitive clit. The sensation was gone as soon as it registered, but the melted water it left behind dripped down and pooled on the leather.

I was smart enough to know this was only a hint of what was planned. A taste of what he had in store for me. *For us*, I corrected, because I could see Travis in my peripheral vision as he sat nearby, watching the scene. I was curious about how he felt. Was he wishing he were the one standing over me right now, rather than the one stuck on the sidelines?

Was he jealous?

Steam fogged my mind. I couldn't help it. The basic woman in me thrilled at the idea of two men fighting over her.

I was still figuring out who they were as people, but I could already tell they were both competitive.

Perhaps Clay knew he didn't have my undivided attention—because he seemed determined to get it back. The melting ice trailed over my stomach, drawing patterns and leaving tracks of water behind. He slid it up over a breast and down the curve to the sensitive side, making me squirm.

He delivered his correction in a soft, yet confident voice. "Stay still."

It was hard though because the ice was incredibly cold and so, so enjoyable. His unpredictable path kept me guessing and my heart racing, and the second time he slicked it through the cleft of my legs, I shuddered with pleasure and discomfort.

His palm trailed behind, smearing the wetness around as the ice skimmed down my thigh. It carved a line along my shin, and then was gone. He set the icicle and the glove aside momentarily so he could use both hands to undo the small buckle of my shoe's ankle strap.

The heel thudded to the floor and he immediately went to work on the other.

I didn't get a chance to enjoy the sensation of the shoes coming off because he re-gloved, scooped up the ice, and scraped it over my instep. The cold was so intense, I yelped, and the sensation reverberated up my leg like freezing lightning. It made the muscles deep in my belly clamp down.

And it made Travis jolt in his seat, but one sharp look from Clay was more powerful than the ropes around my wrists, and it got him to stay in place. As I'd suspected, this scene wasn't just for me. It was meant to push Travis too.

"You're so fucking hot, Lilith." Clay's tone verged on evil. "Do you think I can cool you down?"

My heart leapt into my throat and pounded there as the ice moved along my skin, up over my knee, painting more water trails and ignoring the goosebumps it left in its wake. He'd wandered and meandered with the ice before, but he moved with purpose now. It coasted over the top of my thigh and went straight for the place where I was hot and aching.

I clenched my teeth and air left me in a hiss as he stroked the ice over my clit.

He'd been watching my reaction and power flared in his eyes—or maybe it had been whatever he was preparing to do that had turned him on so much.

"Oh, my fucking God," I cried as my whole body arched, desperate to run from the sensation. He'd slid the shaft of ice inside me—only for a second—but the pain was acute. So cold, it felt like burning.

He raised the ice over me, showering my body with more drips as my body heat had sped up the melting. Freezing drops kissed my skin and he ran the palm of his free hand through it, swirling the water around and caressing me.

The combination of cold and warmth, pain and comfort, was doing things to me. I slipped further under his control, ready to do whatever he desired. If he asked me to go a week without orgasms, I'd agree to it.

"Did you enjoy that?" His question was mostly rhetorical, because he already knew the answer. Maybe he'd asked it so we could make sure Travis knew too.

"Yes," I said.

God, he was so sexy when he was in control. Satisfaction twisted his lips into a smile. "Then, it's all right for me to do it again?"

My heart was still throbbing in my throat, so I nodded.

The ice was set down beside me, and I watched as Clay grabbed the back of his shirt and tugged it over his head, then cast it aside. It was a simple action, but the effect was huge. It felt like . . . escalation.

Tension built inside me.

I gazed at his toned chest and since I couldn't touch, I gripped the rope between my hands instead. My breathing went shallow as his fingers went to the snap of the jeans that hung low across his hips. He was too hot to look at, so I swung my focus away until it landed on Travis.

Well, that was a mistake.

Air evaporated from the room and awareness tingled on the back of my neck. Travis wasn't looking at me for once—his attention was on the other man. He watched Clay undress like a mystery was about to be revealed. He stared at our partner with interest and maybe desire too, but it was hard to tell for sure.

Maybe I just wanted it so badly, I was only imagining it.

Travis blinked away whatever he'd been thinking, his gaze drifted to me, and then there was no doubt about the lust he held. It pooled in his eyes like beautiful ink. I was burning up from the inside, and it was almost sweet relief when Clay pressed the ice to my skin.

He repeated his action from before and the icicle made a

circuit around the sensitive places on my body. Every nerve was awake and tingling, clamoring for more, for attention, for relief . . .

The ice pushed inside me, impaling me with a burning cold I couldn't stay still for, and this time it was longer. "Oh, shit, Clay. *Shit!*"

I whimpered as the cold retreated and I could think again over the sensation. He climbed up onto the table and knelt between my legs, one hand holding the dripping ice and the other clenched around his erection that strained beneath his black underwear.

"Maybe," he teased, "you'd like me to fuck you with my dick instead of this ice?"

I hesitated. Was this a trick question?

He gave himself a pump with his fist, then leaned over and spread my pussy open with his thumb and forefinger. It was so he could hold the ice just above my clit and let the water drip onto it. The impact of each freezing drop made me flinch.

His tone was dark and victorious. "I'll do it if you beg me."

Holy fuck.

I'd told him I didn't beg, and my first instinct was to fight, even when I knew this was a battle I was going to lose. My grip tightened on the rope as I shook my head.

Judging by the smile that flashed on his lips, he'd hoped for this.

I inhaled sharply as the ice plunged inside my body, gliding in as if made of the smoothest glass, but it brought pain so intense, it stole my breath. Years of wearing heels had taught me to be comfortable with pain. I had no problem with a long, lingering ache or a blister. I didn't notice half the time, and occasionally, I found it weirdly pleasurable.

But pain that came on in an instant? And was white-hot? I wasn't prepared.

A panicked whine tore from my mouth and I squirmed on the table, fighting against my restraints, desperate to escape. On some level, I was aware I wasn't the only one wrestling with discomfort, but it wasn't until he spoke that I remembered anything outside of the icy fire existed.

Travis's urgent warning was forceful and verged on scary. *"Clay."*

I gasped with relief as the ice went away, and Clay's attention snapped toward the other man, who'd risen to his feet and stood with a threatening posture. Clay wasn't intimidated, nor was he happy with how Travis had interrupted the scene and the way he'd been challenged.

"Trust me," Clay said. "I know what I'm doing, and unlike you—I have this under control."

It was clear he didn't just mean the scene—this was a dig at how Travis's self-control had faltered both yesterday, and maybe even now. He waited impatiently for Travis to say something else, and when nothing came, his focus shifted back to me.

I'd expected another round with the ice or a reminder I needed to beg, but he kept me guessing, that was for sure. Clay pushed his glasses up the bridge of his nose, as if preparing to study blueprints, set down the ice and glove, and then lowered in to place his mouth over my clit. My satisfied moan was immediate and unstoppable.

Oh, he was good.

If he'd asked me to beg, I was already weak enough I would have done it, but his warm mouth against my numb skin gave me time to recover. It rekindled my desire to resist . . . especially if this was going to be my reward.

My toes went into points as his tongue flickered, and in my contentment, my head lolled to the side. Travis was still on his feet beside the stool, as if he'd been too distracted to find his seat, and now the lust coiling inside him made it impossible to move. His broad shoulders were as tense as the muscle flexed along the side of his jaw, signaling he was clenching his teeth.

Clay had seen another man go down on me several times, but this was a first for Travis, and although he was clearly enjoying it, he also looked like a fragile bomb that had been armed.

One wrong move and he'd lose control.

I suspected he was desperate to join us, and his cock was ready to go. It bulged behind his jeans, swelling enormously to one side. I stared at him through my hazy eyes as Clay's tongue painted pleasure between my legs.

"Fuck," Travis growled. "That's so sexy."

Whatever filter I possessed had been burned away by the ice. "Yeah?" I arched my back provocatively, making my knees and my tits point toward the ceiling. "You like watching him go down on me?"

The tongue between my legs hesitated. Clay wanted to hear the answer.

"I want to watch him fuck you."

There was one final teasing lick and then a half of a chuckle. "Nice try, but she knows what she has to do." I was sure there wasn't a more persuasive, seductive taunt in the world when he whispered it to me. "Beg."

I was a breath away from saying *no* but didn't get the chance.

Travis crossed his thick arms over his chest and tilted his head. "What if I did it for her?"

His question charged the room with chaotic energy, and I could practically hear Clay's mind stumble. He'd planned the scene, and this wasn't part of it, but . . . hearing a dominant beg rather than a submissive? That would be quite the power trip, and he considered it carefully. Would he ever get another opportunity like this?

He straightened, sitting back on his heels, and turned his intense stare toward the other man. "Go on, then."

Travis went still. He hadn't expected Clay to accept his offer and now he fumbled for what to do. His arms uncrossed and hung at his sides as he searched for the right words.

"Please." His voice was unsure. "Please do it. I want to see you fuck her and make her come."

His plea earned him an unimpressed reaction from Clay. "That's it?"

He frowned and adjusted. "Goddamnit, *please*, Clay. I'm begging you. Show me how it is when you're with her." He gave up fighting whatever was holding him back, and his voice went thick with need. "I want to see your cock slide inside her tight, little pussy. I want to find out if her moans are the same as when I'm the one fucking her."

A slow, surprised smile warmed Clay's face. "Yeah?" He hooked a finger under the waistband of his underwear and pulled it down, freeing his erection. "Which cock? This one?"

Jesus.

Travis's unflinching gaze drifted down to take in the display, and my bones threatened to liquify. There wasn't bashfulness from either man—only curiosity.

Travis ran a hand over his lips, maybe muffling a curse word beneath it, but he didn't shy away. I didn't blame him, either. Besides being built for sex, Clay's body was made for admiration.

Travis's hand fell away, a decision made, and his chest lifted with a deep breath. "Yes."

Clay's triumphant smile slid from the man to me, and although he didn't ask with words, he peered down patiently and waited for my consent.

"Yes," I said eagerly.

He pushed his underwear further down and out of the way, and moved over me, supporting himself on one hand while he used the other to steady himself.

The realization sliced through me, nearly as cold as the ice he'd used.

"Wait," I gasped.

He turned to stone and concern filled every inch of his face. "What's wrong?"

"Travis and I," I gulped down a breath, "we didn't use protection last night." My voice went powerless. "I thought you should know, in case you wanted to . . ."

He didn't move, didn't blink. "What?"

"We didn't use a condom."

Finally done processing what I'd said, he turned his head to the man standing nearby, and irritation mixed with disappointment. "Were you thinking about her at all?"

"Are you kidding me?" Travis's tone was surprisingly angry. "I couldn't *stop* thinking about her." He glared at the man lingering over me like he might be the cause. "I'm not proud we didn't talk about it before, or the way I lost control, but I'm clean. Safe. And she said the same. Plus, I got tested a few months ago and she's my first partner since." He set his hands on his hips. "But you already know that, just like I know she's on birth control and you two don't use condoms."

"Because we talked about that *before* anything happened," Clay muttered.

"Yeah, and then you told me too, so I knew I wasn't putting her at risk." He exhaled and visibly released the tension he'd been holding in his body. "Do you want me to get you a condom?"

The man leaning over me struggled, but it seemed more to be with his awkwardness rather than the decision. Once again, things hadn't gone according to plan, and Clay looked unsure of how to proceed.

How to get back into the scene.

I wrapped my legs around his hips and tried to pull him toward me. "I'm still okay without one."

His focus shifted back to me, his eyes darkened with sex, and abruptly an evil smile flitted across his lips. It made me suspicious of what he was thinking about. Whatever new plan he'd just drafted in his head, he was quite pleased with it.

"*Oh,*" I murmured as the tip of his cock brushed over my entrance and began to push inside.

As he eased deeper inside me, all the tension in the room began to fade. I groaned with pleasure when his warm skin flattened to mine, but he only stayed long enough to latch his mouth onto mine and bite my bottom lip. I loved his mean, calculated kiss. It fanned the fire between us.

But then he straightened so we were only touching where we were joined, and he began to fuck me just as cruel as his kiss had been. It was hard, and fast, and premeditated. This wasn't for my pleasure—it was for his.

But if this was supposed to be a punishment fuck, it wasn't working. Clay's brutal thrusts sent sparks glittering across my nerve endings and made me want to roll my eyes back into my head. The ice had numbed me, so now his cock felt like a hot branding iron.

God, it felt good.

He locked his hands on my hips, pinning me against the cushioned tabletop that was wet from the melted ice, and heaved his body into mine. Within seconds we were both panting, and grunts of satisfaction rolled from his lips. His fingers dug painfully into my skin, driving me wild.

"*Yes,*" I moaned.

I kept my gaze on Clay, but I was acutely aware we weren't alone. Travis had taken a subtle step toward the table, maybe to get a closer view, or perhaps he hoped he'd get to participate. It allowed me to see him in my peripheral vision, and although I couldn't make out the exact expression he wore, I sensed both his desire and his envy.

He'd said he wanted Clay to make me come, but then the thought clicked in my head. Clay's evil smile had been a warning. Travis wasn't his submissive and he didn't care what the other man wanted tonight. Plus, Travis valued pleasure over pain. Not bringing me to orgasm could punish us both.

And I'd failed the 'no orgasm' test last night. It stood to reason Clay would want to try again.

His breathing was ragged, and his pulse pounded in his neck, and as his moans began to swell, all the telltale signs were there. My body whined with need. I was close—but not as close as he was, and Clay was determined to get across that finish line before me.

The muscles in his chest flexed and tensed.

His tempo went erratic before jerking to a stop, and a huge gasp rang out like it'd been punched from his chest.

His cock wasn't that deep inside me when he came, but I could still feel the subtle pulses and warmth before he slipped out and retreated. He sat back, admiring the result of his work, and the same smug smile from before lurked on his lips.

His underwear was pulled up as I lay on the table, my body physically cooling but the heat he'd created inside me stubbornly lingered. I bit down on my bottom lip to stay quiet. I'd made it through the scene without begging. No need to start now.

He got down off the table, rescued the ice from the puddle that had formed around it, and strode toward the garbage can. He had to walk past Travis to get there, but pulled to a stop when the man stepped into his path.

Travis's expression was dark. "You didn't make her come."

"No." Clay turned to glance over his shoulder, still wearing the same enigmatic smile. "You are."

NINETEEN

Surprise flashed through Travis and was quickly followed with excitement. I liked this plan as much as he seemed to, but when he took an enthusiastic step toward me, Clay's hand came up and flattened to the center of Travis's chest to stop him.

Everything around the men slowed to a crawl.

Clay's hand was pressed against the front of Travis's t-shirt, and neither man looked prepared for the contact. The touch probably wasn't meant to be sexual, but Clay's fingers splayed out, as if eager to feel more of the hardened muscles beneath them.

Travis's eyes were wide, and he drew in a heavy breath. Clay didn't seem to be breathing at all. This was absolutely not part of his plan, and he looked utterly lost. As if he wanted to draw his hand away, but couldn't.

The moment between them was so shockingly intimate, I felt as if I were intruding simply by being in the same room.

Clay's voice was low and uneven. "Make her come . . . and you can only use your mouth to do it."

Oh, my God.

Travis jolted, breaking his gaze with the man to look at me as I lay motionless, still tied down to the table. Clay had come inside me, and I could feel it slowly dripping out between my legs.

"You want to share her with me?" Clay found his confidence again, and it built with each word. "Then, let's share *everything*."

My heart hammered in my chest as Travis stared at me and considered what he'd just been asked to do. It didn't seem like Clay's motivation was to humiliate the other man—it was a test. How badly did Travis want to be the one to bring me pleasure?

And how comfortable was he with the other man in this relationship?

He closed his hand around the one Clay had resting on his chest, and slowly pushed it away so he could move forward, his expression full of determination.

"Holy shit," I gasped, and a thrill shot through me.

There was a loud thud as the ice dropped into the trash, while Travis moved to the end of the table and set his gaze upon me. It was so sexy and exciting, I could feel it like his hands were caressing me as it moved up my legs.

"This is what you want?" he asked. "Me to clean up after him?"

I didn't know if this was a turn-on for the men, but for me? Fucking *yes*. Not just because I'd get an orgasm, but the idea of it . . . It was so dirty and hot, I couldn't catch my breath. So, I swallowed thickly, gave him a shy smile, and bobbed my head.

Clay looked captivated. Like he didn't want to miss a second of what was going to happen.

Travis urged my legs apart, slid his hands beneath my

thighs, and held my gaze as he lowered in. My pulse was raging, making blood roar through my ears, and I pressed my lips together in anticipation of the moan I'd unleash when his mouth made contact.

His eyes, framed with long, dark lashes, fell closed.

Then his lips brushed against my damp skin and he gave me just a sliver of his tongue. It'd been a featherlight touch, but I jolted with pleasure. His second pass was less tentative. It started at the bottom of my entrance and went all the way up to my clit, and heat gathered inside me, building like a fire storm.

"Fuck." Clay's deeply appreciative word punched through the silence of the room, yanking my attention to him. My face flushed with warmth. Once again, he looked unprepared for the reaction this caused in him. Overcome by how much he liked it. He stared at me bound to the table he'd built, and watched as another man feasted on the pussy he'd just fucked.

Travis had been hesitant in the beginning, but he was all in now. His tongue spun cartwheels on my sensitive skin, and I gulped down air. It wasn't going to take any time for him to make me come since Clay had laid all the groundwork.

Travis issued a soft noise of contentment, like he was enjoying himself, and I squeezed my eyes shut to listen better for a moment.

But my eyes blinked open to find his had too, and his mouth lifted away, just enough so he could speak. "You like this?" His question wasn't for me—it was for the other man, and his tone was sinful. "Do you like how I'm licking the taste of you from her pussy?"

I turned my head, tucking my face into the side of my arm so I could muffle my groan of pleasure. His dirty talk was so fucking hot.

"Yeah, I do." Clay exhaled loudly, still off-balance. "Do you?"

Travis mirrored Clay's evil smile from before, and awareness washed over me.

Perhaps Clay had given this command to Travis to exert his power over him, to put the dominant who'd broken the rules back in his place. But if so, it'd failed *spectacularly*. The tables were turned, the power had flipped, and now it was all Travis's.

Clay wasn't the one in control of the scene anymore, and Travis didn't just know it—he *relished* it. "I could eat this pussy all night."

I writhed beneath his tongue that was determined to finish its task and undo both me and the man standing nearby at the same time. Clay wasn't touching anyone, but he was just as much a part of the scene as everyone else. His hurried breath echoed in my ears the same way Travis's murmurs of enjoyment did.

My legs trembled as my climax approached, growing closer every second. I strained against the ropes holding my wrists together, wanting to put a hand on Travis's head and hold him in place. He'd focus in on exactly the right spot, only to move away as my moans swelled, drawing out my anticipation.

I'd hung so long right on the precipice I couldn't take any more.

"Please," I whispered on a broken breath. "Please make me come."

He lifted his mouth and grinned up at me from between my thighs, his lips wet. "So, she *does* beg."

My head thudded back against the table. He was too sexy to look at when power ripped through his eyes. And I couldn't look at Clay either, but I didn't need to. I could picture him standing there with his mouth hanging open in pleasant surprise. If Travis was his protégé, he had to be proud.

Travis's tone was wicked as he spoke to the other man. "What do you think?"

I could hear his corrupt smile. "She asked so nicely."

Travis's tongue was lush as it massaged my clit, starting so slow and whipping faster to match my ragged breath. Sparks rolled up my shaking legs. My heart sprinted to keep up with the urgency he created. The need for release was so strong, it narrowed my vision to a singular point . . .

And then it burst into unfocused stars as pleasure erupted.

The orgasm wasn't like yesterday's. It went on, and on, and *on*. So long, I wondered if the sensation was ever going to end. As satisfaction gripped my body and mind, it caused me to contract and shudder. I thrashed against my restraints and the hands around my thighs.

I was still recovering when Travis gave a soft laugh of disbelief, but it was the sweetest sound. He loved witnessing how powerful the pleasure was as it washed through my limbs, and then he turned to glance at the other man, as if wanting to confirm what he was seeing was real.

Or perhaps he'd glanced at Clay to acknowledge his part

in the scene. They'd worked as a team to bring me to this point, so he wanted to share the credit. The thought only sent me soaring higher. How the hell did I get so lucky to find—and have—both of these men?

Travis straightened to stand upright, wiped a hand over his mouth, and gazed at me with longing in his eyes. It wasn't sexual desire—it was a different kind of ache, and it made me jittery. I liked the way he looked at me now, but what if it didn't last?

What if I came to dread it like I always had before?

I pushed the thought away as he walked to the other end of the table and undid the knots at the handle, allowing me to lower my arms. He helped me sit up, intent on untying the ropes around my wrists, but when his hands landed on mine, he paused. He saw the opportunity and wasn't going to waste it.

He stepped to the edge of the table, cradled my face in his hands, and lowered in. His lips pressed to mine in a kiss that rivaled the one he'd given me last night. He hadn't asked anyone's permission, but Clay's silence allowed it.

If I weren't already weak, the long, lingering kiss would have made me so. It tasted like gratitude, like he was thanking me for the scene. My brain was foggy and floaty, and enjoyed the simplicity of it. When it ended, I sat dutifully still and let him undo the ropes my other partner had put on me.

Travis hadn't come. The only time he'd been touched was the hand Clay had set on his chest. Yet he seemed satisfied, and without acknowledging it with words, we all sensed it was late and the evening was coming to an end.

Clay picked up his jeans and shoved a leg into them, surveying us as if he felt like an outsider in his own home. As he dressed, Travis fetched my clothes, and while I put them on, he coiled the rope into a neat figure 8 and set it on the workbench.

It was Clay who helped me down off the table, but once I was on my feet, he didn't want to let go of me. Seeing him uncertain was strangely reassuring. He was human, capable of making mistakes, and didn't have every moment of his life figured out.

I didn't want to add to his confusion but couldn't help myself. I rose onto my toes and pressed my mouth to his. The kiss wasn't about possession or ownership. It was meant to show how happy he'd made me, and I was thrilled when he responded in kind. It wasn't in his design, but his embrace strengthened around me and I sank into our connection.

It was over sooner than I wanted, but Clay broke the kiss as if he just thought of something and it needed to be said right that very moment.

"It's important we all understand that while this arrangement works for us now," his voice was serious, "it can change at any time." He searched for the exact words and weighted them. "It's *temporary*."

I exhaled slowly. Maybe he'd said it to be helpful, to protect Travis from falling for me when I wasn't built for the long term. But it also felt like he'd reiterated it was temporary as a reminder to himself, and to me to not become too attached.

It served as a warning to us all.

Dr. Lowe's house was larger than Clay's and had an in-ground pool in the backyard. It was the spot we'd chosen to kick off the celebration for Cassidy's twenty-first birthday, and I sat on the lounger by the deep end, watching the people playing in the pool with mild interest.

The original plan had been a small get-together. Just Cassidy, her boyfriend, and a few of her friends from high school. But there was serious overlap in friends between Cassidy and Dr. Lowe's son Preston, and since it was his house too, the laid-back barbeque had grown into an all-out pool party.

Preston was an ass, and I wasn't the least bit surprised he'd decided to co-opt Cassidy's birthday celebration. When they'd been together, he alway had to be the center of attention, and that hadn't changed when they'd broken up. She claimed he'd done a lot of growing up over the last year and was getting better about her dating his dad.

But I wasn't convinced.

I surveyed the people, trying to remember names and who was dating who. I was older than everyone else—except for Greg—but he was smart enough to pretend he was too busy manning the grill to hang out with the folks in his pool who were considerably younger.

Preston, I knew, because I'd met him before. It was also

easy to remember his friend Troy's name. He sat at the edge of the shallow end, his feet dangling in the water, staying right on the cusp of joining in with everyone else.

Two weeks ago, he'd just been a guy trying to make it in the Music City, but last week he'd won an online competition, and now the whole town was buzzing about the pool boy who could be the next big thing.

Something caught his attention because he climbed out of the pool and hustled over to the grill. Horrible Judy Malinger's house was on one side of Greg's, but his neighbor on the other side had appeared and was deep in conversation with him. I'd met her once or twice before. She was the music agent, and likely Troy's, judging by the way she smiled at him.

A guy plopped down on the end of the lounger, nearly sitting on my feet, but I drew them back just in time. Water dripped down his toned, tan chest, and he slicked his hair back out of his eyes, slinging droplets everywhere.

"Hey, there," he said. "I'm Colin."

He was probably my age or a few years younger, and cute, but judging by his wide grin, he knew it.

"Hi, Colin." I gestured to myself. "Lilith. I'm Cassidy's friend. We work together at—"

"Oh, I know who you are." His eyes sparkled with mischief. "I asked Preston about you, like, a second after I got here." He tucked a foot under himself, swiveling to face me, and his posture was carefree. His gaze swept over my body, taking in the white crocheted cover-up I wore, and I appreciated how he didn't seem to be peering through the small holes to see what was beneath. "How come you're not swimming?"

"I'm not hot enough to want to get in," I lied.

His smile was cocksure. "Gonna have to disagree with you there."

It was so over the top, I couldn't help but laugh. Confidence was sexy, and this guy had it in spades. A few months ago, I probably would have eaten him up. But everything was different now. This cute boy couldn't compare to the two men I was in a relationship with.

"Can I get you another drink?" He glanced at the can of Miller Lite beside me that I'd been nursing the last thirty minutes. Like Cassidy, I'd taken the day off from the clinic, but it was barely six o'clock on a Tuesday night, and it felt weird to be drinking so early. Plus, I assumed harder liquor was coming later tonight when we went out to the bars, so it was best to switch to water until then.

"I'm good, thanks."

Colin wasn't deterred. He wiped at the water dripping down his chest, and I wondered if it truly bothered him, or if he'd done it to call my attention to his muscles. "You going to Troy's show on Saturday? He's opening for Stella."

"I heard, but I—"

"I've got an extra ticket if you want to go with me."

I paused, lifted my eyebrows, and gave him a smile. "Straight to the point," I said. "I appreciate that."

He winked. "I figured you would."

Oh, he was smooth, and I immediately began to catalogue my brain for my single friends. I wasn't interested, but I didn't want to see this guy go to waste. Someone could have fun with him.

I shot him a regretful look. "Thanks for the offer, but I have a boyfriend."

He put his hand over his heart, acting like I'd mortally wounded him, and his tone was teasing. "Do you need another?"

It just came out of my mouth without thought. "No, I already have two. Three is a bit much, even for me."

He blinked and evaluated if I was joking, and must have decided I was, because he laughed and shrugged.

There was a splash and water rained down on us. Troy had returned from his conversation and was gathering up his stuff when Preston had playfully flung water at him. Colin and I were merely bystanders caught in the crossfire.

Preston stood in the shallow end and grinned up at his friend beside the pool, who was stepping into his flipflops.

"Where the fuck are you going?" Preston demanded, but it sounded like he totally knew the answer. The only response Troy gave him was a rueful smile, and then he was off, carrying his bag and towel toward the side gate in the fence.

"Boy," Colin said, "he's sure in a hurry to clean Ms. Graham's pool."

And to make sure I didn't miss his innuendo, he stared at me with an all-knowing look, as if he were letting me in on a big secret. I laughed softly and shook my head. It was always hilarious to me when guys gossiped. Most of them couldn't keep a secret for shit.

Which of course, made my thoughts drift back to Clay and Travis.

This time when Preston splashed us, it was intentional,

and I gasped as I was doused with cold water. It slapped me in the face and soaked my hair. "What the fuck?"

He was oblivious to me; his focus was on Colin. "Hello?" he cried to his friend. "Why am I in here all by myself?"

Fucking Preston. I was drenched, and he didn't care. Hell, he didn't even notice. I swung my legs off the chair and stood, wiping my fingers under my eyes, and probably smudged my makeup.

"I'm getting a new drink," I announced to no one in particular, snatching up my half-empty, warm beer.

Greg's house had a walkout basement, and just inside the door was a small bathroom. With the air conditioning going and my drenched cover-up, it was freezing in the house, and I marched through the kitchenette and straight into the bathroom. I flipped the light on and peered at myself in the mirror, surveying the damage.

Thankfully, it was okay. My mascara wasn't running, and none of my eyeliner had relocated beneath my eyes.

My gaze dropped down to the soaked cover-up. Should I wring it out? Or maybe it made more sense to just change back into my regular clothes and steer clear of the pool. In hindsight, it'd been stupid to put on my bikini in the first place. I knew I was never getting in the pool.

I couldn't, because there'd be questions.

I sighed and pulled the cover-up over my head, then grabbed a towel from the stack on the sink. As I wiped at my damp skin, I peered at my reflection and the faint yellowing purple bruise by my hip. It'd been six days since Clay's rough hand had pinned me to the table, and I wore the memory of it still.

It turned me on just looking at it.

"Who left the light on in the bathroom?" a male voice grumbled to himself.

I was slow to react. I'd just finished turning to face the doorway when Greg stepped in and pulled up short at the sight of me.

"Oh," he said. "I didn't know you were in here."

His innocent gaze swept over me and came to an abrupt stop on my bruise. I shifted the wet fabric in my hands, holding it over my waist to hide the mark, and tried to act natural.

"I got splashed," I said like an idiot.

My clipped voice and quick move to cover up only made it worse, and Greg's handsome face turned serious as he nodded toward my hip. "What happened there?"

"Nothing." I dry-swallowed, buying myself time to come up with a plausible lie. "I caught the edge of an exam table at work."

He kept his tone even, non-accusatory. "And the backs of your legs?"

What?

I turned, realizing dimly he could see all of my back side through the mirror. The worst of the marks were hidden under my bikini bottom, but red-purple lines peeked out beneath and crisscrossed the top of the backs of my thighs.

Clay had instructed Travis to use the flogger last night, and the sweet sting of it had been heaven. I loved the beautiful patterns it'd left on me, but I hadn't realized they would show until I'd slipped into my swimsuit earlier this afternoon.

"Uh . . ." I racked my brain for an explanation.

Greg glanced out into the kitchenette, and when he didn't see anyone, he stepped all the way inside the bathroom and pulled the door closed behind him. He spoke in the low, soothing voice of a doctor. "Lilith, is everything okay?"

I tucked a lock of hair behind my ear, trying not to be embarrassed. "It's fine."

"Is someone hurting you?"

I exhaled and shook my head. "No, no. It's not like that."

"Cassidy said you're dating someone new. Did he do this?"

Dear God, I was going to have to come clean. Greg was a doctor, which meant he had a legal obligation to report suspected abuse. I hated having to tell him though, because Clay was so private, and it was extremely likely Greg was going to figure out who I was talking about. I didn't care who knew I was into the lifestyle, but I didn't want to 'out' Clay to one of our neighbors.

My face heated, but I lifted my chin and tried to look confident. "It was consensual."

"Consensual," he repeated.

"Yes."

"I see." His concern didn't fade. "You sure? No one's making you do anything you don't want to, right?"

I gave a tight smile. "I'm sure. Trust me, I like what we do."

He slowly relaxed a degree. "Okay." He'd probably seen a lot of shit during his residency, so there wasn't judgement in his eyes. Just the conditioned doctor response. "We don't know each other that well, but if you ever need someone to talk to, or start to feel unsafe with your partner . . . you can come to me. I'm here."

My chest was tight with awkwardness, but with warmth too. He was a good guy, and I was glad Cassidy was with him. Despite their age difference, and the messed-up situation with Preston, they made a great pair.

"Thanks, Greg."

He nodded, reached for the door handle, but didn't open it. "I hope he's taking good care of you, during and after."

Maybe I'd sat in the afternoon sun too long, because for the second time today, I spoke without thinking. "Don't worry, they are. One of them is a doctor."

TWENTY

After I'd changed out of my swimsuit, I went back outside and took a seat at the patio table beside Cassidy. Like me, she was drinking water in preparation for the main event tonight.

"You know," she said, "there's plenty of room on the party bus if you want to invite a friend." She pulled at the strands of her hair to tighten her dark ponytail. "Like, say—Dr. Eckhart."

Two girls in the pool squealed with laughter as Colin did a backflip off the diving board and splashed them with water. Nearly everyone here was paired up, or at least they all knew each other. There were inside jokes and conversations about past high school friends I didn't know, and while I was probably Cassidy's closest friend now, it was hard not to feel like an outsider.

She had Greg, and I didn't want to cling to her all night. I was outgoing, but I felt like Clay when I thought about the upcoming evening. Being around unfamiliar people was exhausting.

"Even if Travis is willing," I said, "I don't know how Clay would feel about that." His comment about being jealous ran through my mind.

She said it like I was being silly. "You could ask him."

I opened my mouth to explain it wasn't that simple, and

promptly shut it. She made an excellent point, and we needed to be better about communication. I picked up my phone and thumbed out a text.

Me: I'm going out for my friend's birthday tonight and I don't know most of the people going. Would you mind if I asked Travis to come so I'm not the odd one out?

I sent the message and tried not to hold my breath. Clay and I didn't date, but we hadn't talked about it with Travis. Clay had said he didn't want to stand in the way, and it seemed strange that he would be okay sharing me with another man, but not letting me hang out with one.

The three dots blinked on my screen, and then vanished.

My heart sank. He was struggling with how to respond. Had I just complicated things between us even more?

A new text message popped up on my screen. It was a group message with Clay and a number I didn't recognize.

Clay: I'm looping Travis in on this, hope that's okay. Lilith has something she wants to ask you.

I sat straighter in my chair, surprised and excited enough that Cassidy shot me a look.

"Everything okay?"

"Yeah," I said. If Clay had an issue with me going out with Travis, I doubted the first thing he would have done was give me Travis's number.

Me: Hey, Travis. It's last minute, but are you free

tonight? I'm going out for my friend's birthday, but I don't know most of the people going. Do you want to join me?

I didn't have to wait long for his response.

Travis: Hi. Sure, but I'm still at work. What time?

Me: The party bus is picking us up at 8. My friend's house is just down the street from Clay's.

Travis: Party bus?

Me: It's my friend's 21st birthday. Her boyfriend rented a bus so we can go bar hopping. So...everyone will be kinda young.

Clay: OMG. It's not too late to back out, Travis.

I laughed and pictured Clay as he read the conversation, probably glad for the first time he was down in Florida, because this evening surely sounded like hell to him.

Travis: LOL. It's fine, send me the address.

Travis stood with one hand on the railing and a bottle of beer in the other, and watched Cassidy as she plodded barefoot across the red inflatable mat. "So, the goal is to make her throw up?"

It was loud in the bar, but I heard him and laughed, making my phone shake as I was trying to shoot video. "She won't stay on long enough," I said. "I give her about four seconds."

The male employee at the center of the ring helped her climb up on top of the mechanical bull, and after a quick conversation, he walked to the control panel. People hooted and hollered words of encouragement for her all around the ring. Cassidy's cheeks were pink and her smile enormous as she lifted a hand into the air. It was meant to help keep her balance, but the bull wasn't even moving yet, and she already looked unsteady.

The tequila shots we'd done twenty minutes ago were hitting her. My friend was buzzing hard.

"Four seconds might be generous," Greg said, who stood on my other side against the railing.

To his credit, the guy operating the machine started nice and slow. The bull turned in a leisurely circle and undulated gently, allowing her to get used to the motion. She pumped her fist and beamed to the crowd watching her, acting like this was easy.

But then the bull abruptly changed directions and picked up speed. Cassidy's smile froze as she began to list to one side, and her free hand for balance joined her other one already clinging to the horn of the saddle.

She was rapidly losing the battle to stay up.

The machine swerved and changed directions again, slinging her off into a heap on the red cushion of air. Within seconds she was up on her feet, laughing uncontrollably while trying to fix the gaudy 'Birthday Girl' sash one of her other friends had presented to her at the first bar.

I'd tried to pretend this wasn't a date, but when Travis had parked his fancy SUV in my driveway, climbed out, and flashed a smile, I got the same weird butterflies in my stomach I'd had my first night with Clay.

So, yeah. This was totally a date, which meant it was our *first* date.

Travis looked great too. His fitted, short sleeve button-down shirt was white with navy dots on it, and he'd paired it with dark jeans. His clothes flaunted what great shape he was in, and after we'd walked down the road to Greg's house and boarded the bus, one of the girls in the back had whisper-shouted appreciatively to a friend, "Who's that guy?"

While Cassidy walked toward the exit of the ring, Colin materialized out of nowhere, filling the empty spot at the rail beside Travis. "So," he said to the man that was quite a bit older than he was, "you must be one of Lilith's boyfriends."

He'd said it teasingly, but Travis's expression went blank and my brain stopped working. "Uh . . ." I started.

Colin laughed, not knowing his joke wasn't actually a joke. "She told me she had two boyfriends earlier when we were talking, so no room for me." He continued his teasing tone. "Hope the other guy's not news to you."

Travis tilted his head as if saying *huh, interesting*.

Perhaps he thought since I'd volunteered this info so freely, he was willing to do the same, and his matter-of-fact tone reflected it. "No, he's not."

Colin's smile hung with the realization the man might not be kidding, and what that meant began to dawn in him. Genuine interest filled his expression. "Really?"

Greg had one ear in our conversation, and when he sensed the turn coming, he must have wanted to get ahead of it. "Hey, Colin. Who should we get to go for a ride next? Let's ask the birthday girl."

He practically dragged the kid away, thankfully leaving Travis and me alone to talk.

"It just came out when I was talking to him," I said. "I hope that's okay."

"Calling me your boyfriend?" Travis lifted his beer to his lips, somewhat concealing his smile before taking a sip. "It's okay with me." He leaned his forearms on the rail and turned over his shoulder to give me a good look at his handsome face. "I'm not interested in seeing other people. You—and Clay too, I guess—are plenty."

My breath caught. "Is it weird for you? Being with me while I'm also with him?"

"I didn't think I'd like it. I mean, I'm not supposed to, right? Guys aren't really known for sharing." The sound of the loud bar faded as I focused on him. "But I don't mind it, Lilith, especially now that the rules are gone. It's like you said. I really like what we have."

"Why?" I had my reasons, but I was desperate to know his.

His gaze left mine as he searched how to put it into words. "Clay and I both can give you pleasure, but we do it in different ways. He does things you need, things I don't know if I could do—at least not on my own yet." His focus returned to me. "And I get how pain can be a release. Don't get me wrong, I enjoy what we do. I love the power exchange when we're in a scene, but I'm still dealing with my hang-ups when it comes to inflicting pain. Even when it's clearly what you want." He adjusted so he stood tall, took another swig of his beer, and his expression clouded over. "I struggle whenever I see suffering."

I exhaled, feeling ten pounds lighter. It felt so good to talk about it and understand. We spent our whole lives believing in black and white that causing other people pain was bad. Travis still needed to get comfortable in this new gray area, where I liked the pain he caused.

And I understood the struggle with suffering. Knowing I could help ease the discomfort in an animal, when they couldn't speak for themselves, was the most rewarding part of my job.

"Is that why you became a vet?" I asked.

"It's a big part of it, yeah." He softened. "You know how when you're a kid, you say what you want to be when you grow up? Like, I'm gonna be a fireman, or a football player . . . or a vet." He shot me a lopsided smile. "I just never grew out of it." He absentmindedly picked at the label on his beer. "And also, my parents were super anti-pet."

"Oh, my God, mine too. That's how I ended up jointly owning a cat with Clay."

He hesitated. "What?"

"Noir?" That only confused him further. "The tuxedo cat at Clay's. She's both of ours."

I explained the story to him as we watched Cassidy's

friends fall off the mechanical bull one by one. Since I'd just told him how Clay and I had met, I wondered about him.

"Can I ask you something?" I swirled the ice in my empty glass. "Clay said he 'trained' you. What was that like?"

When Travis's eyebrows pulled together, I wondered if I'd overstepped, so I waived a hand like I could brush my prying question away.

"You don't have to answer," I said quickly. "Clay's a private guy, not the most forthcoming, and I'm—"

"He is private, but there's a reason for that."

"Yeah." I dropped my voice low. "He, uh, told me about her."

Surprise glanced through him. "That's good, then. I'm glad. He's never talked about it with me, but I know the situation was really hard on him."

"Wait." Curiosity ate at me. "If he's never talked about it, how do you know?"

"Because I was there the night he had her removed from the club." His shoulders lifted with a deep breath. "She didn't go quietly, either. She screamed and caused a huge scene, saying all this personal shit about him like his name, where he lived, where he worked. It was bad."

"Oh, my God." That had to be one of Clay's nightmares fully realized. And to have it done by someone he'd cared about? Awful.

"I didn't know him back then, but I'd been right there when it all went down. I saw how upset he was and, even though he was a stranger, I wanted to make sure he was . . . I don't know. Okay." Because Travis saw Clay was suffering and he couldn't tolerate it. He had to help. "So, I bought him a drink and we got to talking, and when he found out it was my first time at Eros, he was focused on that. I think he was happy for the distraction, and I was happy to get some advice."

"Advice?"

"On getting into the lifestyle. I'd been interested in it for a while, but I didn't know where to start." He said it straightforward. "I didn't have friends I was comfortable talking about it with either."

"So, he offered to take you under his wing and train you?"

"No, not at first. For a while, he was just someone to talk to. We mostly texted. After the night his partner got banned, he was pretty cautious."

"Understandable," I said.

"Yeah. After a few months of that, we started coordinating the nights we'd be at the club. If I found a scene partner who was up for it, he'd usually watch, and then we'd discuss afterward."

I pressed my lips together, trying not to smile. "Like, he'd critique the scene?"

Travis's lopsided smile was so fucking sexy, I had to grip the rail to stay upright. "He gave me feedback, yeah." His tone was warm. "I learned a lot from him, and he liked doing it, so when he offered to show me more, it was an easy yes."

My pulse skipped faster, intrigued. "Hmm," I purred. "Tell me about this 'more.'"

He chuckled. "If I'm going to use something in a scene—like, say a flogger," he paused to give time for the memory of last night's scene to burn through my mind, "I need to understand the flogger completely. What kind of sensation the ends of the tails create versus the middle. How much force to use and where on the body to strike to create different layers. I have to know what it feels like, so I can give my partner the right sensations at the right pace."

Holy shit.

My breathing went erratic as I figured out what he was saying. To understand how to use the flogger, he'd had to experience it being used on himself. "You scened with Clay."

He could see how hot the idea made me because he smiled and shook his head. "Don't get all excited. It was instructional. I like pleasure, not pain, plus I'm not submissive. I wasn't sure at the time, thinking maybe I was a switch, but that first session cleared it right up for me."

Meaning he wasn't interested in switching roles between being a scene top and bottom. He was completely dominant.

I was dying inside at picturing Travis under Clay's command. Had he been restrained while Clay demonstrated all the sensations the different implements could give? The bite of the clamps? The sting of the paddle?

The pure fire of the cane?

I was so turned on, it was uncomfortable, but I pretended I wasn't affected. "How many sessions have you done?"

"Two. After the second one, he started to pull away." His gaze darted away for a moment, then returned to me. "Maybe he felt like he'd shown me as much as he could, but then I got a call from him out of the blue." He moved subtly closer. "He told me to go to the club that night because he'd be there, and he was bringing someone he wanted me to meet."

I sucked in a breath at the memory.

But his reaction wasn't the same as mine because his expression twisted with displeasure. "He said I wasn't allowed to speak to you until he'd introduced us, which if you remember . . ."

"He didn't."

"Nope. It's why I was pissed when the scene was over and he made me leave. He didn't give me any feedback that night either. I didn't know what to think. For the three of us to have this amazing experience together, and then to have him act like it had no chance of happening again . . . I was so confused. He wouldn't even tell me your name."

"Because he's so private?" I guessed.

"Yeah, I thought it was a trust issue." His mood suddenly lightened. "But a week later he called, apologized, and explained the situation. You were a new submissive, I was a new dom looking for experience, and he'd been enjoying guiding me. We could all get something from this arrangement he was suggesting." He smiled. "Once again, it was an easy yes."

I knew I shouldn't say it, because I liked him, and it would be better if I didn't like him. It felt as if there were a time limit on our relationship and admitting my feelings would be pushing the start button on the clock. But it was unavoidable. "I'm glad you said yes."

He leaned close, tilting his head down so his mouth hovered right over mine. "Me too."

Our kiss wasn't long, but it contained so much passion, I was buzzing in its aftermath. He was too, although his was literal. I had a hand on his hip and felt the phone vibrate in his pocket.

He checked the email and visibly brightened.

"Good news?" I asked.

"Yeah. One of the trainers giving me an update on a ring-tailed lemur. Jasmina's twenty-two, which means she's nearing the end of her life, and we've been battling this lingering infection. It's been resistant to everything I've tried so far." He pocketed his phone and looked relaxed. "But the new medication seems to be working. She ate all of her food and has been more active today."

"Oh, that is good."

He smiled like he was recalling a memory. "She's a handful. Lemurs are female-dominant and Jasmina's the matriarch of the troop, so I'm sure she's anxious to get back on exhibit and keep everyone in line."

"How long do lemurs usually live?"

"In captivity? Between twenty to twenty-five years. She's a special girl, but I don't know how much longer she'll have a good quality of life. It's been hard watching her struggle with this stubborn infection."

"I get the feeling," I said softly, "you're especially close with her."

His eyes read *guilty as charged.* "Jasmina was my first patient when I took up my residency at the zoo, and you know what they say. You always remember your first."

God, the way he looked at me. I smiled and tucked a lock of hair behind my ear, trying not to think about how we were each other's firsts in our unconventional relationship.

"So, anyway," he continued, "I know it's a fight I'm

eventually going to lose, but I'm going to keep trying anyway."

He held my gaze for a long moment and my heart slowed to a stop. Was he talking about Jasmina . . . or me?

"Lilith!" Cassidy came at me so fast, she nearly ran into me. Her eyes were glassy and full of laughter. "You're next."

"For what?"

She flung a finger toward the center of the ring and the empty saddle that waited.

Travis chuckled, but I shook my head. No matter how good of balance I thought I possessed, I had zero desire to flop down on the mat in front of a bar full of strangers. Which was kind of hilarious when I thought about it. I'd had no issue letting people watch as Travis fucked me at Eros.

But that was different. People hadn't been rooting to see me fail like they would here.

"I'm going to pass," I said.

But she didn't want to take no for an answer. Her warm hand wrapped around my wrist, but when she tugged me toward the entrance, I stayed rooted to the ground.

Travis nodded and a wide, unhelpful grin smeared across his face. "I think you should do it."

"You first," I shot back at him.

Greg appeared at Cassidy's side, handing her a glass of what looked like ice water. "Preston's getting ready to go next."

"Oh, this I gotta see," I said, turning my attention back to the ring.

My phone vibrated with a text message. It was from Travis, sent to our group chat with Clay, and was a photo he must have snapped moments ago of the empty mechanical bull.

Travis: Do you want to see Lilith ride this?

"Don't include him on your peer pressure," I teased.

Clay: I'd rather watch her riding something else. Like your dick.

I lifted my gaze from the screen, pretending to be shocked and scandalized.

"That's *naughty*," I whispered.

Travis grinned as he thumbed out his reply.

Travis: I can make that happen.

TWENTY-ONE

Our group chat was active. The week after my date with Travis, private DMs from a married, conservative politician leaked online, and his atrocious and graphic texts to his mistress gave us a lot to talk about. I'd started it off by jokingly asking why I didn't get horny texts riddled with typos from either of my men.

Me: It's like you don't even care about me.

That set off a slew of filthy texts, and I wondered if each man were trying to outdo the other. The conversation was scorching, and it was a miracle it didn't melt my phone.

As the weeks ticked by, we settled into a comfortable pattern.

Weeknight sessions were carried out by Travis and usually planned by Clay, but not always. The scenes were more of a partnership than they'd been before, and I suspected the same was true of the planning sessions the men had privately. The weekends when Clay was home, things were flip-flopped. Sometimes Travis watched Clay and me on his phone and other times he'd sit over by the workbench, quietly observing.

The summer ended and Cassidy returned to school. A junior now in college, she was so busy, we mostly talked through series of sporadic texts. It gave me less opportunity to tell my friend how I was feeling or about the worry that was growing in my stomach.

Every night I spent with Clay, or Travis, or both of them, felt one step closer to the cliff I knew was coming. It was twice as risky as anything I'd had before. What if one of them fell in love with me? Would they have to exit the relationship, or would the whole thing be over? It was the last thing I wanted.

Rather than be an adult and talk about my feelings like I'd promised Clay I would, I avoided it. Everything was going so great now. I rationalized my worry away, forcing it to a back corner of my mind by telling myself I'd figure out how to cross that bridge whenever I came to it.

The three of us talked every day through the group chat.

It wasn't always a recap of our scenes. It was filled with all sorts of topics, like Travis's story about the crazy lady who kept bringing live lobsters to the zoo. She'd bought them from a tank at the market to 'rescue them' and said the zoo needed to find a way to care for them.

There was also Clay's never-ending quest to find the best pizza in Jacksonville, and my marathon photo viewing session with my folks when they returned from Machu Pichu.

During the last week of September, I came down with a cold, so I had to take a raincheck on my session with the men that evening. Except when I went over to do my nightly check on Noir, Travis showed up with takeout and a movie—under the direction of Clay, he'd said. Our partner in Florida streamed the same movie to his computer as we FaceTimed with him so we could watch it together. I snuggled under a blanket with Noir on my lap, Travis at my side, and Clay on the screen of my phone.

It was wonderful. The men seemed just as satisfied hanging out and spending time together with me as they were when we went down into the basement.

How had this happened?

I didn't break under the impact of a crop or paddle when either of my partners wielded one. But this caring, attentive gesture? It threatened to break me completely. I refused to acknowledge how they made me feel. I had no choice but to stave off my emotions. The longer I held them off, the more time I could have with these men who seemed perfectly attuned to what I desired.

To what I needed.

The next weekend Clay was home, he sent me a text Saturday morning.

Clay: I have dinner reservations for us tonight. 6pm, meet at my place.

I paused. He hadn't sent the message to the group text—it was just to me. Was this a date? And if so . . . what about Travis? Didn't we need to tell him?

It took me forever to pick out what to wear. In the end, I went with a black crossover blouse, a pair of super skinny jeans, and nude pumps. At a quarter to six, I couldn't wait any longer to see him. I scurried down the stone path to the gate, and then strolled across my driveway, heading for Clay's front door.

I rang the doorbell, which was kind of funny since I'd been letting myself into his house for months, but it seemed weird to barge in without warning.

"Hi," he said after he pulled the door open and gestured for me to come in.

He took me in from head to toe and clearly liked what he saw, and it was the same for me. He was dressed nicer than normal, wearing a lightweight sweater and slacks, rather than jeans and a t-shirt.

"Hi." I surprised him by dropping a kiss on his cheek, fast enough I could pretend this was merely friendly and not because I was desperate to kiss him. "Am I underdressed?"

"No, you're good." He shut the door behind me, but kept his hand on the doorknob, suddenly distracted with a thought. "I have something for you though."

"Yeah?" I followed him deeper into the house.

"Hold on, let me get it." He disappeared into his bedroom while I remained in the living room. The television was on, and a bright orange octopus swam across the screen, followed by a woman telling the camera how smart the species was.

When he reemerged, I gave him a dubious smile. "You're watching Animal Planet?"

His gaze flew to the television where the docuseries about the Georgia Aquarium was currently playing, and . . . was he embarrassed? His tone verged on defensive. "I turned it on for Noir."

If that were true, it was super cute, but Clay was flustered. It told me something else was going on. "Is she interested in it?" I looked around for our black and white cat but didn't find her. "Where is she?"

He stood frozen for a single breath, and then gave up. "Okay, I turned it on for me." He rolled his shoulders back and met my gaze head-on. "You and Travis have a lot in common. It's kind of dumb, but I thought maybe I could keep up."

Oh, wow. There were those butterflies again, fluttering in my stomach and making me weak with desire. "It's not dumb."

No, it was *romantic*. He wanted to be into what we were into.

He tried to shift my focus away and held out the box he'd retrieved. It was medium-sized, square, and wrapped in silver paper, complete with a matching silver satin bow.

I mentally noted it was October, and my birthday wasn't for several more months. "Did you get me a present?"

He shrugged. "They offered to gift wrap it."

I took the box, utterly confused. "What's this for?"

"Because you do nice things for me. I wanted to return the favor."

Did he mean how I helped out with his house while he was away? "Bringing in your mail is no big deal. I'm happy to do it."

He was obviously waiting on me to open it, and I was more than a little curious about what was inside, so I sat on the couch and got to work. The wrapping paper was thick, which should have been my first hint this was more than a polite 'thank you' gift.

I peeled back the paper and my hands stilled when the recognizable logo branded across the top of the box came into view. I said it the same way I'd say, *you didn't*. "Clay."

He waited like he was on pins and needles. "Open it."

I almost didn't want to. Like our relationship, I feared

I'd fall in love with something I wouldn't be able to keep, but my hands had a mind of their own. I lifted the lid and gasped. The pair of red leopard print heels were gorgeous and sexy, complete with black soles and the designer name printed in gold.

"Do you like them?"

Of course I liked them. They retailed in the high three figures. "They're beautiful." I looked at the printing inside the heel. "And they're my size."

"I've taken your shoes off a few times." His smile was devious. "I guess you were too distracted to notice I looked at the size. Try them on."

Was he crazy? "I can't."

His confident look hung awkwardly. "Why not?"

"Because if I put them on, they might not ever come off and I can't accept these."

He made a noise like I was talking nonsense and sat beside me, plucking one of the shoes out of the box in my lap.

"Yes, you can, Lilith. I like making you happy, and seeing you wear these will make me happy." He pulled the stuffing out of the toe of the shoe and unfastened the tiny buckle at the ankle strap. "If it helps, I got a nice bonus from my firm for all the travel I've had to do on this project."

"Clay," I repeated in the same tone from before.

His voice deepened and filled with sex. "Think about how good you'll look in these and nothing else."

Damn him. I didn't put up a fight as he moved off the couch and down on a knee to take off the pumps I was wearing. I sat as Cinderella while he slipped on the shoe and evaluated how it looked. “Does it fit?”

“Yes,” I whispered.

“Good.”

He looked so pleased, and I knew I was doomed. The shoes were too much. Way, *way* too much and yet I knew I wasn’t going to refuse them. When he had the other one on and fastened around my ankle, he stood and pulled me up with him.

The sexy heels fit perfectly, and as I looked down at them, I went dizzy with emotions, so I was grateful when his hands closed on my waist to steady me.

“Will you wear them tonight to dinner?”

“For our date?”

He hadn’t expected that response, and his tone was cautious. “Do you want it to be a date?”

My heart rose in my chest, making it difficult to breathe, but I was tired of pretending my feelings didn’t exist. “Yes,” I admitted. “I know you said you don’t date, but . . . Is that okay? This feels like a date and I’m excited about that.”

His mouth fell open and he looked like he had no idea what to say.

In his silence, I shifted my weight on my feet. “We need to tell Travis though. Just so he’s aware.”

I didn’t understand the mix of emotions that played out on his face. Was he happy about what I’d said? Or terrified? His hands abandoned my waist as he stepped back and adjusted his glasses. “There’s no need to tell him. Travis is meeting us at the restaurant.”

“Oh.” All the air went out of my lungs. If we were having

dinner together, why hadn't we discussed it in the group chat? My gaze left him and floated over to the lid of the shoebox.

Okay, well, that made sense. He hadn't included Travis because Clay wanted to give me this gift in private. It probably would have made the other man uncomfortable, or worse. It might make Travis feel like he needed to make a similar gesture, and I hoped to avoid that. I didn't want expensive gifts like I was some kind of kept woman.

Clay put his hands in his pockets, trying to act casual, but then took them out. He looked nervous, and his voice was uneven. "Do you want me to cancel with him? Because I can, it's just—"

"No, it's fine." I pressed out a smile that was probably too bright to cover my awkwardness. Plus, it *was* fine. Better than fine—it was great. It'd be the first time the three of us would go out, and I could pretend it was a date for all of us. "Maybe some other time, you and I could—"

"Yes."

My heart skipped at his sure, confident word.

He stared at me, wordlessly saying he wanted what I wanted, and my knees softened when he surged forward. His mouth was on me the same instant his hands were on my body, and it happened so quickly, I gasped.

His kiss. Oh, my God, his *fucking* kiss.

It was the kind they wrote love songs about. The one at the end of a movie when the lovers finally got together. His lips pressed to mine like he would have died if we'd been separated a moment longer, and I sank into him. His kiss was hungry and consuming and powerful.

I was sure he'd planned to kiss me after giving his gift. It'd probably been designed to happen after I'd thanked him, which I'd gotten sidetracked from and hadn't actually done yet. But *this* kiss? No way he'd planned it.

It felt unleashed. Wild. Passion poured from him like wine spilling from a bottle that'd been knocked over.

He tilted his head, adjusting the angle to deepen the kiss, and his tongue swept in my mouth. I'd never moaned from a kiss before. It was usually just lips meeting lips, but this was distinctly different. It was a statement.

A declaration.

I pictured us in my mind. His arms were cased around my back, and I had fistfuls of his sweater in my hands during the onslaught of his fiery kiss. I was trembling and he was struggling to catch his breath, and if it didn't end soon, I worried we might collapse under the gravity of it.

But, thankfully, he slowed and ended the kiss.

My voice was so hushed, it was barely audible. "What was that?"

His eyes were hazy as he stared at my mouth. "That was . . . unexpected." He blinked his fog away and his gaze sharpened. "It was something I've been wanting to do all week."

His expression shuttered like he'd said too much, and he searched wildly for something to deflect until his gaze landed on the pair of shoes I'd been wearing when I arrived. He scooped them up, put them in the box, and handed it to me.

"We should get going," he said. "I don't want to be late and make Travis worry."

"Right." I hugged the box to my chest, hoping it would cover my rapidly beating heart. I still hadn't recovered from his kiss and wasn't sure if I ever would. "Thank you for the shoes," I said. "I love them."

His smile reached into his eyes, lighting up his face. "You're welcome."

The restaurant had a trendy pub feel, full of distressed, warm wood and exposed brick. Travis had been early and was waiting by the host stand when we arrived, and the three of us were seated at a square table in the center of the dining room.

It felt so fucking good to be here, right in the middle between the two men I cared about, and who demanded all my attention, even when they weren't around. Was it the same for them as it was for me?

Did they like this unusual 'date' as much as I did?

I tried to tamp down my excitement. If this evening went well, perhaps I could convince them we should do it again.

The waitress appeared, wearing a shirt with the sleeves rolled to the elbow and a necktie that was tucked into her white waist apron. "Should I get your drink orders started?" She glanced at the place setting and empty chair across from me. "Or are we waiting for a fourth guest?"

"It's just the three of us," Clay said.

For a moment, I let my fantasies run away with me. Maybe this was how it could be.

Just the three of us.

After she'd taken our orders and menus, the waitress moved on, leaving us to stare at each other anxiously. No one was sure who should speak first, but Clay set his arms on the table, leaned forward, and took in a long, preparing breath.

"My project's moving into phase three at the end of next week."

I tensed, not understanding what that meant, but he'd delivered his statement with such seriousness, it felt like he'd dropped an anvil on us.

Travis had my same confusion, but also suspicion, because his eyes narrowed. "Which means what?"

"My part's over. I'll be back in Nashville for good next weekend."

My happiness at having Clay home full time was short-lived, and immediately trumped by anxiety. With him home, there'd be no need for a stand-in after next week. Pieces began to fall into place, moving too fast for my heart to keep up.

The clock hanging over us was suddenly out of time.

TWENTY-TWO

I'm not ready. That was the thought blaring through my mind as I sat at the table, stunned.

"It's why I wanted to get together tonight." Clay's tone was measured, but gentle. "We need to talk about our arrangement, and how it should end."

It cut through me as a knife that was so sharp, I couldn't do anything but sit there and let it slice me in two.

Travis, however, was still able to speak, and his tone was full of dread. "You want it to end?"

His gaze slid over to me, needing to confirm if I felt the same, but I was just as stunned as he was by this. Hell, twenty seconds ago, I'd had a head full of *what-ifs*, dreaming about a future for the three of us.

Now that I'd caught a glimpse, it was all I wanted. Fuck. How could I choose between these men when I needed them both?

Clay's expression was pained. "I was upfront with you about everything. When I asked you to step in, you knew it was temporary."

"Yeah, you made that clear," Travis said, "but shit has changed since then."

"Yes, just like I warned you. I told you this could happen."

Oh, God. There was an invisible band around my chest,

and every word was cinching it tighter. At that moment, the waitress reappeared with a tray of our drinks in hand. She picked up on the tension at the table and chose to silently dole out the cocktails while the two men stared intensely at each other.

"Can I get you anything else?" she said.

My voice was a ghost. "No, thank you."

She hurried away, which just ratcheted up my anxiety.

"Did you ask me to come here," Travis's tone was equal parts hurt and disbelief, "because you thought it would keep me from making a scene?"

I flashed back to his story about the night Clay had his partner removed from the club. It made sense he'd be gun shy, but I was also hurt on Travis's behalf, and upset with how we'd been ambushed.

Clay's hand on the table curled into a fist, but it wasn't in anger. He realized this wasn't going well and struggled to find the right words. "No, I asked you because I wanted us to talk. You're . . ." He sighed. "Before Lilith, you were my best friend, Travis. And now—after Lilith—you've become something more."

His expression was so stunningly beautiful, it was heartbreaking, and Travis froze in place. It was a statement that hadn't been said out loud before, and its power wasn't lost on Travis.

The rest of the restaurant ceased to exist. There was a force pulling Travis and me toward Clay. An inescapable gravity.

"I don't know what it is," he said, "or how to label what

we are to each other, but I'm not blind. I see what's happening between you two and I'm torn. I don't want to stand in the way, but I don't want to be left behind either."

"No one's leaving you behind," I said.

Clay turned his attention toward me, and it looked like he wanted to believe what I'd said, but the skeptical side of him wouldn't allow it. "Did I fuck this up? I tried to give you what you needed, and I brought him in when I couldn't. Tell me that wasn't wrong and I'm not going to lose you both as a result."

My jaw hit the table as I endured the rollercoaster that was Clay tonight.

"Just wait a minute. I'm not going anywhere." Travis sat straighter in his seat. "I don't think she is, either. Look, I know this isn't what you planned, but we can—"

He flinched as if someone had poked him, and his gaze dropped to his phone which must have vibrated. Whomever was calling him, it caused concern.

"I'm sorry. I have to take this." He tapped the screen and lifted the phone to his ear. "This is Dr. Eckhart."

I was reeling from what Clay had said, and what he *really* meant. With him returning home, he thought I was going to have to choose between the men.

And he was sure he was going to lose.

The urge to reassure and connect with him was so strong, I reached across the table and covered his hand with mine. "It wasn't wrong, and I'm not going anywhere."

Meanwhile, Travis stared at his untouched drink and listened somberly to the person on the other end. "Yeah, I agree with Dr. Khaan. It's time."

"Oh, no," I whispered. He had that same resigned and professional tone I'd heard countless times at the clinic, the one the doctors used when they'd exhausted every option.

Clay kept his voice hushed to not disturb Travis. "What's wrong?"

"They're putting an animal down."

"I appreciate the call," Travis said. "Is she comfortable?" He nodded as he listened, then pulled the phone away for a moment to check the time on the screen. "I can be there in thirty minutes if Khaan thinks it can wait that long." He continued to nod. "Okay, thanks. I'm on my way."

He hung up, and it was as if he just realized where he was. He couldn't have looked more conflicted if he'd tried.

"Jasmina?" I asked, suspecting the answer. He'd mentioned a few days ago the lemur wasn't interested in food and had withdrawn from the rest of her troop.

Sadness filled his eyes. "Yeah."

"I'm so sorry."

It happened so naturally, it wasn't until his gaze dropped to the table I realized what I'd done. My hand rested on his, which meant I was now holding hands with both men.

Neither pulled away. Maybe they felt the connection to each other as it flowed through me.

"I'm not on-call," Travis said, "but I'd like to be there to say goodbye. So, unfortunately, I have to go."

"Is there anything we can do to help?" Clay asked.

Travis considered it. He looked like he was about to say something, but then he made a face, shaking the thought away.

"Tell us," I prompted.

His gaze flicked to Clay. "Weekends are usually yours with Lilith, but after I'm done, I was wondering if you'd . . ."

My breath caught. Clay had *just* confessed he felt like he was being left behind, and now Travis was asking if he'd be willing to give up his time with me this evening. None of this was in his plans, and he hated when they were changed on him.

But he stared across the table at his best friend and evaluated what was more important, and the dominant in him couldn't ignore what was necessary. This was something Travis needed, and Clay would put that over his own desires.

"Of course," he said. "If Lilith is okay being with you tonight instead of me, I am too."

Emotions came on powerfully strong, so I nodded and squeezed their hands, wishing I could tell them both how I felt at the same moment, but we didn't have time. Travis needed to go, and I wasn't going to make him stay while the animal he'd bonded with was suffering.

Yet, he didn't get up from his seat.

His gaze was fixated on how my hand was linked with Clay's, and his chest lifted with a slow breath. "What if that's not what I'm asking?" His gaze drifted up, tracing the line of Clay's body, all the way until he met his eyes. "What if I don't want tonight to be about me and her, or you and her," he paused, "but us?"

My heart lurched.

The men had been scene partners twice, but that had happened before me. Since then, both had respected the other's role when observing. They didn't interact or interfere with who was in charge. The closest they'd come was our first night together in the club—with the day Clay had pressed his hand on Travis's chest coming in as a distant second.

Clay's expression was guarded, so I couldn't tell if he loved or hated the idea, but he hadn't moved. He hadn't pulled his hand away from me. "Together?"

Travis's voice was tight. "Yes."

Light glinted off Clay's lenses as he turned his attention toward me and searched my expression. Could he see how badly I wanted this? That maybe I needed it as much as Travis did? He must have, because his focus moved on to the other man.

His voice wasn't loud, but it rang through my body. "All right."

We didn't talk about Travis during dinner, nor did we on the drive back to our neighborhood. After Travis left the restaurant, Clay canceled his entrée with the kitchen, and then Clay proceeded to give me the date I'd been expecting when I'd come over to his house earlier this evening.

We talked about his project ending and the next trip my parents were planning, still undecided if they'd do Europe or Australia. It led the conversation to what traveling we'd done, and from there . . . his family.

His sister was married with two kids and lived on the

west coast because she worked for a big tech company. His parents moved to Florida after retiring, so he only saw them at the holidays. He was alone here in Nashville, but didn't struggle much with loneliness.

He shared personal things with ease now, and I soaked the information up. How he'd toyed with becoming a full-time carpenter after high school, but a teacher had pushed him to try drafting, and that was it. He loved precision and details and building, plus he was 'decent at math.'

Conversation flowed freely while we pretended our thoughts weren't drifting to what would happen this evening. If Clay were drafting a plan in his head, I couldn't tell, but perhaps he was excellent at multitasking.

Anticipation wound tightly around my body as we returned to his house. Clay was pouring us each a glass of white wine when we received the text message.

Travis: I'm finished. Where are you guys?

Clay: My place. Come over.

His line of text was casual, but it could have just as easily been an order and steam flooded every inch of my body, from my fingertips down to my toes nestled inside the beautiful shoes Clay had given me.

The kitchen renovation was nearly complete, so I pressed my hands to the quartz countertop to try to cool down at least some part of me. It was possible I'd burst into flames when Travis got here, and I frantically looked for something to distract.

"Did you decide on a backsplash?" I nodded to the two samples still taped to the wall.

He stood beside me as we drank our wine and studied the options. "Not yet. Do you have a preference?"

"I don't know if I can pick one. I like them both equally." It wasn't until the statement was out that I heard how it sounded. It could apply to a much larger decision than the decorative bits of ceramic and glass. "I mean, they both look good."

"Yeah. They're both *attractive*," he conceded. "But you don't think one is better looking than the other?"

"No, I honestly don't." I stared at the tiles, pretending I was talking about backsplashes and not my partners. "They're attractive to me in different ways."

He stared at the samples, which were similar, and both cast in varying shades of gray. "I get that." His voice was off. "Well, I can't have both. That's just . . . not how it's done."

"I don't know. Some people do it." My heart was hurrying along. "Maybe it'd create something really unique and amazing."

"It sounds like a lot of work."

I nodded. "I don't think it'd be easy, but it could be worth it."

He picked up his wine glass, took a long sip, and stared at the wall like he wished the backsplash were already installed. "A decision doesn't have to be made tonight," he said. "Let's not talk about tiles anymore."

It wasn't tense between Clay and me after that, but the mood had taken a hit, and conversation was stilted until the doorbell chimed. Clay set his wine glass down on the table beside the couch and moved to the entryway, while I followed behind. When he opened the door, the other man came in and scoured the room until his gaze landed on me, and his shoulders relaxed. As if the sight of me had a calming effect.

"How did it go?" The band was back around my chest, tight with worry, and I squeezed the wineglass in my hand.

His eyes had a hint of sadness, but they were clear. "It was good. Peaceful."

"Good," I said.

The three of us fell into awkward silence for a moment, but Clay rescued us. He motioned that we should move into the living room.

"Did you want something to eat?" he asked Travis. "You had to skip dinner."

"No, thanks. I grabbed something quick after I left the zoo."

"Wine?"

"Sure."

Clay left us, his footsteps growing quieter as he disappeared into the kitchen. Travis held my gaze as he steadily approached, moving in like nothing else existed. It was so intense, I began to retreat, only to bump up against the back of the couch near the center of the room.

He took the glass of wine from my hand, deposited it on the side table next to Clay's, and then cradled my face in his palms. It was so he could hold me still while he leaned down and claimed my mouth with his. I went rigid under his kiss. Not because I didn't want it, but because I could hear the other man in the kitchen as he opened a cabinet and retrieved a wine glass.

But I was pliable in Travis's hands, and even though I didn't know if this was allowed or respectful, I began to soften. His slow, sensual kiss was less about romance and more about seduction. It was dangerous.

Which also made it exciting.

Clay's footsteps grew louder as he approached. There came a soft, surprised intake of breath from him as he discovered what we were doing, but Travis took his time ending the kiss. It made my head spin.

Wait a minute.

Was this . . . a pissing contest?

Anger began to swell in the pit of my stomach. In the right scene, I liked how the men used me. There was a certain kind of enjoyment in being treated like an object, or a toy to bring my partner satisfaction. But we weren't in a scene right now, and—

Travis took the glass of wine that was meant for him from Clay, gave me a hard look, and said it in a dominating voice that would have made any submissive weak. "Now, kiss him."

The muscles low in my belly clenched. Travis didn't often give me orders, and when he did, they'd always come from the other man. But this command was undeniably his, and he stepped to the side to give me room to follow it.

Electricity swirled, charging the air in the room as I took the two steps toward Clay. He wasn't exactly smiling with his mouth, but it lurked in his eyes. He liked our partner's order just as much as I did and looked forward to how I would carry it out.

He tasted like the wine we'd been drinking.

I initiated the kiss, but the second our lips touched, he took over. It wasn't quite as earth-shattering as the one he'd given me earlier today, but this wasn't in his script either, so it was untamed and raw. His palm slid down my back and clenched a handful of my ass, and it drove me deeper into his kiss.

When it was over, I pulled back just enough to turn my head and glance at Travis for approval. He sipped his wine like he was savoring both it and the way Clay had kissed me. Goosebumps shattered across my skin.

The realization hit me then. Travis's kiss hadn't been competitive or territorial—it'd been a test. A hurdle to overcome and help keep jealousy at bay. It meant there was trust even when we weren't in sight. It demonstrated Travis wasn't going to do anything with me he wouldn't be comfortable with Clay also doing.

Travis said it like he was asking me to do something ordinary, and not an action guaranteed to stoke the fire between the three of us. "Again."

I turned my focus back to Clay, but he didn't wait for me to instigate this time. He crushed his mouth to mine, and slid his tongue past my lips, possessing me. His deep kiss was erotic, and the way his tongue moved reminded me of how good he was at using it other places too.

The pleasure of it was wonderful and disorienting.

So, I didn't realize Travis had set his wine down until I heard the *clink* of the glass against the wooden tabletop. He moved in behind me, pressing the length of his body against mine, his chest flattened to my back.

Clay didn't back down. If anything, the proximity of the other man only made him kiss me harder. Fingertips brushed over my neck, gathering my hair, and pushing it out of his way, so Travis could tilt his head down and set his warm, damp mouth on the sensitive spot just below my ear.

I shivered.

Holy God, it was *insane* to have both men kissing me at the same time. When I tore my mouth away from Clay's to gasp for air, he simply moved, trailing his lips over my cheekbone and down to the other side of my neck.

I was trapped between them, one arm around Clay's waist and the other curled back so I could grip Travis's hair while they kissed, and sucked, and softly nipped at me. There was literally nowhere else in the world I wanted to be. I could die a happy woman right here, right now.

They could hear how hard I was breathing, but did they feel my heart as it roared? I was lightheaded and clung to both of them, worried I might fall and take us all down.

Travis tugged at the neck of my shirt, pulling it down to expose my shoulder and his mouth followed behind, feasting on my newly exposed skin. "Let's get you naked."

"Yes," I panted. "Let's."

While Travis tried to get in my shirt from the top, Clay's attack was from the bottom. He slid a hand up under the hem and cupped one of my bra-covered breasts. "Should we go downstairs first?"

Travis's mouth slowed. "I was thinking a bed might be

better." He put a hand on my hip and ground his growing erection against my ass. "Wouldn't you like that, Lilith? Plenty of room for us to fuck you exactly how we want."

I sagged so much, both men tightened their grip to keep me on my feet. "Yes," I babbled. "I want that."

Shit, I wanted it so much it was painful, and that ache only turned me on more.

"All right." Clay's hand slipped down out of my shirt and once he was sure I wasn't going to topple over, he stepped back. "Grab your wine and follow me."

There were three identical glasses on the table, and I wasn't sure he knew which one was his, but he snatched up a glass and lead the way down the hall, stopping in front of the open door to a bedroom and casting a glance back at us.

He hadn't gone to the stairs that lead to the guest bedrooms on the second floor. He waited for us to follow him into *his* bedroom.

Travis eyed the remaining wine glasses. "Which one is yours?"

My voice was urgent as I blindly grabbed a glass and took off toward Clay. "Who the hell cares? Let's go."

Travis's laugh was deep and warm.

TWENTY-THREE

Clay's bedroom was in the same state it'd been in last time. The bed wasn't made, and the dark gray comforter spilled off to one side. The chair in the corner still had a few discarded articles of clothes on it, but otherwise his bedroom wasn't messy.

He went to the bedside lamp and clicked it on before taking a long sip of wine and set down his glass. His focus went to the man who was surveying the room for the first time, and Clay's tone was both playful and serious.

"You're going to let her talk to you like that?"

"No, you're right." Travis gave me a firm look. "Take off your shirt and your jeans."

The shirt was easy and fluttered to the carpet, but the jeans were harder because they molded to my legs, plus I'd have to take off my new shoes. I undid the button and dropped the zipper as Clay sat on his bed, pulled off his shoes and socks, and lounged across the mattress to watch.

I wriggled my hips, pushing down the denim, but when my jeans were wadded around my knees, Travis put a hand on my shoulder and abruptly shoved me forward. I reached out, catching myself with my hands on the mattress, leaving me bent over the end of the bed.

The first crack of his palm on my ass startled me, but not

Clay, because a pleased smile burned across his lips. Warmth bloomed in my center. The spanking hadn't been hard, but I was smart enough to know this was just the warm-up. It was so much better when it built up to the *real* punishment.

Like I'd done to Clay all those months ago in his study, I wiggled my ass to taunt Travis, although this time I wasn't naked. I wore a black and nude bra and matching bikini panties that were trimmed delicately with lace.

"Fuck," Travis growled. "That ass is gonna get it."

It wasn't a new experience to look at Clay while Travis doled out spankings, but now he was right here in the flesh. Close enough to touch me, which he did. He sat up and his fingers curled around my wrists, cuffing them. My eyes widened and my mouth went dry at this type of sexy restraint.

It was what I'd been craving for so long. Domination by my men *together*.

Clay's eyes were electric as he studied my face, watching how every impact of Travis's palm against my body affected me. His satisfaction was rich when I clenched my teeth and moaned. Travis would have to hit me much harder if he wanted it to punish, because this only felt good. His intent wasn't to hurt me anyway. I was a slut for pain, but he was a slut for pleasure.

He did put more force behind his hand, increasing the intensity of each smack.

Did Clay like how he could feel the blows his protégé's gave me? His hold on my wrists made him acutely aware of every jolt and each reverberation as the spankings glanced through my body. I loved it. He peered at me with the artful appreciation of a man watching a chef prepare a decadent meal.

"Mm," I moaned. My skin was warm and tingling.

Perhaps his palm was getting tired, or maybe he just wanted to keep me guessing, because Travis ran a hand over my back. It smoothed over my sensitized skin, wandered over the swell of my ass, and down the back of my thighs. I wanted to spread my knees and encourage him to explore me elsewhere, but the jeans around my knees hindered that.

His touch was gone as he dropped down behind me and worked to undo the straps of my shoes.

"I like these." His voice was heavy with lust. "Are they new?"

My breath caught as I stared at Clay. Did he want me to say where I'd gotten them? "Um . . . yeah."

"I gave them to her," he looked beyond me to the other man, "as a thank you gift for her help with my house stuff."

Travis didn't seem bothered by this, but then again—he was a guy. He probably had no idea how much the shoes cost. He finished undoing the buckles and helped me step out of my jeans, one leg at a time.

He righted himself and cracked a hand against one of my lace-covered cheeks. The loud sound announced how hard he'd hit me, but I just smiled in enjoyment.

"Shit, Clay, you weren't kidding about her ass of steel." His voice thickened with desire. "Do you want to take over for me?"

It was like Clay had just been offered the world. He was up off the bed in a heartbeat, moving to stand beside the other man. The mattress sank as Travis put a knee on it and crawled over to me. His hands tangled in my hair and held me still so he could kiss me as Clay delivered his first blow.

He must have believed I was adequately warmed up because his strike was *serious.* Hot pins and needles danced in the aftermath, making me groan with discomfort and deep satisfaction. Travis's hands clenched tighter, twisting strands so I couldn't run and allowed him to drink up my moans as Clay rained fire down on me.

At some point, Clay jerked down my panties, and it must have been a signal to the other man because Travis's fingertips drifted to the clasp at the back of my bra.

I was naked as I stretched between these two men, and it was hard to hold my position since I was trembling and verged on overload. On one end, I had Clay's brutal hand crashing down, searing me with pain, and on the other, Travis's passionate, seductive kiss was branding me in a different way.

How was it I was overwhelmed, and yet dying for more?

The final spank from Clay was rough enough it made a yelp burst from my lips and I tumbled forward into Travis's arms. He seemed happy with this new development and turned me over so I was seated between his thighs, my back leaning against his chest. It meant he could gaze down the bare slope of my body and watch as Clay took a knee at the edge of the bed.

There wasn't any doubt what he intended to do, but I still gasped as Clay shoved his hands between my thighs and spread my legs open. His gaze dropped to the most intimate part of me, then lifted to Travis, and a smirk tweaked his lips.

Let's make her come, it said.

I shuddered with pleasure as Clay lowered in and brushed his hot mouth over my pussy. I was wet. So fucking turned on, it was almost embarrassing, but that was one of the things I loved about being with these men. There wasn't shame or judgement when we were together.

Clay had given me rough with his hand, and now he gave me oh-so-gentle with his tongue. My breathing was ragged, and my chest heaved, but Travis had his arms around me, and his lips traced the shell of my ear.

When I rocked my hips, he reached a hand down to grip my thigh. "Stay still," Travis urged, "and let him fuck you with that tongue."

Couldn't he tell it was impossible to keep still? My body was primed. It pleaded for release. If either of them asked me to beg with words, I'd do it gladly.

When Clay's lips closed around my clit and sucked, it brought on a sensation that was so intense, I jerked and tried to snap my legs shut. To stop me, he braced the insides of my thighs with his palms, which inadvertently caused him to put his hand on top of Travis's as it held on to my leg.

Seeing his fingers splayed on top of the other man's gave Clay pause. It made the chest behind me swell with an unsteady breath. And it forced my heart to stop, only for it to restart at twice the speed.

Because Clay's hand didn't slide over to let Travis escape, and Travis didn't attempt to retreat. They were friends, had partnered before, and were obviously comfortable with each other . . . yet Clay's confession at dinner echoed in my mind.

You were my best friend, Travis. And now you've become something more.

Heat mounted and I had to take it one moment at a time to survive. Clay nuzzled between my thighs and stared up at me as his pink tongue swiped across my clit. Travis's fingers from his other hand skated across my breast and zeroed in on my hardened nipple, pinching until it changed the uneven cadence of my breath.

My orgasm hit me so suddenly, it surprised us all.

It was a deluge of pleasure, rushing from my center outward as a wave of heat, chased by cold and followed with tingling bliss. The hands on my legs tightened their grip and both men seemed to revel in the ecstasy coursing through my body. Clay's pleased look was complimented by Travis's heavy exhale of satisfaction.

I lay boneless in the middle of them, quaking and gasping and feverish.

It reminded me of the first night when I'd been sandwiched between them at the club, except the men were reversed, and no one was inside me, and . . . I knew these men now. Not just that, but I cared about them so much, I—

Oh, God.

Was it possible I *loved* them?

No, a panicked part of my mind yelled back. *You don't do that, remember?* And Clay didn't either, so what was the point? I couldn't fall in love with both men when at least one of them wasn't capable of loving me back.

He said he didn't date either, but he did that tonight, didn't he?

Just as the thought seized my mind, Clay dragged his hands down my thighs and straightened. He grasped the side of his frames and pulled his glasses off, leaning back to set them on the dresser nearby. It was the first time he'd removed them during a scene, like they might be a hindrance, and I was glad there was nothing blocking his beautiful eyes from me. Nowhere for him to hide.

Wait. *Was* this a scene?

There was no plan or design. No hierarchy, and no real power exchange because tonight wasn't about that. It was the three of us all wanting to connect. To share the experience as a group.

As a unit.

Once his glasses were gone, Clay grabbed the bottom of his sweater, jerked it up over his head, and balled it in his hands before chucking it away. I reached out to run my fingers down his chest, and he allowed it, but his attention was on the man at my back.

"I want to watch her suck your cock while I fuck her."

The muscles inside me flexed so hard, I nearly came again, but I swallowed a deep breath and backed down off the ledge.

Travis moved out from behind me, getting up off the bed so he could begin to undress. His voice turned husky. "How do you want her?"

Clay's gaze swept over me as I lay on my back, propped up on my elbows, and he gave me a dark smile while he undid his belt. "Roll over. On your stomach."

I did, sliding off the bed enough so my knees were buried

in the carpet and my breasts flattened to the mattress. My hands balled the sheets beneath them into fists as the *vrrrrp* rang out of his belt being pulled free from his belt loops.

He didn't have plans to use it on me though, at least not now, because it fell with a thump to the floor. I turned my head to the side, watching Travis as he finished getting his pants and underwear off, but I stayed very aware of the hand that grasped my waist. The naked tip of Clay's dick teased me, rubbing back and forth through the wetness his mouth had created on my skin.

It came from deep inside my chest when he lined himself up and began to intrude. "Oh, my God."

I tipped my head forward, pulling the sheets toward me and over my face as he pushed further inside. It felt so, so good.

"Yes," Travis encouraged. "Take it."

The bed rocked as he climbed on and the sheet was pulled away, revealing he was as naked as the rest of us, and already half hard. At least, I thought he was. It was hard to focus because Clay was inside me, moving in slow, deep strokes.

The room was a thousand degrees and the needle kept rising. I was barely moving, but it felt like I was breathing in steam, struggling to catch my breath. My pulse was a furious drum, banging in my neck. The man behind me found a tempo he liked, and once it was established, moans played from my mouth.

But all this pleasure I was receiving? I didn't have to keep it. I could share it.

I reached out, clasping Travis's impressive cock and

stroked him from tip to base. He groaned through his parted lips and moved closer. Clay had explained what he wanted to see, and Travis was more than willing to oblige.

It was easy to open my mouth and slip the head of Travis's dick inside. It was a bit of a challenge to take more of him, but I did my best. I ringed my fingers around what I couldn't take and pumped my fist in time with my lips. Only a few passes and he was slick with my saliva.

A heavy breath came from Clay, followed by a growl of satisfaction. "That's it," he said. "Get that cock good and hard so he's ready to fuck you with it."

It was impossible to organize my thoughts and my focus yo-yoed between the two men. One was pleasing me while I was intent on doing that to the other. I wondered if it could be the same as when I was holding their hands at the restaurant—only amplified a thousand percent. All the pleasure Clay was giving me could be translated through my body and carried on to Travis.

I pulsed my mouth on him, mimicking the same rhythm Clay used as he thrust into me. So, as Clay fucked me . . . in a way he was fucking Travis too.

My jaw began to tire, and I struggled to maintain the same tempo, but holy hell, Clay felt so good as he moved inside me. Plus, listening to Travis's sighs and moans made the experience all that more enjoyable.

I wished I could see us in this moment, utterly connected and as one. Clay's hips slapped against my ass as he held onto my waist, and I was bent over the bed while Travis knelt on it, his cock lodged in my mouth.

Perhaps Clay wished he could see too, because his hands were on my head, gathering my hair up in a loose ponytail. Or maybe he felt I needed direction, because there was purpose behind his fingers, guiding me to bob faster on Travis.

Spit slung from my lips. The head of his thick cock pushed deeper in my mouth, just past the point of comfort, and I retreated with a choking gag. I'd never found the sound sexy before. In fact, it was a turn-off for me . . . until Travis bent down, gripped my face, and delivered a rewarding kiss.

Clay's hands stayed in my hair, so when the kiss ended, Travis rose upright and put his hands on top of the other man's. They worked as a team to urge me back down, to fit my mouth around Travis and try again.

I did better the second time, mostly because I was distracted. Bliss was pooling in my belly from the rock of Clay's body against mine. Could I come again so soon? And would he let me?

He gasped abruptly, pulling completely out of me at the same time he released my head, sliding his hands out from beneath Travis's so he could drive his fingertips hard across my still-smarting backside. "You're too fucking good, you know that? You're going to make me come if I don't stop."

I wanted to sob at the loss of him, but as the sting of his slap lingered, Clay scooped me up and hauled me against him. His voice was as rough as his spanking had been, but darker and infinitely hotter.

"You want him?" he asked as I stared at the other man.

Clay's face was right beside mine, and although I couldn't really see him, I sensed his gaze was on Travis in the same way mine was. It took in the landscape of Travis's beautiful body and the throbbing dick that was clenched in his hand. It followed the slow stroke of his fist and watched the tendons twist and flex in his powerful arm.

It was said so hushed, I couldn't tell if it was an order or a plea from Clay. "Tell him you want him."

Truer words had never been spoken, and I locked eyes with Travis's intense ones. "I want you."

Lightning crackled around us as he moved to lie down with his back against the pillows at the head of the bed. His sexy expression said it all. *Come here.*

But Clay kept hold of me with an arm around my chest, preventing that, and flung a finger at the man stretched out before us. "Get on him but face me. I want to play with you while you're fucking him."

It injected more heat into me, and I was burning alive. Even the marrow of my bones seemed to be on fire, and lust made me clumsy, so when he released me, it was awkward trying to climb up over the end of the bed. Somehow, I managed. I crawled on my hands and knees across the rumpled sheets toward Travis.

He sat up, meeting me halfway, and kissed me. Maybe he wanted to get it in now, because he wouldn't be able to once I turned around and climbed on top of him.

I handled mounting him with as much grace as possible, and he shifted beneath my straddling legs to help line us up. Clay was on his feet at the end of the bed, watching and waiting, his gaze pinned to the junction of my legs and the man whose rigid cock teased back and forth.

When it began to creep inside, Clay's gaze rose, gliding over my stomach and my bare breasts until it reached my eyes. I was trapped there, unable to look away as I slid down inch by inch. Even as the enjoyable stretch of Travis made my mouth round into a silent *oh*, my gaze didn't waver.

I was barely seated on him before he began to move. The thigh muscles beneath me hardened and flexed with his thrusts—shallow at first, until I could sink deeper on him.

My moan was a starting bell to Clay, who was on his knees on the bed beside us instantly, one hand roughly gripping the hair at the back of my head and the other cupping my breast.

I gasped and panted, but he swallowed it. His mouth slammed over mine, lashing his tongue at me as if I didn't deserve his cruel kiss but he was going to give it to me anyway. Travis drove into me and had a hand on my ass to encourage me to keep up with his demanding tempo, which meant Clay had to follow the rock of my body to keep kissing me as I rode Travis.

This bed was on fire.

I covered Travis's hand on my ass with my own and gasped as Clay's pinch on my nipple went white-hot. It didn't stay there, though. He broke our kiss and replaced his harsh fingers with even meaner teeth.

"Shit," I swore in pain and pleasure, threading fingers through his hair. My body was conflicted, not knowing if I wanted to pull him away or hold his head there. Tremors graduated up my legs, making me vibrate. Groans of satisfaction punched from Travis's lungs, and drew escalating ones from me.

They grew louder when Clay's fingertips traced a line down over the flat of my shuttering stomach, venturing lower.

As his fingers discovered my clit, he pulled back to watch what he was doing. To study how he was touching me and my response to the way he rubbed tight circles and made me moan. Whenever it started to feel a little too good, his stinging pinch on my sensitive nub cured that right up.

And when the pain faded, I couldn't help but think about how intimately close he was to touching Travis. What if that accidentally happened? What if either man *wanted* it to happen?

Clay pinched my clit again, dragging a whimper from me, and his voice was strangled with desire. "Put your hands on his chest and lean back."

Travis's skin was like mine, faintly sticky with sweat, and when I reached back to plant my palms on him, he grasped my arms just above the elbows. It was an added level of support, which I needed, but also domination—which I craved.

I was leaned back but tucked my chin to my chest so I could watch Clay. He gently nudged one of Travis's knees, urging the man to spread them and make room. Travis's tempo slowed to a stop with him lodged inside me, and the sheets rustled as he eased his outstretched legs apart into a V.

My breath came and went in labored gulps when Clay moved, crossing over Travis's leg so he could kneel between them. His hands played over my tits, brushing over my skin like he wanted to leave no spot untouched. I shivered with enjoyment, not just from the way his palms smoothed over me, but how Travis had resumed his slow, deep thrusts.

There was a thought running through Clay's head. I could see it in his eyes. I might not have been able to if he were still wearing his glasses, but they sat on the dresser, out of reach. Whatever he was considering, it made his chest heave with a deep breath.

His hands washed down my body. One stopped at my hip, but the other continued on. It moved down over the top of my thigh, gliding over my knee, and then slid onto Travis's. It didn't rest there. His fingers splayed out so as he began the journey back up, the pad of his thumb traced a line along the inside of Travis's thigh.

The hands gripping my arms tightened, but I got the feeling it was simply surprise and not shock. Travis . . . didn't hate Clay's sensual touch. In fact, he probably enjoyed it because his cock flexed inside me.

Clay's thumb narrowly avoided touching the other man anywhere that would cross a line. It swerved at the last second as his hand moved back up onto my thigh and slid over to touch me just above where Travis and I were joined.

Had Clay been teasing us? Or was he curious and testing the waters with the other man?

He shifted on his knees, maybe to find a more comfortable position, or maybe to give himself a moment to catch his breath, since he was still struggling. Clay's expression was a mix of uncertainty and need, and I wasn't sure which was going to trump the other.

It was at that moment I lifted my hips just a little too much while Travis was retreating, causing his cock to fall out of me. His voice rasped with urgency, like he might die without it. “Oh, fuck, put it back in.”

I’d thought he was talking to me, but the hands on my arms didn’t let go. He didn’t release me to carry out his command.

Time suspended, and the image before me shimmered like I was gazing at it through air so hot it distorted everything.

Clay was impervious to the heat and didn’t hesitate.

He wrapped his fingers around the other man’s dick, positioning it where it needed to be, and guided Travis back inside me.

TWENTY-FOUR

Since we'd entered the bedroom, there'd been an undercurrent we all sensed lurking beneath the surface. It was dangerously powerful, and maybe the men had tried to avoid it. But now it had us, sweeping us away and pulling us down into a place where everything was blurry.

It hazed the sharp edges of fear, and shame, and inhibitions.

My moan mingled with Travis's as he pushed back inside me, sliding deep and hitting the spot that felt so good, it should have been illegal. Clay's hand returned to where it'd been before, rubbing furiously, because he didn't want Travis to be the only one giving me pleasure.

They were supposed to share me, after all.

Sweat beaded on my forehead and tension coiled in my center. Travis picked up the pace, and my heart chugged along so fast, I became dizzy. I was getting close to my orgasm, and my greedy body took over, trying to go faster and find release.

So it wasn't surprising when my attempt to change the tempo backfired, throwing off his rhythm and he came out of me again. He groaned as if in agony, but it wasn't frustration—it was deep satisfaction.

Travis's cock was wet from being inside me, and Clay's

fist tightened around it, pumping up and down in a slick stroke. *Jesus.* It was easily the hottest thing I'd ever seen. It'd be scorched into my memory for the rest of my life, I was sure.

A sound welled up from behind me. It was too strong to call a whimper, but it was heavy with desperation. A victorious smile broke on Clay's face and power flashed in his eyes. He enjoyed having control over the other man. Doing it through pleasure might not have been his preferred medium, but he was still pleased.

"You like watching this?" he asked me.

"Yes," I gasped.

He gave Travis another stroke as he leaned over me, sucking my nipple into his mouth. My arms threatened to buckle. I was turning into a molten mess and was going to drip through the hands of these men who made me melt.

Clay pressed the tip of Travis's cock against my entrance, and this time when I slid down on him, Clay's finger was there too, stretching me. It was shocking and erotic to have a part of them inside me at once.

He had his palm up to the ceiling and moved his finger independently of Travis's rhythm, and my brain emptied of thought. I let the sensations take over and have me in the same way I gave myself over to the men.

"That's so fucking sexy, Lilith," Clay said. "Isn't it?"

"Yes."

"I wonder," his tone was wicked, "if this hot little pussy of yours could handle both of us at the same time."

"Oh, God." It was a knee-jerk reaction to the image he projected in my mind. I saw the two of them, their cocks pushed together as they slid in and out of me. The mental picture just threw gasoline on the fire already consuming me.

He cupped the back of my neck, forcing me to look at him and his sinful eyes. "What do you say?"

"We could," I said between two huge breaths, "try it."

Oh, lord. He looked so happy with my answer, it sent emotional pleasure scattering through my mind. He withdrew his finger from inside me, lifted it to my lips, and pushed it inside my mouth. It allowed him to lean closer and look over my shoulder, down to the man beneath me.

"Do you want to share her with me like that? Because I want to fuck her while my dick's rubbing against yours and feel like I'm fucking you both."

Because Clay's finger, wet with the taste of sex, was in my mouth, it muffled my stunned moan. Travis's entire body jerked, nearly throwing me off. He stopped moving, and as he throbbed inside me, Clay pulsed his finger past my lips.

He'd been so private and reserved, but now it spilled from him without hesitation. He continued detailing his desires without a hint of shame.

"I want to make her come on us, Travis, and then . . . I want to know what it feels like when you come inside her." He gently pulled his finger out and traced the damp pad of it over my lips. "You want that, don't you?"

It wasn't clear whom his question was for, but I nodded at the same time Travis whispered the word. "Yes."

Clay exhaled loudly, laced with relief, and I felt it in my chest. We all breathed it together.

"Turn around on him," he said to me. "I think it'll be

easier that way."

Travis let go of me and both men helped me move, and I was grateful for it because my thighs were tight and strained. Reverse cowgirl was great and all, but I found it more taxing than other positions.

Anticipation and anxious energy made my hands shake as I got on top of Travis, but then his lips pressed to mine in a reassuring kiss that stripped away nervousness and left only excitement.

Was he excited too? In theory, sharing me this way should appeal to both men. Clay would get to design and control the scene, and Travis would get both pleasure and to feel like he was on a level playing field with the more experienced dom.

As soon as I was settled into the new position, my breasts pressed against Travis's chest, I felt Clay's fingers work in alongside the cock that was fucking me. It was a lot to take, but I enjoyed the uncomfortable stretch. I stared down at Travis's bottomless eyes and wondered how he felt about this. Did he enjoy both the concept and the sensation as much as I did?

I didn't get a chance to ask because he jerked me down into a blistering kiss.

The bed shifted as Clay moved behind me, and his warm fingers curled around my hip. Then, there came a sound like he'd spit in his palm and now was using it to lube himself up. I was so wet, he probably didn't need to, but it couldn't hurt. Plus, it was filthy, and I loved the slick sound of him touching himself.

Travis sensed the other man's approach because he slowed to a stop and wrapped his arms around me, caging me in.

Clay sounded breathless. "Ready?"

It wasn't so much a question as it was a warning. His grip on my waist tightened to hold me steady, and then he was there, nudging. Pressure built as he pushed, forcing his way in alongside Travis.

I sucked in a sharp breath. There wasn't pain when he gained entry, but it was a deep ache. A fullness that demanded all my attention. I blinked my wide eyes at it, trying to process the tightness.

Travis's eyes lidded with pleasure, and air escaped him in a quiet moan.

"So . . . fucking tight," Clay groaned.

As Travis held still, Clay continued to fit himself inside me. I had my hands on Travis's shoulders, and when I dug my fingers in, concern streaked through his face. "Okay?"

"Yeah," I whispered. My head was cloudy, and I was a passenger in my own body, but the sensation was amazing.

He'd been tense and anxious, but when I issued a soft sound of enjoyment, he relaxed enough to start moving. And then both men were moving inside me with gentle, shallow strokes, each breathing tight breaths between groans of pleasure.

"Do you like it?" I asked Travis.

He caressed my back and satisfaction burned in his eyes. "It's good," he said. "It's so fucking good."

Hearing that caused Clay to thrust deeper, and it wrung

a deep moan from me. Travis's fingertips traced down the line of my spine, and when he discovered Clay's hand on my hip, he grasped on to it. Both used their hold to urge me to move on them.

It was exactly as it'd been designed. With Clay driving behind me and Travis's slower thrusts from below, Clay was the one in control. He was fucking us both.

God, it was insane. I wanted it to last forever.

The three of us became one body, one unit. Our short gasps alternated with moans, and were punctuated with whispered words of pleasure. It played as a beautiful melody, filling the room.

"Fuck," we uttered.

"*Yes*," we answered back.

Tension built in my core. The position meant I could grind my clit against Travis's pelvis and maximize my enjoyment. I reached back to grab on to one of Clay's hands while Travis's mouth latched onto mine. I wanted to be connected to them in every way possible. I'd never felt this tight, or full or . . .

Complete.

My orgasm tore me apart, but the men held me together with both their hands and encouraging words. They gasped as my body contracted and tried to milk every last drop of satisfaction it could squeeze from them. My vision hazed to black and my heart stopped, but when I finally found air to draw into my lungs, it restarted.

Beneath me, the body solidified into stone. Travis feared if he moved while I was coming, he might not be able to hold himself back, and he wanted to focus on me. Our foreheads were pressed together, and I panted for breath, all while Clay continued to maintain his steady pace.

"It's such a tight fit, Travis." Clay's tone was seductive. "I feel every goddamn inch of you, and you feel so . . . fucking . . . *good*."

Oh, that was the wrong thing to say.

Or maybe it was *exactly* the right thing to say because Clay wanted to be the one to make Travis lose control. To send the other man over the edge.

Travis's body jerked and stuttered as he came, and loud, desperate moans poured from his mouth between ragged gasps for breath. It was the strongest response I'd ever seen out of him and it created aftershocks of pleasure deep between my legs.

"That's it." I couldn't see Clay, but I pictured the commanding look he'd have as he demanded it. "Come all over me and fill her up."

This prolonged his orgasm, judging by his loud exhale and the pulsing throb inside me, but I couldn't be one hundred percent sure. Clay had slowed to an unhurried pace, enjoying the slippery slide in and out of me, and it was hard to focus on anything but that.

As Travis recovered, he pulled me down into a kiss, and when his tongue filled my mouth, Clay picked up speed. I wasn't likely to orgasm another time, but it still felt incredibly good, even when Travis's cock slipped out of me and Clay was on his own.

He seemed eager to find his end as the rest of us had,

and his hard, punishing thrusts that racked my body were perfectly balanced by the gentle, passionate kiss Travis delivered.

And when he came with a guttural groan, he collapsed forward, sandwiching me between the two of them. Our skin was glossy with sweat and everyone's heart seemed to be pumping at a thousand beats a second. Clay began to lean to one side and the three of us fell in a heap of arms and legs and hands and mouths. I lay on my side with my head on Travis's arm and Clay spooning me, and when his palm came to rest on the flat plane of the other man's chest, it made me smile.

It felt natural.

And I was thrilled with how comfortable these men were. Maybe I was in love with them together. So I was grateful they at least seemed to like one another. I put my hand on top of Clay's, which covered Travis's heart.

"Thank you," Travis said, "for tonight."

I knew he was talking to both of us. I smiled and planted a sweet kiss against the side of his neck.

Clay drew in a deep breath. "You're welcome."

I awoke when Noir jumped on the bed and ran her damp nose against my fingers, seeking a hand to pet her. I was happy to do it, until awareness of my situation hit me.

I was in Clay's bed, a man was softly snoring beside me,

and he was not Clay.

Travis lay on his stomach, his hair disheveled but a peaceful look on his face as he slept with the sheets pushed down to his waist.

It was light outside, so it was morning, and I searched the room for both a clock and the man with whom I jointly owned a cat. I found the clock first, telling me it was a quarter past eight, but there were no signs of Clay.

The glasses he'd put on the dresser last night were gone.

I swung my legs over the side of the bed and gingerly climbed out, not wanting to wake Travis. Had we taken up too much room last night and driven Clay from his own bed? I hurried to dress in my clothes from yesterday, then ventured out into the house.

He wasn't in the living room or the kitchen. Cold dread lined my stomach. Had he left?

No. The faint sound of something being nailed could be heard downstairs, and I let out a tight breath.

Plus, there was a pot of coffee that looked freshly brewed sitting on the counter beside two waiting mugs. I poured myself one, added some sugar, and made my way to the basement steps.

He was hunched over the workbench, stretching the leather-like vinyl fabric over a padded piece of wood.

"Good morning," I announced.

I'd either been too quiet coming down the stairs or Clay had been too focused to hear because he jumped and spun to face me, suspicion flaring in his eyes. It dissipated once he recognized me.

"Sorry," I said. "Didn't mean to startle you."

"It's all right. Good morning." He honest-to-God had a pencil tucked behind his ear and I grinned. Why did I find that so sexy? He gave me an evaluating look. "I see you found the coffee."

"Yeah." I glanced over at the tabletop. I wasn't sure what he was working on but could tell this was new. Last time I'd been down here, the space had been empty. "Wow, you've been busy."

His gaze darted away, and he went back to stretching and stapling the fabric. "Trying to play catch-up with orders."

I strove for a causal tone. "What time did you get up this morning? I'm sorry if we drove you out of your own bed."

"You didn't. I couldn't sleep."

Something was off. He seemed distant. "Oh. What'd you do instead?"

He gave his answer by pulling the handle on the staple gun, causing another sharp crack as metal drove into the wood.

I stiffened. "Clay. How long have you been down here?"

"Since three, I guess."

I was suddenly cold and fought a shiver. He'd been down here for *hours*.

It was impossible not to think last night was the cause. I bit down on the inside of my cheek, not sure what to say, and the silence was uncomfortable. Didn't he like what we'd done last night? I still felt the sweet ache of both of them in my body, but he was acting so . . . indifferent.

I flinched as he placed another staple with a loud snap,

making the coffee in my mug slosh.

"Is everything okay?" I asked quietly.

He didn't look at me, perhaps pretending to be distracted by his work. "Yeah. Why wouldn't it be?"

"I don't know." I swallowed thickly. "You seem kind of—"

"Is he still here?"

He'd asked it like it didn't matter one way or the other, but it very clearly did matter. It gave me the impression that whatever Clay was upset about, it had to do with the man upstairs.

"Yeah," I said. "He's still sleeping. Do you want me to wake him up?"

"No, that's fine." He paused, the staple gun hovering over its next target. "Just so you're aware, I have to leave soon to get some more supplies, but you two feel free to stay as long as you'd like."

My mouth dropped open. Had he just *dismissed* me?

He'd told me he didn't date, so it wasn't like I expected snuggling and breakfast together this morning, but after the sex last night he'd been so affectionate and warm. I hated this cold, guarded version of him, especially after everything we'd shared.

It hurt, and not in the enjoyable way, but I refused to show it. My face heated as I plastered on an overly bright smile. "Okay, great. Thanks."

He must have recognized I was upset, but he had no comment. Instead, he pulled the handle on the staple gun, which was like putting a period on the end of our conversation.

"Well," I said, barely keeping the emotion from my voice, "I won't keep you from your work." I turned and strode for the stairs, and it was crushing when he didn't stop me.

TWENTY-FIVE

Travis was awake when I returned to the bedroom. He sat up in the bed and ground the heel of his hand into an eye, but went on alert when I walked in. In total opposition to Clay, he seemed genuinely happy to see me.

"Hey," he said. "I thought I'd run everyone off."

Nope, just Clay, I thought grimly, but it was still early, so maybe I had read too much into my conversation with him. I shot Travis a smile that said he couldn't run me off if he tried.

He patted the empty spot in the bed beside him and sounded hopeful. "Is that coffee for me?"

"We can share, or I can get you your own."

His eyes were warm. "I like sharing."

Oh, lord. He was so handsome like this. I went to sit beside him and handed over the mug, but there was a stone in my stomach, and I fought to keep it from dragging me down. He took a sip and watched me with his intelligent eyes.

"Where's Clay?"

"Downstairs," I said flatly. "Working on a new piece."

He handed the mug back to me. "What's wrong?"

"He's been down there since three, and when I went to talk to him this morning . . ."

Travis didn't seem surprised. "He was weird?"

"Yeah," I said. "Distant. What was that about?"

After I'd come upstairs, I'd stood in the hallway for a long time trying to figure out what was going on. Maybe the answer was simple, and he'd just gotten overwhelmed. He'd told me at the beginning he preferred to be alone. He'd spent two weeks in Florida, and perhaps after dinner and our evening, he just needed space.

"I don't know," he said, "but I wouldn't worry about it." He leaned forward, brushing my hair back over my shoulder. "He did this to me when the two of us scened together. Whatever it is, I'm sure he'll get over it."

I curled my fingers around the mug. "We didn't talk about what's going to happen once he's home."

He pulled at the sleeve of my shirt and seemed distracted by the curve of my shoulder once it was exposed. "We didn't."

His mouth, rough with stubble, brushed against my skin and tendrils of interest awakened in me. But while my body was excited, my mind was fixated on the man downstairs, and the relationship the three of us had. It was wrong to want one when I needed them both.

"Let's just give him some room to breathe and figure out what he wants," he said softly, "He can do that this last week while he's gone. When he's home for good, we can talk about it and everything will be okay."

I wanted to ask him to promise me that, but I knew he couldn't, so instead I chose simply to believe him.

For the first time in my career, I was happy to have long, grueling days. It cut down on the amount of free time I had to check my phone for messages.

Because there weren't any.

The group chat that had been incredibly active until last weekend, had gone almost silent. It was all messages from me and short replies from the guys. More of a question-and-answer session than a conversation. We used to talk multiple times throughout the day, and now—

Nothing.

And we didn't arrange any sessions for Clay to watch Travis and me together either.

Travis had said to give Clay space, but by Thursday I was panicked. I could handle one of them being distant, but quitting them both cold turkey? That was brutal.

Cassidy: Have you heard from the guys?

Yesterday, I'd found thirty free minutes in Cassidy's schedule to get together. I'd met her at a Starbucks on the edge of campus and told her everything. How I'd fucked Travis without knowing his name. The arrangement the three of us had struck. How Clay's project was over now, and I worried Clay might have thought the evening we'd spent together was the end.

A 'goodbye sendoff.'

Me: They both gave me bullshit answers about being busy.

Cassidy: You need to talk to them. Like, for real.

She was absolutely right. There'd been a seismic shift in our group dynamic, and if we didn't address it, it would only get worse or disintegrate completely.

And I did not want to lose either of them.

My phone stayed silent Friday morning, and by lunchtime, I reached my breaking point. I composed my text while I sat in my car, ignoring the salad I'd just gone through a drive-thru to pick up.

I sent the most serious of messages; one that should strike fear in the hearts of the men.

Me: We need to talk.

Clay's response was almost instantaneous.

Clay: Agreed, but I'm about to get on a plane. My place tonight, 8pm?

Travis's text didn't come in until I got back to the clinic and I read it while coming in the back door.

Travis: Yeah. See y'all then.

I wore the red leopard print heels Clay had given me

like they might be a good luck charm. Since I'd worn them the night the three of us had become one, my hope was their magic would work again. Trepidation made my muscles tight as I walked over to Clay's house, and my steps slowed as I came through the gate.

Travis's SUV was already parked in Clay's driveway.

Was he running even earlier than I was, or were they meeting without me?

I swallowed dryly and rang the doorbell. A few seconds later, Clay's figure darkened the glass insert of the door. He wore jeans, a button-down shirt, and a look of anxiety that faded the instant he saw me.

"Hey," I said softly.

"Hi." He pushed up his glasses as he stepped back and gestured for me to come inside, but he seemed transfixed. He gazed at me like there were a million things he wanted to say, but first he just needed to look at me.

My heart skipped.

He'd never gazed at me like this before. It was the reaction I'd hoped for the morning after we'd all slept together, and I was thrilled to see he was back. Not just physically either. This was the man who'd let his guard down that night and let me in.

His focus moved down to note the shoes I wore, and recognition lit his eyes. He was pleased by my choice.

I'd been temporarily distracted by him but snapped back to reality. "Is Travis here already?"

Clay's expression voided out and his shields went back up. "Yeah, he's in the dining room."

I followed behind him and when we stepped into the room, the tension was so thick it nearly knocked me over. It only grew when Clay went around the large table to the far side, standing behind the chair that was directly across from Travis, rather than take the one closest that was beside him.

Sitting on opposite sides made them seem like rivals, and had the added bonus of a choice for me. If I sat next to one of the men, it'd seem I was choosing them over the other. At my entrance, Travis rose to his feet. On the surface, it was merely courtesy. Neither man would take their seat until I did, but it felt like a power play.

So I marched to the end of the table, pulled out the chair at the head of it, and sat, leaving equal distance between me and the men.

The atmosphere of the room was already formal, and the gesture of the men taking their seats after I had only added to it. Was this a fucking business negotiation? I peered over at Travis. "You got here early."

He frowned and cast his gaze across the table. "I wanted to talk to Clay first."

My pulse quickened. "About?"

"I told him that if he truly cares about you, he'll step aside."

I stopped breathing. "You did what?"

He gave me a look that I didn't understand. It was like he'd faced a difficult decision, made his choice, and now he had to see it through. "By his own admission, I can give you things he can't. Lilith, we can be in a relationship that's more than just scene partners."

Clay's tone was curt. "Has she said she wants that?"

The question momentarily derailed Travis, and he blinked, lost. But then his expression firmed up. "I'm not just talking about dating. I'm talking about," he took a deep breath, "love."

It was the same reaction as if Travis had dropped a bomb on the center of the table. I froze, while Clay inhaled sharply.

Love.

The word activated something in Clay. A fight-or-flight response, but instead of getting up and leaving, he leaned forward and spread his hands on the table. He looked like a man willing to fight, to go all in, and it left me breathless.

"Yes," he glared at Travis, "in the beginning I said I couldn't give her those things, but now everything is different. The rules keep changing. Every plan I draft gets altered." His focus snapped to me. "The only thing I can expect is the unexpected."

My hands were in my lap, and they balled into fists from the way his intense stare drilled into me. "I don't understand."

His voice dropped to a hush. "Yeah. Me, either." His gaze fell to the table. "It feels like I'm building a house and all of a sudden, this entire new section got added and now I'm scrambling to keep it together. To understand how to make it work."

I got what he was saying. We'd started to build a relationship together, and when Travis was added, it upended that. Didn't he know he didn't have to figure it out alone? Yes, he was my dom, but I'd never expect him to have all the answers.

Just as I opened my mouth to tell him, his eyebrows

tugged together, and his attention flew to the other man. "The reason why I told you I don't do dating or love is because my arrangement with her excludes those things. She assured me she didn't want them. We had a rule that if one of us started to develop feelings, we'd tell each other."

I somehow sensed where he was going, and tingles washed down my back.

Clay spoke confidently, as if ready to lay it all on the line. "When you kissed her, you broke the rules of the arrangement you had with me." His gaze flicked my direction. "I broke mine with her a while ago. I've had feelings for weeks and not said a thing."

I gasped. "Why not?"

"Because you told me the harder a guy falls for you, the faster you want out, so I kept the way I felt a secret. I don't want to lose you. Shit, Lilith, you're all I can think about these days."

"But," I sputtered, "you said you don't get feelings. You don't do love."

"Apparently, I do."

"Yeah?" Travis's tone was irritated. "Well, I fell in love with her first."

I blinked. *Really?*

"I highly doubt it," the other man fired back.

How was this possible? I had gone into this relationship not wanting to fall in love, and now both men were saying they were in love with me. It created a war in my head. One side was ecstatic they felt this way, and the other was beyond terrified.

I hated how they both turned and looked at me as if I had to choose, right here, right now. And it seemed like they each expected me to pick them over the other man.

I laced my fingers together and moved, slowly and measured, to set my hands on the tabletop. As I considered how to answer, I stared at the way my hands were joined.

"I think I'm in love with you too," I said.

Since my head was tipped down and I wasn't looking at either of them, it wasn't clear who I was talking to. They shifted uneasily in their seats, both ready to ask me who I meant, but I sucked in a deep breath, letting it fill my lungs with air—and hopefully courage.

"I'm in love with both of you," I admitted. "Together. As a unit." I looked at one man and then the other. "So, please don't ask me to choose because I won't. I *can't*. The night when all of us were together? That's what I want." I had to revise that, to make sure they understood. "It's what I *need*."

I unlaced my fingers and pressed a hand to my chest in a desperate attempt to shield my heart from tearing in two.

"I've never been in love," I said softly. "Maybe the reason it hasn't happened before is because I never felt . . . complete." I declared it in the strongest, most sure voice I possessed. "But I feel that way now with both of you."

They looked at me as if they'd been tied to their chairs. I saw the struggle raging in their eyes. Maybe they wanted to leave, but also they seemed desperate to stay. Their unwavering gazes were pinned on me.

"And the thing is," I added, "I think you love each other too."

Their eyes went enormously wide before narrowing to slits and they turned their suspicious gazes on each other.

I raised my hands, gesturing for them to hear me out. "Maybe it's platonic love. Clay, you said Travis is your best friend, but you guys are more than that. You both care deeply for me, but you also care about one another. You're partners to each other, just as much as to me."

Travis's expression was unreadable as he considered what I'd said. He didn't necessarily agree with it, but he didn't disagree with it either.

His tone was skeptical. "Okay, so . . . how does that work?" He made a face, displeased with himself. "What I mean is, how do you see it working? Like, we'd all be dating each other?"

"I don't know." It was the most honest answer I could give. "But I'd like to talk about it, and I think we can figure it out, if we're together."

I wanted to connect with them like I'd done at the restaurant, so I leaned forward across the table, stretching out my hands to both of them in offering. The hope was they would each take one, signifying they were willing to give us a shot.

We could become a throuple. Not an open relationship, but three people committed to each other through sex, support, trust, and love.

Clay's chest moved rapidly, and I expected his heart was beating furiously inside his body. He stared at my hand like it was foreign, something he'd never seen before.

I should have known.

He didn't like surprises and hated when things didn't go

according to plan, which I imagined was exactly what was happening now. Clay had probably spent his flight home figuring out how he was going to handle this talk. He'd have scripted what he was going to say, but then Travis had shown up early and disrupted him, and then I'd said I was in love with both men, blowing up whatever was left of his plan.

"You say you love us both." Clay's body language was stiff. "What happens if one of us doesn't want to be part of a," he said the word with disdain, "unit?" He frowned. "You make it sound like it's all or nothing for you."

"Is it?" Travis asked.

The last thing I wanted was to give them an ultimatum, but I needed to be better about communicating. This wasn't going to work if one of them walked away. My voice was hushed and broke on the final word. "I wouldn't be complete without both of you."

I was risking everything.

If one of them said no, that was it. There was no going back, no way to recover from it.

The mood in the room was fraught. I held my breath painfully in my body, waiting for them to choose to take this leap with me. Couldn't they see how amazing we'd be together?

Travis reached out first, his warm fingers finding mine, and although he looked unsteady, he seemed sure. "I'm willing to give it a try."

It sent me flying, and we both turned eagerly to Clay.

But instead of reaching out, he sat back in his seat and crossed his arms over his chest. "No."

It was a punch to my center, and I made a sound of

shock. "Why?"

For once, he didn't like seeing me hurting and his eyes filled with concern, but they were trapped behind his glasses. "I was with you first. I brought him in because he was supposed to be temporary. You weren't supposed to fall for him." Then, he uttered what was truly stopping him. "That wasn't the plan."

"No," I said, "it wasn't. But I wasn't supposed to fall for you either."

He glared at the far end of the table, unwilling to look at me or the hand I still had outstretched to him. "You're right."

Travis sensed I was suffering, and he gripped my hand tightly for support. Or perhaps he was suffering too. By asking for this relationship, I'd put his friendship with Clay in jeopardy. What was Clay's rejection going to do to him?

Unexpected tears welled in my eyes. I felt him slipping away and yet was powerless to stop it. "Clay—"

"I'm sorry I can't give this to you." He finally looked at me, and when he saw my unshed tears, it caused chaos in him. "I wish I could, but I don't know what I'm doing. I don't know how to love one person, let alone two." His posture was tense, like if he moved he might fall apart.

"Maybe I could," Travis said quietly, "help you, like how you helped me."

Clay's face soured. "No. I don't need help. What I needed was for Lilith to stick to the plan, but that's no longer possible." He retreated into himself, and the distance between us became too great. His tone was cool, professional, and as precise as the lines on the drawings in his study. "I don't think there's anything left to say."

I slowly dragged my empty hand back toward my body, feeling like it was made of lead. But Travis seemed to be made of fire, because he let go of me and jolted forward.

"What the fuck is this?" he snapped. "You're going to throw away what we have because you—what? Aren't getting everything you want for once?" His expression darkened. "Is this another test? Because if you're hoping I'm going to gracefully bow out to keep you happy, keep dreaming."

Color rose in Clay's face, matching the other man's anger. "Isn't that exactly what you asked me to do when you first got here?"

Travis's nostrils flared. He knew what Clay had said was true, but he didn't like it. "You're scared. Terrified to try something new and asking for an 'out' before we've even started."

"I'm not scared, and I'm allowed—"

"You know what," Travis sat back in his chair and tossed his hands up in surrender, "you're right. We shouldn't do this. You always told me if you're afraid of the scene, that's a warning you shouldn't do it." He leveled a devastating look at the other man. "You are *not ready*."

His disapproval was delivered in the authoritative voice he usually reserved for me when we were downstairs, and it fell on Clay like the roof had caved in. I understood what Travis was doing, how he was challenging the other man, but I feared it was the wrong tactic. Pushing Clay could backfire and might make him push back.

"You don't know what you're talking about," Clay said. "As usual." He grabbed his frames and adjusted the way they sat on his face while composing the perfect retaliatory strike. "Mentoring you was a mistake. I wish I'd never done it."

The air in the room went horribly thin.

He'd essentially said he wished they'd never become friends, and it was so hurtful, I felt it deep inside. It was worse than any strike of a paddle and more damaging than the tail of a whip.

But the hurt and the destruction didn't show on Travis's face. It was only his tight shoulders and flexed muscle along his jaw that gave away how he was feeling. "Okay, then." His voice was bitter like he couldn't stand the taste of his words. "Let's correct that." He got out of his seat and pushed the chair in with a loud thump. "See you around."

And when he left, he took part of my heart with him, and any chance of our trio surviving.

My body was locked up, becoming an immobile cage. I simply stared in disbelief at Clay while my anguish ripped me apart. It wasn't until the front door slammed closed and the security system chirped that I was able to move.

It must have been the same for him because he took off his glasses, tossed them down on the table with a clatter, and pitched his face forward into his hands. Frustration seeped from every pore of him as he raked his fingers through his hair.

I couldn't tell if he was speaking to me or himself. "It wasn't supposed to go like that. That's not how I planned it."

He cared more about his design than anything else, and right now I couldn't care less. I sucked in a sharp breath, wiped a tear from my cheek, and placed my hands on the tabletop to push myself up onto my feet.

"You're leaving?" He had the audacity to look betrayed.

It was spoken in my voice, but it sounded distant and cold. "You said it yourself. There's nothing left to say."

TWENTY-SIX

When I came out of Clay's house, I discovered Travis's SUV was gone.

No, not gone—it'd been moved.

He'd parked in my driveway and was sitting in the driver's seat, looking deep in thought. The moment he saw me, he got out and concern filled his face.

It was dark outside, but he was illuminated by the exterior lights on my parents' garage, and I watched him strangle back the desire to rush forward and pull me in his arms. I'd told him I loved him, but also that I loved another man, and he wasn't sure where he stood now.

"I'm sorry," he said. "I didn't mean to walk out on you, but I needed to get out of there. Nothing I said was going to help."

"No, I get it." I didn't blame him for leaving. "But he doesn't mean it. I know he cares a lot about you, so I don't know why he said it."

Travis grimaced. "I do." He nodded toward the gate that led to my house. "Can we talk?"

"Yeah, of course."

He'd been in my place before. The night of Cassidy's birthday he'd stayed over, but we'd both been tipsy and the moment we'd made it through my door, he'd been calling Clay so he could watch us. We'd both had to be up early for work, and Travis hadn't stayed long the next morning.

Tonight, he looked around the space like he was seeing it for the first time. He gave a half-smile at the laundry basket that was overflowing with scrubs, understanding the never-ending battle to keep them clean.

He took a seat on one side of my couch in the living area, and his gaze sought mine. He hoped I'd join him, but I was too frantic inside to sit still. Instead, I paced around the room, wanting to escape my emotions but not sure how.

When it was clear I wasn't going to join him, Travis sighed. "I told him he was scared, but it's not just that. I think he's freaking out."

Irritation directed towards Clay glanced through me. "Because he doesn't like when things don't go according to plan?"

"That's part of it, yeah. He likes being in control and maybe he thinks he's losing that. But he's mostly freaking out because of . . . well, me."

I pulled to a stop. "What?"

Travis wiped a hand over his mouth, hesitating for a moment, before giving in. "The first session I did with Clay wasn't sexual. BDSM can be non-sexual kink, but he didn't have experience with that. So, since we were both straight, we decided one of the goals of the scene would be to gauge our comfort level. Which, as it turned out, was high."

I drifted closer, pulled in by the gravity of him.

"We had our conversation after it was over, and I told him I'm good if he wants to try more. I felt like I was, I don't know, expanding? Two years ago, I wasn't into anything beyond vanilla stuff, and now I can't seem to get enough. I want to learn everything, which made me wonder. What if there's more out there? Stuff I didn't think I'd like, but then it turns out, I'm into it?"

I sank down on the couch, blown away by what he was saying and how freely he was willing to share with me.

"I told him I was . . ." He searched for the right word and then found it. "Open." His shoulders lifted with a heavy breath. "He said he was comfortable with that, so our next session was more intense—and sexual. He made me jerk off, and if I didn't come fast enough for him, he showed me what a riding crop felt like."

Oh, fuck me.

I squeezed my knees together and tried to stop the image in my mind, but it was unavoidable. I saw a naked Travis standing in front of Clay, who impatiently tapped the riding crop on the palm of his hand as he watched the other man pleasure himself.

"I enjoyed the scene," he said, "and it was obvious he did too, but I think that scared him. He didn't *want* to like it. He was fine that night, but the next day he was weird."

I remembered what he'd said when we'd talked about it at the bar. "He started to pull away."

He nodded. "You remember the first time I saw you at the club? I waved to Clay, he waved back, and then he just led you away. I sat at the table for a long time thinking he'd brought you there to prove how straight he was to me, or maybe himself. Which is fine. I identify as straight too." He tilted his head. "Straight, but curious."

I slid closer to him and put my hand on his that rested on the couch cushion. "That's how I'd describe myself."

"I care about him a lot and I love the three of us together. It doesn't turn me off if things get sexual with him, and sometimes . . . well, it's a turn-on, but that's all it is. I don't have romantic feelings for him. Before you, I didn't sit around and wonder what he was doing or how his day was going."

That was surprising. "Are you saying you do that now?"

He gave me a sheepish smile and used a hand to rub the back of his neck. "He's a part of us. You have to know, when we talk and plan out our time together, everything is about you. You're all he's focused on, and every decision he makes is so we can give you the best possible scene. How can I not like a guy who cares so much about the same person I care about?"

I sighed. My heart both swelled and hurt.

Travis turned his hand beneath mine and threaded our fingers together. "The threesome rattled him. He let his guard down, we got inside, and now he's freaking out. He puts up a good front, but he's not as comfortable as he pretends to be."

God, he was so right. I'd seen hints at Clay's insecurity, but I hadn't paid enough attention. "And then I sprang being a throuple on him."

"It's going to be okay. You told him you want this, and he loves you. He's going to want this as badly as we do, he . . . just hasn't figured it out yet. Do you trust me?"

"Yes," I breathed.

"Good. He may know what you need," he lifted our joined hands and dropped a kiss on my fingers, "but I know what *he* needs, and that's time. He has to get comfortable with who he is, and what we could be."

Fuck, I hoped he was right.

Travis didn't stay overnight. He didn't ask, and he probably felt the same as I did. Even though our relationship with Clay was now a huge question mark, it would have been wrong to sleep together. Instead, I let him tuck me under his arm and distract me with talk about his work. At times, his days weren't that different than mine, except he cared for a much wider and more exciting variety of animals.

We didn't hear from Clay over the weekend. I had a short text exchange with Travis, but he was on-call both nights because one of the zebras was pregnant and he was on foal watch.

Monday also passed without a word from Clay.

As I came home from work, I tried not to look for signs he was home. Travis had said to give him space. That he needed time. Since he was back in Nashville, I didn't check on Noir, even though it killed me not to. He was always good with her on the weekends when he was home, so I assumed he had it covered.

Eventually we were going to have to talk though, even if it was a post-divorce custody discussion.

Tuesday afternoon, when I was helping prep a dalmatian

for radiographs, my phone vibrated with a text. I finished my work, then ducked into a corner to check the message.

Clay: Can we talk?

Me: I'm at work.

Clay: I meant this evening.

I lifted an eyebrow. The days of silence from him had left me hurt and angry. He'd said he was falling for me, and yet he'd given up on us so fast. I missed him. How wasn't he missing us?

Me: Will Travis be there too?

The dots flickered and disappeared. Finally, his text came through.

Clay: I'd like to talk to you alone.

Me: Sorry. I'm busy tonight.

It was a lie, but I wasn't going to meet with him on my own because we needed to talk about this together.

Clay: How about tomorrow?

Me: If Travis isn't there, then I'm still busy.

He had no response to that.

Since he'd reached out, I figured now was as good a time as any.

Me: I haven't been over to see Noir. How's she doing?

Clay: Fine. She misses you.

My breath caught because there was no way he was talking about our aloof cat. Noir was a paradigm of the independent woman. As long as she had food, she didn't need anyone. Every now and again she liked affection, but it was always on her terms, and the rest of the time she was indifferent.

Me: I miss her too. A lot.

No new messages came through. I wanted to arrange some alone time with her, but we were swamped at the clinic, and I couldn't leave patients waiting on me any longer. I tucked my phone back into my pocket and made a mental note to set something up with him later.

Time dragged as I went about my work trying not to think about the two men I loved, and my frustration that we couldn't be together. It was one of those days where nothing went right. I banged my head on an open cabinet during an exam, which hurt like hell and made me look like an idiot in front of the patient's owner. I spilled my water on a vaccination chart and had to start over. When I put on my latex gloves, the finger tore, and I nearly burst into tears.

I was coming apart.

What if Travis was wrong? What if Clay wanted to talk to me alone because he was going to try to convince me we should go back to the beginning before Travis entered the picture?

The clinic stopped taking patients at four, which meant it was at least five before I was usually done. I was still getting the overnight patients settled for the evening when a text came through.

Travis: Got a second to talk?

Me: Sure.

My screen changed as he called, only it was through FaceTime. Which, of course, because I looked like garbage. But I was too eager to see him. I tapped the icon to accept.

"Hi," I said.

Like me, he appeared to be at work. The background behind him was just a white wall, but he was in his zoo uniform scrubs and had a stethoscope hanging around his neck.

"Hi," he answered back. He had a huge smile, possibly the biggest I'd ever seen from him. Much too big for it simply to be him happy to see me.

Some of the animals in their crates around me were vocal with their displeasure about their accommodations for the evening, and it was hard to hear Travis over the barking.

"Hold on." I darted out into the empty and quiet staff breakroom. "What's up?"

"I meant to call you earlier," he disappeared as he flipped the phone around, "but I got sidetracked by this little guy."

A stall came into view, and the first thing to leap out was the black and white stripes. The camera panned from mom down to the newborn foal resting amongst the hay on the floor, his legs tucked to the side. As his mom ambled toward him, his dark ears twitched, and he turned his head to briefly nuzzle with her.

"Oh, my God! He's gorgeous," I said. The baby zebra was just as vividly striped as his mother, only his were more brown than black. He was just the cutest thing ever too. "How'd it go?"

"Great. He's been up and walking already. Mom's doing good too."

This explained Travis's huge smile. It was the first live birth he'd overseen since starting at the zoo, and I was so thrilled for him that it had been uneventful.

The camera swung back around so he came into view, and then he was on the move, walking away from the stalls.

"So, I don't have a lot of time to talk," he said, "but Clay called me."

I paused, surprised. "Oh, yeah?"

He went through a door and out into a big hallway, which made his voice echo. "You should go over there tonight and talk to him."

I was dubious. "Without you?"

"Yeah. I'm going to be here at least another eight hours, and it's okay. We talked already." There was a lightness in him, and I wondered if it was all from the new foal, or if part of it was a result of his discussion with Clay.

"What'd you talk about?"

Travis got to wherever he was going to, which must have been his office. He shut the door, unclipped his radio from his belt, and set it down on his messy desk so he could take a seat behind it. In the corner, I saw the cot where he'd probably slept last night.

"He apologized and he," Travis's voice filled with weight,

"told me he loved me."

The phone slipped out of my hand, landing with a loud thud on the breakroom table, and I scrambled to pick it up. "He did?"

"Yeah. It's not the same way he loves you. Like you said, it's more of a platonic thing."

"What'd you say?"

His smile caused warmth to flood across my skin and my heart to go out of rhythm. His voice was as soft as his kiss could be, and just as powerful. "I told him I love him too."

I lifted a shaky hand and pressed it over my mouth, overwhelmed. Holy shit. "What does this mean?"

"It means he really needs to talk to you."

The radio on his desk crackled, and although the call wasn't for him, it reminded us both that he could be pulled away at any moment. He leaned closer to the phone, looking so handsome and happy, I wished I could touch him through the screen.

"Okay," I said. "You don't want me to wait for you?"

"No, you can call me afterward though." He blinked, considering something. "Hey. I love you."

We'd spoken about it but hadn't actually said it to each other. Not even Friday night when he'd been at my place. Was it strange that I liked how the men had said it to each other first, before me?

I grinned. "I love you too."

We said goodbye, and as soon as the call disconnected, I thumbed out my message to Clay.

Me: My schedule just cleared up. What time do you want me to come over?

TWENTY-SEVEN

After a shower, I got dressed in a cowlneck sweater, jeans, and a pair of plaid pumps with a pointed toe. I didn't head over early to Clay's house like I used to. I'd stick to the plan of meeting at seven and rang his doorbell at precisely that time, so there'd be no surprises.

When he opened the door, I was struck by how different he looked.

He brightened and a big smile widened on his lips, announcing how glad he was to see me, but dark circles clung below his eyes. He looked tired. Maybe even exhausted. While I was sad to see him suffering, I wondered . . . were Travis and I the cause?

He gestured politely for me to come in, and once I stood in his entryway, he reminded me of how Travis had been after he'd left this house on Friday. His hands seemed to ache to reach for me, but he knew better.

Tension wove between us so thickly, it strangled back his words, and he barely got it out. "I'm sorry."

Okay, that was good.

I'd expected him to say more, but then he just stood there, looking lost. Did he not have a plan for how this was supposed to go?

Noir peeked her head around the corner, saw it was me,

and gave a friendly meow in greeting. She brushed up against the wall before turning around and doing it back the same way she'd come from, trying to entice me to follow her.

So, I did, which added to Clay's confusion. He fell in behind me as I strode into the living room.

I pulled to a stop when I saw the new addition. Noir seemed proud to show off this custom piece of furniture. She went to the base of the tree and vaulted up it, passing by the first platform and continuing to climb higher. There were several platforms to choose from, but she stopped at one in the middle so she could dig her claws into the sisal rope section that was wound tightly around the center support.

It wasn't like the cheap, two-tiered cat tower covered in carpet I'd bought her months ago, which she'd mostly destroyed instead of Clay's furniture, thankfully.

For one thing, this piece was taller than I was. The center support was a bare, whitewashed tree trunk with a natural curve and a fork halfway up, splitting off into two smaller branches. The platforms were covered in thick, white faux fur, which gave the impression there were clouds floating around the tree.

Like everything else he did, it was beautiful. How in the world did he do that? He'd created a cat tower, but it was also gorgeous art. And it looked even better when Noir finished sharpening her claws and climbed up onto the next platform, nestling in on her cloudlike bed. The black of her coat popped out and complimented the monochromatic piece.

I reached over and scratched her behind the ears, enjoying the contented purr she awarded me.

"When did you make this?" I asked him. "It's amazing."

"Oh, thanks. I did it over the weekend." He looked at me like the tree was no big deal, and not what he wanted to talk about right now. "Lilith, did you hear what I said?"

"Yes." My tone was cool. "What are you sorry about?"

He sighed. "Everything."

"Be more specific." We needed to work on our communication, and I wanted that to start right now.

My request didn't frustrate him. Instead, he nodded. "First, I'm sorry for what I said to Travis about our friendship being a mistake. I've already apologized to him, but I wanted to make sure you know too. He was right. I was scared." He made a face. "I was fucking terrified."

This was a good sign, and my pulse quickened. "I'm glad you two talked."

"Me too." He motioned toward his couch. "Do you want to sit? I have a lot more to apologize for."

Another good sign. "Sure."

I sat, but he didn't. It made it feel as if he were giving a presentation, selling himself to me, but I didn't mind that. I could use a little persuasion after the weekend he'd put Travis and me through.

"Second," he said, "I'm sorry for not saying anything when I started to develop feelings for you. It's not an excuse, but when I made that promise, I never expected it to happen to me, and when it did—"

"You got scared."

He set his hands on his hips and hung his head. "Yes. I didn't want to drive you away."

"So, you're saying you're not scared now?"

He shot me a sad smile. "Oh, no, I'm definitely still scared, but I'm no longer too scared to say so. The last week has been miserable without you."

It was such a huge step for him to admit what he was feeling. He was genuine and willing to be open. I'd never seen him vulnerable before, and . . . lord. He hadn't a clue how sexy it was.

"And third," he came over and sat beside me, close but not too close, "I'm sorry about how I reacted all of last week. I felt like what we'd done—what I'd done—during the threesome crossed a line with Travis. I didn't ask him if he was okay with what I did, and afterward, I . . . struggled with how I felt and what it meant."

I turned, tucking one leg beneath the other so I could face him, and softened my voice. "Did it mean something to you?"

"Yes, and no. Travis and I talked about it today. How I liked what we did because it gave me control and power." He tossed a hand up. "And physically it felt good."

I couldn't stop my smile. "It did."

"I'm not romantically attracted to him, but sexually?" He hesitated, but then pushed through. "I'm trying to get comfortable with the idea that . . . might be a gray area for me. How do you feel about that?"

He looked so nervous, and I put a reassuring hand on his cheek. "I'm more than fine with that. As someone who's incredibly attracted to both of you, let me say this—I *get* it."

I wasn't trying to make light of what he'd just shared, but dear God, did I understand, and thankfully, he chuckled.

It seemed to break some of the tension he had, and he lifted a hand to touch mine on his face.

"I'm sorry for Friday night," he said. "I felt ambushed and it was a knee-jerk reaction. Everything went off the rails, and when you said it was all or nothing, I thought I'd already lost you. I can't compete with him."

He nearly broke my heart all over again, "Oh, my God, Clay." I leaned in, pressing our foreheads together. "It's not a competition. I love you both."

His mouth found mine, and this kiss was as unexpected as they came. He was the confident and in control dominant who could make me tremble, but when my lips pressed against his, I discovered he was shaking. It wasn't in fear—this was relief. He hadn't won or lost me to another man.

He was realizing he had us both.

"I'm going to do better," he said as soon as the kiss ended, "and I have a plan. If you don't like it, I'll throw it out, and we can draft a different one." The corner of his mouth quirked up. "Very little with you goes according to plan anyway, but do you want to hear it?"

I gave him a knowing look. "Sure."

"The three of us start a relationship together. Everyone is equal, no one person gets to make the rules." He stared deep into my eyes like he was pleading with my soul, even though he was asking for the very thing I wanted. "We all love each other, and we all want this to work."

"Yes," I nodded. "So far this plan is good. Fully on board with it."

He laughed, then turned serious. "The next step is Travis

moves in here."

My mind skidded to a stop. "What? In your house?"

"I bought this place as an investment. The plan is to renovate and eventually sell it for a profit, but there's a lot of space. More than enough room for him. He'd have the whole second floor to himself. He'd be closer to his work here, plus . . . he'd be a lot closer to us."

Having both men right next door sounded amazing, but . . . "Do you think he'd go for it?"

"He was interested when I asked him, but said it depends on how you feel about it."

Holy cow, he'd *already* asked him.

And Travis was considering it. I had to control myself and not get my hopes up, just as another thought stormed into my mind. "Wait a minute. Clay, this is your home. Your," I struggled to find the right words, "sanctuary. What about having your own space to escape to?"

He shrugged. "I have my workshop. It's where I spend most of my time when I'm home." His hand tangled with mine, lacing our fingers together. "Our schedules are a challenge. This will make it so we can see more of each other. It'll improve communication. The longer I'm around you, the easier it is for me to open up. If I start sliding or don't know how to share what I'm feeling," he took an uneven breath, "Travis is there to help."

Oh, my God. He was taking up Travis's offer to help him emotionally, and I fucking loved that. They'd mentor each other in different areas of their life.

There was a soft thump as Noir jumped down off her

perch and hurried toward us on the couch, distracting me. She rarely came to me on her own; most times she had to be enticed. I watched with surprise as she leapt up onto the cushion and flopped down . . .

Right in Clay's lap.

"What's this?" I demanded. "Do you have catnip in your pocket or something?"

He looked at me like I was speaking gibberish. "What?"

"She hardly ever sits on my lap."

"Really?" He sounded dubious as he stroked her back. She curled into a tight ball with her belly exposed and stretched an arm over her eyes. "She, uh, sits on me a lot. Kind of whenever I sit down."

My mouth dropped open while I stared at our traitorous cat. "Oh, my God. She likes you more than me." I leaned over and rubbed her cheek. "I guess I can't blame her. Me and this cat have a lot in common."

He looked confused. "Such as?"

"She forced her way into your house, and I forced my way into your heart."

He smiled like I was being silly. "I'd tell you you're wrong and you can't force me to do anything," his gaze deepened with a love I wouldn't have thought possible, "but the truth is I'd do anything for you. I mean it. If, down the road, you and Travis need me to step aside—I'll do it. I'll go with the satisfaction that at least I brought the two of you together."

Now it was my turn to look at him like he was being silly. "You're the architect of *this* relationship, Clay. You built this, the three of us together. You're so good at turning everything you make into working art. I can't wait to see what we become."

"Fuck," he said, blinking back the unexpected emotion I'd caused in him.

"Take off your glasses."

"What?" This was yet another unexpected thing to come from me, and he looked confused. "Why?"

"Because you said you'd do anything for me, and right now, I don't want anything between us."

He liked what I'd said, so he pulled them off and set them on the cushion beside himself. His tone was teasing as he gently evicted Noir from his lap. "You know they help me see, right?"

"Well, I guess you'll just have to get closer," I whispered.

Travis gave his landlord notice, and in early December, during an unseasonably warm weekend, we loaded Clay's truck with a batch of things to start moving Travis in. The guys gave me shit about wearing heels while carrying boxes into the house, but I just laughed.

I hoped to still be wearing them and nothing else later when we went downstairs to celebrate having both my boyfriends so close.

All that was left were the big, heavy pieces, so I stood back and admired the view of the men as they grappled with an enormous headboard. It had their arm muscles tensing and twisting beneath their t-shirts in the most delicious way.

Out of the corner of my eye, a woman dressed in black appeared down the road and walked swiftly our direction. I turned to see it was Judy Maligner, the head of the HOA. Maybe she was out on a power walk, but I suspected that was just an excuse so she could keep tabs. She was wearing athletic clothes, but they were contoured to her perfectly trim body, flaunting her figure, and I tried to remember when I'd seen her in anything else.

Also, she had on a full face of makeup. Who did that?

"Hi, Lilith!" She was slightly winded from her fast stride, and it made her sound breathlessly excited. "How are you?"

"I'm good, Ms. Malinger."

"Oh, please, honey." She gave me a smile that managed to chide. "Call me Judy. I'm not that much older than you."

Had math changed recently? Because she was in her fifties, which meant she was twice my age. I plastered on a polite smile and kept the math to myself. I couldn't stand the woman and hoped if I didn't engage, she'd move on.

She asked it innocently, waving a hand toward the men. "What's going on here?"

The guys were focused on their task, not noticing us as they disappeared into the house with the headboard.

"Clay's friend is moving in."

The smile on her face hung. "His 'friend?'" Her gaze flew to the open door, her eyes narrowed, and she didn't bother to hide her disgust. "I didn't know he was gay. I thought he was dating you."

For a moment, I got so angry, my vision blurred. She

wasn't just judgmental—she was a huge bigot.

It didn't surprise me she thought we were dating. I'd been going over to his house nearly every day for months. I turned and gave the darkest grin I possessed, while keeping my tone sugary sweet. "Yes, he's my boyfriend. Not that it's any of your fucking business who he chooses to date, *Judy*."

She reared back in shock. I'd stunned her speechless, but I watched the thought in her head play out on her face. *Well, I never.*

The guys reappeared and I waved at them. "Travis, come here. There's someone you should meet."

She couldn't move. Her strict manners said it wouldn't be polite to walk away, even when I'd been rude to her. As Travis approached, she was locked in place.

He sensed something was off and his confused look bounced between us.

"This is Dr. Travis Eckhart," I said. "My boyfriend."

She was captivated by his looks, and probably the title of doctor too, but then her mind tangled over the last part. "Boyfriend? I thought Clay was—"

My tone was plain. "They both are."

Travis held out his hand in an offered handshake, but she stared at it like if she accepted, she'd go straight to hell.

I gestured to her. "Travis, this is Judy Maligner, the homophobic president of the HOA, who probably wakes up every morning thinking about how she's going to ruin Dr. Lowe's day, all because she disapproves of his relationship with Cassidy." I tilted my head and smiled brighter at her. "Which, once again, really isn't your fucking business, is it?"

She gasped. "I'm not going to stand here and let you talk to me like that!"

"Okay." I waved and said it in a sing-song voice. "*Bye*!"

She scoffed again, and when she realized she was going to have to carry out her threat of leaving, she turned on her heel and marched away in a huff.

"What was that?" Travis asked.

I looped my arm around his waist, and we walked toward Clay, who'd climbed into the bed of his truck to undo the rachet straps on the footboard.

"Sorry," I said. "I thought I'd give Judy a new target to aim for, instead of Greg and Cassidy."

"Us?" he said.

Well, shit. I hadn't thought it all the way through. I was fine taking the heat, but Clay and Travis might feel otherwise. "Well, hopefully she just fixates on me." I pointed to the house across the street and a few doors down. "See that 'for sale' sign? It just went up. The O'Briens would rather move than put up with any more of Judy's bullshit."

"She's the worst," Clay said. "Even worse than carrying all this stuff upstairs is going to be."

I used a sultry voice. "Mm, but you're a bunch of big, strapping men, and the faster you finish, the faster we can go downstairs."

Lord, I couldn't have given them better motivation.

Greg's house was decorated for Christmas, and there were touches of Cassidy visible. For instance, three stockings hung on the mantle, and the one with the C initial had to be hers. I expected it wouldn't be long before he asked her to move in. Probably as soon as her spring semester was over. She spent most of her free time over at his house anyway, and like it was for me and my boyfriends—schedules were tough. Living together maximized chances of seeing each other.

I stood by the window at the back of the house, which overlooked the pool. It was covered for the winter, and the patio furniture had been put away. It'd been four months since I'd been down there, celebrating Cassidy's birthday. God, so much had changed.

It was so much better than I could have imagined.

I sipped my wine while other people began to arrive for the meeting. Most people already knew each other, but there had been some introductions, and a few people had mentally stumbled when I explained Clay, Travis, and I were a throuple. I was glad how instead of judgmental looks, we received mostly curious ones.

Travis and I fielded any questions we got. It's not that Clay was embarrassed of our relationship, but he was private with strangers, so it became a fun game to see how fast I could steer the conversation in a new direction if someone began to pry.

The furniture in Greg's living room had been pushed to one side and folding chairs set up, but most of the folks were still in the kitchen, hovering around the table where the fruit and cheese platters were.

Did Judy know what was happening?

A vengeful smile twitched on my lips. I hoped so. She thought she had all the power, but she'd be powerless to stop us.

Starting a recall petition had been my idea, but Greg fully supported it and had offered his house as the meeting space. I'd scoured the association bylaws, learning what percentage of homeowners we'd need for a quorum and then how many signatures it'd take to remove Judy from the board.

Clay, Greg, his neighbor Erika, and me as my parents' proxy made four, but we'd need twenty-eight more. Looking around, I was encouraged. Not everyone could make the meeting tonight, but there were a lot of people here and once folks got to talking to their neighbors . . .

It was only a matter of time.

Clay had been standing beside me, and we watched as Travis strode toward us, a fresh glass of wine in hand and an easy smile on his face. Was I ever going to get used to how handsome these men were? Since we'd fallen in love, they'd only become more attractive.

If they kept getting hotter, it was going to burn my retinas.

"I was just talking to Jeremiah Abbott," Travis said. "He got fined a hundred bucks for his stone bird bath being two inches too tall."

I paused. "The Abbotts have a bird bath?"

"It's in their backyard. He said his neighbor saw Judy out there one morning with a tape measure. She'd gone through the fence and everything."

Clay groaned it under his breath. "Unbelievable."

"She's drunk with power." I leaned in and dropped my voice low. "And not in the sexy way."

Both men gave me a look of desire. When Travis had come home from work last night, we'd had a pretty intense session. Clay had taken the lead during the scene, Travis had been in charge during the aftercare, and we'd discovered the shower in Clay's bathroom was just big enough for the three of us together.

I was so grateful I'd found these men. I couldn't even remember what it was like before they were in my life, and I never wanted to go back either. Sure, no matter how much planning and designing Clay did, we wouldn't know what the future held for us, but I wasn't scared.

Our hearts were big enough for the three of us.

THANK YOU

There are so many people to thank and I don't know how to adequately express what they did for me.

This book was incredibly stressful, and I would have had a complete emotional breakdown without the love and support of my husband. I love you so much, Nick!

Also, a huge thank you to Aubrey Bondurant for her daily check-ins, and Andrea Lefkowitz and Rebecca Nebel for being cheerleaders.

Thanks to the fantastic ladies from my "2020 Sucks" virtual writers retreat. I miss your faces!

Thank you, Lori Whitwam. God, I was such a mess. I can't believe you put up with me. Thank you a million times.

And thank you to everyone for being so understanding about why this book was delayed. 2020 was a rough year, but we made it. Please know my readers are so, so, SO important to me. You kept me going when the words stopped coming and I wanted to give up.

MORE BY NIKKI SLOANE

THE BLINDFOLD CLUB SERIES

Three Simple Rules

Three Hard Lessons

Three Little Mistakes

Three Dirty Secrets

Three Sweet Nothings

Three Guilty Pleasures

One More Rule

THE SORDID SERIES

Sordid

Torrid

Destroy

SPORTS ROMANCE

The Rivalry

THE NASHVILLE NEIGHBORHOOD

The Doctor

The Pool Boy

The Architect

FILTHY RICH AMERICANS

The Initiation | The Obsession | The Deception

The Redemption

The Temptation

ABOUT THE AUTHOR

USA Today bestselling author Nikki Sloane landed in graphic design after her careers as a waitress, a screenwriter, and a ballroom dance instructor fell through. Now she writes full-time and lives in Kentucky with her husband, two sons, and a pug who is more slug than dog.

She is a four-time Romance Writers of America RITA® & Vivian® Finalist, a Passionate Plume winner, a Goodreads Choice Awards semifinalist, and couldn't be any happier that people enjoy reading her sexy words.

www.NikkiSloane.com

www.twitter.com/AuthorNSloane

www.facebook.com/NikkiSloaneAuthor

www.instagram.com/nikkisloane